I0688474

PRINCESS OF LANFOR

HEROES OF RAVENFORD

BOOK 4

F.P. SPIRIT
K.J. FOGLEMAN

BOOKS BY F.P. SPIRIT

The Heroes of Ravenford

Ruins on Stone Hill

Serpent Cult

Dark Monolith

Princess of Lanfor

The Baron's Heart

Rise of the Thrall Lord

City of Tears

Protectors of Penwick

Arinthar Collections

Tales From Thac

BOOKS BY K.J. FOGLEMAN

Tales of the Wovlen

The Dragon's Son

The Dragon's Due

Arinthar Collections

Tales From Thac

PRINCESS OF LANFOR

HEROES OF RAVENFORD
BOOK 4

Copyright @ 2017 F. P. Spirit
Cover Art by Jackson Tjota
Cover Typography by Amalia Chitulescu
Interior Design by Designs by Shannon
Edited by Sandra Nguyen
ISBN 978-1-7364377-0-4

All rights reserved. No part of this publication may be reproduced, stored in retrieval system, copied in any form or by any means, electronic, mechanical, photocopying, recording or otherwise transmitted without written permission from the publisher. You must not circulate this book in any format.

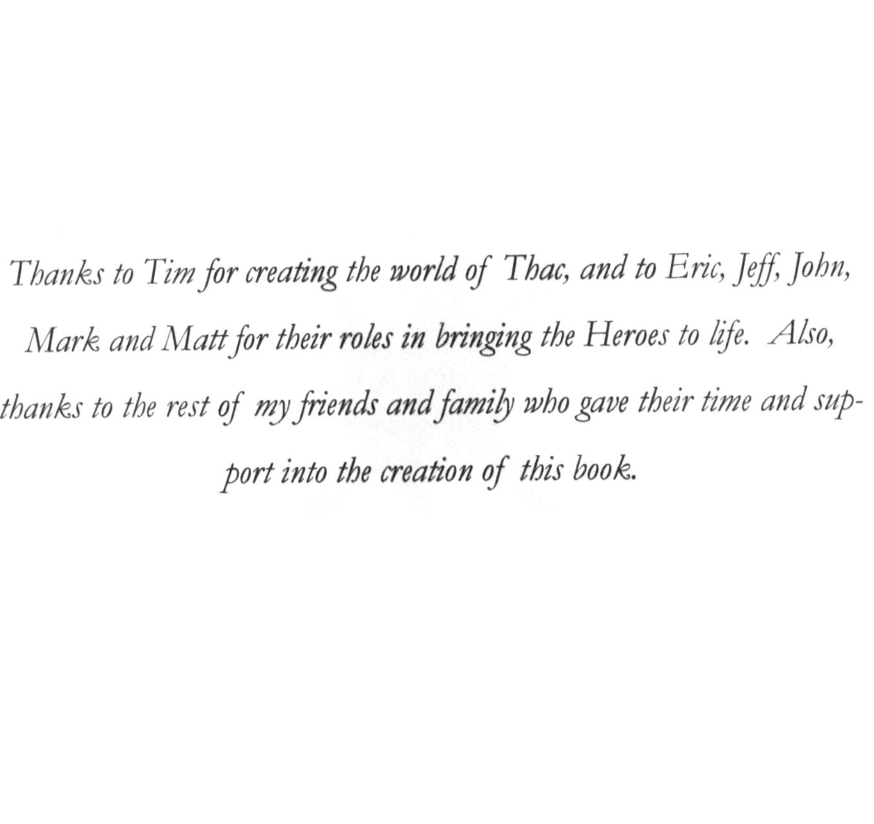
Thanks to Tim for creating the world of Thac, and to Eric, Jeff, John, Mark and Matt for their roles in bringing the Heroes to life. Also, thanks to the rest of my friends and family who gave their time and support into the creation of this book.

TABLE OF CONTENTS

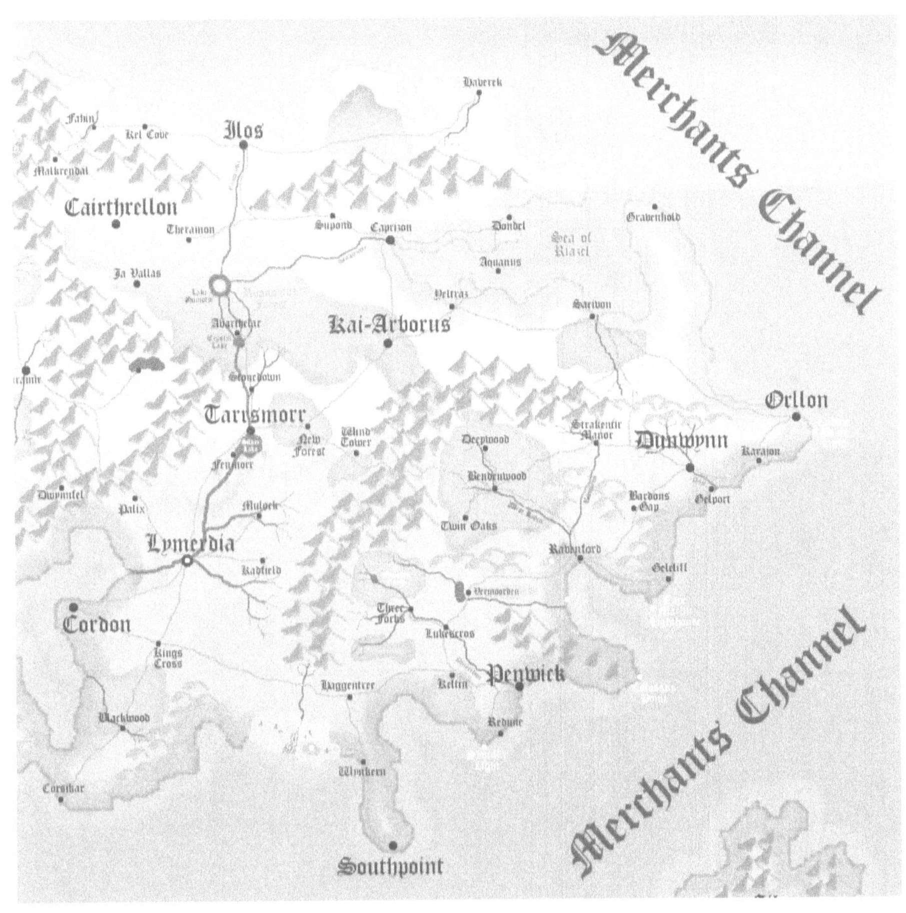

There was not the only one Thrall Master—there were many, some lesser, some greater. Aside from the Golem Thrall Master, Larketh, there were three others who rose higher than the rest, and with their great powers of mind, enthralled veritable armies of minions. One of these great masters in particular was the Dragon Thrall Master. His identity lost to antiquity, he nonetheless had the power to bend the mightiest of creatures—dragons—to his will. His army was powerful and terrible, raining death and destruction across the land. No dragon could resist him with the exception of one, and yet that was his eventual undoing…

- Lady Lara Stealle, High Wizard of Penwick

1
A WICKED WIND

A great dark shape descended from above and landed in the mist

The moon waxed a shade from full in the inky black sky, its soft glow washing over the forest, giving a silvery sheen to everything it touched. It was already deep into the night, the woods quiet except for the chirping of crickets, and the occasional whinny of a sleeping horse. A makeshift hitching post stood at the edge of a wide clearing, a dozen or so slumbering horses tethered to it.

A short distance away, a spike-pitched wooden fence had been hammered into the ground, erected around a small encampment. Inside the fence lay a ring of tents, all in a circle around a single large pavilion. The campfires had all but died down, nothing but dull red embers visible as the last bits of wood slowly burnt away. The camp's occupants had bedded down for the night, a scant few sentries standing vigil over them.

Martan stood watch at the edge of the forest, near the head of the path that led into the woods. Tall trees encircled the glade, so close together that little was visible of the forest beyond. Even the silvery moonlight brought no cheer to those woods, twisted tree trunks and gnarled branches creating shapes that fueled the fearful imagination.

A wry smile crossed Martan's lips. *Hence the name Darkwoods.*

The solitary archer spun away from the ominous trees, his eyes fixing on a tall black structure glistening in the moonlight far above him. The building rose well above the treetops, its dark silhouette framed by the inky, star-filled sky. Martan stared at the structure with awe, and perhaps a touch of fear.

The Darkwoods Monolith.

The monolith had once been the stronghold of the Golem Thrall Master, Larketh, a wielder of great magic, unparalleled even to this day. The Thrall Masters, and all their works, were thought destroyed in the last great war, some hundred and fifty years ago. Yet earlier this week, the existence of the Golem Master's monolith had been unearthed.

The *Heroes of Ravenford* had set out in search of the spire to stop the murderous *Serpent Cult* from gaining the Golem Master's secrets. In the wrong hands, those secrets would spell certain doom for the island continent of Thac. It was a truly heroic undertaking, one in which Martan was certain he did not belong.

Martan Folke was a simple man, an archer and a tracker, not some hero like the tall warrior, Lloyd, or a knight akin to the valiant Dame Alana. Neither was he a wizard such as the tall elf, Glolindir, or an assassin similar to the halfling, Seth. He was certainly no agile swordsman like the slight elf, Donatello, nor did he carry a lightning sword as did the young shapeshifter, Ruka. He couldn't even heal wounds in the manner of the little cleric, Aksel.

With the exception of his expertise in the woods, it was beyond Martan why he was even there. Nonetheless, he was here, and he faithfully took his turn at guard duty. Martan had only run away once in his life, and he had regretted it ever since.

A deep sigh escaped the lean archer's lips. *The past was the past.*

Martan swept his eyes across the wide clearing—there was not much to do on watch. Despite the eeriness of the surrounding woods, the night was relatively quiet, the air cool, stars twinkling brightly in the crystal-clear sky. The scene would have been idyllic, if not for the sinister shadow of the dark monolith.

The Heroes, along with the *Knights of the Rose*, had reached the monolith by midday yesterday. After confirming that the cultists had gone inside, the Heroes went in after them, leaving the knights outside to stand watch. There had been no sign of either group till noon this day, when Glolindir, Donnie, and Ruka re-emerged. The trio had reported no trace of the cult, thus far finding only strange devices and deadly traps inside the Golem Master's stronghold. After a short stay, the threesome returned to the monolith, carrying food back for the rest of their companions. There had been no sightings of the Heroes since, with the exception of the halfling, Seth.

Martan had not actually seen Seth, only hearing about his appearance later from the head knight of the encampment, Sir Craven. The Heroes had finally encountered the cultists, with only a single dark mage making an escape. Seth sought to track the mage back to his home base, so the cult could be uprooted once and for all. A knowing smile spread across Martan's lips. *If anyone could pull that off, it would be Seth.*

The dour archer stood at his post, idly stroking his short-cropped beard, when out of nowhere, he was hit by a cold gust of wind. Martan shivered involuntarily, slapping his arms together to abate the sudden chill. He glanced upward, half expecting to see storm clouds rolling in, but the night sky remained absolutely clear.

Martan's brow furrowed into deep ridges. *That's strange.*

The tracker suddenly froze, the hairs on the back of his neck standing on end. The forest around him had gone deathly silent. He cocked his head to one side and strained his ears, but not a sound came from the surrounding woods, not even the chirping of crickets. Something was definitely amiss. Nearby, the horses fidgeted against their reins, whinnying nervously as if they, too, sensed something wrong. Martan squinted into the dark forest, but saw nothing, not even down the trail that he guarded. The horses grew more anxious as the seconds passed, whinnying louder and prancing around nervously.

Martan spun slowly around, his keen eyes sweeping both the

forest and the clearing, yet still he saw nothing. That was when Martan heard it—a loud hissing noise from somewhere above. He snapped his head back just in time to see the moon and stars disappear from the sky. A strange cloud had appeared out of nowhere, completely blotting out everything overhead.

Martan's jaw dropped. *Where in the world did that come from?*

The tracker's eyes remained glued to that cloud, watching in astonishment as it billowed out in all directions. Then the treetops disappeared, and Martan realized the cloud was falling—in mere seconds, it would envelope the camp. Perhaps it was just some strange natural phenomena, but with the knights depending on him, did he really want to take that chance? Deciding to err on the side of caution, Martan cupped his hands together, and screamed as loud as he could, "To arms! To arms!"

Similar shouts echoed from all corners of the encampment, Martan's cry spurring the other sentries to action. The camp immediately stirred in response, armored men and women spilling out of their tents just moments before the strange mist settled upon them. The fog swiftly fell across the camp, people and tents alike now nothing more than dark shapes in the mist. An acrid smell reached Martan's nostrils just as the first screams started. The dark forms cried out in pain, flailing their weapons wildly in all directions, as if the very mists were attacking them.

Martan's eyes went wide with horror. *Is there something in the mist? Or is it the fog itself?*

The archer swept his gaze around, frantically looking for an answer, when his eyes fell on two small forms next to the nearest tent. That had to be Syndir and Lamorn, the two squires who had befriended him over these last few days. The young men screamed in anguish, waving around violently in all directions, yet Martan saw nothing around them. *It must be the mist.*

Martan now realized he couldn't help the others, but he would not abide the boys' suffering. Without another thought, he vaulted into the mists, pulling up his hood and scarf as he went. The damp fog caressed the exposed parts of his skin, and within seconds it began to burn. Martan bit down a cry, still plunging toward the beset boys.

As luck would have it, they had turned his way, the smart lads making for the safety of the forest. Martan reached them moments later, throwing an arm around each, and dragging them the rest of the way out of the mists. The three of them broached the edge of the fog, and fell to the ground panting with exhaustion, yet their exposed skin still burnt with pain. Martan ripped off his scarf, and wiped himself off, then swiftly did the same for the boys. Moments later, their skin dried, all three of them sighed with relief.

"Is that you, Mart..." the one boy began.

"Shhhh," Martan hissed. He did not know what spawned the deadly cloud, but he had a dreadful suspicion. He grasped the two boys by the neck, pulled them close, and whispered, "Free the horses and get away into the forest."

"But…" the other boy interrupted him.

"No buts," Martan hissed sharply. "Stay hidden until I come for you. Understand?"

Both boys nodded. They swiftly got up and rushed toward the horses, the mounts thankfully still outside the burning mist. With the squires safe, Martan turned his attention back to the fog. The painful screams of the people inside were suddenly overshadowed by a bone-shuddering roar. Martan watched in horror as a great dark shape descended from above, and landed in the middle of the mists. Sharp gusts accompanied the ominous silhouette, swiftly dissipating the deadly fog. Pale moonlight seeped through the thin remains of the mist, illuminating the large figure. Martan's eyes went wide, his worst fears confirmed.

A dragon!

The great beast had landed in the middle of the camp, directly atop the pavilion. The thin structure now lay flattened on the ground under four large clawed feet, no match for the dragon's massive weight. Martan gulped, a lump sticking in his throat. The great beast was a terrifying sight to behold. It dwarfed the large tent, easily fifty feet long from its massive head to the tip of its long, sinuous tail. The dragon had landed in a crouch, its belly low to the ground, powerful legs taut beneath that thick, muscular torso. The great, bat-like wings were partially folded back, the dragon's tail twitching, as the large head whipped around on its long, snake-like neck.

Loud squeals and nickers had been echoing across the clearing since the dragon's first roar. Back at the hitching post, Syndir and Lamorn wrestled with the horses' reins, desperately trying to cut them without getting trampled. At the same time, across the campsite, a small group of men and women had miraculously survived. In the midst of them stood the dark-bearded Sir Craven, tall and unflinching, like a rock in the storm. Holy sword in one hand, shield in the other, he faced the great dragon and shouted to his remaining troops, "Stand fast! You are Knights of the Rose!"

Abruptly, the great head turned toward the knight, large, serpent-like eyes fixing upon him. A deep, menacing growl emanated from the beast, sending an involuntary shiver up Martan's spine. The dragon regarded the knights for a few moments, then slowly reared up to its full height. Martan's breath caught in his throat. The dragon was incredibly large—its long legs raising the massive torso twice the height of a man. Yet that swan-like neck, lifted the great head more than double that height.

Martan was stunned, his eyes nearly popping out of his head, as they swept across the great beast's body. In the pale moonlight, he could not tell the dragon's color, but he did notice dark spots speckled here and there across its torso. Leathery plates ran up the sides of the neck all the way to the giant head, the head itself crowned with a tall crest that ran all the way down the dragon's spine. The beast had no outer ears, but there was a ridge of horns over each of those great eyes. The dragon's head ended in a long snout with a heavily curved jawline, its large mouth filled with a row of wicked, dagger-like teeth. A slender forked tongue flicked in and out of the dragon's mouth, as it glared down at the remaining men and women.

Martan knew his arrows would be no good against the scales of a dragon, and he was terrible with a sword. Yet he knew, from his days in Deepwood, that the best way to fight any enemy was to gain the high ground. There was a tall tree at the edge of the clearing twice the height of the dragon. Martan now made for that tree, keeping one eye on the great beast. He had almost reached the base when the dragon reared its head back, and with a loud hiss, let loose a stream of liquid directly at the remaining knights. The fluid engulfed them all, those brave men and women completely disappearing from sight.

Martan felt the blood drain from his face, not sure anything could survive such a terrible onslaught. After what seemed like forever, the dragon finally stopped, the stream of liquid fading as it drew back its head once more. One lone figure now stood where those last knights had been—Sir Craven glared up at the dragon, his face a mask of rage. He pointed his sword at the foul creature and screamed, "I'll send you to hell for that, you filthy beast!"

Martan drew in a deep breath and forced himself to start climbing. Sir Craven was certainly brave, but he was no match for that dragon alone. If Martan could just climb high enough, he might be able to plant an arrow in the dragon's eye. It was a long shot, but it was the only chance he had of helping the valiant knight.

Below him, Sir Craven advanced on the dragon, sword and shield at ready. Martan wasn't sure if it was the bravest, or the dumbest, thing he'd ever seen—perhaps it was a bit of both. The determined archer redoubled his efforts, climbing as fast as he could, when something large passed overhead, blotting out the moon and stars. Martan froze in place as the moonlight returned, illuminating the huge form that had flown over him. It was a second great dragon, its vast wings sending gusts of wind across the clearing as it landed right next to the first.

Martan suddenly began to shake, his entire body gripped with fear. This second dragon dwarfed the first, nearly twice the size! Sir Craven had stopped his advance—despite the impossible odds, the valiant knight did not appear afraid. Instead, he adjusted his stance to face both dragons, and cried out a challenge. "You may indeed kill me, foul beasts, but I promise it will cost you dearly!"

The first dragon started to advance on the lone knight, but then a strange thing happened. The larger dragon lunged in front of it, and growled at the first dragon menacingly. The smaller dragon froze in its tracks, yet did not back off, emitting a low growl of its own. For the first time, Martan noticed a rider on the huge dragon's back, seated just above those vast wings. The rider appeared to be an armored knight, dressed in full plate similar to that of Sir Craven and Dame Alana, but with one glaring exception—this knight's armor was totally black. It glistened dully in the pale moonlight, making it very hard to see the wearer. The black knight turned its horned helm toward the first dragon, and with a negligent wave of his hand, dismissed the fearsome creature. To Martan's great surprise, the dragon immediately obeyed, backing away from the knight, head bowed and tail between its legs. With the first dragon out of the way, the dark knight spun around in his saddle, turning his attention back to Sir Craven.

Sir Craven had not lowered his guard, instead eyeing the other knight with caution. He shouted up to him, "If you intend this to be a fair fight, you'll come down and face me man to man!"

The strange knight's mount began to growl, but immediately stopped at another wave of its rider's hand. The black knight regarded Sir Craven quietly for a few moments, then responded in an almost unearthly voice. "It would not be a fair fight either way."

Before Sir Craven could answer, the dark knight waved a hand at him. The valiant Knight of the Rose abruptly crumpled to the ground in a heap. Martan's mouth fell open—the knight had felled Sir Craven without so much as lifting a sword. He had to be some sort of caster, but Martan doubted that even Glolindir could have done that to the valiant knight.

Martan watched in astonishment as the rider spurred his mount over to the fallen knight. The huge dragon reached down, and with surprising gentleness, scooped up Sir Craven, carefully cradling him in its front claws. The creature's vast wings then spread apart, and with a few large beats, lifted into the air. As the huge dragon slowly rose higher, its dark rider called down to the first dragon. "Guard this monolith. Let no one in or out until I return."

With those final words, the huge dragon rose above the treetops, and with a great beat of its wings, took off, swiftly disappearing into the night sky.

2
DARK DREAMS

There was fighting… and a lot of blood…
The knights were not winning…

Glolindir Eodin woke with a start. He hadn't exactly been asleep, more like in a waking trance, as was the way of Elves. Yet something had roused him from that peaceful state—a strange sound that didn't belong there. The young wizard pushed himself up onto his elbows, casting a quick glance around.

Everything appeared peaceful. He was in a wide chamber, an expansive rug across the floor beneath him, and several chairs spread about. A long couch sat a short distance away, in front of a small fireplace, the warm glow of its golden fire dimly illuminating the otherwise darkened room. A translucent crystal statue of an elf-maiden stood next to the hearth, holding up a tray in one hand. The only other source of light came from the stairwell, where a solitary figure stood guard.

Glo immediately recognized the tall, broad-shouldered young man in red armor with a shock of tousled brown hair—it was Lloyd, one of his closest companions since he had ventured here to the east coast of Thac. The young warrior seemed relaxed, unaware of whatever noise Glo had heard. The elven wizard sat up further, squinting his eyes as he swept them across the large chamber.

Most of his friends lay around that room, the little gnome, Aksel, curled up into the soft cushions of a plush chair, his white robes pulled tight around him, and his copper-colored hair glowing red in the firelight. Across from Aksel, his fellow elves, Donnie and Elladan, lay stretched out at either end of that long, comfy couch. Donnie, the smaller of the two, had the lighter complexion capped with a mop of sandy blonde hair. He lay sleeping soundly in his leather pants and white puffy shirt, his brown leather vest and knee high boots lay strewn on the floor next to the sofa. Elladan's boots and cloak also lay by the couch, the elven bard curled up into a mound of pure white except for the neatly combed head of jet-black hair that adorned his decidedly handsome face.

On the floor beside Glo lay the lovely seeress, Elistra, her long blonde tresses down for once, as she snuggled into her warm blankets. The seeress had doffed her black and red cap decorated with yellow stars, as well as her black stockings and boots, sleeping only in her red skirt and short black and red top. Deep creases furrowed into Glo's brow as he gazed around the quiet room. Nothing appeared out of place. The door to the next room lay open, the young elf's keen eyes fixing on a large four-poster bed where Alana and Ruka slept. The lady knight had stuck by the young teen's side ever since she had been poisoned.

Poisoned…

The thought brought yesterday's events rushing to the forefront of Glo's mind. The small company had finally made it past the numerous traps and puzzles that riddled the Darkwoods Monolith, only to be confronted with an astonishing find. A huge cavern lay hidden beneath the sub-basement, containing a weapon of unparalleled magnitude—a colossal stone golem, stretching to an incredible height of nearly seventy feet. No sooner had the companions made this amazing discovery, than the Serpent Cult reared its ugly head.

During the deadly battle that ensued, Ruka was forced to reveal her true form—the teen shape-shifter was in reality a young bronze dragon. The party won out in the end, but their victory did not come without a price. Ruka had been severely poisoned. Yet thanks to Aksel's ministrations, and a strange karmic bond that Elistra had forged between Ruka and Donnie, the young teen's condition had stabilized. Still, the toxins remained in her system, taking a toll on her strength.

"Nooo…"

The soft moan caused Glo to spin around, his eyes fixing on Elistra. The seeress was still asleep, but her brow was knit together, her expression almost pained. "Nooo…" she moaned softly once more.

Glo reached over and gently shook the sleeping seeress. All of a sudden, she shot up out of her blankets and screamed, "Nooo!"

The entire room came awake, the overhead lights magically flaring to life in response to the loud shriek. Glo grabbed Elistra by the arms, and spun her toward him. Her violet eyes were glazed over, as if she were in some kind of trance. Glo, now extremely worried, shook her and called out her name. "Elistra! Elistra! Are you alright?"

Her violet eyes turned toward him, finally coming into focus. Elistra stared wide-eyed at him, tears forming in the corners of her eyes. "Oh, Glo…it was terrible." She threw her arms around him, and buried her head into his chest, sobbing uncontrollably.

Glo gently stroked her long, lustrous hair, and cooed to her softly. "It's okay. It's okay. You're safe. You're safe." Glo abruptly remembered they were not alone. Aksel, Donnie, Elladan and Lloyd stood over them, wearing expressions of curiosity and concern.

"What happened?" Aksel asked in a quiet voice.

Glo slowly shook his head. "I'm not sure."

"What's going on out here?" a familiar voice called from across the room.

Glo peered past the others to see Alana standing in the doorway to the bedroom, the statuesque lady knight dressed only in the form-fitting garments that she wore under her armor, her holy sword grasped firmly in one hand. Alana's brow was furrowed under her striking head of fiery-orange hair, her deep brown eyes sweeping around the room. A bleary-eyed Ruka trailed behind her, the young teen barefoot, but still wearing her dark leather tunic. She gingerly rubbed the sleep from her emerald green eyes, and peered out from under her shoulder-length, sandy-blonde hair. "Yeah. What's all the screaming about?"

Donnie turned to face the duo, and replied in a soft tone, "We're not sure. Elistra suddenly started screaming."

Alana and Ruka came over to join them, the lady knight placing a gentle hand on Elistra's shoulder. Even the usually aloof Ruka eyed her with concern. Elistra slowly lifted her head and looked up at Alana. "I'm… I'm alright." Her eyes shifted back to Glo, still brimming with tears. "Thank you," she said, attempting a smile, then gently sat back and wiped the moisture from her eyes.

This mysterious woman had firmly captured Glo's heart, which now ached to see her so distraught. He spoke to her in a gentle tone. "Was it a dream?"

Elistra responded with a short nod. "More like a nightmare."

"Oh," was all Glo said, but he implicitly understood how she felt. Elistra, being a seeress, would sometimes get visions of the future. Sometimes those glimpses came to her in dreams. Glo himself had some experience with that, and he knew how overwhelming it could be. The tall elf got up on his knees, placing one arm around Elistra's shoulder, the other sweeping under her legs. He then lifted her up and carried her over to the couch. She seemed surprised at first, but then rested her head on his shoulder, gazing up at him with a grateful smile. Glo gently put Elistra down and sat on the sofa next to her.

Alana and the others followed, the lady knight covering the seeress with her blanket. Elistra peered up at Alana gratefully, then sat back and laid her head on Glo's shoulder, pulling the blankets close around her body. Donnie handed her a cup of water, which she gratefully accepted, taking a small sip before handing it back. Once she was settled down, Glo spoke to her in a quiet voice. "Why don't you tell us about it?"

Elistra glanced up at him and nodded, then sat up and swept her eyes around the room. Everyone was gathered nearby, either on the floor, or in those comfy chairs, listening intently as the seeress described her dream. "I'm not quite sure where to begin… There were many images, some jumbled, some crystal clear… but one image was prominent throughout… a large… green… dragon…"

Ruka let out a soft hiss. All eyes turned toward the young teen. She peered back, the corner of her mouth rising. "Never really liked green dragons. They talk way too much."

Elistra cocked her head to one side, and squinted at the teen. "Trust me, in my dream it wasn't doing much talking."

Ruka responded with a casual shrug of her shoulders. "When greens aren't talking, they like to fight. Doesn't take much to set them off. Even reds aren't as bad as greens… well at least not in that respect."

Glo arched an eyebrow. He was aware that none of the chromatic dragons were friendly, but this type of insight was not well known outside the dragon community.

Elistra gave the young teen a weak smile and continued. "As I was saying, there was a large green dragon… and there were knights. There was fighting… and a lot of blood…" Her voice fell to almost a whisper. "The knights were not winning…"

Glo felt Elistra shudder next to him. He put an arm around her, and pulled her close. Alana, a dark look upon her face, leaned forward, her tone grim. "Did you recognize any of the knights?"

Elistra met Alana's gaze, the two women locking eyes. "I'm not sure. One may have looked a little like Sir Craven."

Alana stood up and retrieved her nearby sword. "That does it! I'm going to check on my men."

"Wait!" Elistra cried, holding a hand up in front of her. "There's more."

Alana had started for her room, most likely to retrieve her armor, but halted, spinning around to face the seeress. Elistra's eyes took on a faraway look. "There was one more knight… a man in blue armor… I can't see his face… but he drove the dragon off."

Alana's expression was positively grim. "What about the other knights?"

Elistra slowly shook her head. "I'm not sure."

"Then I'm going to see for myself," Alana stated determinedly, her eyes afire as they swept across the group, daring anyone to challenge her decision.

"I'll go with you," Lloyd declared firmly, striding over to stand next to the lady knight.

"I'll come, too," Donnie said, standing up as well.

Alana held up a hand, her eyes still ablaze, yet her tone understanding. "I appreciate the offer, but you're still weary from that karmic bond. I think it better if you wait here."

"I agree," Aksel said, before anyone else could speak.

"But…" Donnie began.

Elladan grabbed his fellow elf's shoulder, and strode around in front of him. "Don't worry, Donnie. I'll make sure the two of them stay out of trouble."

Mixed emotions played across Donnie's face, but then a thin smile won out over them. "That's all well and fine, but then who's going to watch you?"

Elladan chuckled softly, but Aksel interrupted him before he could answer. The little cleric gazed at Alana, his eyes filled with compassion. "I would offer to come as well, but it is probably best for Glo and me to prepare our spells for the day. We will be better able to help you if we have all of them readied."

Alana gave the little cleric a nod. "No doubt. And do not worry. We will only do reconnaissance for now, but I must know if my men are alright."

Aksel gave her a short nod. "Understood."

Alana shifted her gaze from Lloyd to Elladan. "Just give me a few minutes to throw on my chain-mail." The duo both gave her a brief nod, then the lady knight marched off to the bedroom, slamming the door shut behind her.

Ruka, still looking thoroughly exhausted, threw herself down on the couch next to Glo and Elistra. A loud yawn escaped her lips, followed by a few fading words as she drifted off back to sleep. "Wake me when… they get… back…"

Elistra reached over and covered the young teen with her blanket, then shifted her gaze back to Glo. "Maybe you should check with Raven before they head out?"

Glo had, in fact, just been thinking the same thing, and told Elistra as much. A genuine smile graced her lips for the first time since she had awakened. She winked at him and said, "Didn't you know I was a mind reader?"

Glo gave her a wry smile, then closed his eyes, emptying his mind. Raven was Glo's familiar—she had come to him when he started studying magic, some forty years ago. Glo had a special bond with the black bird, and could detect her feelings from over a mile away. It was both a blessing and a curse, Glo sometimes experiencing emotions for no apparent reason, only later finding that they were actually from his familiar. Yet now for some reason, he felt nothing from Raven. Glo redoubled his efforts, but to no avail. After a few more minutes of trying, the young wizard finally opened his eyes, and let out a deep sigh.

Elistra grabbed his hand, and gazed up at him questioningly. "Is something wrong?"

Glo looked at her and shrugged, his shoulders sagging in defeat. "I can't feel anything from Raven. Either she flew off away from the monolith, or all these layers of stone above us are somehow blocking our link."

Elistra cocked her head to one side, her lovely brow creasing. "Any chance that huge anti-magic field around the colossus could be interfering with it?"

Glo raised an eyebrow as he mulled it over. "I guess it's possible. I won't know for certain, though, until we head back upstairs."

Elistra placed a soft hand on the side of his head, and gently stroked his hair. "Later. Right now, you need to prepare your spells, as Aksel said."

Glo gave her a brief smile, then grabbed her hand and kissed it. "You are right, as usual."

Just then, the bedroom door flung open, and Alana strode out, garbed in chainmail, her white tabard with a red rose draped over it. Her eyes swept from Lloyd to Elladan. "Ready?" The duo both nodded. "Good. Then let's go."

Alana marched purposely to the stairwell, Lloyd and Elladan in her wake. Donnie followed as well, catching the lady knight at the bottom of the stairs. He caught Alana by the arm, the lady knight spinning around to face him. She seemed annoyed at first, but her face swiftly softened as she saw the look in Donnie's eyes. He flashed her a brilliant smile, and said, "Good luck up there. Please be careful."

Alana responded with a warm smile. "Thanks Donnie. We will. I promise."

The slender elf let her go and stepped back. Alana motioned for the others to follow, then swiftly disappeared up the winding stairwell that led to the cavern above. Donnie watched them go, then took up a guard position at the bottom of the stairs.

Glo shifted his gaze to Elistra and whispered, "Any idea what they'll find up there?"

Elistra wore a worried frown, as she whispered back, "Yes. That's what frightens me."

3
ENTER THE DRAGOON

Who in his right mind would hunt such a ferocious beast?

Martan believed in the gods, he just didn't think they necessarily listened to, or cared about, ordinary folk like himself. Still, when he needed to pray, his prayers would go to the goddess Synopei. He supposed it was a throwback to his days in Deepwood, that his prayers would go to the goddess of the hunt. Yet that didn't really matter right now, for Martan could think of nothing else that would help other than prayer.

All the Knights of the Rose were gone, deserted by their god, Cormar. Once the greater dragon had winged away, the large dragon had disappeared as well, slinking off into the forest. Martan had been amazed that something so big could move so quietly, but he wasn't stupid, either—he knew the great dragon hadn't gone far. It was hunting in the surrounding woods, looking for survivors.

Martan had feared for the young squires, Syndir and Lamorn, and prayed fervently that the dragon would not find them. Thankfully, it had not. Martan had heard the loud cry of a horse suddenly silenced somewhere off in the woods. A short while later, the great dragon returned with an equine carcass in its large jaws. The foul creature re-entered the clearing, parked itself in front of the monolith, and proceeded to feast on the spoils of its hunt.

Martan watched unmoving from his perch, waiting until the great beast was done and had apparently drifted off to sleep. Just prior to sunrise, the wind began to shift. Martan was forced to finally move, the need to stay downwind of the large predator paramount. He carefully climbed his way down the tree, and circled around the outskirts of the clearing, one eye always on the great dragon. Thankfully, the creature did not move. Just as the sun rose, Martan found a relatively safe spot under a thick hedge of brambles, near the head of the trail that led out of the clearing. He had just been deliberating what to do next, when the man in blue first appeared.

Martan was amazed. He hadn't heard a thing, the blue-clad figure moved so stealthily. Martan barely caught a glimpse of him, the man keeping well to the trees only a short distance from where he lay. Whoever he was, he appeared to be stalking the dragon. Martan was incredulous. *Who in his right mind would hunt such a ferocious beast?*

The figure shifted slightly, affording Martan a better view. The man wasn't that tall, perhaps a shade shorter than Martan. From this angle, he could just see his face, long brown hair covering most of it, but the man appeared young, probably not much older than Lloyd.

This young man was lean, but muscular, garbed in a blue knee-length sleeveless tunic, a studded belt around his waist, loose beige pants tucked inside brown boots, and a pair of brown gloves. A tarnished steel armguard sat on his right shoulder, his right arm wrapped with a matching steel wristband, and his left arm with a similar bracer. A matching set of dull steel greaves covered his legs all the way up to the knees. There was a large tattoo on his bare left shoulder in the shape of a dragon's head.

The warrior carried a wickedly sharp spear with a deadly-looking curved axe head near the top of the shaft. Martan had never seen that kind of weapon before, but he had heard of them—it was called a halberd.

Martan was not typically trusting of strangers, or anyone for that matter, but the circumstances were dire. He extricated himself from the brush, careful not to make any sound, then stole his way over to the man in blue. Martan silently approached the blue-clad warrior, from an angle where he was sure to be seen. The last thing he needed to do was startle the young man. That would spell certain death for the both of them. To his credit, the young warrior didn't even flinch when he saw Martan, merely responding with a slight nod. Martan replied by signaling for the young man to follow him, then carefully led him away, back into the woods.

Martan kept silent until they were a good half mile into the forest, then called for a halt, spinning to face the young man. The blue-clad warrior held that wicked-looking spear in one hand, his face a stony mask. Martan was taken aback for a moment—the warrior seemed awfully young for such a grim expression. He silently wondered what had befallen this youth that had made him so serious. When the young man spoke, there was a sharp edge to his voice. "What do you want?"

The curt response caught Martan by surprise. He eyed the youth warily as he replied. "You wouldn't by any chance be hunting that dragon?"

The young man's eyes narrowed as he glared at him intently. "What does it look like I was doing? Of course I was hunting the dragon."

Martan's eyes went wide. *So he is crazy.*

Before he could respond, the young man nodded his head back toward the clearing. "What happened back there?"

Martan paused before answering, not sure he trusted this grim young man, but then decided there was no use in keeping it secret at this point. He described the dragon's attack on his camp, the appearance of the greater dragon and its rider, and the black knight's orders before taking off. The young man listened intently, not interrupting the entire time. When Martan finished, he finally spoke. "Never heard of anyone ordering a dragon around, especially not an adult green."

Martan shrugged in response. "I don't know much about dragons, but I was as surprised as you."

The young warrior eyes narrowed. "Dragons don't hang around for no reason. What's inside that monolith that it wants?"

Martan let out a short sigh. "My friends—they went in the day before, chasing after this group of evil magicians."

The young man frowned for the first time since Martan had met him. "Evil magicians? Are you sure they're still alive?"

Martan responded with a short nod. "They're alive. They're a pretty resourceful group."

The man in blue spun around and peered through the woods back toward the monolith. After a moment or two, he spoke to Martan without turning around. "Do you think they'd be any good in a dragon fight?"

Martan's eyes widened, all sorts of alarm bells going off in his head. *This guy really is crazy… but then again it is probably going to come down to that anyway. The dragon certainly isn't leaving anytime soon.*

"I can't say for certain—though I have seen them make short work of a bunch of large serpents."

The young man, still turned away from him, was silent for a few moments. Finally, he spoke again. "How large?"

Martan thought back briefly to the battle at Ravenford Keep. There were several large serpents there. Most of them were a good two heads taller than Lloyd, and the last one was two heads taller than that. Martan knew a bit about snakes—they could only rear up the first third of their body. Based on that, he estimated the serpents' size. "Between twenty-five and thirty feet long."

The young man responded with a curt nod. "That'll do."

He began to stride forward, motioning for Martan to follow. "Let's go pay a visit to your friends."

Martan stared after the man in blue incredulously. "And just how are we going to do that with the dragon in the way?"

"That won't be a problem," the young man said without stopping to look at him.

Martan spiked an eyebrow. *Yup, definitely crazy—and I must be nuts to follow him.*

Still, the others needed to be warned about the dragon before it was too late. If there was any chance of getting past it, Martan supposed they would need to try. The dour archer let out a deep sigh and took off after the man in blue. "Wait for me!"

A short while later, Martan was positioned under a row of bushes at the north end of the clearing. The man in blue had told him to wind his way around there, and wait for his signal. Martan still thought him crazy, but the truth was, he really didn't have any choice.

The large green dragon had not moved, still apparently asleep, its great head facing the entrance to the monolith. A few minutes went by until the blue-clad warrior silently entered the clearing. Martan watched incredulously as the young man walked straight toward the dragon, stopping maybe thirty feet from it, in a wide stance with his left foot forward. Weapon held firmly in his right hand, he peered at the creature over his left shoulder and called out, "I know you're not asleep."

His statement was met with a deep rumbling that reverberated throughout the clearing. Martan arched an eyebrow in disbelief. *The dragon is laughing?*

The great head lifted and spun around on the long neck to face the blue-clad warrior. Unexpectedly, the dragon spoke in the common tongue, its voice a deep, rumbling baritone. "Heh, heh. And what do we have here? A little man playing hero?"

The young warrior stared grimly at the dragon, appearing completely confident in its fearsome presence. "Oh, I'm no hero. I'm something far worse."

The dragon laughed again, the ominous sound sending shivers up Martan's spine. "Hmmm… something worse? Should I be quaking in my boots?"

The dragon suddenly reared up, and slowly spun its large body around, still crouching low to the ground. Its large head jutted out on the long neck, stopping maybe ten feet from the young warrior. "So then, little man, tell me… are you impressed with what you see?"

The young man let out a deep sigh. "Typical dragon. Are you going to talk me to death, or are we going to fight already?"

The dragon did not laugh this time. The serpent-like eyes fixed on the young warrior, the large creature baring a deadly row of dagger-like teeth. "Interesting. If you are really so eager to die, then who am I to stop you?"

Without warning, the dragon's head shot forward, its mouth opening wide as it sped toward the young warrior. Martan thought him a goner for sure, but at the last possible second, the blue warrior leaped high into the air, narrowly avoiding the dragon's jaws. The dragon's great maw snapped shut on thin air, causing the creature to momentarily flinch.

The young warrior landed a few yards back with a loud cry. "Now!"

Martan immediately spurred into action, jumping from underneath the brush, and taking off at a dead run for the monolith. The dragon swiftly recovered, its serpent-like eyes fixing solely on the figure in blue. The creature's voice rumbled across the clearing. "You're pretty quick for a squishy little fleshling…"

The dragon paused a moment. When it spoke again, its tone was extremely menacing. "…though I wonder if you can outrun my breath?"

As the great creature finished speaking, its large maw opened wide and began to draw in air. Yet the blue warrior seemed unphased by the dragon's threat. He answered the creature in a tone as cold as ice. "I don't run from anything."

Without warning, the young man charged forward, his wicked-looking halberd pointing straight at the dragon's head. His brazen move must have taken the beast by surprise—it suddenly stopped inhaling, its dark eyes fixed on the crazed figure rushing toward it.

About ten paces from the dragon's snout, the blue warrior suddenly leapt forward high into the air, straight over the head of the stunned creature. At the last moment, the great beast lifted its head and snapped at the young man, but it was too late. The warrior had already vaulted over its head, landing on the dragon's neck.

Martan had raced like mad to reach the monolith's entrance, yet he halted there, staring in wonder at the sight of the young man racing at incredible speed down the dragon's back. The great head swiveled around and followed the warrior, snapping violently at him.

Yet whenever those jaws came too close, the man in blue would just leap out of the way. As soon as he reached the dragon's tail, the young warrior took a huge leap off its back, straight for where Martan stood. His grim eyes fixed on the frozen tracker, a shout erupting from his lips. "Run, you fool!"

The irate cry spurred Martan into motion. The dour tracker spun around on his heel and dashed into the monolith, the darkness within quickly enveloping him.

When Alana, Lloyd, and Elladan reached the top of the monolith, it was already daylight outside. Alana led the way to the window facing east, and peered out over the edge. The lady knight let out a short gasp—down in the clearing, the camp was in shambles, pieces of tent lay shredded and scattered, the spike-pitched fence mostly flattened, the troops nowhere to be seen.

Lloyd stood next to Alana, just as surprised as she to see the wreckage below. He placed a comforting arm around her shoulder and said, "I'm sorry, Alana."

Alana glanced up at him, tears brimming in her eyes. She quickly brushed the tears away, and set her jaw. "They were brave men and woman—willing to make the ultimate sacrifice for the greater good. Their names will not go unspoken, nor their lives unavenged."

Lloyd smiled grimly at the lady knight. "I would like a hand in that."

Elladan nudged Lloyd in the side. The young man shifted his gaze to the bard questioningly. Elladan pointed a finger straight down the side of the monolith. "Look down there, directly below us."

Lloyd followed the bard's finger. A large green mound sat on the ground directly below them. It had been easy to miss, the way it blended in with the grass surrounding the monolith. Lloyd squinted his eyes—the mound slowly grew and shrank. It was a rhythmic motion, like… breathing. Lloyd looked all over the strangely moving mound. There were a couple of sections that, when traced out, looked just like wings. Lloyd shifted his gaze to Alana. "I think we've found the object of our vengeance."

Alana nodded, her expression stony. "I see it as well. By Cormar, I swear, before this day is over, my blade will taste dragon blood."

"As will mine," Lloyd agreed.

"Hold on there, you two," Elladan interrupted them. Lloyd took a step back, so that both he and Alana could face the bard. Elladan's gaze shifted from Alana to Lloyd and back again, his expression keenly sympathetic, yet his eyes filled with concern. "I realize the loss you just suffered, but I'm not sure, even with all of us combined, that we can stand against an adult green dragon."

Alana's eyes narrowed as she stared intently at the bard, her reply strained at best. "I cannot let such a vile act go unpunished. It is against everything I stand for."

Elladan put his hands on his hips and returned her steely gaze, unflinching. "What good will that do if you're dead?"

The two of them stood there staring at each other, neither batting an eye. The tension in the air was so thick, it was almost palpable. Alana finally broke the silence. "If I die, then so be it. At least it will be for what I believe in."

Lloyd stood there the entire time with his arms folded across his chest. He implicitly understood both sides of the argument. Elladan was concerned for the lives of his friends, while Alana felt compelled to stand up for her beliefs. They were both right, and yet, his own beliefs were similar to Alana's. His gaze shifted back and forth between the two, when his eye caught a hint of movement down in the clearing below. "Look down there, over by the treeline."

Alana and Elladan followed Lloyd's gaze, just in time to see a man step out of the trees and approach the green dragon. The warrior wore a blue tunic and carried a long spear. Alana's mouth fell open, her tone hushed. "Could that be the blue knight from Elistra's dream?"

They all watched incredulously as the man in blue strode up to the dragon, stopped, and called out to the creature. The dragon responded by lifting its head, spinning it around to face the man. A short exchange took place, the man purposely trying to antagonize the dragon. The dragon then got up and shifted its entire body to face the man.

"He must have a death wish," Elladan murmured quietly.

There was another short exchange, then abruptly the dragon lunged at the warrior. The large creature was surprisingly fast, but the man was faster. At the last second, he leaped out the way, the dragon cleanly missing him. The warrior landed a short distance away and cried out, "Now!" Yet instead of turning and running, he stood his ground. The dragon momentarily flinched, but then quickly recovered.

"He's going to get himself killed," Elladan cried, his voice rising an octave.

Lloyd glanced at Alana, their eyes meeting for a brief moment, then the young warrior spun around and rushed toward the stairs. Alana was right behind him.

"Not if we can help it!" Lloyd cried over his shoulder.

"Wait!" Elladan shouted after them. "Wait for me!"

Martan had run into the monolith, only to find himself in pitch blackness. Unsure what was in front of him, the tracker pulled out his bow and used it to feel out the ground ahead. He had only made it a short distance when a voice shouted from behind him, "That's too slow!"

As if responding to the loud voice, the room around them suddenly flared to life. Strange glowing tiles were embedded in the floor and ceiling every so many feet, illuminating the entire area. They stood in a vast chamber, easily the largest Martan had ever seen. The huge room was basically empty, except for some large, ornate tapestries that hung on the wall, and a thick central pillar that rose from floor all the way to the ceiling. A spiral staircase wound around the outside of the column, disappearing into the ceiling far above. Martan felt a hand on his arm, the blue-clad warrior running past and dragging him with him. "No time to gawk. Make for that pillar."

Martan took off behind the young warrior, but a loud roar made him cast a glance over his shoulder. "Get back here, you puny little humans!"

The dragon had stuck its head through the archway, its jaws

opening wide as it chased after them. The blue warrior abruptly halted, pulling a small rod from the pack on his back. The rod swiftly expanded into a full-sized spear. The man in blue launched the spear at the dragon's open maw, with the cry, "You're making this way too easy!"

Martan watched in awe as the flying spear turned into a lightning bolt in mid-air. The dragon realized its peril far too late. Before it could close its mouth, the bolt shot forward directly into the dragon's maw. Electrical arcs flew out of the dragon's mouth, dancing all around its snout and eyes. The large beast shuddered in pain, its entire head sizzling from the barrage.

The man in blue spun around and slapped Martan on the arm. "That won't last long. To the pillar, quick!"

Martan took off after the young man, the two of them racing toward the central column. They had just made it to the base when the dragon roared yet again. "I'll get you for that!"

"Quick," the man in blue urged, "up the stairs and around the back."

Martan raced up the staircase just behind the young man, the spiral leading them around and behind the large pillar. The blue warrior halted there and held up a hand, Martan coming to a halt beside him. It was not a moment too soon.

They had no sooner stopped than a barrage of thick green liquid went flying past them on either side of the pillar. Martan flattened himself against the wall—he had seen what the dragon's breath could do, and wanted no part of it. The liquid barrage lasted for almost a minute, the acrid smell causing Martan's eyes to tear. Finally, it subsided, the dragon having exhausted its deadly breath.

The warrior in blue nudged Martan in the arm. "It won't be able to do that again for a bit. So which way do we go, up or down?"

As if in answer to his question, a familiar voice drifted down from above. "Quick, this way! We're up here!"

Martan immediately recognized that voice as belonging to Elladan. The stairs above them were in the way, but there was no doubt in his mind that it had been the bard. Martan grinned for the first time in a long while. "You heard the man, up it is!"

Martan ran past the young man and raced up the winding stair-well, the man in blue right behind him. Down below, they could still hear the dragon raging, throwing an oversized temper tantrum.

"Get back here, you filthy little humans. I will kill you, and eat you, and grind your bones between my teeth, until there is nothing left of you but dust!"

The blue warrior let out a cold laugh. "Heh. Guess I got under its skin."

"You think?" Martan spiked an eyebrow, not bothering to look down as they continued their ascent.

Lloyd waited impatiently at the top of the stairs with Alana and Elladan. The bard had forced the two of them to stop there, point-ing out that Martan and this strange man in blue had already made it safely to the stairwell. Alana appeared as impatient as Lloyd, the lady knight still thirsting for revenge against the dragon. Less than a minute had passed when Martan and the newcomer appeared on the stairwell just below them.

"Quick, this way!" Elladan urged them. He motioned for Lloyd and Alana to head back up the stairs to the next floor.

Lloyd glanced at Alana and shrugged. "I guess we might as well."

Alana gave him a brief nod, then turned and climbed back up the winding staircase, not stopping until they made it to the room above. The light in this room was rather dim, the only source of light com-ing from a group of dancing balls that Elladan had cast on their way down. Elladan, Martan and the newcomer in blue soon joined them. Elladan turned to face the duo, still sweaty and somewhat flushed from their encounter with the dragon.

"Well that looked like fun. Who's your friend?"

Martan shifted his gaze to the man wearing the blue tunic. "Sorry, but I never quite got your name."

The young man gazed at him with a cold expression. "Cyclone."

"Cyclone?" Martan trailed off.

"Just Cyclone."

Martan gave the young man a wan smile, then introduced himself and the others. "I'm Martan. Martan Folke. This is the Dame Alana, Knight of the Rose, Lloyd Stealle, Spiritblade of Penwick, and Elladan Narmolanya, Bard from Kai-Arborus."

Cyclone eyed them all wordlessly. Alana, however, seemed impressed with the young warrior. "That was some exchange you had out there with that dragon."

Cyclone's expression remained stoic. "Green dragons are stupidly predictable. Now if that had been a red, it would have been more of a challenge."

Lloyd eyed the newcomer curiously. He seemed to know an awful lot about dragons. "That's funny. Ruka said almost the same thing."

Cyclone turned his intense gaze toward Lloyd. "Who is this Ruka? Sounds like she might actually know a thing or two about dragons."

Before Lloyd could answer, Elladan cut him off. "You'll meet her in a bit. First, tell us Cyclone, how do *you* know so much about dragons?"

Cyclone spun his gaze toward Elladan, and regarded the bard coldly. "That's because I'm a dragoon."

Lloyd stared at him blankly for a few seconds. "A what?"

Before the man in blue could respond, Alana answered for him, her voice slightly strained. "He's a dragon hunter."

Lloyd exchanged a worried glance with Alana and Elladan. The bard raised an eyebrow. "Well this could be interesting."

Lloyd wasn't quite sure what to make of this Cyclone. It was just short of amazing how he handled that green dragon below, and saved Martan's life in the process. Still, he didn't seem like the friendliest person in the world. Lloyd silently wondered how he would react when he met Ruka. Of course, they didn't need to tell him what she was, but what if he figured it out?

Martan was staring all around at the encroaching darkness. "Why haven't you turned on the lights in here?"

Elladan stared at the archer as if he were daft. "Turn on the lights? What do you mean, turn on the lights? How are we supposed to do that?"

Martan cocked his head to one side, his brow furrowed as he looked at the bard. "Just like downstairs, I suppose." Martan cupped his hands together, and cried out, "Turn on!"

The room suddenly flared to life, tiles on the floor and ceiling glowing brightly, illuminating the entire room. Lloyd glanced all around, then back at Elladan and Alana. The bard slapped his palm to his forehead. "What do you know? They were there the entire time."

Cyclone let out a derisive snort. "You mean, all this time you were roaming around here in the dark?"

Elladan fixed the dragon hunter with a strained smile. "Not exactly."

Martan swept his eyes across the little group. "So where are the others?"

"Downstairs," Lloyd answered immediately.

Martan cocked his head to one side and stared at Lloyd quizzically. The archer then pointed a thumb towards the floor. "Isn't that in the other direction?"

Alana answered this time, a faint smile spreading across her lips for this first time this day. "You would think so, but no."

Martan slowly shook his head. "I don't think I'm quite following you."

Elladan let out a short laugh. "That's okay. You must understand Larketh. Nothing is ever straightforward in here."

"Lar-who?" Cyclone gave him a dark look.

"Larketh," Lloyd answered, waving his hands at the surrounding room. "The Golem Thrall Master. This is his monolith."

Cyclone folded his arms across his chest. "Never heard of him."

Elladan peered curiously at the young man, a single eyebrow raised. "Never studied much history?"

Cyclone responded with a curt shake of his head. "No. Just dragons."

Elladan arched an eyebrow at the young man. "You know, there's a lot to be learned from history."

Cyclone unfolded his arms and strode past all of them toward the stairs. "Don't care. I'm a dragon hunter. I hunt dragons. It's that simple. Now are we going to meet the rest of your friends, or not?"

Lloyd exchanged surprised glances with Elladan, Alana, and Martan. This Cyclone was definitely not the warm and fuzzy type. Still, he had a point. The dragon should be their first priority. Lloyd shrugged at the others then strode past the young warrior toward the stairs.

"Follow me." He motioned to Cyclone, then headed up the stairs toward the top of the monolith.

4
THE DRAGON MASTER

Glolindir had finished memorizing his spells for the day, and now sat with Elistra and Aksel, waiting for the others to return. Ruka was still fast asleep on the couch, while Donnie stood guard over by the stairwell. Aksel peered at Glo, his brow creased with deep lines of concern. "Still nothing from Raven?"

Glo let out a short sigh. He had tried once more to reach his familiar, but still felt nothing. "No. I just hope she's okay."

Elistra placed a gentle hand on top of his. "I'm sure she is."

Donnie suddenly called out from the stairs. "Someone's coming."

Glo, Elistra, and Aksel all stood up and turned to face the door. Ruka stirred on the couch. Over at the staircase, Donnie took a few steps back, a hand resting on his sword hilt, until a familiar voice drifted down the stairwell, causing them all to relax. "…and that was the end of the first age, Hai'Valan. Luckily, the dragons won."

The corners of Glo's mouth upturned slightly. Elladan was

discussing history, one of his favorite topics. The slight smile faded from Glo's lips, and turned into a frown, as an unfamiliar voice answered the bard. "Why are you still talking? Did I ask for a history lesson on dragons?"

A moment later, the bard appeared around the corner of the stairs, a stranger dressed in a blue tunic decorated with sparse pieces of armor walking next to him. Glo cast a quick glance at Elistra, her eyes widening as she stared at the newcomer.

"The blue knight," she murmured under her breath.

The warrior carried a long, pointed spear with a wicked-looking curved axe-head at the top of the shaft. Glo immediately recognized the weapon—it was a halberd. The combination axe and spear was typically used for fighting mounted soldiers… or large creatures.

Alana and Lloyd appeared immediately behind Elladan and the warrior in blue. Martan trailed behind them all, his long brown hair a bit disheveled, and his normally close-cropped mustache and beard a bit more ragged than usual. The rest of the companions strode forward to greet them, even Ruka begrudgingly lifting herself off the couch, shuffling over with her blanket still wrapped tightly around her.

Aksel was the first to speak. "So, what did you find up there?"

Elladan cast a quick glance at Alana, then slowly shook his head. "It wasn't good. The camp was gone."

Glo's eyes narrowed, sweeping over Alana, Lloyd, Martan, and the man in blue. The lady knight hung her head in sorrow, while Lloyd's face flushed with anger. Martan closed his eyes, his expression pained. The newcomer's face remained solidly neutral, though Glo noticed a momentary trace of sadness in his eyes.

"Gone? What do you mean, gone?" Donnie cried, his eyes wide and mouth agape.

Lloyd responded through gritted teeth. "Trampled, shredded, completely torn apart."

The blood had drained from Aksel's face. When he spoke, there was a trace of hysteria in his voice. "What about all those people? The cavalry, the squires, Sir Craven?"

Martan's voice sounded from the back of the group, thick with emotion. "The troops were all killed… I think it was over before they even knew what hit them. Thankfully, the squires got away, but Sir Craven… he was taken."

Elladan, Lloyd, Alana, and the blue warrior all stepped aside as the archer strode forward. Glo was aghast—all those brave men and women gone. Yet he also felt confused. "What do you mean, taken?"

A deep sigh escaped Martan's lips. "It's a long story."

Elistra finally spoke up, her voice hushed. "Was it a dragon?"

The blue warrior shifted his eyes toward the seeress. "An adult green."

"I hate greens," Ruka commented from inside her blankets.

The man in blue shifted his gaze toward the blanket-wrapped teen, his expression remaining neutral. "You and me both."

Aksel waved everyone forward. "How about we all sit down. You can introduce us to your new friend, and then Martan can tell us the whole story."

The dour archer gave a nod to the little cleric, a slim smile crossing his lips. "Much obliged."

They all adjourned to the couch and chairs that surrounded the fireplace. There was a slight pause in the conversation, as the crystal-blue statue of the elf-maiden came to life, bread, cheese, and water magically appearing on her tray. By now, the companions were used to Larketh's exotic taste in constructs, but Martan still eyed the creature cautiously.

Elladan had to take a piece of cheese and pop it in his mouth before the sensible archer would touch any of it. Even then, he seemed reluctant as he grabbed a slice of bread. While they ate, Martan introduced Cyclone to everyone. There was an interesting pause in the conversation when Cyclone explained he was a dragoon—a dragon hunter. Everyone did their best to refrain from looking at Ruka.

The young teen sat forward in her chair, and eyed the warrior with keen intensity. "A dragon hunter, huh? You must be really brave, going after a dragon with that glorified pig-sticker… or really stupid."

Cyclone stared back at her for a moment or two, his eyes narrowing and his expression turning hard. "Yeah, and I'm not the one who's clearly dying."

There was a long silence as Ruka regarded the newcomer. There was a quick flash of amber across the girl's normally green pupils, and a sudden palpable tension in the air, made even more ominous by the rumble of thunder off in the distance.

Things could have gone from bad to worse, if Martan hadn't spoken up just then. "I don't mean to interrupt…"

Ruka's amber-flecked eyes turned on the dour archer, practically burning a hole into him with their intensity. Martan visibly flinched, the blood practically draining from his face, but somehow he found the courage to continue. "…but we would have never gotten past that green dragon… if it weren't for him…"

Ruka glared at the archer for a few more moments before responding, her voice filled with barely checked anger. "Go on…"

Martan hesitated, still appearing rather nervous, but then went into a description of his meeting with Cyclone. He detailed the hunter's confrontation with the dragon, how it had allowed Martan to slip past, the amazing leap over the dragon, and their mad dash through the monolith.

When he was done, Ruka spun her gaze back toward the young dragon hunter, and looked him over again with those piercing green eyes. "You… are… nuts…"

Cyclone glared back at her without batting an eye.

She eyed him for a moment more, her lips twisting as she flopped back in her chair. "Fine… he can stay…"

The tension in the air suddenly faded like the popping of a balloon. Nearly everyone breathed an audible sigh, including Glo. Lloyd, however, seemed far too intrigued with the dragon hunter to notice the sudden change in atmosphere.

"Sounds like you're pretty fast on your feet. Are you any good with that halberd?"

Cyclone's gaze shifted to the tall warrior, his eyes narrowing. "I can hold my own with it."

Lloyd's eyes lit up with excitement at the prospect of a new challenge. "Maybe we could spar sometime?"

"Fine by me." Cyclone's tone was as impassive as his expression, but the light in his eyes betrayed more than a passing interest in fighting the tall warrior.

Now that the threat of a confrontation with Ruka was over, Glo had to admit that he was as impressed with the dragon hunter as Lloyd. Cyclone's outmaneuvering of the green dragon was nothing short of amazing. Sooner or later, their little group was going to have to face that dragon, and when that time came, Cyclone could prove to be a valuable ally.

With the tension in the room dissipated, Aksel turned back to Martan. "Ahem, Martan, you never did finish your story. What exactly happened last night?"

Martan's eyes swept around the gathering, the horror of what he had seen quite apparent in those dark pupils. The dour archer's gaze came to rest on Alana.

The lady knight stared back at him, her normally placid features turned stony. She gave the archer a grim nod. "Go ahead."

Martan nodded back, and then went into a detailed description of the green dragon's attack. He described the cloud of gas that had descended upon the camp, how the knights had immediately responded, the large form of the dragon landing in their midst, and the subsequent devastating breath attack. He then explained how Sir Craven had valiantly stood up to the deadly creature, until the greater dragon arrived.

Cyclone's eyes narrowed at Martan's description of the second dragon. He cast a glance at Ruka. "Sounds like an ancient green."

Ruka stared back at him and nodded slowly. "Probably." She said nothing more, but from the expression on her face, it was obvious that a lot more was going through her mind.

Martan then told them about the dragon's rider, the black knight. Everyone was astounded that both dragons simply obeyed his commands, yet Glo felt more than just astonishment—he had a sinking feeling in the pit of his stomach. The elven wizard exchanged a quick glance with Aksel and Elladan. "Could it be?"

Both gnome and elf gazed back at him with equally troubled expressions. The three of them slowly turned to gaze at Elistra. The seeress appeared as disturbed as they, her violet eyes wide, her mouth partially agape. She responded to their non-verbal question with a slow shake of her head. "I just don't know…"

"Care to share what the four of you are going on about?"

Glo and the others turned as one toward Donnie. The sandy-haired elf sat on the couch next to Alana, gently holding the lady knight's hand. Glo pursed his lips together as he decided how to best explain the feeling of dread that had suddenly come over him.

"Remember what Elistra told us when we first met her… that the Thrall Masters might not have been destroyed?"

Donnie's eyes widened as the realization of what Glo was implying struck him. "You mean to say, this guy with the dragons could have been a Thrall Master?"

Glo gave him a short nod. Donnie sat forward, his eyes shifting from Elladan, to Aksel, then Elistra. "And you all think this?"

The trio exchanged a glance, then turned back to Donnie.

"Yeah," Elladan replied.

"I believe so," Elistra agreed.

Donnie sat back in his seat, his expression suddenly grim. Alana, quiet up till now, addressed Martan, her voice just above a whisper. "Thank you for saving Syndir and Lamorn." She paused a moment, her voice catching in her throat. "Was… was Sir Craven still alive?"

Martan gazed at the lady knight with keen sympathy. "Yes, I believe so. It looked like he had just been put to sleep."

"Thank Cormar…" Alana said with a huge sigh.

She trailed off, unable to speak any further. Her distress roused Donnie from his dark thoughts, the thin elf placing a comforting arm around the lady knight's shoulders. No one else spoke for a bit, the fate of Sir Craven playing on all their minds. It was Cyclone who finally broke the silence.

"What's a Thrall Master?"

Glo, roused from his own dark thoughts, arched a single eyebrow, the question catching him by surprise. He thought that everyone knew about the Thrall Masters. Aksel appeared equally astonished. The little cleric stared at the young man for a moment, then turned to Elladan, and motioned toward the young dragon hunter. "Maybe it's best if you explain?"

Elladan gave Aksel a curt nod, and then turned his gaze back to Cyclone. "I know you don't have much background in history, but have you at least heard of the Thrall Wars?"

Cyclone's face remained impassive. "Heard the name… not much else."

Elladan let out a long sigh. "Looks like I've got a lot of ground to cover with you. Let's make this as simple as possible."

The elven bard took a deep breath, and then started his narrative. "One hundred and fifty years ago, the Thrall Masters rose to power. There were many of them, some lesser, some greater, but four rose above the rest. Those four had incredible power, with armies of formidable creatures at their disposal, creatures that normally couldn't be controlled. One of the four was the Dragon Master, a mage who had the power to bend the mightiest of creatures, dragons, to his will."

The elven bard paused, his eyes sweeping around the room, then continued his story. "The Thrall Masters sent their armies spilling across Thac, raining terror and destruction wherever they went. They quickly spread across the island, the individual races rallying against them too late, and before anyone knew it, most of the continent had fallen."

Elladan paused again, his tone rising in intensity as he told the next part of his tale. "Yet just when all seemed lost, an alliance of races was formed. Led by a group of then-unknown heroes, the alliance waged a bloody war against the Thrall Masters that lasted for years. Many lives were lost, but in the end, their armies were defeated, and the Thrall Masters themselves were overthrown, each in turn."

When Elladan was done, he took a long breath, his eyes coming to rest on Cyclone. The young man sat with his arms folded across his chest, his expression rather skeptical. "A man who could control dragons? I don't believe it."

Martan gave the young hunter a feeble smile. "I've seen it, and I still don't believe it."

Elladan swept his gaze across both men, a semi-smile forming on his lips. "Trust me, I get it. It isn't easy to believe. I'm not sure I would have either, if I hadn't read Dreamweaver's original works for myself."

Cyclone, arms still folded, did not appear convinced. "Who's this Dreamweaver?"

Elladan eyed the young hunter as if he had just climbed out from under a rock. "You really didn't study any history, did you?"

Cyclone stared at him with a deadpan expression. "Nope."

Elladan let out a long, drawn out sigh and shook his head. "Dreamweaver was one of those heroes I mentioned earlier. He was also a bard, and at the end of the Thrall Wars, he wrote a three-volume text on it."

Cyclone responded with a cold shrug. "So?"

Elladan cast a quick glance at Glo, his eyes betraying his thinly worn patience. Still, to the bard's credit, he did not show it otherwise, instead flashing his typical half-smile at the dragon hunter. "Yeah… well, that text covers quite a bit about the Dragon Thrall Master. Even the Knights Argentum, the great order of silver dragons, fell under his sway. No dragon could resist him, with the exception of one, but that was his eventual undoing…"

Ruka, quiet through Elladan's narrative till now, began to cough violently. She sat up in her chair, unable to stop the spasms. Donnie shot out of his seat, rushed over to her side, and patted her vigorously on the back.

"Are you alright?" he blurted out, worry written all over his face.

"I… I'm… fine…" Ruka managed in between coughs. A few moments later, the fits subsided and she pushed his arm away.

Donnie knelt in front of the young teen. "Are you sure?"

Ruka glared back at him, a hint of yellow appearing in her green eyes once more. "I said I'm fine!"

A muffled roll of thunder could be heard far off in the distance. Glo arched a single eyebrow. He had noticed the same phenomenon whenever the young teen was angry, but now it finally made sense. Bronze dragons were electric in nature, thus when Ruka grew emotional, it would stir up the very currents in the air.

The distant thunder quickly subsided, the young teen's eyes returning to their normal emerald green. Ruka then flopped back into her chair, pulling her blankets tight around her. Donnie, looking rather hurt, quietly went back to his seat next to Alana.

An awkward silence pervaded the room afterwards. Glo steepled his hands in front of his mouth. Right now, they needed to face the problem at hand—dealing with anything else would have to wait. Glo took a deep breath, and broached the subject. "Well, it doesn't sound like that dragon is going anywhere soon. The question is, what are we going to do about it?"

Alana had been rather withdrawn since her return from the world above. Now the lady knight sat forward in her seat, a fire in her brown eyes, her voice as hard as steel. "It may be pure folly, but I can't in good conscience let the deaths of my comrades go unavenged."

All eyes fell on Alana, filled with mixtures of empathy and concern. There was a moment of silence, then Lloyd stood and faced the lady knight, his expression deathly serious. The young warrior drew his black star-metal sword, held it blade-up, and spoke in a solemn tone. "My sword is yours, lady knight. I swear to you on my oath as a Spiritblade, this evil dragon will not go unpunished."

The moment Lloyd finished his speech, the black blade burst into flames, emphasizing his fiery resolve. Glo had to admit, his display was moving, but strength and determination alone would not be enough. When it came to pure brawn, they were severely outclassed by the large dragon. What they needed was to somehow outsmart the creature—find a way to catch it off guard, if that were at all possible. Thankfully, Elladan was thinking along the same lines.

The bard also stood, mixed emotions playing across his face, as his eyes shifted between Lloyd and Alana. "I truly understand how you feel. In fact, I feel the same way… but taking that dragon head-on would be certain death. What we need is a strategy, something that will give us an edge against the beast." Elladan shifted his gaze to Cyclone. "Maybe someone with experience fighting dragons could give us an idea."

Cyclone eyed the bard for a moment, then sat forward, his gaze slowly sweeping over the group, as if gauging each one of them individually. His eyes lingered for an extra moment over Alana, but finally settled on Lloyd. When he spoke, his tone was harsh. "Tell me Mr. Spiritblade, you got any idea what a dragon's weak spot is?"

Lloyd cocked his head to one side, and eyed the hunter carefully. "Wouldn't it be the underside… where the scales are smaller?"

Cyclone let out a cynical laugh. "Heh. Good try… but no. It's the wings. A dragon in the air is almost unstoppable, but ground it, and you have a fighting chance."

Ruka sat forward in her chair, her emerald eyes practically burning a hole into the dragon hunter. "And then what? Now you have a pissed-off adult green dragon on your hands. Wings or not, you're facing a death machine."

Cyclone returned her stare, unflinching, the side of his mouth lifting slightly. "I was wondering when you were going to speak up. You're right… grounded or not, a dragon is still a dragon. What you really want to avoid is being grappled, or pinned. Of course, getting chomped isn't the best, either. The trick is to avoid as many of those as possible, and the best place to do that… is on its back."

Ruka eyed the hunter as if he were crazy. When she spoke, her tone dripped with sarcasm. "And how is that going to stop it from breathing acid on you?"

Cyclone sat back in his chair, and let out a short, sarcastic laugh. "Heh. That is the real trick, isn't it?"

A hush fell over the little group once more, the dragon hunter and dragon girl locking eyes. The staring contest went on for a few moments, before the silence was finally broken by Donnie.

"I think I just might have an idea that could help with that…"

5

GREEN DRAGONS & SILVER TONGUES

You would paint a portrait? Of me?

Donatello crept silently across the ground floor of the Dark-woods monolith, toward the open archway the led to the outside world. His ears pounded with the rapid beating of his heart, nearly drowning out the loud, heavy breaths of the huge creature that lay just beyond the nearby arch. Every fiber in his being screamed at him to turn around and run, yet this had been his plan, and he wasn't going to back down now.

Donnie paused and took in a deep breath, slowly calming his nerves. He could feel dampness across his brow and on the back of his neck, beads of sweat already forming there. The agile elf wiped a single hand across his forehead, silently reminding himself he was not alone. Alana and Aksel waited only a short distance away, behind the huge pillar in the center of the room. Donnie had argued against the lady knight and little cleric following him, but now found himself glad they had.

His other hand brushed against the hilt of the strange weapon that hung from his belt. It was none other than Inazuma—the sentient sword had agreed to accompany him for this treacherous battle. Donnie had been astounded by the offer—not only was the sword a priceless artifact, but it was also Ruka's family heirloom. Donnie found it hard to believe that he was worthy in the slightest to wield such a weapon, but Elistra had put it into perspective for him.

Ruka was at death's door, yet you risked your very life by bonding it to hers. Although you no longer share life-forces, a bond like that can never be completely severed. Thus, you are truly one of the few people in this world who can safely wield her blade.

As if that hadn't been enough, Ruka had also bestowed upon him her dagger, the Ruchan. A hint of moisture welled up in Donnie's eyes as he recalled her words.

Among my kind, a life debt is not something to be taken lightly. I do not have much to give, but I would like you to have this dagger. It was carved from a scale closest to my heart. With it, know that you can always call me and I will come.

Those thoughts hardened Donnie's resolve. He was no longer the carefree artist, traveling from town to town, making a quick exit after painting a nude portrait of some nobleman's wife. He had more purpose now, and with it, more responsibility—and, for the first time in a very long time, he had friends. Donnie was doing this for them, to give his new friends a fighting chance against the ferocious green dragon that now guarded the entrance to this monolith. The slight elf wiped the moisture from his eyes, and slowly crept forward, toward what might just be his last breath.

* * *

On the topmost floor of the Darkwoods monolith, the rest of the companions prepared for the upcoming assault. It was almost midday, the sky clear and the winds calm as the sun neared its zenith overhead, the warm rays of the golden orb filtering over the lush treetops of the surrounding woods. The forest spread out like a dark green ocean before them, not stopping until it met a tall range of black peaks, the Korlokesels, far off to the north and west. In the clearing directly below, a large green mound sat near the entrance to the monolith. Though it blended in well with the surrounding grass, the mound was not a part of the wood—it was, in fact, the green dragon.

Glo gazed out over the edge of the open archway, a few hundred feet above the great beast, mentally preparing himself for the battle to come. Elladan stood beside him, Ruka pacing the floor nearby. The others were scattered about—Cyclone and Martan quietly readying their weapons, Lloyd and Elistra meditating before the impending battle.

The companions had hatched a daring plan to take on the great beast below, a strategy based on timing and misdirection. If it worked, they would have a fighting chance against the otherwise invincible creature. Yet their entire plan hinged on the slim shoulders of the irrepressible Donatello. The slim elf insisted he could pull off the most pivotal role in their strategy, yet declined to tell the others exactly how he intended to do so. Now, they all did their best to while away the minutes, tensions running high as they waited for the sandy-haired elf to play his part far below.

Donnie peered through the open archway, the green dragon laying no more than twenty yards from the door. Though on its stomach, the great beast towered above him, its massive body reaching a height more than twice that of a man, not including the tall crest that ran along the length of its spine.

The great head curled in close to the body, turned sideways so that a single large eye faced the door where Donnie stood. Thankfully, that eye was closed. The dragon continued to breathe in heavy, rhythmic breaths, as if fast asleep. Though its mouth was shut, Donnie caught a glimpse of wicked, dagger-like teeth protruding down the length of its jaw. The sight sent a cold shiver up his spine. *Just one of those teeth could skewer me like a spit.*

Donnie firmly pushed the thought aside. He had promised his friends he would do this, and he always kept his word. The anxious elf took a deep breath, then silently passed through the archway, out into the grassy clearing. The full light of the late morning sun fell upon Donnie's face, causing him to momentarily flinch. Thankfully, his elven eyes quickly adjusted to the change in brightness, and he was able to focus once more on the dragon.

The great creature still loomed over him, its breathing deep and regular, that single great eye closed. Donnie let out a long, silent breath, then took another couple of steps forward. Abruptly he froze—the dragon's huge mouth suddenly opened, a deep rumbling voice emanating from it. "I don't need to see or hear you. I can smell you, little elf."

Donnie's first instinct was to turn and run, but his knees had gone weak, and he found that he couldn't move. Thankfully his wits had not entirely left him. He steeled himself, and spoke in as calm a tone as he could muster. "Well met, good sir!"

That had come out an octave higher than Donnie had wished. His reply was met by a deep rumbling sound that reverberated throughout the clearing. Donnie arched a single eyebrow. *The dragon is laughing?*

A moment later, that deep voice rumbled at him again. "Faced with certain death, and the best you can come up with is 'well met'?"

Donnie gulped, his feet rooted firmly in place. Fortunately, his verbal talents kicked in, the words practically tumbling out of his mouth. "It was meant as an earnest greeting to one of such noble stature. I had heard of your arrival, and merely wanted to gaze at your magnificence for myself."

That had come out a bit faster than he would have liked, but at least his voice hadn't cracked that time. The dragon's eye abruptly snapped open, a large black slit the size of Donnie's head focusing on him. The tone of the dragon's response was practically scathing. "Really?" The creature paused a moment, as the great head lifted a few feet off the ground. "And?"

It took every ounce of Donnie's will to stop his knees from quaking together. He kept his eyes firmly fixed on the dragon, his voice filled with false reverence. "…and what I see most definitely lives up to your reputation. The stories say you single-handedly decimated an entire company of knights this last evening."

Once again, a deep rumbling sound reverberated throughout the clearing. "Ah… so the little scamps that ran into the tower must have told you that. Good… now I'm glad I let them get away."

The dragon's head lifted further, then spun around on its neck so that the large mouth faced Donnie. The slender elf involuntarily shivered as he gazed into that giant maw. An entire row of those deadly, dagger-like teeth lined its heavily curved jaw, looking perfectly capable of snapping a man—or elf—in half with one bite. A wicked-looking forked tongue flickered in and out from the great throat, easily wide enough to swallow him whole. It took every last bit of courage for Donnie not to spin around and scramble for the door.

The dragon's deep voice rumbled across the clearing once more. "Maybe I'll let one of you live after all… to spread my reputation."

A glimmer of hope rose from somewhere deep within Donnie. The dragon was vain, as he had suspected. Donnie had dealt with pride before, and man, or dragon, it was something he could exploit. "Oh, and what a reputation it is!" Donnie cried, warming up to the role he needed to play. "A destroyer of men and beast alike. A decimator of entire companies of warriors. A scourge to all human kind."

The dragon laughed yet again, the evil sound sending chills up Donnie's spine. "You paint an accurate picture of me, little elf."

A faint smile graced Donnie's lips for the first time since he had accepted this deadly task. This was going better than he had hoped. The thin elf struck a nonchalant pose, crossing one leg over the other where he stood. "Well, I am an artist, after all."

"Indeed," the dragon rumbled, its serpent-like eyes firmly fixed on him. "Both an elf and an artist. I've never tasted one of those before. You will make an interesting snack."

Donnie nearly jumped out of his skin as the great head slowly bore down on him. A quick glance over his shoulder showed him to be only a few yards from the archway. Yet even if he were to make it, he still had a fifty-foot run to the pillar in the center of the monolith. He would never make that in time.

Donnie had no choice but to go through with his plan, and hope to the gods that it worked. He threw up his hands, and cried out to the dragon. "Whoa there, great and noble creature. While I can think of no finer way to end my life than serving as a snack for one as glorious as thee, it would be remiss of me not to offer to immortalize your likeness for all time."

The dragon suddenly halted its menacing advance. For the first time in their conversation, the great creature sounded uncertain. "Eh? And just how do you propose to do that?"

Donnie forged on with his desperate ploy—the only thing now standing between him and certain death. "As I told you before, I am an artist. While I would make a meager meal at best for one such as yourself"—the wiry elf motioned with both hands at his thin form—"I am rather talented with the brush. If it would please you, allow me to paint your portrait. Consider it my gift to you."

Donnie held his breath, uncertain if that last bit had been too much. The dragon glared at him in silence, causing the erstwhile artist to break out into a nervous sweat. Finally, the creature answered him, its deep voice filled with skepticism. "You would paint a portrait? Of me?"

Despite its apparent disbelief, Donnie detected an underlying hint of doubt in the creature. If he continued to play to its vanity, he might yet live to tell the tale. "Can you think of a grander subject than yourself?" Donnie spread his hands out in front of him. "Just think of it... these lesser creatures, Lords and Ladies of elves and men, constantly having their portraits painted. Shouldn't a greater being such as yourself have one? Think of how splendid it would look."

Donnie flashed a sparkling smile at the huge beast, hoping beyond hope that his ruse would work. The dragon still hesitated, appearing as if it were mulling over his idea. "Hmm," a loud murmur escaped from the creature's throat. A few seconds later, it addressed him again. "You make a salient point, for a lesser being... and I suppose in payment for this 'gift' of yours, you would ask me to spare your puny life?"

All sorts of warning bells went off in Donnie's head. He needed to be careful here—if he asked for too much, the dragon might decide to eat him here and now. Yet, if he asked for too little, the creature would know that he was up to more than just saving his own skin. "Well… I was hoping that if you really like your portrait, you might consider it."

Those serpent-like eyes bore into him, making Donnie's skin crawl. It was as if the dragon were trying to read his mind. Finally, the great beast reached a decision. "Very well, get out your implements. I shall grant you leave to capture my likeness on canvas. If you manage to portray my true splendor, then perhaps I shall not eat you after all."

The dragon finished by baring its large row of teeth, another rumbling laugh emanating from its throat. The creature obviously enjoyed terrorizing its victims. Donnie had to admit, it was working—he was terrified. His mouth fell open, the words nervously spilling out of it. "I'll do my best, your magnificence. Just let me get out my brushes, and my paints, and my easel, and my canvas…"

Donnie swiftly doffed his pack, knelt, and pulled out everything he had just described. He stood up and unfolded his easel, noticing the dragon still watched him intently. *Okay Donnie, you've got its attention. Now what?*

Alana Benefilla peered out from behind the large central pillar of the monolith, just as Donnie reached the archway. The lady knight thought it foolish to stay all the way back here, especially since there was a spell over the door that prevented anyone from seeing inside. Yet according to Cyclone, dragons had such incredible eyesight, that the spell might not work on them. Thus, Donnie had insisted that Alana and Aksel stay hidden.

Alana gritted her teeth together as Donnie stepped through the archway. *It should be me out there.*

It was her people that the dragon had killed, so she should be the one acting as bait. She had argued as much, but Donnie insisted, pointing out how much faster he was on his feet. Alana had grudgingly given in, with the caveat that she come with him. Donnie had balked at first, but when Aksel declared that he would also accompany them, the reluctant elf finally agreed.

Now Alana felt helpless as she watched Donnie step out into the clearing. From this vantage point, she could only see a portion of the large green mound that was actually the dragon. Alana's hand went to her sword hilt when the deep rumbling voice of the great beast filtered in through the archway, and echoed off the walls of the vast chamber. She could not hear Donnie's reply, but her heart nearly stopped when the great head suddenly lifted into view, then bore down on the slight elf.

Alana launched herself forward, all else forgotten except for the sandy-haired elf who did not yet know he had captured her heart. She had not made it halfway across the gap to the door, when a hushed cry reached her ears.

"Alana, wait! Look!"

Ahead of her, the dragon had stopped its advance, and instead seemed to be conversing with Donnie. Alana pulled up short, her eyes narrowing as the slim elf answered the dragon, waving his hands around as if putting on some sort of show. She watched in astonishment as Donnie removed his pack, pulled out his easel, and planted it firmly into the ground.

Alana glanced sideways at Aksel, the little cleric having caught up with her. She whispered to him softly, "Do you have any idea what he's doing out there?"

Aksel appeared as puzzled as she, his head tilted slightly, nose scrunched up, and mouth partially agape. "It looks like he's… painting the dragon?"

Glo, Elladan, and Ruka watched the exchange between Donnie and the dragon with great concern. When the dragon suddenly advanced on the slight elf, Ruka nearly launched herself off the side of the monolith. Thankfully Elistra stopped her in time.

"Ruka, wait!"

The young teen halted at the very edge of the window, flashes of amber in her emerald eyes as she spun her head toward the seeress. Elistra drew up next to Glo, and spoke to Ruka with an air of certainty. "He'll be fine."

Mixed emotions played across the young teen's face, until she finally regained a measure of control. Ruka folded her arms across her chest, and continued to glare at the seeress, a menacing edge to her voice. "You better be right."

The exchange had drawn everyone's attention, Lloyd, Cyclone, and Martan joining them at the wide-arched window. Lloyd was the first to speak, his voice rife with confusion. "What in the name of Arenor is Donnie doing down there?"

Glo shifted his attention back to scene below, and was met with a sight so strange that it left him speechless. Luckily, Elladan was never at a loss for words, though his tone one of utter disbelief. "Donnie just took out his easel…"

Glo swept his gaze around the little group—there were looks of bewilderment and confusion all around—all except for Elistra. Seeing his baffled expression, the seeress gently grabbed him by the arm, and smiled at him reassuringly. Glo managed a wan smile in return, but could not shake the sinking feeling in the pit of his stomach. *Donnie, I just hope you know what you're doing.*

Back down below, Donnie furiously sketched out the dragon's likeness, his focus on the great head and those terrifying jaws. The young artist struggled to keep his hand steady—not exactly an easy task with those huge reptilian eyes watching his every stroke. *Talk about your killer critics.*

Donnie had met his share of detractors before, but never one quite so fatal. *Then again, there was that one husband back in Lukescros…*

Donnie mentally chastised himself. *Now is not the time. Think Donnie, think! How do I get this beast inside the monolith?*

The elven artist continued to work feverishly, his mind racing all the while. Before he knew it, he had finished the great head along with the upper portion of the neck. Donnie roughly sketched out the rest of the body, then drew some trees in the background. With much of the drawing done, he began to paint in earnest, starting with the dragon's head, then jumping over to the surrounding trees. He had only added a few strokes, when the answer hit him.

Donnie dropped his brush to the ground, and slowly backed away from the canvas, covering his head with his arms, and whimpering. "No, no, no. This will never do. Now I will be eaten for sure."

"What's wrong, little artist? Having trouble capturing my splendid likeness?" the dragon rumbled, its assertion ending in a wicked laugh.

Donnie's eyes darted up to the dragon—the young artist didn't have to pretend he was nervous—he truly was. "No… it's not that… it's just…"

The dragon was quickly losing patience, its voice growing louder and angrier. "It's just what? Spit it out already."

The dragon's shout was so loud, it made Donnie flinch. "It's just… green on green will never do. The surrounding vegetation totally detracts from your emerald elegance."

"Hmm," the dragon let out an elongated murmur, "let me see that."

Donnie froze in place as the great head snaked forward on that long, sinuous neck. It swiveled around behind him, the dragon's hot breath beating down on the back of his neck. As the dragon peered over his shoulder, Donnie braced himself for the worst. After a few moments, another deep murmur escaped the creature's throat. "Hmm… not bad, little elf. Not bad at all—you have managed to capture my likeness."

Donnie peeked over his shoulder—the dragon's head twisted from side to side, its gaze intent upon the canvas. "Yet I do see what you mean. That green background does take away from my beautiful scales."

Donnie carefully weighed his next choice of words. He needed to get the dragon inside the monolith, but a straight-out suggestion would definitely raise the creature's suspicions. *Maybe if I propose just the opposite…*

"Perhaps we could go somewhere else—like one of those streams just north of here? The blue waters would be a much more suitable background for those dazzling emerald scales."

The dragon slowly snaked its head around in front of him, those large, reptilian eyes boring into him once more. Donnie felt as transparent as glass, as if the great beast could see right through his ploy.

The dragon regarded him for a few moments before answering. "Why go so far away, when we have a perfectly suitable background standing right before us?"

Donnie had to bite his lower lip to keep himself from crying out in triumph. He spun his head around and peered at the monolith. "You can't mean in there? It's so dark, and dingy." He shifted his gaze back to the dragon, and waved a dismissive hand. "Totally the wrong lighting for a subject of your magnificence."

"That's funny, I seem to recall it being rather splendid in there. The stonework is quite refined, and there are some decent tapestries on the walls." The dragon paused, the great head coming uncomfortably close to Donnie. "Unless, perhaps, there is some reason you don't want me in there?"

Got you! Donnie thought with glee, outwardly maintaining his nervous demeanor. It was not exactly difficult, with the dragon's lethal maw a mere few feet away. Donnie threw up his hands, his voice cracking outrageously. "Oh, no, no, no, your magnificence... Why would I want that?"

The dragon's hot breath washed over him, the acrid smell nearly bowling him over. After what seemed like an eternity, the creature responded in a commanding tone. "It's decided, then. Take your implements and set up inside. I will follow shortly, and you shall finish the portrait which you promised me."

Donnie nodded vigorously—"Yes, yes, your magnificence!"—then hurriedly gathered up his easel and paints, and scrambled toward the monolith. As soon as he broached the archway, Donnie saw Alana and Aksel out in the open. He motioned for them to hide, the duo quickly disappearing behind the central column. Still, that wouldn't be enough. As soon as the dragon entered the monolith, it would catch their scent.

Donnie scurried across the chamber, almost to the pillar, then dropped everything, and reached into his bag. He swiftly pulled out a jar of clear liquid, and popped off the top, just as the dragon's head passed through the archway. Donnie took a step forward, and "tripped," the jar flying from his hands, clattering to the stone floor in front of him. The clear liquid spilled all over, a pungent odor immediately rising from it, making Donnie's eyes water.

The dragon snaked its way farther into the monolith, the great head swiveling around, those large eyes carefully sweeping the vast ground floor. Donnie felt his heart skip a beat as the dragon suddenly halted its advance, its large nostrils warily sampling the air. After what seemed like forever, the great head turned toward the artist, the beast's deep voice reverberating throughout the huge chamber. "Whatever is that horrid odor?"

Donnie hadn't realized he'd been holding his breath. He let it out now, and swiftly executed a deep bow. "Many pardons, your magnificence. It is merely paint thinner." He pointed toward the dropped canvas. "I need to remove that horrible background before I can continue with your portrait."

The dragon regarded him in silence, those serpentine slits sending shivers up his spine. After a long pause, its deep rumbling voice echoed around the chamber once more. "Very well… let's get this over with."

The dragon lifted its head higher and glared down at the artist, striking a fierce pose for its 'portrait.' The corners of Donnie's mouth upturned slightly as he brought his thumbs and forefingers together, framing out his large subject. A great purple tapestry, with the flowing symbol of Larketh on it, hung just behind the dragon's head, covering a large portion of the dark stone wall. The huge tapestry was suspended by a single great spike, embedded in the wall far above.

"Perfect," Donnie murmured softly, throwing himself into his work to hide the slight smile on his lips.

6
DEATH FROM ABOVE

The dragon hunter rushed toward his target...

Glolindir watched in astonishment as the green dragon followed Donnie, inserting its great head into the entryway of the monolith, far below. Somehow the slight elf had done it—he had coerced the fearsome creature into placing itself in a most compromising position. The others were lined up at the wide window next to Glo, staring down in equal amazement at the strange sight below.

Cyclone shook his head. "Yeah… he's gonna die."

Ruka cast a sidelong glance at the hunter. "Nah. He'll be fine. Donnie's pretty resilient."

A sudden crash of thunder echoed up from down below.

Elladan spun around to face the others. "Well that doesn't sound good. I think you need to get down there pronto."

The bard immediately stepped back, a golden-hued lute appearing in his hands. He launched into a lively tune, laced with magic to inspire courage amongst his comrades. The rest of the party took the bard's cue, and spurred into action.

Cyclone poised himself at the edge of the window, wicked-looking halberd in one hand, cautiously gauging the wind with his other. Martan lined up next to Cyclone, the archer also carefully testing the wind.

Lloyd grabbed the edge of his flying cloak, and spoke the single word that invoked its magic, *"Fugere."*

The young warrior then drew his black sword, the blade harder than ordinary steel—so sharp that it could cut through other metals with ease.

Glo swiftly cast the same spell as Lloyd, weaving his arms in a distinct pattern, that same word flowing off the wizard's tongue. Elistra weaved a spell as well, the air shimmering where the seeress pointed, a short distance back from the window. A moment or so later, a translucent creature appeared in that space, looking vaguely like a horse-sized hummingbird.

Yet the most dramatic action belonged to Ruka. The young teen rushed back a few paces, then halted, an expression of deep concentration across her brow. Her entire body began to glow, growing brighter and brighter until all that was visible was a brilliant white light. The glow then transformed, expanding into a much larger shape.

The torso shifted onto all fours, the neck elongating drastically. A pair of large, bat-like wings sprouted from its back, and a long, serpentine tail extending from its hindquarters. The brilliant radiance faded, and in the young teen's place, there now stood a magnificent, young, bronze-colored dragon.

Glo gazed in awe at the breathtaking sight. The creature's scales positively gleamed in the midday sun, with a warm, yellow-brown metallic sheen, light green stripes interlaced across her neck, torso and tail. Still, she was far smaller than the green dragon outside, perhaps half the size of her adult 'cousin.'

"Knew it," Cyclone remarked, the dragon hunter peering at the bronze dragon with a self-satisfied smile. The dragon's head swiveled toward the blue-clad hunter.

"Sure, you did," Ruka responded, her voice still recognizable, just a bit deeper in her true form. Her statement was punctuated by a loud roar echoing up from down below.

Cyclone let out a gruff laugh. "Heh. Think what you want. I've got better things to do."

With that, the dragon hunter spun around, and leapt out of the wide archway. Glo and Lloyd took off immediately after him, launching themselves away from the tall black structure, out into the open airspace above the clearing. A moment later, a large shadow passed over them—Glo glanced up and saw the graceful form of the bronze dragon sail past them at nearly twice their speed.

A minute or so earlier, Donnie frantically wiped a cloth soaked with paint thinner against the canvas to wipe the background clean. He reached down for more paint thinner, knocking the jar over once more.

"Dragon dung!" Donnie swore under his breath.

The green dragon's deep voice rumbled around the inside of the great chamber, a dangerous edge to it. "You suddenly seem quite nervous, little elf. Did you really think you could play me for the fool? I shall extricate myself now, and foil whatever plot you puny elves and humans have brewing."

Donnie suddenly went cold inside, yet to his credit, he kept his voice smooth and steady. "Whatever could you mean, your magnificence? There's no trick, only a poor itinerant artist, trying to barter here for his life."

The black eyes of the great creature glared down evilly at him. "Do not fret, little elf. I will be back for you soon enough."

Donnie knew the jig was up, but he still had one last trump card to play. He dropped the canvas, in one swift motion drawing Inazuma from its sheath and pointing it at the dragon. "We shall just see about that!"

The dragon let out a deep, wicked laugh. "And just what do you think you are going to do with that puny stick?"

"This!" Donnie cried. As Inazuma began to glow, Donnie shifted his aim slightly above the dragon's great head. A moment later, a bolt of lightning shot out from the blade, flashing past the dragon's head, hitting the wall of the monolith far above.

The dragon momentarily winced at the flash, the crash of thunder bouncing off the inner walls of the monolith. As the rumbling noise died down, it was replaced with the sound of deep, wicked laughter. "You missed, little elf."

Donnie arched a single eyebrow in response. "Did I?"

A huge length of purple fabric suddenly fell from above, the dragon's great head and upper neck disappearing beneath Larketh's huge tapestry. At the same time, a familiar voice sounded from behind Donnie. "I trust that is what you meant to do."

The slim elf spun around and saw Alana standing behind him, a skeptical expression on the lady knight's face. Donnie peered at Alana with a hurt expression. "Of course I did. How could you ever doubt me?"

Behind him, the dragon let out a great roar, accompanied by the sound of ripping cloth. "I'll melt you to your bones, you puny little elf!"

Aksel's voice rang out from the pillar, a few yards away. "Get back here, you two! Before it breaks loose!"

The artist and the lady knight exchanged a quick glance, then grabbed each other by the arm, and sprinted back behind the central column of the monolith.

Outside the monolith, Cyclone hurtled head first toward the exposed back of the unsuspecting green dragon. The dragon hunter's wicked-looking halberd jutted out in front of him, a glint of light reflecting off the deadly weapon's sharp tip. Lloyd and Glo exchanged a fleeting glance, then banked into a steep dive, scrambling to get into position in time. The dragon hunter rushed toward his target... one hundred feet... fifty... twenty-five...

The dragon hunter slammed into the dragon's back, the added force of his high dive driving the long halberd well past the thick green scales. The deathly-sharp weapon dug deep into the great beast's flesh, just above the base of its wings, next to the dragon's tall crest. Blood spurted from the wound—the acid blood of a green dragon—hissing as burned through everything it touched.

In an amazing feat of agility, Cyclone avoided the spray of blood, flipping his body around and firmly planting his feet on either side of the impaling weapon.

The dragon's reaction was immediate, and violent—its large frame bucked like some huge, wild horse, the large wings flaring out wide on either side, the long serpentine tail whipping around furiously. A bone-shattering roar gushed from the entryway, sending chills up Glo's spine.

A moment later, the dragon was struck again, this time from multiple sources. Lloyd strafed over the creature's large left wing, his black blade engulfed in flames as it bit deep into the thinly stretched portion of skin between two of the long phalanxes. Three arrows rained down in rapid succession from above, planting themselves in a row along the length of the dragon's other wing.

Glo shook off his fear and sent a bolt of lightning cascading through the air, into the same area as the three arrows. A moment later, another bolt of lightning flashed past the wizard, Ruka expertly hitting the very same spot that Glo had.

The great dragon flinched with each and every hit, arcs of electricity dancing across its wing, as the loud crash of twin thunder strikes reverberated throughout the clearing. The thin membrane of the dragon's wing was left scorched and sizzling from the relentless attacks. Its other wing was even worse, Lloyd leaving a huge gash in his wake, rendering the appendage useless for flight.

From above and behind Glo came a triumphant roar. The great beast had been effectively grounded. Now came the hard part—facing the wrath of an enraged full-adult green dragon.

Down near the ground, Lloyd performed a tight bank, blade readied for another pass at the great dragon. Cyclone yelled to the flying warrior, "Attack the underside!"

Lloyd responded with a curt nod, then dove underneath the large creature, his black blade rending several angry red tears along the dragon's underbelly. Once again, acid blood spurted from those wounds, some of it landing on the flying warrior. Yet before it could burn him, a green aura rose to meet it, causing the acid to dissipate. It was a good thing Glo had cast an absorption spell on the young warrior. Otherwise, that blood would be eating through his armor and skin.

Meanwhile, Cyclone gave a great heave, yanking out the long shaft of his halberd. The dragon hunter then leapt high up into the air and slammed his razor-sharp weapon back down into the deep red oozing wound. The dragon flinched at the blow, another roar of rage exploding within the confines of the monolith.

More blood spurted upward, the hunter performing a crazy dance to move out of the way. He managed to avoid most of it, but some got on his armor and skin, causing them both to sizzle—yet somehow Cyclone seemed able to ignore the pain.

For the life of him, Glo couldn't understand why the hunter had refused his absorption spell. Perhaps it was a matter of pride. Yet there was nothing to be done about it now.

Without warning, the dragon backed completely out of the entrance, moving with frightening speed. Its head swiveled around, the dark-slit eyes focusing with clear hatred on the blue-clad hunter. Seeing Cyclone's imminent peril, Glo shifted the direction of his next bolt, and loosed it straight at the great beast's head.

The dragon flinched as the flash of light blasted its long snout, arcs of electricity dancing around its jaw and eyes, but the beast was so enraged that it immediately shook it off. The green dragon opened its large maw wide, inhaling deeply as it prepared to spew out a deadly stream of acid breath.

"Watch out!" Glo cried in horror, his cry punctuated by the receding roll of thunder.

Yet before the dragon could exhale, a golden-brown figure streaked down between it and its prey, letting loose a bolt of lightning straight into the larger creature's open maw. The smaller dragon swiftly sped past, leaving the greater green sputtering and choking on its own acid. Before it could recover, blue bands of force suddenly appeared around its snout, forcing the great jaws shut with a snap.

Glo spun around and saw Elistra hovering on her 'hummingbird' in the air nearby, her brow deeply furrowed with concentration, beads of sweat already forming across her forehead. Down below, the dragon's eyes practically bulged out of its head, streams of acid spewing out the sides of its mouth.

"I can't hold it much longer!" Elistra cried, her voice strained with the tension of fighting the dragon's incredible strength.

Down below, Lloyd strafed in again, rending more red-streaked tears in the dragon's underbelly. At the same moment, Alana, Donnie, and Aksel poured from the entryway of the monolith. The lady knight, sword and shield in hand, rushed forward with a loud war cry, Donnie right behind her with Inazuma in hand.

As the duo assaulted the dragon's front legs, Cyclone yanked his halberd out of the deep, bloodied wound and crouched way down. The young dragon hunter then launched himself upward higher than before, and came down with all his might, slamming the deadly weapon well into that same wound yet again. The sharp halberd went all the way in this time, down to the very end of its long shaft.

Blood spurted in all directions from the great wound, the blue-clad hunter twisting and turning to avoid the spray. Yet some of it still got on him, eating away at everything it touched. Large welts appeared all over the hunter's arms and one appeared on his cheek. Still, Cyclone ignored the pain, firmly hanging on to the end of his weapon's shaft.

Abruptly the dragon's large serpentine eyes went glassy, one last terrifying roar escaping the great maw as the bands of blue force disappeared from around its long snout. Beneath the young hunter, the dragon's body shuddered, the great knees buckling.

"Fall back!" Aksel's cry reverberated around the clearing.

Alana and Donnie pulled back just as the monster's long, thick legs gave out altogether, the green dragon falling to the ground with an earth-shaking *thud*. Everyone looked on in amazement as green liquid spilled from the creature's mouth and formed an acrid pool on the ground in front of it. The huge torso twitched a few times, then the whole body shuddered and the green dragon finally lay still.

Cheers of victory went up all around. Lloyd landed next to Cyclone, the young warrior eyeing the dragon hunter with clear concern. Cyclone glanced at the tall warrior, and gave him a brief nod. Glo, Elistra, and Ruka flew down and hovered around the pair. The young dragon's voice was filled with a mixture of sarcasm and awe. "Remind me never to piss you off."

Cyclone peered back at her, clearing trying not to wince from the pain. The side of his mouth upturned somewhat. "After that stunt you just pulled, I could say the same."

7
JOY AND SORROW

His father had been a dragon hunter, like his father before him

Moments later, Elladan and Martan emerged from the monolith. The duo stopped next to Aksel, their eyes falling on the still form of the green dragon. Alana and Donnie skirted around the body of the large beast, while Lloyd and Cyclone jumped down from the dragon's back.

The latter still winced in pain, the welts on his arms and face an angry red. Aksel came rushing over and insisted on healing his wounds despite the proud hunter's protests. Cyclone eyed the little cleric sharply at first, but finally gave in. "You're going to keep on hounding me if I don't let you do this."

Aksel's responded with a curt nod, his jaw firmly set.

"Fine!" Cyclone practically spat the word, plopping himself down on the ground facing the remains of the green dragon. "Just don't block my view."

As Aksel set to work on Cyclone's wounds, Glo, Elistra, and Ruka landed, the latter swiftly transforming into a teenaged girl once again. The small group stared in wonder at the carcass of their once invincible opponent. The great head lay still just in front of them, the black-slit eyes unfocused, the long-forked tongue sticking out of its open maw.

Donnie turned to Alana and grasped the lady knight, drawing her into a tight embrace. The slim elf rocked her back and forth, crying for joy. "We did it!"

Alana held on awkwardly to Donnie, her face turning a bright scarlet. At the same time, Elladan clasped Martan on the shoulder. "Nice shooting there! What was that, like three hundred feet?"

Martan gave the elven bard a sidelong glance and responded with a slight smile. "Something like that."

Glo spun toward Elistra. The seeress appeared quite tired. He put his arms around her, and drew her to him, a warm smile on his lips. "What you did was amazing. Are you alright?"

Elistra gazed up into his eyes, her own gleaming with affection. "I'm fine… just tired."

"Not too bad," Cyclone agreed in a gruff voice.

Aksel still hovered over the hunter, divine white light pouring from his palms and bathing the young man's arms and face with healing energy. Cyclone nodded in the direction of Ruka. "You definitely saved me and the suicidal bronze here from an acid bath."

Ruka stared back at the dragon hunter with a twisted smile. "Maybe next time I'll let the nice green dragon give you that toasty little bath."

The corner of Cyclone's mouth lifted, a short laugh escaping his lips, but Lloyd interrupted any retort he might have had. "That leap from the top of the monolith was rather impressive."

Cyclone shifted his gaze toward the young warrior, his expression turning impassive once more. "That was no big deal. It's a dragon hunter thing."

At that point, Alana gently disengaged herself from Donnie's embrace, and turned toward Martan. "Can you please help me find Syndir and Lamorn? I would like to make sure they are all right."

Martan responded with a curt nod. "Follow me."

The tracker took off with Alana in tow, the duo swiftly disappearing into the thick surrounding woods. Ruka watched them go with the others, but as she swung back around, her face suddenly went pale. The young teen swayed where she stood, looking as if she were about to fall over. Donnie immediately rushed forward and grabbed her, Ruka doing little to resist. She melted into his arms, laying her head on the slender elf's chest.

Aksel, still working on Cyclone, watched the dragon girl with deep lines of concern across his face. "Now that that's settled, we need to get you permanently cured of that poison."

Elladan placed a hand on Aksel's shoulder. "Vermoorden is still the closest town. It would probably be our best bet."

Aksel glanced up at the bard, and gave him a grateful nod, then shifted his gaze back to Ruka, his eyes narrowing. "Do you think you can make the flight?"

Ruka pursed her lips together, not lifting her head from Donnie's chest. "Well… I won't be able to fly at my normal speed, but I should still be able to get us there in just under half a day."

Elladan gazed up at the sun, the golden orb now just past its zenith. "If you leave soon, you should be able to make it there by late evening."

Donnie grasped Ruka by the shoulders, his eyes filled with worry. "I'll go with you, that is, if you don't mind carrying me on your back."

Ruka's cheeks reddened slightly. She shook her head, an embarrassed smile crossing her lips. "No… I don't mind at all."

Aksel abruptly cleared his throat, drawing everyone's attention back to him. "Ahem, actually, I should probably go with her. If you get there and there is no immediate cure, then you will need another spell to delay the poison from spreading."

Donnie eyed Aksel for a moment, then nodded. He shifted his gaze back to Ruka and spoke in a soft voice. "He's right. Your health is paramount. I would never forgive myself if something happened to you."

Ruka's cheeks reddened even further. The young teen stared at the sandy-haired elf for a moment, her emerald eyes filled with more than just a touch of affection. Her voice was just barely above a whisper. "I feel the same way."

Donnie flashed her a bright smile, then let Ruka go and stepped back. He drew Inazuma from his sheath and held it out in front of her. "Thank you for the use of your family's blade."

"You're welcome," Ruka responded with a satisfied smile, reaching out to take back the ancient sword. Her small hand lingered on Donnie's for a long moment before drawing the weapon away.

Donnie gazed warmly at the young teen, then shifted his eyes toward Aksel. "Before you go, take these."

The thin elf bent down and removed his Boots of the Spider, and dropped them next to the little cleric. "These will help you hang on and not slow Ruka down."

Aksel gave Donnie a grateful nod. "Thanks."

White light gradually stopped pouring from the little cleric's hands as he stepped back away from Cyclone. The angry welts on the hunter's arms and face had disappeared, only a trace of reddish skin remained where they had been. Cyclone pushed himself off the ground and made circles with each arm, one after the other, then cast a glance down at Aksel. "I suppose I should thank you."

Aksel, in the interim, had sat down and removed his boots, pulling on Donnie's. He smiled back up at the hunter. "No thanks are necessary. Just doing my job."

Cyclone gave the little cleric a short nod, his face expressionless, but there was a slight twinkle in his eye. Meanwhile, the magical boots Aksel had pulled on abruptly shrank to fit the gnome's smaller legs. Aksel stared at them in wonder for a moment, then got up and turned to face Ruka. "Shall we?"

The young teen nodded. She cast one last reluctant stare at Donnie, then spun around and walked a short way from the others. Ruka's body glowed once more as she shifted back to her natural form. Once the transformation was complete, she lay down on the ground, allowing the little cleric to climb up onto her back.

Aksel perched himself on her shoulders just above her glistening golden-brown wings. Ruka then stood, her great wings fanning out on either side of her sleek bronze torso. With a few steady flaps, the duo gently lifted off the ground, slowly rising above the tree tops. The gleaming bronze dragon hovered there as she spun toward the east, then shot off out of the clearing, swiftly disappearing behind the treetops.

Cyclone watched with interest as the dragon girl flew off with the little gnome on her back. The amount of concern this strange group showed for the young bronze seemed unnatural to him. What was more surprising, was that the dragon girl had risked her life for him—a dragon hunter.

In truth, he had not thought much of Ruka at first. From everything she had said, and the way the group acted around her, he suspected she was some kind of dragon. Yet that didn't impress him much. She was obviously sick, and Cyclone considered her more of a liability in a fight than not. Yet the girl had proven herself in battle, and that was something the young hunter could respect.

Cyclone was also impressed with the rest of the group… well, some of them at least. The tall warrior, Lloyd, had proven to be quite useful in the fight. With his ability to fly, and those burning blades, he had done significant damage to the dragon. Cyclone had to admit he was curious how the warrior would fare against him in a one-on-one battle.

The wizard had also done an adequate job. Cyclone didn't care much for casters. They were only good as long as their spells held out. Once those were gone, they were useless on the battlefield. The knight and the wiry elf had acted bravely, rushing the dragon's legs. Neither had done that much damage, but their attempt had earned the hunter's respect.

What had really surprised Cyclone, other than the actions of the bronze, was the other caster… the gypsy, Elistra. That little parlor trick she had pulled had given him just enough time to deliver the killing blow. Maybe casters weren't so useless after all… well at least not this one.

Cyclone glanced over at the blonde gypsy. She looked tired, her head laying heavily on the tall wizard's shoulder. This elf, Glolindir, seemed quite concerned with her condition—it was written all over his face. Cyclone watched on curiously as the elf reached down and lifted her chin.

"You really should rest, you know."

The gypsy gazed up at him, a delicate eyebrow arched. "I'm not…" A sudden yawn interrupted her response. "…tired…"

A knowing smile spread across Glolindir's face. "You were saying?"

A tiny, bell-like laugh escaped Elistra's lips, followed by a mischievous grin. "Very well… but only if you join me."

The elf's smile turned into genuine laughter. "How could I possibly resist an invitation like that?"

Cyclone wasn't one for pleasantries, but something about these two amused him. He kept his expression neutral, but watched on with curiosity as the duo excused themselves and disappeared arm-in-arm through the entryway to the monolith. Once they were gone, the slight elf, Donatello, spun back around, wearing a wide grin. "Well, there go the love-birds."

The elven bard, Elladan, playfully shoved his friend in the arm. "You're one to talk. You've got not one, but two women chasing after you!"

Donatello placed his hands on his hips, his jaw set as he eyed his fellow elf with mock anger. "First of all, Alana is far from 'chasing' me. Second, Ruka is *waaaaay* too young to even consider."

The tall warrior, Lloyd, gazed from Donatello to Elladan with a perplexed expression, his brow furrowed into deep creases. "But Ruka's a dragon, so wouldn't that make her older than she looks?"

Donnie shifted his gaze toward Lloyd and grimaced, his tone plaintive as he addressed the young man. "Not you, too."

A sheepish grin crossed the young warrior's face, his hand going to the back of his neck. "It was just an observation."

Cyclone's lips bent to one side as he listened to the three friends banter back and forth. They were an interesting lot. They fought hard together, but harassed each other with equal enthusiasm. Cyclone was not overly fond of strangers, but he found himself intrigued by this strange little group.

As Elladan continued to needle Donatello, Cyclone decided to weigh in on the conversation. "If I had to guess, your friend Ruka appears to be somewhere on the border between a juvenile and a young adult dragon. That would make her around fifty."

Lloyd turned to gaze at him, the young man's eyes filled with curiosity. "So, what would that be in human years?"

Cyclone folded his arms across his chest as he mulled it over. "Roughly around fifteen."

Elladan's lips pursed as he cast a sidelong glance at Donatello. "How old did you say you were?"

The thin elf gazed back at him with a triumphant expression. He pointed a finger and cried, "Ah ha! One hundred and seventeen—far too old for her, even in dragon years."

A crafty smile spread across Elladan's features. He wagged a finger back at his friend in response. "Ah, but that would make you only seventeen in human years—that's only two year's difference."

Elladan held up two fingers in the air, a wide smile on his face as he peered at his elven friend. The sandy-haired elf glared back at him with obvious discomfort, his complexion slowly reddening at the bard's suggestion. Cyclone found himself enjoying the exchange probably far more than he should, but any further banter was cut short by Lloyd.

"Guys?"

Everyone turned their attention to the tall warrior. Lloyd nodded toward the remains of the camp at the edge of the clearing. "All things considered, maybe we should clean that up, before Alana returns with the squires."

Any traces of a smile swiftly drained from Elladan's face. The bard gazed over at the campground, his expression turning dreadfully somber. "You're right, of course."

Donatello gazed at the young man with clear appreciation. "Thanks for thinking of that."

The three of them started across the clearing. Cyclone hesitated, gazing reluctantly at the huge dragon carcass before him. What he really wanted to do was cut off some scales and flesh. The scales made a decent trophy, and if you collected enough, would make a tough armor. Or you could even sell them for a nice price. Dragon meat was also a delicacy if cooked and seasoned right. It would be a shame to let the carcass sit for too long, but Lloyd was right—they needed to take care of the knights who had fallen in battle first.

The hunter let out a deep sigh, then followed the others across the clearing. Upon reaching the edge of the campground, they were met with a grisly sight. The men and women of the small company had been dissolved away, only parts of their skeletal structure still left intact. Donatello went pale at the sight. "I'm just glad Alana hasn't seen this."

Elladan reached out and placed a hand on Donatello's shoulder. "Let's clean this up quick, so she never has to."

Elladan and Donatello set to work gathering all the remains, while Cyclone and Lloyd dug out a deep pit. The two elves stacked those remains in a pile next to the hole they were excavating. After a few trips back and forth, Donatello broke the heavy silence. "Not that I'm worried right now, mind you, but what would happen if someone was to, say, resurrect the green dragon?"

Cyclone stopped digging for a moment, and peered up at the slim elf. A short laugh escaped his lips. "Well, hypothetically, you'd be the first one he'd eat."

Donatello's face turned absolutely pale. "Uh…I was afraid you might say something like that."

Elladan drew up next to them, respectfully adding more remains to the pile. "From my understanding, green dragons are the most aggressive of the chromatic side of the tree."

"That's the colored dragons, right?" Lloyd asked, as he threw another shovelful of dirt over his shoulder.

Cyclone shifted his gaze toward the tall man and nodded, digging in with his own shovel while answering. "Whites, blues, greens, blacks, and reds are all your 'not so friendly' dragons. The metallics, like your friend, Ruka, are supposed to be the good ones, but personally, I still don't believe that."

Donatello raised an eyebrow, but did not comment. The conversation died down after that, 'til the slim elf returned with another armful. "So how do we prevent anyone, like that black knight guy, for instance, from coming back and resurrecting this dragon?"

He finished with a nod toward the great carcass, still lying near the entrance to the monolith. Lloyd, now knee-deep into the pit they were digging, proposed a solution. "What if we burn it?"

Cyclone shifted his gaze toward the tall man, and eyed him cynically. *Is he truly that stupid?* When he answered, there was more than just a trace of sarcasm in his tone. "That's a lot of dragon to burn. It's not like we can just gather some firewood, and light it up."

Lloyd responded with a short nod, as he hefted another shovelful of dirt. "Yeah, I know, but we do have a wizard with us… and he definitely has fire spells…"

"…which he absolutely loves to use," Donatello finished, as he carefully unloaded another armful.

Cyclone peered up at the sandy-haired elf, his eyes narrowing. "Are you just flapping your gums, or is there a story behind that?"

"Oh, there's a story, alright," Donnie said with a grin. He motioned to Elladan as the handsome elf rejoined them. "You're the master storyteller—care to do the honors?"

Elladan paused a moment, then launched into the tale of how the elven wizard single-handedly burnt down the Cape Marlin lighthouse. The elven bard finished with the words, "The lighthouse burned most of the night, and the wreckage was still smoking when they left the next day."

"That's Glo for you," Donnie added with a wry smile. "He never does anything halfway."

A short laugh escaped Cyclone's mouth as he stepped firmly on his shovel and dug out another spadeful. "Heh. That might just work."

The corners of Elladan's eyes crinkled as he broke out into a grin. "Oh, it will work, alright. Let's just hope he doesn't take the monolith down with it."

The bard's comment drew a round of laughter. Even Cyclone found it amusing. It wasn't much longer till they finished with the pit. Elladan and Donnie had gathered all the remains, and the four of them carefully stacked the bones in the grave. When they were done, they piled the loose dirt back on top, creating a large mound.

Donnie recovered the knights' pennants and carefully planted them in the ground around the perimeter of the mass grave. When he was finished, he wiped the sweat from his brow, and nodded toward the trail that led into the clearing. "Looks like we finished just in time."

Cyclone shifted his gaze in that direction, and saw Alana and Martan had returned, the pair accompanied by two young boys. A few horses trailed after them, led by the reins. While Lloyd and Martan tended to the horses, Donnie gently escorted Alana and the boys over to the grave. The lady knight and the two young squires stood over the mass grave, their expressions grim. After a few moments of silence, Alana finally spoke.

Great Cormar:
Please receive these stalwart men and women into your open arms.
They were brave souls to the very last, giving their lives in defense of that which is good and righteous.
Please reserve a place for them by your side, so that their souls may dwell in peace.

Cyclone listened to the lady knight's heartfelt prayer, with his head bowed in respect for the fallen. He was not personally a great believer in the deities, preferring instead to depend on his own two hands to get the job done. Cyclone's father had lived his life that way, and raised his son to do the same. But just the same, Cyclone was all too familiar with loss.

His father had been a dragon hunter, like his father before him. Their family spawned from a long line of hunters going well back before the Thrall Wars. Cyclone began training the moment he could hold a spear. His father was a tough teacher, but Cyclone never complained. In a few short years, he won the right to carry a halberd.

Cyclone went on a few hunts with his father, but those had been younger dragons. There were not many of the creatures left on the east coast of Thac these days. So when an adult red, the most ferocious of dragons, appeared off the coast a few years back, it was a strange occurrence. His father had gone on that hunt alone, leaving Cyclone behind. He never returned.

Alana and the squires finished their prayers, then the lady knight escorted the two boys inside the monolith to eat and rest. Over by the edge of the forest, Martan and Lloyd were busily fixing the broken hitching post. Elladan motioned for Donnie and Cyclone to follow him, leading the pair to what had previously been a large campfire pit. Miraculously, the cauldron was still intact, but the wooden frame was smashed and the kindling scattered. Elladan stood over the pit, his hands on his hips as he appraised it carefully. "This shouldn't be too hard to fix."

Donnie cocked his head to one side and stared at the pit speculatively. "Once this is fixed up, I can get Martan, and the two of us could go hunting."

Cyclone swept his eyes across the duo. "Ever taste dragon?"

The pair turned to face him, their mouths agape. Elladan's eyes narrowed. "Are you serious?"

Cyclone responded with a curt nod.

Donnie glanced across the clearing toward the huge dragon carcass lying in front of the monolith. "Isn't that thing just a little big to eat?"

Cyclone glared at the slight elf as if he were daft. "We're not gonna eat the whole thing."

Elladan held a hand to his chin, his brow furrowed in concentration. "It would have to be prepared right. We'd need to drain that acid blood, and then add the right seasonings."

Cyclone strode over and threw an arm around the elf, shaking him roughly. "Now you're talking!"

The elf stared back at him, his mouth twisting into a half smile. The bard then turned to Donnie. "I'll give you a list of herbs to hunt down in the forest. Meanwhile, we'll get things set up here."

Donnie went to fetch Martan, while Cyclone helped Elladan erect the frame and re-attach the cauldron to it. When they were done, Cyclone saw the slim elf disappear with the tracker into the woods. A few moments later, Lloyd drifted over to join them. Cyclone motioned for the young warrior to follow him, then headed back toward the dragon carcass.

"What are we doing?" Lloyd asked curiously.

Cyclone glanced at the tall man, his mouth curving sideways. "Ever filet a dragon?"

Lloyd's eyes went wide as they strode together across the clearing.

After a restful afternoon, Glo returned to the clearing with Elistra, Alana, and her two squires. It was late in the day, probably an hour before nightfall, the sun gaining a reddish hue as it approached the horizon. The others were already gathered around a large campfire, Elladan busily preparing an evening stew from the dragon they had killed.

Glo had balked at the idea at first, but Elladan assured him that he had prepared it so that it was safe. The smell of the simmering cauldron reached Glo's nostrils, making his stomach grumble. If Elladan said it was okay, he supposed he could give it a try.

Yet before he could sit down with the others, Donnie pulled Glo aside and asked him to use his magic to light up the rest of the dragon's carcass. The slight elf confessed his worries about the dragon being resurrected and hunting them all down. Glo cast a glance at Cyclone, but the dragon hunter offered no comment, merely sitting near the fire with his arms folded across his chest.

Glo felt two slim hands wrap themselves around his arm. He gazed down and saw Elistra looking up at him with those big violet eyes. "Could it really hurt?"

Glo let out a short sigh and smiled affectionately at the dulcet seeress. "I suppose not."

Glo retraced his steps, slowly circling around the huge dragon carcass as he estimated the power he would need. It was still mostly intact, other than a large chunk along the flank where the scales had been removed and strips of flesh had been sliced off. In the end, a couple of fireballs did the trick. The dragon's carcass lit up nicely, looking like a giant bonfire next to the tall, dark monolith.

"Dinner's ready!" Elladan announced from across the clearing.

Everyone converged on the campfire, as the bard gingerly ladled out bowls of stew, handing them over to be passed around. Glo's mouth watered with each bowl that went by—even with dragon meat, Elladan's seasonings were a delicacy not to be missed.

Once everyone had a bowl in hand, the bard set down his ladle and cleared his throat. "I'd like to take a moment to thank the gods for this bounty we have received, and to honor the memory of our fallen comrades. Brave men and woman, all, they gave their lives for the noblest of causes—the safety of others. May their souls find peace in the afterlife."

The entire gathering bowed their heads in silence. Glo briefly thought of the last time he had seen all those brave souls alive, just a little more than a day ago. It was heartbreaking that they were all now gone.

The young elf cast a furtive glance at Alana. The lady knight's head was bowed, a single tear flowing down one cheek. Donnie stood next to her, his head bowed as well, silently holding her hand. Lamorn and Syndir stood on the other side of the lady knight, their faces ashen. After a full minute of silence, Alana raised her head, her eyes falling on Elladan. "Thank you for your kind words. Our comrades will be sorely missed."

They all sat down and quietly began to eat. As the meal progressed, sporadic conversation broke the silence, eventually growing into full-fledged discussions. Much of it concerned their hectic adventures over these last few days, but Alana also shared a few stories about her fallen comrades. Overall, it had a cathartic effect, helping Alana and the squires to deal with their grief.

Although Glo had not known them personally, he felt deeply for the loss of all those good people. It made him miss his family, and those friends who were not currently with them. Glo briefly wondered about his mother and father. He hadn't seen them in a few months now, and he hadn't exactly left on the best of terms, especially with his father.

His mind then drifted to Aksel and Ruka. It was almost night now, the sun fallen behind the trees, darkness already blanketing the sky to the east. It was too soon for the duo to have reached Vermoorden—they were probably still in flight.

Glo let out a deep sigh as his thoughts turned to Seth. The halfling had been gone for almost an entire day now, chasing after the one black mage who had escaped their battle with the Serpent Cult. Glo silently hoped that wherever he was, his small friend was alright.

8
DEEPWOOD SNIPER

In the blink of an eye, three arrows suddenly
appeared in the mage's body

The forest had grown thicker during the last day or so of travel—much thicker and wilder, but notably less oppressive, and far more peaceful than the Darkwoods—perhaps too peaceful. Seth Korzair might have enjoyed the quiet of the forest, if it weren't for his current mission and the ever-present nagging feeling that someone, or *something*, was watching him. He glanced around at the large trees suspiciously, noting a few evening stars peeking through the canopy above, then he refocused on his quarry's trail.

During the fight with the Serpent Cult inside the monolith, one mage had escaped—he had left the monolith, stolen a horse, and fled into the woods. Being a halfling with a very particular skill set, stealth being king among them, Seth followed the mage, hoping he would lead him to the rest of the Serpent Cult—the viper's nest, so to speak. The mage had mostly kept to the road that ran toward Bendenwood, the capital of the Druids, though he had been sure to circumvent any towns, especially Bendenwood itself.

Seth had stayed one step behind him all the way, using a magic spell he'd learned to keep from exhausting his riding dog, and double its speed. He suspected that the mage was using the same magic on his stolen horse, because he had only stopped twice during the last twenty-four hours to refill his water.

Now they were on a small, underused road that was heading directly toward a small town nestled somewhere deep in the forest— Deepwood Fort was the name. Seth had seen an old, weather-beaten sign on the road near Bendenwood, with the smaller town's name scratched into it.

For some reason, the name rang a bell, though Seth wasn't sure why. He vaguely remembered having heard of it as he passed through Bendenwood, on the way to Ravenford about a month ago, but he was sure he'd heard of it elsewhere as well. As his eyes cautiously flitted around the lush green canopy above him, he wondered what sort of people could live in a place like Deepwood—a place so wild and remote.

They're probably all flowery, plant hugging druids who cry when a fly dies, Seth thought dryly.

A few silent moments passed before Seth reined his dog to a halt. There was a small trail that branched off the road, and the mage's horse had gone down that path. Seth turned his dog down the trail. He traveled it for a few twists and turns, until the main road had disappeared behind him, then his riding dog halted abruptly. It sniffed the air and whined, taking a step back. Seth looked ahead and squinted, but only saw a small clearing in the trees a short distance ahead. Still, that didn't mean there wasn't anything there.

Good place for a trap, actually.

He patted the dog on the shoulder and turned it to the side, moving it up to a fir tree with low branches. He slipped from the saddle and tied the dog to a low branch, then he moved forward as quietly as possible, shrugging on his magic cloak as he did and turning invisible. He crept up to the edge of the small clearing and peered around a tree.

The mage stood in the middle of the clearing, his horse tethered to a log, and he chanted and weaved his hands in a spell.

What is he trying to do?

Seth only had a few seconds to wonder. As the mage finished, a shimmering light surrounded Seth, outlining his body and illuminating the shadows he was hiding in. The mage had cast a spell to reveal the invisible.

Crap baskets…

A hiss from above made the hairs on the back of Seth's neck stand on end. He rolled away from the tree, barely avoiding the coils of a giant green snake. He spun around to face the beast, drawing a knife from his belt. The creature hissed, its red eyes locked on him, as it slowly dropped from the tree. Although not the largest snake Seth had seen by far, this one was still a good eight feet or more in length and could undoubtedly squeeze the life out of him in seconds if it could get its coils around him.

Seth tried to take a step back, his mind racing, but his muscles stiffened. His arms fell to his side and locked into place. He glanced to the side and saw the mage pointing a glowing finger at him while chanting.

He's trying to bind me!

With that thought, the spell suddenly ended and Seth's limbs returned to normal. The mage snarled.

"You cannot escape us!"

As the snake struck at him, Seth rolled to the side, springing back up to his feet. He darted for a large oak tree, glancing over his shoulder once to see the snake in hot pursuit.

If I time this correctly…

He slowed his pace just a little, waiting for the snake to come within range. The snake, seeing an opportunity, brought its coils in close behind it and sprang forward, maw open.

Seth put all his energy into his legs, running up the side of the oak tree and flipping in the air, drawing another dagger. As he came down, the snake slammed into the side of the oak tree beneath him, sinking its fangs into the thick bark. Before it could recover from its mistake, though, Seth dropped onto its head, jamming both daggers into its skull and giving them both a sharp twist.

The snake's mouth fell open, and it slumped to the ground, its lifeless body writhing. Seth pulled his daggers free and rolled away from it in one fluid motion. Suddenly, a brilliant flash of light exploded in his face. He stumbled backward, blinking rapidly as the shadowy world around him became a haze of multicolored lights.

Two big hands grabbed him by the wrists and wrenched his knives from his hands. Then he was lifted from the ground and held against a tight chest by two thick arms that squeezed him until he could barely breathe. The world gradually came back into focus, and when Seth look down at the arms restraining him, he found that they were green in color.

It's an orc!

"Ha!"

Seth looked up and blinked, his eyes slowly focusing on the mage, who danced on one foot in glee. The mage gloated. "I have you now!"

Crap baskets!

Seth knew he was in serious trouble, but he wouldn't let the mage see that. He forced his lips into a lopsided grin. "Did you learn that victory dance from a three-year-old, or did you come up with it on your own? It's pretty cute. All you're missing is a diaper."

The mage stopped and scowled at Seth. "Let's see how witty you are after I'm finished with you!"

A look of concentration crossed his face as he started to mutter and weave his hands in a pattern.

Seth struggled against the orc, but the brute only chuckled, then squeezed harder. Seth continued to wiggle and struggle, his fingers groping for one of his knives hidden in his cloak. There was a soft sound of rushing air, and then, in the blink of an eye, three arrows suddenly appeared in the mage's body. The first arrow punched through his right hand. He faltered mid-spell, his eyes going wide and his mouth dropping open in pain, but before he could cry out, another arrow punched into his left shoulder, making him stumble backward a couple of steps and fall against a tree, where another arrow sliced through his right shoulder and tacked him to the tree like a doll.

The orc howled in surprise, loosening its grip on Seth. Seth wrapped his fingers around a blade and whipped it out, twisting in the orc's arms and slicing the blade across the monster's jugular. Before the brute could drop him or react, an arrow tip punched through the middle of its forehead. Its eyes rolled back and it crumpled to the ground. Seth shoved away from the orc as it fell, barely avoiding being crushed. He rolled across the ground in a somersault, jumping back up to his feet. He looked back at the motionless orc, bewildered.

Never saw that coming. But who…?

Suddenly, Seth's head started to swim and the world twisted sideways. He fell onto his knees, his ribs screaming in pain as his lungs gulped in shallow breaths of air. That orc had squeezed him a little harder than he realized. A soft rustle made Seth look back up.

A young woman, perhaps in her twenties, dropped from the tree above the orc. She slipped a bow over her shoulder, her sharp gray eyes looking him over carefully. She pushed a long strand of reddish-brown hair behind her ear, keeping a hand on her bow.

"You alright?" She asked, somewhat timidly, the words rolling from her mouth in a drawl.

Seth nodded, but said nothing, focusing on getting his lungs to work properly so he didn't look so pathetic.

She sighed, pulling a rag from a pocket on her long green tunic. "I gotta say, I'm impressed; not just anyone can handle a giant snake the way you did. You sure are tough for a lil guy!"

She grinned and winked.

Seth frowned. He watched as she leaned down and pulled the arrow from the orc's head, wiping the rag over it to clean the gore from it. Suddenly, a big silver lynx dropped onto the orc's body. It fixed Seth with stern golden eyes and growled low, then it sat down, making itself comfortable on top of the orc. It kept its eyes locked on Seth, making it clear that he was not to move.

"Now then…"

Seth turned to where the mage was pinned to the tree, moaning, and watched as the young woman approached him, tapping the arrow across the palm of her hand.

"I know a guy who had that same tattoo," she said, using the arrow to push back the right-hand sleeve of the mage's robe, revealing a snake tattoo. "We never exchanged names, or anything like that, but he had an unforgettable face. He was bald and had a half-skull tattoo on the left side of his head. Maybe you know him?"

The mage rolled his lips together and kept his mouth closed tight.

The young woman sighed. "I see how this is gonna be."

She reached out and wrapped her fingers around the end of the arrow sticking through the mage's hand, making him flinch. "I'll give you the benefit of the doubt and say that maybe you don't know the guy with the half-skull tattoo. But I'll bet a shiny new bow that you two are in the same club, huh? Mind telling me what that club is?"

"I could save you some time and tell you that." Seth crossed his arms as he spoke, glancing to the side as the lynx growled at him. "He's with the Serpent Cult."

The young woman looked back at him, raising an eyebrow. "The Serpent Cult, huh? Is that the same as the one that crashed the birthday party at Ravenford a few days back?"

Seth raised an eyebrow, but nodded his head. "How did you know about that?"

She shrugged. "Word gets around these parts fast, especially if it has anything to do with humiliating the Duke of Dunwynn." She turned back to the mage. "So, the Serpent Cult, huh? What's a Serpent Cultist like you doing in a forest like Deepwood?"

The mage kept his lips rolled tightly together for several moments until the young woman started to twist the arrow into his hand slowly, pushing it farther in. The mage jumped and cried out.

Seth raised his other eyebrow as she pushed the arrow all the way out of his hand, dropping it to the ground and letting the wound bleed openly. *Not afraid to get her hands dirty, but what's her angle?*

"What are you doing in Deepwood?" She demanded. "Is the Serpent Cult responsible for the disappearances here?" Her voice took on a sharp edge.

The mage started to laugh. Before he finished, the young woman pinched his nose and covered his mouth with her free hand, raised the arrow that had killed the orc, and slammed it into the mage's knee, right above the kneecap, slowly twisting it. The mage let out a sick, stifled cry, trying to pull his face away from her hand so he could breathe.

She snarled as she continued to twist the arrow in his knee. "I can do this all day, you dribbling, clay-brained, goblin licker."

Seth grabbed his sides to stop himself from laughing out loud. *Dribbling, clay-brained, goblin licker? She must be new to this.*

"So, you either make this easy on yourself and answer my questions, or I spend the entire day making you wish you'd made this easy on yourself."

She stopped twisting and jerked the arrow out, letting go of his nose at the same time. The mage gasped as the arrow was removed, and started panting heavily. The young woman cleaned the arrow off again.

"Not so tough when you're not picking on someone half your size, are you?" With that, she moved the arrow up to his nose. "No piercings? Well, I can fix that." She reached out with her free hand and grabbed the end of his nose, "Hold still, I want to make the hole big enough to fit a chicken bone through." With that, she pulled the arrow back and tensed her muscles.

The mage screamed. "Wait! Wait! Serpent's Hollow! I was just passing through to Serpent's Hollow!"

Seth's eyes narrowed. *I was right—he was headed to the cult's 'home.'*

The young woman cast a quick glance at Seth and winked, dropping both hands to her sides. "Good boy. Don't stop there, though. Keep talking."

The mage licked his lips. "I was just passing through. I didn't have anything to do with the disappearances, I swear."

The young woman raised her arrow and twisted it nonchalantly between her fingers, pretending to stare at it. "Go on."

The mage licked his lips again, the corners of his eyes pinching up in a cringe. "Oh please, I've said too much. They're going to kill me for what I've said already."

The young woman smiled. "Aha! So, this Serpent's Hollow is your nest! Anything else you want to tell us? Like, did the Serpent Cult have something to do with folk disappearing here in Deepwood?"

The mage squirmed, moaning in pain. "The cult has kidnapped people from everywhere. It's not my job to keep a list."

The young woman moved the arrow up to his nose again. "Actually, I think two chicken bones could fit in a nose that size…"

The mage tensed and started panting. "Yes! Yes! The cult has taken people from Deepwood! You guys are the closest. It's easier to snatch one or two of you if we need more."

"More what? What are you taking people for?" she asked, still keeping the arrow tip up by his nose.

He narrowed his eyes, his voice losing some of its fear. "Slaves."

"Slaves? What the heck do you guys need so many slaves for? What's been happening to them? Are they still alive?"

The mage stiffened, and silence reigned for several long moments. The young woman began to tap the arrow against her hand impatiently.

The mage took a deep breath. "Do your worst. I've said too much all ready. I'll not give you any more information."

"Okay." The young woman stood and walked over to Seth. "He's all yours, short-stack. Do what you want to him."

Seth glared at the young woman, trying to decide how much of this interrogation he actually believed. It seemed real enough—he had already established the mage was a chicken, the way he ran from the battle in the monolith. It wasn't very likely that he would willingly subject himself to the pain she inflicted on him.

The young woman shrugged, cocking her hip to the side and resting her free hand on it. "You might be able to get some more information out of him." She glanced over her shoulder uncertainly at the mage, "I've got all I'm gonna get out of him, I think, which is just enough for me to know what I need to do."

Seth tilted his chin and narrowed his eyes. She seemed genuine enough. Either that, or she was a consummate actress. "So, I take it you're from Deepwood Fort?"

The young woman's mouth fell open, and she gave him an incredulous look. "No. I'm a dragonborn that fell from the sky. I mean, really, it doesn't take a wizard to figure out where I'm from."

Seth snorted. She was cocky, he'd give her that, even if her jabs were a bit lame. The real question was could he trust her? If people were disappearing from Deepwood, as she said, then her interest in the Serpent Cult *might* be genuine. "Heh… and folks are being kidnapped from that town?"

She shrugged and nodded uncertainly, straightening her posture, then used her free hand to rub her other arm awkwardly. "No one believes they've been kidnapped... 'cept me, of course. Most say they just ran off, or something like that. But folk have been disappearing left and right around here for about four months now. Probably more."

She shrugged and sighed. "At least my suspicions have been put to rest and I know I ain't crazy. Still, I think I would have settled for crazy over my neighbors becoming slaves, and no one knowing about it or trying to rescue them."

She ended softly on a sad tone, looking away and twisting her mouth to the side to hide the emotion that Seth saw creeping into her face.

Seth knew that look only too well—he had seen it on Aksel many times, in quiet moments when the little cleric thought no one was looking. This young woman had suffered a loss—a painful one. That was something you couldn't fake. Seth let out a short sigh, the tension releasing from his shoulders. He wasn't quite sure yet just how much he trusted this woman, but he no longer thought this some elaborate ruse. "Do you have any idea where Serpent's Hollow is?"

She looked back at him, her eyebrows narrowing and her shoulders slumping forward. "No." She shook her head dejectedly, but then her face lit up as her eyes grew wider. "But, I know someone who might! Sure as a dead man knows where his grave is!"

Seth's mouth rose to one side. This young woman's colorful phrasing was definitely growing on him. "Who would that be?"

She cocked her hip to the side again, "Someone we can trust more than the gods themselves."

Seth spiked an eyebrow. "That's putting a lot of trust in one person."

"She's just that trustworthy." She winked, then became serious again. "Hey, what're you after in Serpent's Hollow?"

"Nothing." Seth shook his head. He wasn't ready to trust her with that information just yet. Too many lives were at stake.

She crossed her arms and grinned. "I'd buy a goblin's left ear over that steaming pile of troll snot."

Seth rolled his eyes. Gods she was corny. "I just wanted to find out where the Serpent Cult was based."

"For who?"

Seth held his breath and stared at her for a moment, weighing his choice of words. "For myself…"

The young woman tilted her head and spiked an eyebrow, looking unimpressed. "Gonna have to do better than that if I'm gonna trust you, pint-size."

Seth grit his teeth and crossed his arms, pretending to be angry. The fact that she didn't trust him, actually made him trust her more. His response positively dripped with acid. "I have a name."

She mimicked him. "You didn't tell it to me."

Seth knit his brows, still pretending to be perturbed. This was starting to get fun—nearly as fun as needling Glo. "You didn't ask."

"Sure didn't! Didn't look like you were in the mood to give it to me after that orc hug." She grinned and cleared her throat. "I'm Kalyn Rhan, and that's my buddy, Elfar." She jerked her thumb back at the Lynx still sitting on the orc corpse. "And now, you are?"

"I'm Seth." He answered curtly, seeing just how much more he could goad her.

"Okay." There was silence between them for several moments, then she rolled her hand in the air slowly, prompting him to continue. "And you want to find the Serpent Cult headquarters for…?"

"I already told you," Seth replied, still gauging the young woman's reactions.

She nodded and continued to roll her hand in the air. "And you're looking for it, because…?"

Seth huffed. This Kalyn was stubborn as hell. He glanced over at the black mage, still pinned to the tree. He was obviously going nowhere soon. If Seth wanted to find Serpent's Hollow now, he was going to have to work with her. "I'm working for the Baron of Ravenford…"

"The Heroes of Ravenford!" The young woman let out a high-pitched squeal, interrupting Seth and startling him as she suddenly broke into an awkward dance of happiness. Just as quickly as she started dancing, she stopped, her cheeks reddening with embarrassment.

Seth's smirk widened into a dry smile. That awkward outburst was in sharp contrast to the hardened façade Kalyn had portrayed up till now.

"Oh. Um. You are the halfling that is with the Heroes of Ravenford, are you not?" She asked.

Seth eyed her as he nodded slowly.

"I knew it!" She tucked a rogue strand of hair behind her ear. "The stories about the Heroes are the only exciting stories I hear in Deepwood Fort anymore."

Seth let out a derisive snort. "I didn't know we were that popular."

"Oh, y'all are making an impression, that's for sure. Me and most of the folk in Deepwood think y'all are slicker 'n snot!" She giggled, then she cleared her throat and crossed her arms, changing her tone. "Anyway, I'm gonna go to Serpent's Hollow, and check it out for myself, so you can tag along if you want, free of charge."

Seth knit his brows, trying to determine exactly what was driving this girl. If he had to guess, it probably had to do with that painful loss she'd experienced. "What do you want to go to Serpent's Hollow for?"

She frowned. "Well, to get the slaves out of there, of course!"

Seth shook his head. She wasn't telling him everything. "That's not all. You mentioned something about knowing someone with a snake and skull tattoo."

At that, she tensed and crossed her arms, shuffling her feet. Her jaw settled into a firm line, and her eyes grew dark and harsh as they darted to the side.

"I've got a score to settle with him." Her tone was soft, short, and dark, mimicking her demeanor for a moment, but then she shrugged and sighed, her mood lightening a little. "But first, I gotta figure out how to help the people who've been kidnapped and get them home. They come first, score settling second."

Seth nodded his head slowly. He had been right. This was personal. Someone she knew had been kidnapped by the cult—someone close to her. "And you know someone who can get us to Serpent's Hollow? Someone you can trust?"

"Oh, I know someone, and she *ain't* no Serpent Cultist, that's for sure!" She shifted on her feet then, her face growing a little sheepish. "She *might* be able to tell us where Serpent's Hollow is. She can't take us there, though… but I can."

Seth narrowed his eyes again. "I take it you're a tracker."

An indignant look came over her face. "Darn straight. I'm one of the best trackers in all of Deepwood forest! Possibly *the* best. You just ask anyone here'bouts about the Rhan family and they'll tell you we're the best! Yes sir! You tell me where you wanna go, and I'll get you there faster than a rust monster can chew through an iron pile."

Seth couldn't help but smile. "So, if your friend can tell us where Serpent's Hollow is, you're sure you can get us there?"

She grinned with a half wink, then slipped her arrow back into the quiver on her back. "I always know where to go, especially when I don't know where to go." She turned to the mage's stolen horse and untied it from the log.

"Wait, you aren't just going to leave me here, are you?" The mage asked breathlessly.

Kalyn looked at Seth. "Your call, tough stuff."

Seth shifted his gaze to the black mage. He was badly wounded, and Seth wasn't about to waste his own energy healing him. And even if they did bring him along, Seth wouldn't trust him any farther than he could throw him. Leaving him here was also out of the question. If by any chance, one of the other cultists were to find him, they could warn the rest of the cult. If that happened, he and his friends would be walking straight into a trap.

Seth peered back at Kalyn. She seemed very sure of herself. He didn't doubt her tracking ability—she seemed very at home in the woods. And the way she handled a bow was probably as good as, if not better than Martan. The real question was, would her friend know where to find Serpent's Hollow? Seth finally decided that he had to chance it.

"He's not useful to me anymore." With that, Seth flicked his wrist, sending a small blade singing through the air, straight into the front of the mage's skull. The mage stopped moving immediately. The lynx got up and stretched with a yawn, then it stepped up to Kalyn and rubbed its face against her leg.

Kalyn sighed. "Well, Seth, I must say that you really kicked butt a moment ago. Very impressive what you did to that nasty snake."

Seth narrowed his eyes—he swore he saw her shudder at the mention of the snake. "That was nothing. You finished off the other two."

She shrugged. "Well, for being a tiny person stuck on the ground, you did better than I probably would have." With that, she walked over to the mage and pulled Seth's knife from his skull, tossing it back to him. "I was equally impressed by how quiet you were. Most folk sound like a herd of angry centaurs when tromping through these woods, but not you. I watched you for about ten minutes or so, and you ne'er made a sound."

So, I was *being watched…*

Seth cleaned his knife off and sheathed it.

"Though I should warn you—don't try sneaking past a Deepwood archer while you're invisible. You aren't *that* quiet. They might think you're a green hag skulking about and shoot you, no questions asked. That would be bad. And it wouldn't be the first time it's happened."

Deepwood Snipers! Of course! Now I remember where I've heard of Deepwood Fort.

Seth mentally slapped his forehead. Deepwood was home to a group of archers that were so skilled in their craft, it was said they rivalled those of elvish archers. There were stories and legends spanning back hundreds, perhaps even thousands of years, about these guys almost single—handedly demolishing entire races, crushing empires, and turning the tide of war. But many argued that the legendary skills of the Deepwood Snipers were nothing more than good stories for little children. Not so much as an arrow had been seen leaving this forest in a very long time, much less an archer, and Deepwood Fort was little more than a tiny dot on the map.

Seth spiked a skeptical eyebrow. "You can't shoot something you can't see."

She shrugged, a mysterious smile creeping onto her face. "That's what a few green hags have thought." Her smile grew, as did the twinkle in her eye. "Well, come on!" With that, she turned on her heel, and walked away.

Seth narrowed his eyes. She seemed awfully certain of herself. Not even Ruka had heard him a few nights ago, on the deck of the Rusty Nail. Still this was a forest, and it was definitely harder to be quiet here, with all the twigs and what-not strewn across the forest floor. He swept his eyes around the clearing, at the dead snake, orc, and mage. "What about the bodies?"

"Something'll eat 'em before dawn tomorrow. Or the Patrol will find 'em and sound the alarm at the fort. Either way, they ain't our problem!"

The big lynx padded past Seth, sniffing at him as it went by before haughtily raising its tail and trotting after Kalyn. Seth sighed and shrugged inwardly.

This is the path I decided on. For now, I have to follow her, and hope that I made the right choice.

He picked up his feet, and quickly caught up with her.

"We'll fetch your doggy, then we'll go see my friend. She ain't far off, so we don't have far to go. By the way, are you hungry?" Kalyn asked.

Seth's stomach growled involuntarily.

Kalyn giggled. "I thought you might be, 'specially after what you just went through. Well, rest assured, my friend is a tremendous cook. You won't be disappointed.

9
FLIGHT OF MERCY

Oh, my apologies. I was just checking to see if you were a chosen one

The lights twinkled softly on the other side of the lake, as Ruka and Aksel sped just above the water, toward the little town of Vermoorden. It was late in the evening; the sun had set long ago, and midnight was only a couple of hours away. The moon, full the previous night, now waxed gibbous in the star-filled sky, its silvery rays lighting a path across the lake in front of them.

Their flight had been extremely smooth, the ground left far below as Ruka flew them effortlessly across the countryside. Aksel was amazed at how fast the dragon girl could travel—even faster than Ves when she had taken the form of a giant eagle. The little cleric could only wonder at the speeds the teen might hit once she was fully recovered.

Ruka veered north as they approached the shoreline, heading for the woods just outside of town. A short while later, they swept over a low embankment, the lakeside here dotted sparsely with lights from the few farmhouses that populated this end of town. They swiftly reached the edge of the woods and skirted over the treetops, safe from any prying eyes.

The young dragon touched down a few moments later in a small clearing just north of town, the woods around them dark and silent. Ruka slowly craned her neck in a circle, silently scanning the surrounding trees. Satisfied that they were alone, she squatted down and allowed Aksel to dismount. Ruka then shifted to the familiar form of a sandy-blonde haired human teen. The two travelers left the clearing and weaved their way through the dark trees, quickly finding the road that led south into town.

After a short walk, a walled structure came into view, seated atop a hill to the southeast—Vermoorden Keep. Aksel had seen the structure before, on their last visit to the small town just a few days ago. The keep's windows were dimly lit at this late hour, the citadel a tall, dark shadow against the starlit backdrop of the night sky. The castle walls were lined with torches, the shadows of the occasional patrol of guards visible along the parapets.

The duo continued down the road, soon striding past the general store. The small building was closed and dark at this time of night. The Theater of the Festive Spirits appeared to still be open, as the lights were still on, and the sound of music was drifting down the road from the lively establishment.

The duo passed a few more darkened stores before an inn appeared on their right. The lights were still on, and probably would be for most of the night. Aksel cast a glance at Ruka as they walked beside the fence line that surrounded the establishment. "I think we should stop here at Barmann's, and rent some rooms for the night."

"I don't need to sleep," Ruka responded immediately, with more than a hint of impatience in her voice.

Aksel came to a stop and turned to face the young teen. Ruka halted as well, and stared at him with her arms folded. Aksel was quite aware of how frustrated she must feel, but he also knew that sometimes things could not be rushed. He let out a short sigh, and attempted to pacify the anxious teen.

"It may not be quite that easy. We can try the church, but they may not be open at this hour. Even if they are, there's no guarantee that one of the clerics prayed for a spell to cure poison this day."

Ruka glared at him and slowly shook her head. "Did anyone ever tell you that you're too damned practical?"

Aksel responded with a short, closemouthed laugh. "More often than I care to admit."

Ruka stared at him for a few moments, then let out a long sigh. "Oh, very well, but you might as well just get one room since I'll end up sleeping on the roof anyway."

"Fair enough," Aksel responded with a slight shrug of his shoulders.

When they reached the front gate, Ruka stopped and leaned against the fence post. "You go ahead," she waved him on. "Wouldn't want people to see us together and get the wrong idea."

Aksel paused a moment, but even in the pale moonlight, he could see the twisted grin on Ruka's lips.

"Suit yourself," Aksel responded, then spun around and strode through the gate, leaving the young teen behind. What she hadn't seen was the slight smile on his lips as he walked away. Ruka was very much like Seth, and the little cleric had sorely missed his friend's biting sense of humor this last day or so.

"You're no fun!" Ruka called out as she rushed after him, swiftly drawing up to his side. Aksel said nothing more as they strode together toward the inn, but inside he was still smiling.

A short while later, the duo stood outside the town church. They had appropriated a room at the inn as planned, but once there, Ruka's fidgeting prompted Aksel to reconsider his original stance. The church was a modest stone structure, with arched windows, and capped with a tall green steeple. The twin symbols of the goddesses Thena and Zesstara, the Lady of Nature and Lady of the Seas, respectively, stood above the tall steeple—a not-unexpected sight for a community whose livelihood was based on farming and fishing.

Not surprisingly, the church was closed. It was slightly more than an hour till midnight, and evening services were well past over. Aksel took a few steps back and peered around the corner of the building. On the one side stood a small cemetery with nondescript headstones, surrounded by a short picket fence. Around the other corner stood another stone structure that was most likely the church rectory. Aksel, with Ruka in tow, strode up to the building and knocked, but no one came to the door. Ruka pointed out a small house situated behind the rectory. There was a light in one of its windows.

"At least somebody's there," Ruka noted, with obvious frustration.

Having grown up on church grounds, Aksel was certain the dwelling belonged to the groundskeeper, but he decided to keep that to himself for the moment. He shrugged his shoulders. "Might as well."

The resigned duo walked over to the house, and knocked on the front door. After a minute or so, an elderly gentleman, with wisps of white hair around his otherwise bald head, slowly opened the door. Despite his advanced age, the man seemed quite sharp, his eyes shifting carefully from Aksel to Ruka, then back again. He pulled his thick robe closer around his body as the chill of the night air hit him, then spoke, his voice low and raspy. "What can I do for you at this late hour?"

Aksel waved a hand toward Ruka. "My friend here has been poisoned. I've managed to delay the effects, but she needs a cure as soon as possible."

The elderly gentleman nodded thoughtfully, as he appraised the young teen from the open doorway. "I see." His eyes shifted back toward Aksel. "Based on your diagnosis, and your attire, I take it you are a cleric."

It was more of a statement than a question. Aksel responded with a single nod. "I am—but neutralizing poisons is currently beyond my abilities. Is there anyone at the church who could cure her? Or perhaps you might have a curative potion?"

"Hmmm," the elderly gentleman pondered, his hand briefly stroking his chin, "I'm sorry to say, but there is nothing we can do for your friend at the moment."

Aksel cast a glance at Ruka, and gave her a sympathetic smile. He shifted his gaze back to the old gentleman, about to thank him for his time, but the elderly man stepped back from the door and ushered them inside. "But please come in and sit down. I'll pour us some tea, and then maybe we can put our heads together, and figure something out."

Aksel exchanged another glance with Ruka. The young teen shrugged, then strode forward through the entryway with an extremely polite "Thank you."

Aksel raised an eyebrow, and followed close behind.

"Oh, where are my manners?" the old gentleman said, as he led them through a narrow hallway and into his kitchen. "My name is Lothar. Lothar Feltain. I am the groundskeeper for our little Church of the Two Ladies."

A rather appropriate name for the church, Aksel thought to himself. He placed a hand on his chest, and executed a deep bow, finishing with a wave toward Ruka. "I am Aksel Alabaster, Cleric of The Soldenar, and this is my friend Ruka."

"Ah," Lothar slowly drawled, "a cleric of yet another goddess. Well met," he added, his eyes sweeping over the pair. Lothar pointed toward two chairs at a rather quaint kitchen table. "Please be seated while I fetch us our tea."

Ruka wore a bemused look as she sat down at the small table. Aksel sat down next to her, then shifted his gaze back to the old man. Lothar stood at the kitchen hearth, pouring a few cups from a small kettle that hung over the fire. The old gentleman called over to them as he filled up their mugs. "I wish we could have met under better circumstances."

Aksel couldn't help smiling. This Lothar was a quintessential gentleman. He peered at Ruka, and noted the soft expression on her face. The normally sardonic teen seemed rather reverent of the elderly gentleman. Aksel silently wondered if it was indicative of dragon kind, or if it had something to do with Ruka's 'grandfather.'

Lothar came over to join them, carrying a tray of tea and some small cookies. He placed a mug on the table before each of them, then sat down in an empty kitchen chair. Lothar took a small sip of tea, then set his mug down on the table and folded his hands in front of him. "Now then, let's think about your problem."

Aksel took a sip of tea as well. It was quite good—elderberry root, if he had to guess. He watched the old man carefully as he spoke. "Most of the priests are already bedded down for the night. And out of them, only the High Priest, Harper, or Canon Harmin, would be able to cast the spell." Lothar paused a moment as he mulled things over. "Although I'm not sure we'd be able to count on the High Priest. He's not quite all there anymore, and we never know what spells he's going to pray for…"

Aksel nearly spit out his tea. He cast a quick glance at Ruka. The young teen had a hand over her mouth, doing her best to stifle a giggle. Meanwhile, Lothar continued to think out loud. "…and the temple's supply of potions were recently depleted." He paused, his eyes suddenly coming alight. "Wait, that's it! There's a potion vendor in town. He operates out of the inn. He goes by the name of Philmar."

Aksel had not really looked for a potions shop last time they were in town, having no need for one. He thought it somewhat dubious, though, that this vendor sold potions out of the inn. Aksel cast a glance at Ruka—she gave him a nod, and started to rise. Aksel stood up as well. "Thank you for your hospitality, Lothar, but we really must leave now. We are kind of in a rush."

Lothar stood as well, and gave the duo a knowing smile. "Such it is with youth. Always rushing here and there." He escorted them to the door and stood to one side. "Anyway, I hope you find your cure."

Ruka gave the old gentlemen a genuine smile and said, "Thank you," before exiting the house. Aksel thanked him again as well, then followed her through the threshold. The little cleric glanced up into the night sky as they hurried up the road back toward the inn. It was nearing midnight, and they still hadn't found a cure for Ruka. The prospect of dealing with a potion vendor out of the inn nagged at the back of his mind. He could just imagine what Seth would say about it.

Potion vendor, my ass. Probably just colored water jacked up at three times the price. The thought brought a smile to Aksel's face, as they rushed through the night toward the House of Barmann.

When the duo reached the inn, Barmann pointed out Philmar to them. Despite the late hour, the vendor was still up, nursing a mug of ale by himself at a corner table in the common room. Aksel eyed this Philmar carefully—he was a rather seedy-looking character, with long, straggly black hair and a chin thinly covered with dark stubble, wearing a patched and stained what-used-to-be-tan longcoat.

Aksel exchanged a quick glance with Ruka. The young teen wore a distrustful expression that mirrored Aksel's thoughts, but she merely shrugged at his silent query. The two of them left the bar and strode over to the potion vendor's table.

The shabby-looking Philmar watched them out of the corner of his eye as they approached. Aksel stopped in front of the man's table, and spoke in as polite a voice as he could muster. "Excuse me sir, might you be Philmar?"

Philmar peered out over the top of his mug, and responded with a sneer. "Who wants to know?"

Aksel took a deep breath, immediately regretting it. This Philmar actually smelled worse than he looked. With a lake at the edge of town, Aksel could not fathom why anyone would go more than a day or two without a bath. The little cleric steeled himself, and carried on. "My friend here has been poisoned, and is in need of a cure." He nodded toward Ruka. "They told us at the church that you sold such potions."

Philmar slowly set his mug down, a greedy twinkle in his dark eyes. "I do indeed, but they aren't cheap."

"How much?" Ruka demanded, stepping in front of Aksel and leaning over the table. The teenager's eyes gleamed as much as Philmar's at the prospect of bargaining."

The vendor's eyes narrowed as he appraised the young teen. "Well, little lady, let's see…" He began ticking off on his fingers as he itemized the price. "There's the cost of the ingredients, the magic required, the current market demand, and, of course, a restocking fee… let's say"—he paused and pursed his lips together—"fifteen hundred gold pieces."

Aksel's eyes nearly popped out of his head at the outrageous price.

"Fifteen hundred? That's double the market price!"

The shady merchant shifted his gaze toward Aksel, a shrewd look upon his face. He sat back in his seat and gave a slight shrug, his hands going out to either side. His tone was as smooth as silk as he replied. "Well, that particular potion is currently in high demand, so the price has gone up."

Ruka did not seem perturbed in the slightest by the blatant price-gouging. A slight smile crossed her lips as she shot back with a counter offer. "Eight hundred, in your hand right now."

"Fourteen hundred," Philmar countered in a casual tone, though his eyes were alit with the thrill of haggling.

"Nine hundred," Ruka countered immediately, leaning in closer this time.

The enthralled pair went back and forth a few more times, finally settling on the midway sum of eleven hundred gold pieces. Ruka seemed rather pleased, although Aksel was not thrilled with the outcome. He leaned in close and whispered in her ear. "That's still highway robbery."

Ruka let out a soft snort. "Heh. I know, but I still want to leave first thing in the morning."

Any further comments Aksel might have had were cut off as Philmar gulped down the rest of his ale, slammed the empty mug down, and rose from the table. He motioned toward Ruka and Aksel. "C'mon, follow me." The seedy vendor shuffled his way toward the hall that led from the common room to the guest rooms on the first floor of the inn. "I keep the potions back in my room."

Aksel raised an eyebrow, but followed Ruka, who had fallen in right behind Philmar. The potion vendor led them down the dimly-lit hall, and around a bend toward the back of the inn. He stopped at a door near the end of the hallway and slid in a key. The door unlocked with a soft click, and the shady vendor passed through the threshold, gesturing for the two of them to follow.

Aksel walked into what appeared to be a typical guestroom, if somewhat unkempt. There were clothes and various cases strewn all around the room. Philmar walked over to the bed and pushed it aside, revealing a trap door in the floor. The shabby merchant knelt and pulled it open, reached in, and pulled out a small box. He pushed some clothes out of the way, and placed the box on top of the un-made bed.

Philmar pulled a small key off his keychain and inserted it into the chest, turning it with a click. The box popped open—it was filled with numerous vials of liquid of a variety of colors. The seedy vendor rummaged through the vials, eventually picking out one containing a black liquid. He spun around and lifted it up for them to see. "Here it is."

Aksel leaned forward and examined the vial closely. He peered at Ruka and nodded. "It's the right color."

Ruka reached out a hand for the vial, but Philmar swiftly pulled it away. "Ah, ah," he said waving the index finger of his other hand back and forth, "the money first."

"Fine!" Ruka exhaled with clear exasperation. She turned away from the shifty vendor and unbuttoned her tunic, reaching a hand inside. Aksel swiftly spun his head away, feeling the heat rise to his cheeks. A soft chuckle made him inadvertently gaze back at Ruka. Thankfully, her tunic was closed once again, and in her hand she held a small purse.

Ruka undid the ties and dug her hand into it, pulling out a mass of platinum coins. She threw them out onto the bed in fistfuls of ten, until she reached a count of one hundred and ten. When she was done, she closed the purse and pulled the drawstrings tight. She fixed Philmar with an acid stare, her tone dripping with sarcasm. "There you go. Eleven hundred gold. May I have my potion now?"

Philmar's eyes were glued to the coins on the bed. He absently held the potion out toward Ruka. "Absolutely…"

Ruka whipped the potion from his hand, unstopped the cork with a single thumb, and gave the contents a sniff. After a moment or two, she held it out for Aksel to smell. The little cleric leaned in and took a whiff. It had a very mild odor. He then dipped his finger in, pulling it back out with a drop of the tincture at the tip, and placed it in his mouth. The liquid had a gritty texture and tasted quite foul. Aksel let out a few coughs, then nodded. "Yup… that's it… alright…"

Ruka gave him a curt smile, then downed the potion in one gulp. Almost immediately her breathing deepened and the full color returned to her skin. It appeared that the potion had already worked, but a moment later a purplish glow encircled her body. Aksel felt the faint tingle of magic as well, but it faded away as swiftly as the glow.

The little cleric cocked his head to the side, his mouth twisting with it. The potion should not have had that effect on Ruka, let alone himself. Aksel cast a glance at Philmar—the shifty vendor swiftly tucked his hands behind his body, but it was too late—Aksel recognized what he had done.

He pointed at Philmar with an accusing cry. "He just tried to put us to sleep!"

Aksel could feel the electricity stir in the room as Ruka glared at the vendor. Flecks of yellow suddenly appeared in her otherwise emerald eyes, her pupils turning almost cat-like. The shady Philmar's expression went from surprise to absolute fear. He scrambled back up onto the bed and grabbed a pillow, hugging it in front of him. "Whoa, whoa, whoa! Please don't hurt me!"

Ruka took a step forward, her voice low and menacing. "What was that for?"

Philmar's eyes went wide with fright. At some subconscious level, the sleazy vendor realized he had awoke a beast, and his life was in mortal danger. The hapless merchant stammered his reply. "I…I…I just wanted to see if…you were the chosen ones…you know…from the prophecy."

A dreadful smile crossed Ruka's lips. She reached out and placed a hand on Philmar's chest, the vendor so frozen with fear that he could not move. Sparks flew from the young teen's fingertips, sending electrical arcs across the merchant's body. Philmar shook uncontrollably, his eyes going glassy, until Ruka finally stopped. The hapless vendor fell back on the bed, his body still jerking at odd moments.

Ruka stepped back and spoke, her tone exceedingly mocking. "Oh, my apologies. I was just checking to see if you were a chosen one. Guess not."

Aksel strode forward and ran his hands over the prone vendor. He was out cold. Aksel stood up and peered at Ruka, with a tight-lipped smile. "Remind me to never tick you off."

"Duly noted," Ruka said over her shoulder. The young teen had taken the potion box, and was rummaging through it. A moment later, she withdrew another potion of the same black color that Philmar had sold them.

"What are you doing with that?" Aksel asked softly.

Ruka held out the vial toward Aksel. "He was going to rob us. Consider this compensation for our trouble."

Aksel took the potion without further argument. Philmar had tried to charge them double for the first potion, and who knows what else he would have stolen from them if they had fallen under his spell. Meanwhile, Ruka had knelt next to the trap door. She beckoned for Aksel to join her. "Look at this…"

Aksel knelt next to her and peered into the hole. There was a small shelf on one side where Philmar must have stored his potions, and across from that stood the top of a ladder. Aksel followed it down with his eyes as far as he could see, until it disappeared below into utter darkness. He shifted his gaze to Ruka, the young teen staring intently down into the hole. "Can you see where it goes?

She glanced up at him, her eyes aflame with curiosity. "It ends about twenty feet down, at what appears to be some kind of tunnel."

Aksel spiked an eyebrow. *Why is there a tunnel underneath the inn? Is it Philmar's doing? Aside from being a shady vendor, is he also a smuggler?*

Ruka appeared torn. Aksel had to admit he was curious about the strange tunnel, but who knew how far it went? And they needed a good night's rest if they were going straight back to the monolith in the morning. He said as much to Ruka, half expecting an argument, but the young teen surprised him, getting up and closing the trap door without another word. She strode over to the bedroom door, pulled it open, spun her head toward Aksel, and uttered a single word. "Coming?"

Aksel couldn't help grinning at the young teen. She reminded him more and more of Seth with each passing minute.

The next morning, Aksel woke up to a commotion outside his window. His first thought was that Philmar had finally come to, and had roused the town guard. The little cleric rolled out of bed and hurried over to the window, but pulled up short, as a familiar form swung in from the outside.

Ruka fixed her eyes on him, her face red with anger. "That idiot, Calipherous! He can't shapeshift, so instead he decides to land right smack in the middle of town."

Aksel cocked his head to one side and scrunched his nose. "Calipherous? I thought you girls didn't want to be seen by him? Last I remember, you jumped ship to avoid him."

Instead of immediately answering, Ruka rushed past him and started gathering up her things. "Yeah, well… a lot has changed since then. I'll explain later. Right now, get your stuff. We need to get down there before things get out of hand."

Aksel didn't have to be told twice. He spun on his heel and gathered his gear, throwing on his robe as they rushed out the door. Ruka practically vaulted down the stairs, then raced through the hall and the common room, bursting out of the front door of the inn in less than three minutes. Aksel slipped through the doorway just behind her, huffing as he tried to catch his breath.

A crowd had gathered in the courtyard of the inn, but it was not hard to see what they were gathered around. In the very center stood a copper dragon, covered from head to tail with warm reddish-brown scales, speckled here and there with small spots of blue.

Though not large by dragon standards, Calipherous still towered above the surrounding mob. Aksel swiftly scanned the crowd, but did not see any town guards yet. Ruka rushed forward, pushing her way through the throng, Aksel trailing right behind her. When they breached the inner circle, a familiar voice cried out, "Ruka!"

A little golden-haired girl, barely taller than Aksel, came rushing up to greet them, jumping straight into the young teen's arms. It was Ruka's little sister, Maya. The little girl hugged Ruka tight, all the while cooing, "We found you. We found you."

"Yeah, yeah, it's nice to see you too," Ruka responded, gently pulling the little girl's arms from around her neck. She continued to carry her as she strode purposefully up to the tall dragon, with Aksel still in tow. Ruka stopped a few feet away from Calipherous, and spoke in a semi-hushed voice. "What are you two doing here? Are you crazy? Do you know how much attention you're drawing?"

The young teen swept her eyes around the crowd—Aksel did the same. The throng, curious as they were, still gave the dragon a wide berth. Meanwhile, Calipherous seemed taken aback by Ruka's admonishment. "Yes, well, um… when you told us you would be in Vermoorden, Maya just couldn't wait. I tried to restrain her."

Ruka shifted her gaze back toward the dragon, fixing him with a hard stare. "Next time try harder. We could have met outside of town and avoided all of this." She nodded toward the growing crowd of townsfolk surrounding them.

Calipherous responded with a deep sigh. "Unfortunately, your sister is not that easy to rein in. Once she has her mind made up…"

Maya sat back up and grabbed Ruka on either side of her face, turning her head toward her. "But Ruka, we can't find Ves!"

Can't find Ves? Aksel's brow furrowed, his gaze shifting from the little girl to Calipherous, then back again. Ves was Ruka's and Maya's older sister, the eldest of the three Greymantles.

The companions had first met the sisters on the beach at Cape Marlin, during their search for the disappearing ships. The eldest Greymantle sister was a very capable, strong-willed young woman, who, upon reflection, was in fact a huge bronze dragon. To hear that she had disappeared was troubling news indeed.

Maya's eyes welled with tears as she buried her small head in Ruka's shoulder. Ruka proceeded to pat the little girl gently on the back, and spoke to her in a reassuring tone. "Don't worry, Ves can take care of herself."

Despite her nonchalant attitude, Ruka's eyes were filled with concern. As she continued to calm Maya down, the young teen turned an eye toward Calipherous and mouthed the words, *what happened?*

Calipherous replied in a surprisingly soft voice for a dragon. "The Glittering Isles were attacked by a flight of chromatics."

Ruka's face twisted in shock. "What?"

Maya lifted her head back up, her tiny face streaked with tears. "Ves took off with the chromes chasing her, and we haven't heard from her since!"

A flight of chromatic dragons? Aksel spiked an eyebrow. As far as he knew, there hadn't been any confrontations between dragons since the Thrall Wars. So why would a group of chromatic dragons suddenly attack their metallic cousins?

He shifted his gaze back toward Calipherous when something caught his eye. A contingent of castle guards marched down the hill from the keep, armed to the teeth with spears and shields. Aksel peered at Calipherous and Ruka, and nodded toward the keep. "Um, guys… you might want to continue this conversation somewhere else."

They both looked toward where he had indicated, then Ruka gazed back at Calipherous. "We'll talk more later. Right now, you need to carry us out of here."

Calipherous gave a slow nod of his large head. "Very well."

The copper dragon lowered his body, allowing Ruka, Maya, and Aksel to climb up onto his back. The crowd backpedaled as the copper dragon unfolded its wings and gave them a few slow beats, stirring up a cloud of dirt in the surrounding courtyard.

Aksel swung his gaze toward the approaching guards as they slowly lifted off the ground. They were leaving none too soon—the contingent had just reached the main road, and would be in spear range in less than a minute.

Ruka pointed a finger toward the west. "Quick, out over the lake."

Calipherous rose above the two-story inn, then with a single beat of his great wings, shot past the roof and out over the town of Vermoorden. Aksel watched the town flash by below. In no time, they had left it behind, flitting past the docks, and were out over the waters of Lake Strikken.

The morning sun was behind them, its golden rays reflecting a path across the clear waters beneath them. The copper dragon carried them all the way to the other side of the lake, a short while later landing on a small stretch of sand along the opposite shore. Once they had all dismounted, Ruka turned to face Aksel.

"Would you mind watching Maya for a few minutes? Cal and I need to talk in private. I'm sorry, but there are things about our island that must remain secret."

Aksel responded with a brief nod. "I understand. Don't worry, Maya and I will be fine." He shifted his gaze to the little girl. "Right, Maya?"

"Can we skip stones?" Maya asked, her eyes wide, two dimples forming on either side of her mouth.

Aksel couldn't help but smile back at her. "Certainly."

Maya clapped her hands together, and spun around in a circle with a cry of "Yay!"

Ruka's face softened into an uncharacteristic smile as she gazed with fondness at her little sister. It was only for a moment, though, her expression swiftly turning serious once again. She gave Aksel a curt nod, then spun around and walked off with Cal a short way down the beach.

Maya grabbed Aksel by the hand and dragged the little cleric down toward the water. Once there, he bent down and began his search for a good stone to skip across the lake waters. About twenty minutes passed before Ruka and Cal rejoined them. Ruka pulled Aksel aside, and talked with him in a hushed voice. "We'll drop you off back at the tower, but then we're going to have to go and search for our sister."

Aksel gazed at her with keen sympathy. He knew only too well what it was like to have a loved one disappear. Aksel placed a reassuring hand on Ruka's arm and gave her a slow nod. "I completely understand. Please let us know if there is anything we can do to help."

A small smile creased the young teen's lips. "I think we'll be fine, but thanks for the offer."

Ruka and Maya both shifted into dragon form since it was the fastest way to travel. Aksel marveled at the sight of the three dragons side-by-side, though he did note some differences between them. Ruka and Maya both glistened with a yellow-brown metallic sheen, though Ruka was perhaps just a bit darker than her sister. Still, both were far lighter in comparison to Cal's deep reddish-brown scales.

Further, Maya was probably about half the size of her older sister. Yet Ruka was just as large as Cal, both dragons almost thirty feet long. Aksel remembered Glo saying that copper dragons were smaller than their brethren, but the little cleric never realized by just how much till now. He felt a sudden wave of empathy wash over him—Aksel was very aware of what it was like to live in a world where most beings were twice your size.

After a few moments' reflection, Aksel climbed on Ruka's back, and the three dragons lifted off the ground. The small flight then shot out away from the lake, headed northwest toward the Dark-woods. Aksel had previously wondered about Ruka's top speed, but now the air rushed by so fast, the little cleric could hardly breath. He silently thanked Donnie for the loan of his spider boots as he hung on for dear life.

10
STIRRING THE POT

Ach! Not another one of them snake cults!

hen Kalyn talked, she talked a lot, but when she wasn't talking, she was as silent as a stone. Seth had been following her on his riding dog for several minutes now. She rode the horse ahead of him, her head constantly swiveling about and tilting, as if listening to the nighttime crickets, or the very trees themselves.

After a moment, a new sound made Seth perk up, as it was completely out of place in this silent forest. A woman's voice sang a cheerful ditty somewhere in the trees. Seth looked at Kalyn and saw her shake her head with a smile.

> *One day as I was gone a-hunting*
> *I saw'er an orc wearing a bunting*
> *He danced a jigged and was laughing*
> *His kicked up his heels to a lute staffing*

He carried a jug with a passel o' flowers
I followed him to a twisted tree
Where many a folk danced full-a glee
They passed about drinks and all sang:

Come down to the Twisted Tree
Where the weather is always right as rain
We'll give ya a hearty cheers times three
And together we'll sing, "Crane! Crane!"

Seth cocked his head to one side and squinted his eyes. "What the heck is that?"

"Depends on which you are referring to, the noise, or the noise maker." Kalyn giggled. "The noise is a popular tavern song in Deepwood Fort. The noise maker is my friend. She loves to sing."

Kalyn turned off the road and led the way down a deer trail that wound its way through the trees for a short distance, before opening into a glade. In the middle of the glade sat a middle-aged woman on a large stone, wearing a straw hat with decorative flowers all around a pink band. She was bent over a small fire that did not smoke, and a pot of steaming liquid hung over the licking flames.

"Oh good! Yer here. Supper's 'bout ready. I cooked enough for three." She looked up at them, but her bright blue eyes did not focus, instead staring into nothingness.

Kalyn halted her horse and whipped around to look back at Seth, her brows knit in confusion. "Wait a moment!" She turned back to face her friend. "How'd you know there were gonna be three of us?"

The other woman smiled slyly. "I said I *cooked* enough fer three. I didn't say I knew there'd be three."

Now that they were closer, Seth was able to get a better look at the older woman. Her dress was a patchwork puzzle of greens, browns, and grays, and a belt of braided grass was tied around her waist. Her pale gold hair, streaked with gray, was tied to the side in a messy braid, and her tanned face was covered with smile lines. On her shoulder, nestled close to her messy hair, was a small, one-legged owl that peered at Seth with large, inquisitive eyes.

Kalyn dismounted her horse. "Okay, I have to ask—do you know *who* I've brought with me?"

The other woman frowned. "What kind of a silly question is that, child? 'course I don't!! But I knows that he's a short feller. Probably a halfling, judging by the way his dog pads 'cross the ground."

Kalyn shook her head with a sigh. "Fran, you do beat all."

Fran smiled. "Aw, now, you'll be makin' me blush if ya keep up with that flatterin' talk. Now, get yerselves o'er here and sit down! Can't tell me yer tales when yer starvin' fer a bite to eat."

Seth tilted his head down and put his hand over his mouth, almost snorting out his nose. *Do they all talk like this? I better watch myself, or I'll start doing it, too.*

Fran raised her arm and waved her hand, motioning for them to come closer.

Kalyn looked back at Seth. "This is my oldest, dearest, and strangest friend, Fran. And when I say strange, I mean you ain't seen nothin' till you've seen Fran."

Seth slipped off his dog and eyed Kalyn dubiously. "I don't know. I've seen some pretty strange stuff."

Kalyn bent over and dropped her voice to a whisper. "Not this kind of strange. Trust me."

"Ho! I may be blind, but I ain't deaf! Watch how you talk 'bout me, or I'll show you some strangeness alright!" Fran shook her spoon in Kalyn's direction, though a smile wrinkled the corners of her bright blue eyes.

Kalyn giggled softly, then cleared her throat. "Fran, this is Seth. And you're right—he is a short feller."

Seth shot Kalyn a glare that could have curdled milk, even though in reality he was too amused to be angry. Yet his dark look only made her grin grow larger.

Fran slapped her knee. "Well, for Druids' sakes and Dunwynn unda'pants! I plum missed an opp'tunity to win a bet."

Seth looked back at the older woman, the corners of his mouth slowly upturning. *I am going to start talking like this if I stay here much longer.*

"So, young Seth. Where you wander in from, eh? Been travelin' long?" Fran asked him. "Do come sit yerself down. I'll serve ya up some food. Might not be fit for a duke, but I'll bet my two pretty eyes that it makes yer belly stop a-growlin'." She angled a gentle, warm smile in Seth's direction as she motioned to a large stone opposite of her, near the fire.

Seth tied his dog to a log, next to where Kalyn was tying the horse, then walked over to the fire, climbed up on the rock, and sat down. The savory smell of the stew in the pot wafted toward him and made his belly rumble. Seth regarded the older woman with a slight bend to his lips. "Do you have a particular duke in mind?"

I could think of one...

Fran poured some of the stew into a wooden bowl and stood, holding it out toward Seth. "Duke a-Dunwynn." She spat into the fire, "May rust monsters eat his armory." She made a sign in the air with her free hand, as if casting a spell, though nothing happened.

Seth's smirk widened as he sat up tall and reached high to take the bowl from her. *It appears the Duke's 'charm' extends even all the way out here.*

"Fran, you keep putting all those curses on the Duke, and none of them have come true yet." Kalyn said as she sauntered up and sat down on a stone next to Fran.

"They ain't wishes, sweetie. Curses take their time. The longer they take, the bett'r they 'er." Fran sat back down and nodded toward Seth. "You'll havta slurp that slop up from the bowl, honey. I ain't got no spoons 'cept this one," She held up her serving spoon as evidence, "An' I might need to use it to whoop on Kalyn 'fore the night is gone."

"Hey now! I've been a good girl, I have!" Kalyn protested. "And you'd better dip us both some food before you dirty that spoon on me."

"Eh, I might not eat. Had too many 'shrooms." Fran said as she leaned over and poured some stew into another bowl.

Kalyn's smile faded, and her eyes grew bigger. "You... you didn't put none of those nasty hagstools in this stew, did you?"

Fran sat up and glared. "I wouldn't share my 'shrooms with you if you was the las' person on this here green earth!"

Kalyn sighed and smiled, then took the bowl from Fran. "Oh good. I'm glad."

Seth had been holding his bowl politely in his hands, the mouth-watering smell begging him to eat it, but Seth wasn't about to eat food offered by strangers, even if one of them had saved his life. He would wait until one of the women sampled the stew, no matter how good it smelled.

Fran shook her head, then turned it back in Seth's direction. "Now then, has ya forgotten my question, young man? Where is ya comin' from?"

Seth shook his head, then remembered he was shaking it at a blind woman. "I'm coming from the South."

Kalyn coughed forcibly, with great exaggeration. Seth shifted his eyes toward Kalyn and narrowed them. Kalyn raised her eyebrows expectantly, then frowned. "Oh, come on! That was so vague! Brag a little!" she said before taking a slurp of her stew.

Fran chuckled softly, presumably at his reluctance to tell her anything about himself.

Seth blew across his stew. "Why should I when you are clearly going to do it for me?"

Kalyn huffed, then pivoted toward Fran. "Seth is just being modest. He is none other than one of *the* Heroes of Ravenford."

"Well! Ain't that a fine howdy-do!" Fran slapped her knee, then paused abruptly. "Who are the Heroes of Ravenford? They impo'tant?"

Kalyn's mouth fell open.

Having determined the stew as safe to eat, Seth took a quick gulp to keep down the laugh that was creeping up his throat.

"But, Fran, I told you all about them as we were traveling!" Kalyn said.

Fran blinked. "Oh? Oh! Ya mean them ones that was doing all the magic, snake killin', and lighthouse burnin'?"

This time, Seth snorted stew through his nose, and the rest that was in his mouth spewed toward the fire, making the flames hiss.

Fran sat up with a frown. "My stew ain't good 'nough to breathe, young feller!"

Seth wiped his nose, his eyes watering as he gasped for air while his muscles seized with laughter. *Oh gods, do I wish Glo was here right now to hear this!*

Kalyn turned a light shade of red, her manner growing sheepish. "Oh. Well, I just told you that the lighthouse burned down after they left town on a mission. I didn't say *they* burned it down." She glanced between Seth and Fran several times.

Seth wiped the stew from his mouth and laughed. "*We* didn't burn it down. Glo was the one who did that."

"Glo?" Kalyn and Fran both asked simultaneously.

Seth realized he had mentioned the elven wizard's name without thinking, but before he could retrace his steps, Kalyn sat forward eagerly, almost spilling her stew into the fire.

"Oh! Oh! Is he the elf feller with all the wizardy powers? Is he?"

Seth nodded, trying very hard not to laugh.

"Yes! I knew it!" She smiled with satisfaction, then took another sip of her stew.

Fran sighed. "So then, young adventurin' Seth, what 'er ya doin' all the way out here away from yer comrades, and how did Kalyn find ya?"

Seth and Kalyn exchanged glances, then the halfling leaned back in his seat. "Maybe I'll just let you explain it to her."

Kalyn shook her head. "No-can-do, holy cracker muncher! I don't know how you got out here, because I didn't ask, because I don't ask questions of a more personal nature. I just killed the guys who were trying to kill you, because I'm nice like that." She gave him a big, cheesy grin, then winked before slurping her soup again.

The corners of Seth's mouth upturned slightly once more. He was having a very difficult time holding back his amusement. Much as he tried to retain his composure, this young woman's open nature and simplistic view on things continued to grow on him.

Fran snorted and shook her head. "Don't ask pers'nal questions, my fat goose." She muttered under her breath before folding her arms over her chest. "So then, young Seth, what is ya tale?"

Seth narrowed his eyes, taking a moment to size Fran up. She seemed rather genuine, but just how much could he actually trust her? As he stared at her, she angled her sightless eyes in his direction, almost looking directly at him, her expression completely serious. "Yer out here for the darkness that I've been seein' creepin' o'er the land in my visions, ain't ya?"

Seth kept his eyes narrowed. "Are you a seer?"

Fran waved her hand dismissively. "Don't skirt 'round my question. Jus' answer it."

Seth let out a wicked laugh. "Wow. Rough crowd!"

Kalyn shook her head. "Don't include me in this! I ain't the one asking questions."

Seth gazed from one to the other yet again. He had to tell them something if he was ever going to find Serpent's Hollow, but he still wasn't completely sure about them. "First, tell me what you two are doing out here all alone."

Fran pointed in Kalyn's direction. "She's takin' me to Bendenwood."

Kalyn pointed a thumb back at Fran. "I'm takin' her to Bendenwood."

Seth shook his head. "And you accuse me of being cryptic!"

Kalyn shrugged. "What? That's what we were doing! We ain't being cryp-tic!"

Seth fixed Kalyn with a hard stare. *They couldn't be that dense.*

"Is there any particular *reason* you're going there?"

Kalyn pushed her shoulders back. "Well, duh! Sure, there is."

"I has a meeting with some friends in Bendenwood. We has one 'bout once a month." Fran explained.

Seth cocked his head and squinted with one eye at Fran. *A once-a-month meeting in Bendenwood?* When he spoke, his tone was quite deliberate. "The moon is almost full, isn't it?"

Fran smiled mysteriously. "Yep. Sure is." She reached up and gently stroked the little one legged owl perched on her shoulder.

Seth continued to stare at the older woman. Even though she was being vague, he was certain she was referring to the monthly meeting of the Druidic counsel. If she was truly attending that, then she had to be someone fairly high up in the druid ranks.

"Am I missing something?" Kalyn asked, looking between Seth and Fran.

Fran moved her hand up to her neck and pulled out a crescent shaped pendant hanging from a leather cord, fiddling with it almost absently. "Nah, ya ain't missing much, honey."

Seth sat forward for a closer look at the pendant in her hand. It gleamed silver in the firelight, like a quarter moon. Seth had seen a similar pendant only just recently. It had been worn by Almax, the druid representative to Ravenford. If this Fran wore that same pendant, then she was indeed a druid. Seth let out a short sigh. Perhaps he could trust her after all. At least somewhat. "Very well. You guessed right. My friends and I are after the darkness. They're called the Serpent Cult." He said the last part slowly while staring at Fran, trying to gauge her reaction.

Fran's eyebrows slowly lifted and relaxed. "Ach! Not another one of them snake cults!"

That was certainly not the response Seth was expecting. "What do you mean *another*?"

Seth and Kalyn had asked the question simultaneously. The duo cast a brief glance at each other before turning back to Fran.

"Oh, this here goes *way* back—back a 'fore the Thrall Wars, even a 'fore the Galinthral elves went off n' disappeared to gods-knows-where."

Seth eyed Fran carefully. "How long ago was that?"

Fran frowned in his direction. "Well I done told ya that it was a 'fore the Thrall Wars!"

Kalyn let out a deep sigh. "Could you be a little more precise for us younger folk? We aren't as ancient as you."

Fran raised the spoon and swiped it in Kalyn's direction, but the young woman ducked under it deftly, a grin spreading from ear-to-ear.

"Oh, all right. If ya needs to know a number, I'd say it was more or less 'bout five hundred years ago, give or take."

Seth raised an eyebrow. That was half a millennium. *So Glo's people have been hidden away all that time?*

"But I don't knows that 'cause I'm ancient, young lady. I knows it 'cause I'm smart." Fran smiled.

"Okay…" A goofy grin spread across Kalyn's face. "So then, oh great smart woman, what did you mean by 'another'?"

Fran sighed. "Well, make yerselves comf'table, 'cause this is a long tale."

11
TO TRACK A SNAKE

How could you possibly get a location out of all that gibberish?

Seth lost track of the time as Fran recounted the tale of the old Serpent Cult that existed over five hundred years ago. The story was chilling. The cult back then had become a scourge on the land. They would wipe out entire towns, taking captives for slaves or to use as sacrifices for their serpent god.

At the mention of sacrifice, Kalyn became noticeably uncomfortable, shifting in her seat.

"Whoa. Whoa. Hold it." She stopped Fran, the shadows of the camp fire painting a deadly serious expression on her face. "Sacrifices? You mean they were sacrificing people?"

Fran nodded. "Yep. Sure was."

Kalyn shivered, the color draining from her face. "Do you think this cult is doing the same thing?"

Fran raised her eyebrows and pursed her lips. "Well now, can't say for sure. But, a'fore you go to frettin' too much, I also know they had a bunch of slaves for building stuff, too."

Kalyn didn't look reassured, and the pained expression of loss that Seth had seen on her face before had appeared in her eyes once again.

"That lines up with what that mage told us." Seth reminded her. "He did say they were kidnapping people for slaves."

Kalyn nodded, but remained somber.

Fran continued with her story, telling how the humans and elves of that time came together and marched into the cult's lair, wiping them out and destroying their temple, thus saving the land from a dark, unknown fate.

"As far as anyone know'd, that was the end o' them snake worshipers." Fran ended.

Seth couldn't shake the feeling that this new cult was still somehow connected to the old one. There were too many similarities to ignore. It wouldn't surprise him at all if the new cult had set up shop in the same exact spot as the original one. Seth narrowed his eyes as he gazed at Fran. "You mentioned they had a temple. Do you know where that was at?"

Fran chewed on her lip for a moment. "It was somewhere 'long the North'rn branch of the Korlokesels. Almost direct north o' us here. As I recall, I'm believin' it was called Serpent's Holler."

Seth and Kalyn exchanged glances, his recognition of the name mirrored in her eyes. Seth crossed his arms, his gaze shifting back to Fran with a curt nod. "The mage also mentioned that name."

Fran cocked her head to the side. "What mage?"

"The one I was tracking until Kalyn killed him." Seth's mouth twisted into a lopsided smile.

"Hey!" Kalyn sat up straight. "Technically *you* killed him!"

"Yeah, yeah, potato-potahto. You tortured him till he was practically useless."

"What?" Fran exclaimed, twisting to the side so sharply she nearly toppled her one-legged owl off her shoulder. "Kalyn! You didn't."

"I did! And Seth thought it was cool, admit it." She put her hands on her hips and stuck out her tongue at the halfling.

Seth sat back in his seat and placed his hands behind his head, the smirk on his face widening. "Nope. I ain't admittin' ta nothin.'"

Kalyn giggled and Fran grinned. "We're a-rubbin' off on him, I think."

Seth rolled his eyes, although inwardly he was rather pleased with himself. Their thick dialect practically rolled off the tongue. "Sooo, anyway. Serpent's Holler… how do we all get thar?"

Kalyn giggled once more. "Yeah, what he said."

An impish smile came to Fran's face. "I'll tell ya after you tell me your side o' it." She angled her face in Seth's direction. "I get the feelin' that ya has a tale to tell that leads up to ya meetin' Kalyn."

Seth fixed her with a long stare. He was starting to like these folks, but he still didn't want to reveal too much. After mulling it over for a few moments, he shrugged. "Oh, what the heck?"

Kalyn sat forward, her eyes widening with excitement. "Oh! More Hero stories!"

Seth cast a dubious glance at the strange young woman, then launched into a short version about the Serpent Cult's attack on Ravenford, how he and his friends had foiled it, but also how that wasn't the end of it. After the battle, Seth had found out there were still more cultists skulking about. The cult was still very much alive— and plotting to take over Thac.

When he was done, Fran let out a derisive snort. "Take o'er Thac? Mighty big piece o' land to take over. Just how is they plannin' ta do that?"

Seth paused a moment, deciding just how much he could safely tell these two women. He settled on giving them the gist of things without mentioning Larketh or the monolith.

"Let's just say that the location of some weapons left over from the Thrall Wars fell into their laps. My friends are stopping them from getting those, and I was supposed to track that moron mage back to his lair. That's when Kalyn bumbled in and killed him. So, poof! No more trail."

Kalyn huffed. "Get your story right! *You* killed him. I didn't." She crossed her arms and glared at him darkly.

Seth's mouth twisted into wry smile. "Well, he wouldn't be dead if you hadn't come along."

"Yeah, but you'd be!" Kalyn half stood from her seat and pointed at him accusingly.

Before Seth could fire back a response, he heard a loud clap. They both turned and saw Fran with her hands clasped together, a look of irritation on her face. "Oh, shut your pie holes! He's dead, and that's that. Now, do y'all wanna know the location of Serpent's Holler, or not?"

Seth sat back once more, casting a smug glance at Kalyn. "Fine by me."

Kalyn glared at him, though there was a mischievous twinkle in her gray eyes. "You're despicable." With a huff, she sat back down.

A snicker escaped Seth's lips, earning himself another glare from the girl.

Fran took a moment to think, then launched into a series of convoluted directions that left Seth's head spinning. There were "stone's throws," "hop-skip-'n-a-jumps," "jigs," and other slang that Seth didn't understand.

"Oh! I know where it's at!" Kalyn exclaimed as Fran finished.

Seth looked at her as if she were crazy. "How could you possibly get a location out of all that gibberish?"

Kalyn's eyes gleamed as she peered back at him. "Born here. Learned to speak the language. What's your excuse?"

Seth gave her an acid look. "Um… not born here. Don't speak the language. Don't really want to, either."

Kalyn fixed him with a dark glare, her hands going to her hips. After a moment or two, she began to laugh rather loudly.

Seth rolled his eyes. *What have I gotten myself into? I might have been better off with the dead black mage.*

His thoughts were interrupted by Fran. "If what ya say is true 'bout them findin' some weapons from the Thrall wars, then I has ta warn the Druidic Counsel."

Kalyn's mood instantly shifted to a more somber one. "You're right. I'll take you the rest of the way to Bendenwood, then Seth and I will go to Serpent's Hollow and check it out."

Fran shook her head. "Nah, that'd take too long. I gotta sense that you needs ta find this place soon-a than later. The both a-ya needs to make for Serpent's Holler first thing in the morning.'"

Kalyn's mouth fell open. "Fran! I'm not going to abandon you! How are you going to get to Bendenwood without my help?"

Fran smiled. "Now, I ain't lived all by myself for years on end without learnin' a few tricks." She waved her hand dismissively. "I'll convince ya in the mornin.' Fer now, the both a-ya should get some rest. Eh, do ya has a bedroll or a blanket for yerself, young Seth?"

Seth caught himself nodding his head at a blind woman again. He shot a glare at Kalyn when she stifled a giggle at his expense. "Yes. I have a blanket."

"Good! Now then, don't be shy. Feel free to scoot close to the fire n' keep yerself warm." Fran got to her feet, turned, and carefully shambled over to a tree, running her hand down the bark until she reached a backpack, which she opened and pulled a blanket from. "Here, Kalyn." She held the blanket out, which Kalyn took, then she reached in and pulled another out, unfolding it and wrapping it around her shoulders.

"I'll take first watch!" Kalyn said as she wrapped her blanket around herself.

Fran clicked her tongue. "No ma'am! I'm gonna stay up. The both of ya needs as much sleep as ya can get for tomorr'er." Kalyn opened her mouth to protest, but Fran interrupted her, "I can sleep plenty when I is dead! So, I won't tolerate no arguin' from you, young lady! Now lay yerself down and get some rest."

Fran slowly, with Kalyn's help, lowered herself to the ground near the fire, and sat down cross-legged. Kalyn sat down beside her, curling her legs in close to herself.

Seth slipped off his rock and moved over to a tree, making himself comfortable between two roots. Although he was really starting to like these two, he learned a long time ago that going to sleep in the company of strangers was a sure way to lose all your belongings, or worse.

There was a rustle in the tree above and suddenly, Elfar, the big lynx, dropped to the ground directly in front of Seth. The big cat looked back at him, its bright yellow eyes a-gleam with a smile, then it sauntered over to Kalyn and curled up next to her.

Kalyn stroked the silvery cat fondly, then she laid down, placing her head on Fran's lap and closing her eyes. Fran almost absently began to stroke Kalyn's hair and hum a tune. After a short while, her humming turned into soft singing, her gentle voice crooning out a slow, melancholy song.

Stone to wood
Break the bows that reddened the forest
And leave them behind
Light the fire
Curse his name who brought you to this end
And let the trees burn

Oh!
The Tears of Hiranzara
Are what make the rivers flow tonight
Oh!
The blood of Galinthrae
Rises with the smoke to the sky
Lift your voice!
Let the gods curse the soul of Valanor
And dry the tears of Hiranzara

Blood on blood
Elf and man all pay the same debt
And give death its due
Free at last
Those at rest will never bear the shame
Of a haunting memory

Oh!
The Tears of Hiranzara
Are what make the rivers flow tonight
Oh!
The blood of Galinthrae
Rises with the smoke to the sky
Lift your voice!
Let the gods curse the soul of Valanor
And dry the tears of Hiranzara

Seth's eyes popped open. He sat bolt upright and looked around. The light of the sun was just beginning to pale the sky above the trees. Fran herself was still sitting in the same spot, though her eyes were closed and her hands were resting on her knees as if she were meditating. Kalyn was sleeping next to her, curled into a ball around Elfar, who stared at Seth groggily.

I never fall asleep like that… Seth looked back at Fran, narrowing his eyes. The last thing he could recall was her song.

He stood and slowly crept toward the smoldering embers that used to be the fire.

"Marnin'," Fran spoke softly, "Sleep well?"

Seth froze, then relaxed, crossing his arms. "Too well."

She smiled softly, keeping her eyes closed. "Forest made ne'er a sound last night, though there were some wolves not far off that put up a howl 'bout some blood n' carcasses to feast on. Can't guess what they would-a been talkin' 'bout." Her last sentence was thick with sarcasm, "But all in all, t'was a peaceful night fer sleepin' under the stars."

Seth stared at her for a long moment, until a bird entered the clearing and began to circle overhead. He looked up and saw Fran's small owl slowly circling in toward them.

Fran lifted her arm, and the owl swiftly alighted on it with its one leg. It hopped up Fran's arm and to her shoulder, snuggling in close to her hair and looking at Seth with wide eyes.

Fran slowly opened her eyes, sighing. She stretched her arms, then she reached over and ruffled Kalyn's hair harshly.

"Up n' at 'em!"

Kalyn sat bolt upright, weaving slightly as her eyes flickered open, "I's waked," she mumbled groggily.

Fran chuckled. "Sure, you is. Let me know when ya's really awake." She got to her feet and carefully leaned over the fire, "I made some rocks. They is s'pposed to be biscuits, but I'm a-feared they is more like rocks." She lifted a small lump from a flat stone sitting in the embers, fingering it gingerly. She cocked her head and bit down on it, tearing a piece off. She nodded. "Not quite as hard as I thought they'd be, n' they taste decent 'nough to swaller. Help yerselves!"

With that, she picked up her blanket from the ground, shook it, then folded it as she ambled toward the backpacks, presumably to put the blanket away.

Kalyn reached out and grabbed two biscuits, chucking one at Seth before biting down on the other.

Seth caught the lumpy biscuit, fumbling with it for a moment as the heat from it stung his hands.

"The two of ya needs to be gettin' gone soon." Fran said, "The sooner ya learn more 'bout them cultists, the better. But I don't want ya to be takin' unnecessary risks, ya hear me? Yer just goin' to make sure that Serpent's Holler is their base, n' yer gonna have a look 'round and see what ev'ry one's up 'gainst, then yer gonna leave and meet me in Bendenwood, ya hear me?"

"I understand, but," Kalyn shook her head, "I still won't leave ya to go to Bendenwood by yourself."

"She won't be going by herself." An unfamiliar voice spoke up from the woods.

In a flash, Seth drew two daggers, crouching low. Kalyn jumped to her feet, dumping Elfar from her lap, and drew two knives from her boots, but she relaxed as a girl her age stepped into the clearing.

The newcomer had vibrant red dreadlocks and bright green eyes that twinkled as a wide, cheery smile spread across her freckled face. Her clothes were a strange mish-mash of different fibers and colors, all styled to look like bark and leaves. Feathers were also tied to her dreadlocks and clothes in different places, and she wore no shoes.

Druid. I'd bet money on it. Seth thought wryly.

"Raina!" Kalyn put her knives away and ran up to the girl. They clasped hands and bounced in a circle together excitedly, complete with girly giggles.

"It's been too long since we last saw each other!" Kalyn said as they finished.

"It has! It's been, like, an entire month. I would love to catch up sometime, but I get the feeling this is not a good time for that." Raina dropped her hands to her side and looked directly at Seth. "Hello there."

Kalyn instantly launched into introducing Seth, not forgetting to mention that he was a Hero of Ravenford, and she even took the time to sing a few of his praises. When she was done, she turned to Seth.

"Seth, this is my longtime friend, Raina Belkin. She's a druid!"

Knew it.

Raina gave Seth a weak wave and a sheepish smile. "Hi, Seth. Nice to meet you."

Seth narrowed his eyes at her. "Taking an early morning stroll through the forest?"

Raina shook her head, her dreadlocks swaying from side-to-side. "Oh no. Well, sort of. I've been walking all night, actually. I was on my way to see Fran. I usually come to see her about once a month."

Seth spiked an eyebrow. "For the monthly meeting?"

Raina tilted her head just slightly with a curious expression. "Why, yes actually."

Seth crossed his arms. "Well, that's convenient."

Kalyn mimicked his pose, her eyes narrowing. "Yeah. Very convenient."

Raina smiled and shrugged innocently.

Fran spoke up. "Raina's the one that usually takes me to the meetin.' If it ain't her, then it's that ol' fire lovin' maniac who ne'rly burnt my house down and roasted all my geese alive. Troll-brained fool." She muttered the last part under her breath as she tied her backpack closed and lifted it to her shoulder.

Raina put a hand over her mouth, trying to stifle a giggle, while Kalyn bent down to Seth's level to explain. "She's talkin' about Qualar, a rickety old man from Bendenwood. Though neither admit to it, Fran and Qualar are as stuck on each other as a dragon is on gold. I sometimes wonder if these mysterious 'monthly meetings' are just secret little rendezvous for the two of them."

Fran cleared her throat. "I hope y'all ain't spreadin' more untruthful rumors 'bout myself and that ol' goblin fart."

Seth covered his mouth with his fist and coughed into it to hide a laugh. If he stayed with these two much longer, it was going to ruin his snarky reputation.

Kalyn and Raina both stood straight to attention.

"Us?" Kalyn asked.

"We would never." Raina added.

"Didn't think so." Fran grabbed a staff leaning against the tree. "Now then! Did ya bring us some wings, Raina?"

"Yes ma'am, I did!" Raina put her fingers to her lips and whistled.

A soft buzzing sound began to thrum in Seth's ears, steadily growing louder and louder. The horse nearby whinnied loudly as faint shadows fell over them, making Seth glance upward. He nearly went slack jawed as he watched two giant dragonflies, one green and one blue, swoop into the clearing and circle around the trees.

Kalyn covered her head and ducked as the green one swept over her, nearly hitting her with its long black legs. "Holy gurgling gargoyles! Watch where you're going, you googly-eyed brain buzzer!"

The giant dragonflies landed on either side of Raina, twitching their large antenna and dancing on their dainty legs.

Raina giggled. "Compliments of the Archdruid."

Kalyn stood with a huff, straightening her clothes.

"Kalyn, you n' Seth take these o'ersized bugs to Serpent's Holler. It'll be faster." Fran said. "Raina n' I'll take that horse and dog to Bendenwood with us."

Kalyn and Seth exchanged glances, then looked back at Fran.

"You mean we have to ride these things?" Kalyn asked.

Fran nodded.

"Yes!" Seth pumped his fist in the air.

"What about Elfar? Can he ride with me?" Kalyn asked.

"It might be best if he came with us. The added weight might be too much for the dragonfly." Raina said.

Kalyn looked down at the big lynx, who yawned with a bored expression, seeming oblivious to her plight.

She sighed. "Oh, fine. If I must, then I must. But I'm sure he'll miss me."

At that, Elfar stood and, with his tail in the air, sauntered away into the woods without so much as a glance back at Kalyn.

Seth's mouth curved to one side. "Yep. Looks like he's gonna miss you *real* bad."

Kalyn glared at Seth with a lofty expression. "He is. He's just going to hide it behind a mask of stalwart independence."

Seth rolled his eyes. "Sure, he is."

"All right, chil'ens. Ain't got the time for bickerin'." Fran shambled up to Seth and held a pack out to him, "Take this, young feller. Iff'n all goes well, ya won't be needin' none of it, but I don't want to be sendin' the both o' ya off without some food n' supplies."

Seth took the pack from her, then paused as she bent down and dropped her voice low. "I know you is the distrustin' type and don't has much faith in us, and that's good n' well. So, you'll unda'stand when I say that I don't trust you much neither. That said, I 'spect my Kalyn to come back safe n' sound. If she don't, I swear by my pretty straw hat, I *will* end you."

Seth spiked an eyebrow, a little taken aback by the colorful wording, but then a wicked grin broke across his face. "No promises. She's pretty annoying, and I get the feeling there might be a few really big, hungry snakes 'round where we're going."

Fran stood back to her full height to reveal Kalyn standing right next to her, arms crossed.

Kalyn cleared her throat. "If the two of you are done making pointless threats..." She jerked her thumb back at the dragonflies, "I'd like to get this done and over with as soon as possible. I have all I need, and if you've got the food, we should be set."

Seth shouldered the pack. "Fine. I call the blue one."

"Not if I get to it first!" Kalyn shot toward the dragonfly, but Seth dashed under the creature, scrambling up a leg, bounding up to its back and seating himself before Kalyn could make it around the creature's long, outstretched wings.

Kalyn skidded to a halt, her mouth falling open. "Hey! No fair!"

Seth crossed his arms and shrugged. "What can I say? Being a *lil' feller* has its perks."

Kalyn grinned, seemingly in spite of herself. "Fine. Take the blue one. I really wanted the green one anyway."

"Have either of you children ever flown one of these before?" Raina asked, hands on her hips, as Kalyn mounted her dragonfly.

Seth shook his head. "Nope!"

"Nope. Is it hard?" Kalyn asked.

Raina shrugged. "Oh, not really. Especially for a Deepwood

tracker." She quickly explained the best techniques for guiding the creatures while in the air, "It just mostly involves leaning in the right direction. It's really not too hard."

Seth and Kalyn looked at each other, and a mischievous smile slowly twisted up the corners of Kalyn's face. "Last one to Serpent's Hollow is a rotten zombie?"

"You're on!" Seth nudged his dragonfly in the sides and held on tightly as it took to the air with ease, Kalyn's dragonfly right on his heels.

"Don't take unnecessary risks! Remember!" Fran shouted after them.

No promises! Seth laughed in his mind. He angled his dragonfly in the general direction he knew they needed to go, grinning from ear-to-ear as the cool wind rushed by his face.

12
AIRSHIP

How does something that big stay airborne in the first place?

The golden orb of the sun rose over the lush green canopy of the forest far to the east. Birds flitted across the treetops, playing "Follow the Leader," their morning song permeating the waking wood with sweet music. Traces of morning dew evaporated off the leaves of the tall surrounding trees. The lingering smell of smoke filled the air, the burnt remains of the large green dragon still smoldering down in the clearing far below.

Lloyd Stealle stood on the upper floor of the Darkwoods monolith, gazing out the wide-arched window that faced the eastern horizon. The young warrior had relieved Martan halfway through the night, taking up the second half of the overnight watch.

They all had agreed on this necessary precaution, especially after the surprise appearance of the large green dragon the night before. Furthermore, there was no telling if, or when, the other larger green dragon would make its reappearance. Yet the night had passed quietly, the morning sun now on the rise as the surrounding forest woke up for another day.

Lloyd circled around the top floor of the monolith, scanning the area through all four windows—yet all he saw was a peaceful ocean of green treetops spread out before him, ending to the north and west in a jagged wall of tall black peaks. It was the beginning of a beautiful sunny day, with clear blue skies in every direction.

As the young warrior returned to the east window, something caught his eye. There was a tiny black speck on the horizon, far off in the distance, that hadn't been there a few minutes before. He wasn't sure what to make of it at first, but after a while, the spec appeared to grow in size. *Whatever that is, it's headed this way.*

Lloyd squinted his eyes, his immediate concern that the spec was the returning ancient green dragon. Yet he saw no hint of green from the object in the bright morning sun. Still, whatever it was, it continued to grow larger. Lloyd got the sense that whatever it was, it was fairly big. *I better go tell the others.*

The young warrior climbed up the short flight of stairs, to the floating dais above the monolith's central pillar, and spoke the word that made the disc magically descend to the sub-basement.

Glolindir's eyes snapped open—once again he was in his blankets on the floor of the wide oval chamber that had once served as Larketh's living room. The room was dim, lit only by the golden flames of the small fireplace that magically never went out.

Two darkened forms lay in blankets next to him—Elladan and Donnie, if he remembered correctly. Martan and Cyclone were both curled up in chairs near the fire, while the two squires, Syndir and Lamorn, lay strewn across either side of the long couch.

This time, however, Glo immediately knew what had stirred him from his elven trance—the sound of heavy footsteps echoed from the stairwell at the other end of the room. Someone was charging down those spiral stairs at breakneck speed. The loud noise had woken the others as well. A loud clapping noise sounded next to Glo, the lights in the room flaring to life.

Elladan sat next to him, the bard's hands firmly clasped together. Donnie and Martan swiftly scooped up their weapons, and rushed over toward the base of the stairs. A moment later, Alana came bursting out of the bedroom, sword in hand as she hurried to join the others. Elistra, trailing behind her, cried out, "What is it this time?"

Cyclone, still sitting in his chair, rubbed his face with his hands and grumbled, "They're all nuts. It's probably just Lloyd…"

As if on cue, the warrior's voice cascaded down the stairwell. "Don't worry, it's only me!"

Cyclone sat back in his chair, and folded his arms across his chest. "Told ya."

Glo, Elladan, Donnie, and Martan all exchanged an embarrassed glance, the latter two lowering their weapons. As Lloyd spilled out of the spiral stairwell, Cyclone gave him a dark stare. "You better have a good reason for waking me so early."

Lloyd stopped at the base of the stairwell and bent over, his hands on his knees as he huffed to catch his breath. "Some… some… something's coming…"

Elladan cast a quick glance at Glo, a single eyebrow raised, then pushed forward through the others. "What do you mean, something's coming?"

Lloyd took a deep breath, and stood back up. "There's something headed… this way… something flying… something big."

Glo felt a chill run up his spine. *Could it be the other dragon? The huge green one?*

Elladan spun around, his eyes sweeping from Glo to Elistra, his anxious expression mirroring Glo's thoughts. "We better go and have a look."

Glo swept his eyes across the room, seeing grim faces all around. They had been lucky in their battle with the first green dragon. The chances of fooling another dragon into an equally compromising position were slim at best. Alana gave Elladan a nod.

"You go on ahead—the rest of us will gear up."

The lady knight spun on her heel and marched swiftly back toward the bedroom, motioning for her squire, Syndir, to follow. At the same time, Cyclone pushed himself out of his chair, and pulled out his pieces of armor.

"Wait one moment, and I'll join you," Donnie declared, rushing back over to his blankets to fetch his vest and sword belt.

Glo shifted his gaze toward Martan. "Can you join us as well? Your eyesight is probably the best out of all of us."

Martan gave him a dubious look. "I'm not so sure about that, but I'll come if you want me to."

The archer went to gather the rest of his gear. Meanwhile, Elistra strode quietly up to Glo and whispered softly to him. "I'm going to stay here and meditate on this. Please be careful up there."

Glo gazed down into those bright violet eyes and saw the genuine concern in them. He grasped the seeress by the hands and gave her a warm smile. "I promise."

Elistra gave him a small smile back, then stood on her toes, and kissed him soundly on the lips. It was a short kiss, but Glo's head swam from it nonetheless. The seeress then pulled away, went over to a chair, sat down crossed-legged, and firmly shut her eyes. At that point, Donnie and Martan returned.

"Ready," the rapier-toting elf announced to them.

Lloyd and Donnie led the way, with Glo and Elladan next, Martan bringing up the rear. As they swiftly ascended the spiral stairs, Glo silently wondered to himself if they would survive this day.

When they reached the top of the monolith shaft, Lloyd led the way to the eastern arch, the others following close behind. The "speck" was now noticeably larger. In fact, in the short time it had taken him to get the others, it had grown large enough to clearly see its shape—it appeared to be a ship, floating in the air.

"An airship!" Donnie exclaimed, his voice filled with wonder.

Lloyd had heard of airships before, but he had never seen one. This one was close enough now that you could definitely see the shape of its hull. It did not appear very different from a sea-faring vessel, but there were no masts or sails visible above the deck. Instead, there was a bright blue pulsing ring of energy that encircled the ship, close to the aft. Lloyd was familiar with how the ring worked, his mother, the High Wizard of Penwick, having explained it to him. Yet now that Lloyd actually saw an airship, it brought more questions to his mind. His face scrunched up as he shifted his gaze to Glo. "Can you explain something to me?"

Glo's eyes remained fixed on the airborne craft. "You want to know about the ring?"

Lloyd shook his head. "No, I already know that. The blue ring is powered by a great air elemental—the ring spins like a giant propeller, pushing the ship through the air."

Glo responded with a slow nod. "That's basically it. So, what is it you want to know?"

"Well…" Lloyd hesitated, feeling foolish about even asking the question. After a moment's deliberation, he took a deep breath and plowed ahead, the words practically spilling from his mouth. "… even with the power of a great air elemental, how does something that big stay airborne in the first place?"

Glo finally turned to face Lloyd, a slight laugh escaping the wizard's lips. "That is a good question. If the craft were made of normal wood, it would never even lift off the ground."

"You need special wood," Elladan said from behind him. Lloyd spun his head toward the bard, and saw the quasi-smile on his face. "The wood has to have magical properties that makes it lighter than air. That's how airships float in the first place."

Lloyd reached up and scratched his head. "Magical wood? Is that even a thing?"

Elladan let out a short laugh. "It is… and don't feel too bad, Lloyd. It's not exactly common knowledge."

Lloyd was still digesting this new information about 'magical wood' as he turned his gaze back toward the airship. The vessel was nearer now, but still appeared to be a few miles away. Lloyd narrowed his eyes, scanning the vessel for any markings that would indicate its name, or point of origin, but he could see none. "I wonder what fleet it belongs to?"

Martan, quiet up till now, chimed in. "It's running a purple flag with a golden design of some sort, but I can't see what it is from this distance."

Lloyd gave the archer an appreciative nod. "Good eye, Martan. I can barely see the flag from this distance."

Glo commended the archer as well, then steepled his hands together in front of his mouth. His expression grew more pensive with each passing second. "Well, wherever they're from, the next question is, what are they doing out here?"

No one had an immediate answer. It was Donnie who broke the short silence. "Well, I don't know why they're out here, but it sure looks as if they are heading straight for us."

Lloyd returned his attention to the airship. Sure enough, the sandy-haired elf was right. The airborne vessel had altered its course, and was now headed directly for the monolith. Elladan leaned forward, his eyes glued to the approaching craft. "I think it best we find out their intentions."

Glo shifted his gaze to the bard and eyed him curiously. "And just how do you plan to do that?"

Elladan spun his head toward Glo, and gave the elven wizard a sly wink. "I'm going to send them a note."

Glo arched an eyebrow, but listened in earnest to the bard's idea. A short while later, Elladan had scribbled out a message on some parchment, and handed it over to Glo.

Lloyd skirted around behind the tall elf, gazing over the shoulder not occupied by Raven. The errant bird had reappeared a day earlier, once the green dragon had been dispatched. She had not left Glo's side since.

Lloyd completely understood how the fearsome creature might have scared Raven away. The dragon had been huge from their perspective, so he could just imagine how large it appeared to the tiny bird. Lloyd gave Raven a brief smile then glanced at the note the bard had crafted.

Greetings to those in the approaching airship. If your intentions are peaceful, then please halt your approach to the monolith. We will gladly meet with you to parley in a neutral location. However, if your intentions are not peaceful, then be aware you are trespassing on territory belonging to the Baron of Ravenford, and will be dealt with accordingly.

Best Regards,
Elladan Narmolanya, Emissary of Ravenford

Lloyd glanced at Elladan skeptically. The Baron never sanctioned them to claim ownership of the monolith in his name, nor did he give them the right to act as his emissaries. Glo seemed equally concerned, the elven wizard arching an eyebrow yet again at the bard as he rolled up the parchment. "You sure you want to send this?"

Elladan placed a reassuring hand on the wizard's shoulder. "Trust me, it'll be fine."

Elladan seemed quite sure of himself. Lloyd glanced at Donnie, but the slight elf merely shrugged. Martan remained quiet throughout the entire discussion. Glo hesitated a moment longer, then let out a deep sigh. "Very well."

The wizard handed the parchment to Raven and spoke to her briefly in elvish. "*Revia an i' gwelu cair.*"

The bird squawked once, then took off and winged her way across the sky toward the approaching airship. The black bird's tiny form dwindled as it sped across the distance to the airborne vessel. Lloyd was watching her progress when a dark shape suddenly detached itself from the ship's hull. He squinted his eyes, trying to determine the identity of the dark form. *That looks like a…*

"Dragon!" Martan interrupted his thoughts with a choked cry.

The five of them leaned forward as one. Indeed, the archer was right. The dark form had a sleek body, adjoined on either side by a graceful bat-like wing, and trailed a long, lithe tail. Yet there was something off about the dragon-like figure. Lloyd couldn't quite figure out what it was at first, but then Elladan put it into words.

"If that's a dragon, it's either tiny, or that airship is a lot bigger than we think."

Lloyd nearly laughed aloud at the bard's observation, but then he noticed that Glo's face had gone pale. Lloyd nudged his elven friend in the shoulder. "Are you alright?"

The wizard shifted his eyes toward Lloyd, a strained smile spreading across his lips. "I'm fine. It's just Raven—dragon or not, that thing has her spooked."

They all watched anxiously as the small, dark, dragon-like creature closed on Glo's anxious familiar. The gap between them grew smaller and smaller, till without warning, Raven banked and veered away. The note the black bird carried dropped from her claws, unfolding and fluttering down through the air. Raven's tiny wings flapped like mad as she sped away, but the dark creature did not pursue her, instead diving after the fluttering parchment. The small, dragon-like beast snagged the note out of the sky, then gracefully arced around and headed back toward the airship from whence it came. It receded swiftly, and reached the vessel well before Glo's familiar would make it back to the monolith.

"Whatever that thing is, it's certainly fast," Donnie noted with a wry lilt to his tone.

"What's fast?" a familiar voice sounded from behind them.

Lloyd spun around in time to see Alana, Cyclone, Elistra, and the two squires spill out of the shaft in the center of the room, none waiting for the floating disc to finish its ascent. It was Alana who had asked the question, the lady knight and the dragon hunter leading the way across the chamber. Cyclone answered her before anyone else could speak.

"The little black dragon headed for that airship."

Lloyd spun around and took another look at the fast-flying creature. *So Martan and Elladan were both right—it is a dragon! A little black dragon.*

The others drew up next to them and peered out the archway just as the little dragon reached the airship and disappeared behind the forecastle. Alana shaded her eyes with her hand and stared intently at the approaching vessel. "Anyone care to explain what we're seeing here?"

Elladan turned to face the others, his eyes fixed on Alana as he went through a brief explanation of what they had missed. When he was done, the lady knight closed her eyes and shook her head, a pained smile upon her face. "Really, Elladan? Claiming the monolith in the Baron's name?"

Elladan's mouth twisted into that all-too-familiar half-smile. "Easy there, Alana. No one's actually claiming anything. It was just a ploy to deter that airship—at least until we know who we are dealing with."

Donnie strode up next to the lady knight, and waved a hand

through the air in front of him, a mischievous smile across his lips. "Emissary of Ravenford… you have to admit, it does have a nice ring to it."

Elladan tilted his head to one side, and squinted at his slim friend. "Give me a break, will you? It was the best I could come up with on such short notice."

A quick retort formed on Donnie's lips, but before he could speak, he was interrupted by Martan. The somber archer pointed out the archway. "Don't look now, but I think your plan worked."

Lloyd cast a glance back over his shoulder—the airship was still a couple of miles away, but it had visibly slowed. Abruptly, the bright ring around the vessel disappeared, and the airship came to a complete halt. It sat there, floating in mid-air, a little more than a mile away.

Elladan pointed a triumphant hand toward the airship as his gaze shifted back toward Alana. "See, what did I tell you?"

"It must have been that awe-inspiring emissary title," Donnie quipped with a shameless grin.

Elladan let out a short, close-mouthed laugh. "Guess I just have that effect on people."

Donnie opened his mouth to fire off another retort, but was cut off once again, this time by Cyclone. The dragon hunter nodded toward the open archway. "We've got company."

Lloyd glanced out the window once more, and saw the little black dragon again, this time zipping away from the airship. The creature swiftly banked, and headed straight for the monolith at an incredible speed. Lloyd squinted at the little black dragon. It appeared to be carrying something in one of its claws—a note, most likely.

Cyclone must have seen it as well. The dragon hunter folded his arms across his chest, and shook his head. "A dragon acting as somebody's messenger? Disgusting."

Lloyd sympathized with the dragon hunter. Since he had left Penwick, his entire world had been turned upside down. The young warrior had seen many strange things, some of which he never even knew existed. From skeletal wizards to stone golems, giant serpents and wolf-like demons, Lloyd had faced more bizarre foes in these last few months than in all his eighteen years. The young warrior cast a sidelong glance at Cyclone. "Kind of goes against everything you believe, doesn't it?"

Cyclone kept his eyes fixed forward. "Did I ask for your opinion…"

Lloyd was taken aback by the dragon hunter's harsh response. Yet before he could say anything, Donnie drew up next to the duo.

The slight elf gazed out the archway at the approaching dragon. "Trust me, I've seen some strange things in my lifetime, and I've learned one thing from it. Much as the scholars would like you to believe, not everything fits into a nice little pigeon hole." The elf's expression grew distant, his voice somewhat hollow. "There are things in this world that just can't be explained."

Donnie's little speech was capped with a series of coughs. Lloyd spun his gaze toward Elistra. The seeress had a fist in front of her mouth, her face turning red as she coughed into it. Glo swiftly stepped behind her, and patted Elistra gently on the back, his eyes filled with concern. "Are you alright?"

Elistra swiveled her head toward the wizard, and gave him a feeble smile. "I'm… fine. Wrong… pipe…"

Glo placed an arm around her and held the seeress until she calmed down. Once her impromptu coughing fit subsided, everyone's attention returned to the little black dragon. As the creature drew closer, it became apparent that it was truly tiny for one of its kind, barely larger than a man. Lloyd glanced at Cyclone once again. "Is that a baby dragon?"

The dragon hunter responded with a single shake of his head. "Nah. A baby would be half that size." Cyclone's eyes narrowed as he sized up the young dragon. "I'd guess this one is no more than twenty—not even a teen-ager yet in dragon years."

The little black dragon's dark scales glistened in the morning sunlight as it drew near the monolith. When the creature reached the clearing, it slowed and executed a wide arc. The little dragon let out a derisive snort as it flew by and casually released the parchment in its claw. The young black dragon continued its arc until it faced away from the monolith, and with a few great flaps of its bat-like wings, shot out over the forest, back toward the waiting airship.

Lloyd overheard Glo speaking in elvish to his familiar, the tiny black bird planted firmly on his shoulder since her frantic return. *"Revia. Gad i' lekmee."*

Raven seemed unwilling to move at first, but after a bit more coaxing, finally flew out the window and dove down after the fluttering parchment the dragon had dropped. The black bird caught the paper a few feet above the ground and returned with it a few seconds later. She hovered in front of Glo, holding what looked like the original note that they had sent to the airship. The elven wizard gingerly took the parchment from his tiny friend, then let her light on his arm, softly cooing to her.

"Quel gwenn. Quel gwenn."

Elladan held out a hand to his elven friend. "Let me see that."

Glo proffered the parchment to the bard, then fed Raven something from a pouch on his belt. The elf then stroked her tiny head, still cooing to her softly. The small black bird appeared to settle down, and hopped back up onto the elven wizard's shoulder. Meanwhile, Elladan unrolled the parchment and read it aloud.

Dear Elladan,

You have made me laugh. If you ever want a job as a jester, please feel free to apply at my court. However, as my intentions are peaceful, I have complied and parked my airship. I will set up a meeting place in the meadow south of here, where we can discuss any claims on this territory. Please be kind enough to join me there in an hour from now.

Regards,
Anya, Princess of Lanfor

Elladan responded with a short chuckle. "I've been called many things in my life, but never a jester."

Lloyd paid little attention to the bard, his mind focused on the last line of the written reply. "Princess of Lanfor? That's on the other side of the Merchant's Channel. What would a princess of Lanfor be doing all the way out here?"

Lanfor was a small island kingdom directly east of Thac. While nowhere near the size of the island continent, Lanfor was nonetheless a powerful nation. Yet their strength did not come from a wide-reaching naval presence, like Lloyd's home city of Penwick, but rather from their queen and the great army that supported her. Lloyd had heard rumors of the Queen of Lanfor. It was said that she was a powerful sorceress who had ruled that kingdom for nearly three hundred years.

Lloyd cast a curious glance at Glo. The wizard appeared as perplexed as he, a single eyebrow arched across his forehead. "And why, of all places, would she be headed straight for this monolith?"

A wry smile graced Donnie's lips as he stared out the window at the hovering airship. "If she came all this way for take-out, she's going to be sorely disappointed."

"Unless she likes roast dragon," Cyclone added, with a quick glance toward the great carcass still smoldering in the clearing below.

Snorts and chuckles erupted from the group, until Glo spoke up once more. The elven wizard eyed Donnie and Cyclone with a raised brow. "You can ask her about the roast dragon when you see her, but right now what I really want to know is, how does she know about the monolith in the first place?"

Glo's query left everyone in silence. Not many folks knew about the existence of the monolith. As far as Lloyd was aware of, it was just this group, the Knights of the Rose, and the first family of Ravenford. It didn't seem likely that any of them would contact Lanfor about it. Lloyd's eyes went wide once more as a sudden thought occurred to him. *The only other group that knew about the monolith was the Serpent Cult…*

Lloyd opened his mouth to speak, but Elistra beat him to it. The seeress sounded hesitant as she broke the silence. "I had meditated on this a bit before we came up here…"

All eyes turned to the seeress, as she paused for a moment's reflection. Glo placed his arm around Elistra again, and gently prompted her. "And…"

Elistra cast a brief smile at the tall elf, then continued. "…and while I didn't have any visions, I got the distinct impression that there is some sort of connection between the green dragon and this airship."

Glo peered down at the seeress, his eyes narrowing at this startling new revelation. "Connected in what way?"

Elistra slowly shook her head, deep creases lining her comely brow. "I am not quite sure. It's just a feeling, but my intuition is seldom wrong."

Lloyd reached up and scratched the top of his head. Elistra had proven her abilities time and again on this journey—he wasn't about to question her now, but something just didn't add up. Feeling even more confused than ever, Lloyd swept his eyes around the group, looking for answers. "Let me get this straight. First, we have this black knight who commanded the two green dragons. Now we have this princess, who has a little black dragon as a 'pet.' But the only person who could ever control dragons was the Dragon Thrall Master."

Glo's eyes fell on Lloyd, the blue orbs lit with a keen intensity. "Go on…"

Lloyd responded with a brief nod, then pressed on with his thoughts. "Well, yesterday you were thinking that this black knight was the Dragon Master, somehow still alive after all these years. But if this princess can also control dragons, then what does that make her?"

Glo let go of Elistra and steepled his hands together in front of his chin, his eyes remaining fixed on Lloyd. "You bring up an excellent point. I doubt this black knight is on board the airship, or we would have seen that huge green dragon by now. That being said, how is it this princess has a little black dragon running errands for her?"

Cyclone folded his arms across his chest. "Maybe a metallic dragon, but a chromatic—no way."

Donnie peered out the window again, eyeing the floating airship suspiciously. "I don't like this. I don't like this one bit." The slight elf folded his arms in front of him and bit his lower lip. "I just wish there was some way we could warn Ruka to stay away from here—at least until we know it's safe."

Alana strode up next to the worried elf and placed a gauntleted hand on his slim shoulder. "So do I."

Donnie cast a brief glance at the lady knight, then put his hand on hers and gave her a strained smile. Glo, still standing next to Elistra, responded to both their concerns in a soft voice. "There might just be a way."

Donnie spun all the way around this time, and cocked an eye at the wizard. "How?"

Glo took a deep breath, then reached underneath his tunic and pulled out a bronze chain from around his neck. At the end of that chain hung a perfectly round moon-colored gemstone, the size of a large pebble, inset into a bronze border.

A low whistle emanated from Elladan, the bard leaning in for a closer look at the amulet. "I've never seen such a large pearl. Where in Thac did you get that?"

A thin smile spread across Glo's lips as he gazed down at the bard. "It was a gift from Ves before we left. She called it a 'Pearl of Friendship.' She said that I could use it if we needed to get in touch with her."

As Elladan stepped back, Elistra peered up at Glo. "May I?" Glo responded with a single nod. Elistra gently grasped the amulet and brought it up to her eye. Her gaze remained fixed on the large pearl as she spoke. "Yes, I am familiar with these. They are used for communication over long distances. They are also typically made as a set." Elistra gazed back up at Glo. "If Ves has one, then Ruka most likely does as well."

"Can you please try to contact her?" Donnie implored, his normally carefree features lined with concern. Alana stood quietly next to the slim elf, her face filled with equal apprehension.

Glo gazed at the duo with a resigned smile. "I'm not quite sure how it works, but I'll do my best."

Elistra grabbed hold of the tall elf's hand. "Let me help you."

The wizard and seeress walked off toward the center of the room, most likely in search of a quiet place to concentrate. Lloyd watched after them for a few moments, then turned his attention back to his friends. "So, we have less than an hour till this meeting with the princess. How do we want to handle it?"

13
A PICNIC WITH THE PRINCESS

*Her elegant outfit bespoke of nobility, at the same time
exposing as much skin as possible*

The sun peeked through the canopy of trees above, already well on its journey across the clear mid-morning sky. Elladan practically strutted along the wooded path through the dark forest, his bright white fringes dangling in time to the jaunty tune he whistled. Birds in the nearby trees heard his song and responded in kind, creating a beautiful woodland harmony in the surrounding forest.

The squire Lamorn marched next to the bard, decorated in the formal white flower-covered tabard of the Knights of the Rose. Elladan purposely did his best to make a spectacle of himself in the woods, attempting to catch the attention of any prying eyes in the area. The young squire walked proudly next to him, but Elladan sensed the lad was just a touch nervous. He whispered to him out of the side of his mouth. "Don't worry son… help is close at hand."

Elladan cast a furtive glance toward the woods to the left of the path. The vaguest hint of a fleeting shadow passed through the trees, barely seen by even his sharp elven eyes. Martan was quite adept in the woods—the tracker could stay hidden from even the most discerning of observers. Elladan gazed briefly to his right, but there was not even the remotest of signs that Donnie was there.

Glo had cast a spell on the already-stealthy elf to make him invisible. Yet Martan had declined the offer of magic, steadfastly claiming that he would be fine as long as he stuck to the trees.

The path they were on led south from the glade where the monolith stood, entering another meadow about two miles to the south. Raven had scouted out the area ahead for them, the reluctant familiar turning tail as soon as she had spied the clearing. Elladan had wished the bird could have given them more information as to what they were facing, but Glo said she was too spooked by the little black dragon to fly into such a wide-open area alone. Thus, the need for their current deception with Martan and Donnie covertly flanking them.

Lloyd, Cyclone, Glo, and Elistra had all stayed behind at the monolith, to guard the structure in case this meeting was merely a ruse to get inside unchallenged. It would be a while yet till Aksel and Ruka returned. Glo was able to contact the dragon girl, and had warned her about their current situation. After hearing what was going on, Aksel decided it best they come in on the ground—that would slow their progress, but help them to remain unseen.

Elladan and Lamorn, surrounded by their silent companions, continued their colorful march a short distance further, until the canopy of trees opened, signifying a break in the forest. At that point, Elladan raised his hand, signaling a halt. Unlike the glade surrounding the monolith, this meadow was not clear, with trees and brush strewn across their path.

Elladan bobbed and weaved his head around, trying to get a better view of what lay ahead through the tangled mass of vegetation. Something gleamed white in the late morning sun, just above the brambles in front of them. Elladan squinted his eyes for a better look—it appeared to be the top of a large white canopy. Elladan laughed silently to himself. This princess obviously didn't do things halfway.

"What's so funny?" Lamorn asked.

The bard shifted his gaze to the young squire, the lad staring at him curiously. Elladan waved Lamorn over next to him, and pointed toward the top of the white canopy. "It looks like they've got a fancy little welcome set up for us already."

Lamorn sidled up next to him, and followed his gaze, the lad visibly relaxing at the sight. "That looks like a friendly sign."

Elladan pursed his lips together. "Maybe… then again, looks can be deceiving."

The bard had dealt with diplomats before, and he wasn't about to let his guard down just yet. The squire gazed at him questioningly, but before Elladan could respond, he felt a sudden presence at his side. Elladan nearly jumped out of his skin. He swiftly spun around, but there was no one there.

A soft whisper reached his ears. "Wait for a bit while Martan and I go ahead."

Elladan responded with the barest of nods, acting as if he had never heard Donnie's voice. Instead, he turned to Lamorn and gave the lad a quick wink. "Either way, let's stop here a few moments, and make sure we're presentable. After all, this is a princess."

Lamorn broke out into a genuine smile as the two of them straightened their attire.

Donnie moved on silent feet as he stole around the thick mass of brush ahead. The slight elf cast a quick glance toward the woods, but there was no sign of Martan. The rustle of a leaf or two was the only indication of the tracker's passage through the nearby trees. Donnie skirted the edge of the brambles, the thick mass ending just a few dozen yards beyond. The path abruptly opened into a wide, sunny meadow. Donnie halted in his tracks, astonished by what stood before him.

In the very center of the clearing sat a large white canopy, underneath which stood a long table covered in a cloth of pure white silk. Heavy chairs of gleaming mahogany surrounded the table, upholstered similarly to the silk tablecloth. The table itself was decorated with candelabras, several fancy place settings, and a wide variety of food.

Each plate was accompanied by an ornate silver goblet. A few crystal decanters were scattered between the settings, glittering vividly in the bright sunlight. Beneath the fancy table and chairs lay a fine woven carpet, with intricate red and black designs, creating a strange oval island of luxury in an otherwise rough and unfinished setting. It was an incongruous sight that made Donnie raise an eyebrow.

Yet that was not the most striking sight in the otherwise plain meadow. Donnie's gaze was drawn to three shapely figures at the far end of the table. The woman in the center of the trio was a statuesque figure with alabaster skin, and long, flaxen blonde hair that draped over her creamy white shoulders, reaching down nearly to her waist. Yet it was her outfit that immediately drew Donnie's attention. It was rather revealing, composed of a short black bodice, separate black sleeves that ran from above the elbow down to the wrist, and a long black skirt, slit all the way up the front, revealing a good portion of her shapely legs.

The entire ensemble was trimmed in gold, including an ornate choker and a V-shaped belt that was tightly fitted to her slim waist. White ruffles hung from end of her sleeves, the center of her bodice, the ornate belt, and peaked around the edges of her skirt.

Donnie stood there, his mouth agape for a few moments, till he finally caught himself. Reddening with embarrassment, he thanked the gods that he was invisible at that moment. The chagrinned elf returned his gaze to the woman's face and noted the thin tiara atop her light blonde head of hair. This was quite obviously the Princess Anya of Lanfor.

At the left and just behind the Princess stood a figure with long, wavy, light brown hair, adorned in formfitting white robes, laced with gold symbols and trim. A golden belt hung at her waist, the hilt of a long sword protruding from the scabbard attached to it. Donnie narrowed his eyes—he had seen those golden symbols before. It struck him just moments later—that was the mark of the goddess, Lenara, the *Lady of Battle.*

This woman was none other than a battle priestess. Donnie

arched an eyebrow. Such an adversary could be deadly, wielding the blade as effectively as divine magic. Donnie's eyes lingered on the priestess a moment or two longer, noting how eagerly she fingered the sword hilt at her waist. *I'll have to keep an eye on that one.*

The slim elf then shifted his gaze to the woman at the Princess' right. A sultry figure with bronzed skin and a wild mane of curly red hair dangling down her shoulders lounged casually in one of the ornate mahogany chairs. The woman was garbed exclusively in scarlet, a tight-laced leather bodice over a long-sleeved dress with a full skirt. She wore no visible weapons, but spoke softly with the Princess, the two of them breaking out into a grin as if sharing some private joke.

At first Donnie thought her a lady in waiting, but there was something odd about the way she sprawled across that chair, like some great jungle cat waiting for her prey.

Donnie was still trying to figure her out when a movement behind the Princess caught his eye. At the other end of the meadow, a solitary figure leaned against a tree, a long bow held casually in its hand. Donnie squinted and saw that the figure was a slim woman with straight, shoulder-length chestnut hair, wearing the brown and green leathers of a forest tracker.

Not far from the archer, another figure stalked the meadow like some caged animal anxious for a fight. The figure was quite obviously female, her trim physique accentuated by a sleek black leather outfit. His interest piqued, Donnie silently circled around the canopied table for a better view. This woman was most definitely a warrior, her outfit adorned with an intricately tooled black leather epaulet, corset, bracers, and belt, all decorated with silver buckles and studs that glistened in the bright morning sun. Hanging from that belt on either side were two long scabbards, each capped with an ornate silver hilt. The warrior's long golden-blonde hair was braided into a single ponytail that reached down between her shoulder blades.

The slim elf stole softly closer, his eyes riveted to the intricate silver designs on her outfit. His eyes went suddenly wide. *Those are mithril!*

Donnie had never seen such intricate craftwork before. It put even the elves to shame. His musings were interrupted by a regal voice. "Make sure the wine is properly chilled."

Donnie shifted his attention back to the table in the center of the meadow. The Princess had spoken her directive to no one in particular, but as Donnie watched, the decanter of wine in front of her suddenly frosted over. A moment later, the crystal decanter lifted into the air of its own accord, and poured its contents into a silver goblet in front of the Princess.

Donnie narrowed his eyes—none of the three women at the table had lifted a finger, let alone cast a spell. That could only mean one thing—there was another party present in that glade, an invisible person with the ability to cast spells. *A wizard most likely.*

Donnie wanted to seek out this mystery figure, but time had run out. The Princess peered up and past him, her eyes coming alight with keen interest. Donnie spun around and saw that Elladan had entered the meadow with the young squire, Lamorn, by his side.

Elladan marched purposely past the thick mass of brush and into the wide meadow with Lamorn at his side. His gaze immediately fell on the lavish spread laid out before them—it was a *Heroes' Feast.* Elladan was quite familiar with the spell. The Duke of Dunwynn had used it to salvage the Lady Andrella's birthday party.

His eyes swept across the table, falling on the figures at the far end. They were three lovely women, the one in the center possibly one of the most beautiful he had ever seen. Her appearance rivaled that of Shalla, the attractive bardess Elladan had left back in Ravenford. Yet in contrast to Shalla, this woman was fair, with hair so blonde that it bordered on white, a complexion like porcelain, and striking eyes the color of burnt gold. She also dressed far more provocatively than the lady bard. Garbed in fine black and gold, her elegant outfit bespoke of nobility, at the same time exposing as much skin as possible.

Still, Elladan was not thrown by her beauty. He had met many attractive women in his time—it kind of came with the territory in his line of work. He quickly assessed the young lady, noting the tiara atop her brow, and the regal way in which she carried herself. This was most definitely the Princess Anya of Lanfor.

Elladan flashed the Princess one of his best smiles as her amber eyes turned toward him. He nudged Lamorn and shifted his approach toward her, noting the way she blatantly stared him up and down. Elladan immediately revised his assessment of this young lady. She was quite obviously used to getting what she wanted. *I'll have to be careful with this one.*

As he approached the Princess, her two attendants casually, yet protectively flanked her. Elladan smiled to himself. *Not exactly a trusting lot, are they?*

He halted a few feet from the Princess, then executed a deep bow. "Elladan Narmolanya, of the House of Narmolanya, at your service, your majesty."

The Princess continued to look him up and down, her voice breathy and her cheeks somewhat flushed. "My my, Elladan, we are very pleased to meet you. I hope that I can count you among my friends."

She had placed particular emphasis on that last word. Elladan maintained his composure, smoothly replying, "I was hoping the same thing, your majesty."

The young princess motioned for her two attendants to step aside, then strode over to Elladan, her slit dress exposing far more of her fair legs than would be considered appropriate in an elven court. Elladan cast a quick glance at Lamorn, and noted the squire's face had turned a bright shade of scarlet. Attempting to spare the lad any further embarrassment, Elladan spoke softly to him. "Wait here, lad."

Lamorn responded with a slow nod, the young squire unable to tear his eyes away from the visage of the sultry Princess. Elladan stepped forward and met the young princess halfway.

Princess Anya extended a porcelain arm, her eyes dancing playfully as she stared at him. "Attend me?"

"Certainly, your majesty." Elladan grasped her slim hand in his, noting how cool her fingers felt to the touch. He silently hoped that signified a warm heart, though that remained to be seen.

The Princess spun around and led him back to the table, her tone regal, yet with playful undertones. "Please join us for lunch. After all, we wouldn't want this feast to go to waste, would we?"

Elladan responded politely, while noting how closely her one attendant, the red-head dressed in scarlet, stuck to her side. "That would be a shame, your majesty."

She stopped and stared at him, a sensual smile gracing her lips. "Anya. Please call me Anya."

Elladan smiled back. "Anya, then."

Anya let go of his hand and leisurely sat down at the head of the table, her eyes firmly fixed on Elladan's as she slowly crossed one long leg over the other. The Princess' eyes continued to dance as she motioned an arm toward the chair at her right. "Please sit down."

"Thank you… Anya," Elladan responded as he smoothly slid into the proffered seat. As expected, it was quite comfortable, despite its high back and ornate design.

Anya reached over and pulled a grape from a nearby bowl, delicately chewing on it as she regarded her guest. "Tell me, Elladan, how did you manage to take control of the monolith?"

Elladan knew he had to be careful here. He could not risk telling this young, pampered noble too much about his friends and their mission. The elven bard reached for a grape as well, buying himself a few moments to carefully word his reply. "That is quite a tale, milady—one I've yet to put into song, but it is filled with cunning and bravery."

Anya eyed him carefully, her expression taking on a shrewd cast. "Oh, of that I am sure… but weren't there safeguards and traps and such?"

Elladan sat back and fixed the Princess with a partial smile. "There were a few… but nothing that we couldn't handle."

Anya raised a blonde eyebrow as she lounged leisurely in her chair. "We? Is it a large group that you are traveling with?"

Elladan kept his tone casual as he reached for another grape. "Not really… but enough to get the job done."

Anya narrowed her eyes, her slim arms folding across her chest as she assessed the weight of his words. "Obviously, if you were able to secure the Golem Master's monolith."

Ah, so she does know about Larketh. Somehow, the discovery of the Golem Master's stronghold had reached all the way to Lanfor.

Elladan maintained a neutral expression as Anya continued to eye him shrewdly. The Princess unfolded her arms and placed a hand on the table, gently rapping it with her fingertips. "That is no trivial feat for a small group of travelers… tell me about them."

Elladan shrugged, that same bent smile twisting his mouth as he continued to verbally fence with the Princess. "Oh, there's not all that much to tell. A few warriors, some magic users, a couple of folks that are handy with a lock pick… your typical crew for a job like this."

Anya's amber eyes bore into him, as she remained silent for a few moments. Finally, she responded with a slow nod. "Typical, and yet not so typical… I think it would take more than the 'usual' crew to break into one of the Golem Master's strongholds."

Elladan cast a brief glance at the red-haired woman who stood just behind the Princess. Her dark eyes were fixed on him, a brooding malevolence behind them that sent a cold shiver up his spine. Elladan quickly shrugged it off, and responded warmly to the Princess. "Thank you, Anya, but I can assure you that we are just a simple band of travelers."

"Hmm," Anya murmured, as she reached for another grape. This one she brought up to her lips and sucked on for a few moments before popping it into her mouth.

Elladan suddenly felt very warm. He nodded toward the crystal decanter that sat on the table between them. "May I?"

Anya, an amused smile on her lips, responded with a brief nod. "Be my guest."

Elladan poured the clear liquid into the silver goblet in front of him and took a brief sip. It was ice cold. He placed it down on the table, and returned his attention to the Princess. "Thank you, Anya."

Anya sat there watching him with clear amusement. "My pleasure."

The Princess eyed him for a moment longer, then moved forward in her seat. She leaned over the table toward him, exposing more of her bosom than most folks would have been comfortable with. "So, tell me, Elladan… have you found the Colossus?"

To his credit, Elladan kept his eyes firmly fixed on Anya's, not flinching at the mention of the Colossus. Yet how could she possibly know of the existence of the huge stone golem? Not even Telvar, the mage the Serpent Cult had tortured to obtain the location of the monolith, had mentioned the colossal construct. All this flashed through Elladan's mind in a moment. He responded to Anya without missing a beat. "Of course we did, Anya."

The Princess reached out and placed her hand on top of Elladan's, gently caressing it as she spoke. "Would you be a doll then, and do me a tiny little favor?"

Elladan kept his eyes focused on Anya's. "If it is in my power."

Anya flipped Elladan's hand over and held it there, while drawing circles in his palm with her finger. She was doing her darnedest to rattle him, but Elladan was no novice when it came to flirtation. The elven bard took a deep breath and continued to smile at the Princess.

Her voice took on a sickly-sweet tone as she continued to draw on his palm. "Would you destroy it for me?"

Elladan's eyes widened momentarily at her request. He had to admit, it was not what he had expected. Elladan had thought it more likely that she would want the Colossus for herself. He pulled his hand away from hers and gazed at her curiously. "Destroy it? Why would you want to do that?"

The Princess sat back in her chair, and waved a nonchalant hand at him, her tone sounding almost bored. "Because it's dangerous... and... my advisors have warned me that it must be demolished."

Her voice grew sweet again, a sparkle returning to her eyes. "Now won't you do this little thing for me? I'll make it worth your while."

Elladan sat back in his chair, his mind racing. *Her advisors warned her?* There is no way they could have known about the Colossus. The creature had an antimagic field around it that hid it even from magical eyes. It suddenly dawned on him, *Elistra was right!* There was a tie between the Princess and the green dragon—it had to be the Dragon Master. Only another Thrall Master could have known of the existence of the Colossus. Thankfully, the Dragon Master himself had not returned, instead sending Anya to do his dirty work.

Elladan gazed at the Princess with a mournful smile. "I'm sorry, Anya, but even if we could, I'm not sure how to destroy something that large."

Anya let out a short sigh, the young lady nonchalantly twirling a lock of her long blonde hair. "Ah well, that's too bad."

A blonde eyebrow suddenly arched across her forehead. Anya sat up and gazed at him curiously. "Tell me, Elladan, are you and your companions good friends?"

Elladan cocked his head to one side, a single eye narrowing. "We haven't known each other long, but I would say so."

The Princess picked up a spoon in front of her and casually played with it. "So, say something were to happen to you. Would they do anything to save you?"

Elladan did not like the sound of that thinly veiled threat. He threw up his hands in front of him. "Now hold on there, little lady. I thought we were going to be friends."

A wide smile spread across Anya's lips. "Oh, my dear Elladan. I wouldn't dream of harming a hair on that gorgeous head of yours."

Before he could respond, the Princess dropped her spoon, and waved her hands at him in a circular motion, two words falling from her lips. "*Tristis Mutatio.*"

Elladan tried to stand up, but the sudden tingle of magic surrounded him. Abruptly he felt himself sinking downward, the top of the table disappearing above. Elladan tried to summon his lute, but it would not appear. He attempted to cry out, but no sound came from his throat. He gazed around in panic, and saw that his hands had grown smaller, his fingers shortened, and that grey hair had sprouted out of them.

A pair of large hands suddenly grabbed him and lifted him up into the air. Anya's red-haired attendant towered over him, a wicked smile across her dark features. The scarlet woman carried him to the Princess and handed him over, Anya snuggling him against her soft bosom. Elladan, panic setting in, tried to escape from her grasp, but the Princess held him firmly in place. She gently stroked his head and back, while softly cooing to him.

"Now, now, Elladan. Don't be scared. I'm sure your friends will soon be here to rescue you."

14
A BUNNY GOOD TIME

The slim elf spun on his heel and saw a huge figure towering over him

Glolindir stood at the top level of the Darkwoods monolith, Lloyd and Elistra beside him, the trio peering anxiously out the southern archway. The lush green forest spread out before them, reaching all the way to the horizon, the only visible break in the canopy being a parting in the trees about two miles south of there. That was the meadow in which they were supposed to meet with the Princess Anya.

After the delivery of her invitation, the Princess' airship had moved off, briefly hovering over that glade before parking itself above the forest a few miles farther south. Not knowing what to expect, the group had split up. Alana, Cyclone, and Syndir guarded the entrance while Glo, Lloyd, and Elistra kept watch from above.

Meanwhile, Elladan led the others to rendezvous with the Princess. That had been almost an hour ago. Glo was aware it would take his friends the better part of an hour to reach the meadow, but for some reason he was still anxious.

Lloyd seemed to share his concerns. The young man's brow was knit, as he squinted out the wide archway. "I have a bad feeling about this."

Elistra turned her violet eyes upon the two of them, a small frown across her forehead. "Normally I would say give it time, but I too feel uneasy about this 'Princess.'"

Glo steepled his hands in front of his chin, and slowly nodded. "I feel it as well."

The young wizard paused a moment, pressing his hands together like a spider on a mirror as he decided what to do. Their best chance to keep tabs on their friends was Glo's familiar, but Raven, spooked by that little black dragon, had flatly refused to go near the meadow.

Glo let out a deep sigh. "I'm going to try Raven one more time."

Elistra smiled at him encouragingly. "Good idea."

Glo closed his eyes and reached out with his feelings, swiftly making contact with the little black bird. She was still flitting around the forest to the south, not far from the glade where the meeting was taking place. Glo tried once again to steer her toward the meadow, but the stubborn bird continued to veer away.

Finally, Glo lost his patience. *We need your help! Just go to the edge of the darned meadow—you don't even have to leave the trees.*

He was met with a mixture of emotions, fear, shock, and a touch of remorse. He had never yelled at his familiar before, and she seemed quite hurt. Yet Raven finally gave in, and headed off toward the clearing.

Now it was Glo's turn to feel regret. A soft hand touched his shoulder. Glo opened his eyes and saw Elistra staring up at him with clear concern. "What's wrong?"

A smile spread across the wizard's lips as he reached up and grasped her hand. "It's nothing, really. I convinced Raven to go to the meadow, but I think I hurt her feelings in doing so."

Understanding dawned in the seeress' eyes. "Oh. Well… she was being a bit of a pill."

Her observation elicited a short laugh from both Glo and Lloyd. Glo winked at his two companions. "Just don't tell her that."

Elistra pressed her lips together and drew two fingers across her mouth as if closing a zipper. "My lips are sealed."

A broad smile swept across the wizard's face, but was quickly swept away as his gut went all awry. Elistra immediately noted the change in him. "What's wrong… and don't tell me nothing this time."

Glo responded with a short nod. "It's Raven. Something's happened."

Lloyd grabbed the end of his cloak, as if preparing to fly off, but Glo reached out and grasped the warrior's shoulder. "Wait! She's flying back here to tell us what happened."

Lloyd spun around to look at Glo, his eyes filled with concern. "But that might be too late! Shouldn't we just meet her halfway?"

Glo shook his head. "She's clearly upset, but not totally panicked. I think it best if we get the others, and hear what she has to tell us first."

"I'll go fetch them," Elistra offered. The seeress spun around and hastened toward the stairwell before Glo could utter a response.

Lloyd's shoulders slowly relaxed under his grip. The young man let go of his cloak and stepped back, gazing at Glo with a sheepish grin. "I guess I'm just on edge is all."

"You and me both," Glo agreed.

Only a few minutes passed till Raven winged her way through the monolith archway and onto Glo's waiting arm, but it felt like an eternity. The moment she landed, she began squawking in elvish.

"*Elladan querna vardor! Querna vardor!*"

Glo's face scrunched up as he stared at the bird incredulously. Had he heard right? "*Querna vardor?*"

Raven hopped up and down on his outstretched arm. "*Elladan querna vardor! Querna vardor!*"

"What's she saying?" Lloyd asked.

"Something about a rabbit?" came a familiar voice from behind them.

The duo spun around and saw Elistra rushing toward them with Cyclone in tow. Glo gazed at the seeress curiously. "I didn't know you could speak elvish."

Elistra and Cyclone drew up next to them, the seeress giving him a weak smile. "Speak would be an exaggeration. I know the odd word or two."

Glo peered at her uncertainly, till Lloyd shook him by the shoulder. "Why is Raven talking about rabbits? I thought I heard her mention Elladan."

Glo swept his gaze across the trio, not quite believing what he was about to tell them. "Well, according to Raven, Elladan's been turned into a rabbit."

Lloyd's eyes went wide.

Elistra's head cocked to one side, a delicate eyebrow arched.

Yet, Cyclone's response surprised them all. The hunter let out a gruff laugh. "Heh. What a fool."

Lloyd eyes widened, his mouth partially agape as he stared at the hunter. "Seriously?"

Cyclone merely shrugged. "It's what he gets for letting his guard down."

Lloyd's face reddened with anger, but Glo interrupted him before he could retort. "This is no time to argue. No matter how he got into this situation, Elladan still needs our help. What I'd like to know is why she turned him into a rabbit in the first place?"

"They're easy to control," Elistra answered almost immediately.

Glo eyed the seeress curiously. "That may be true, but what does it gain her?"

Elistra folded her arms across her chest, her face taking on a grim cast. "It's a test. She wants to see what will we do."

"Well Princess or not, she needs to learn that she can't just go around and do whatever she wants to people," Lloyd declared vehemently.

Glo saw the d expression on his friend's face—he couldn't have agreed more. Having grown up in a noble household, Glo had been raised with the privileges of position. Yet he had also been taught the responsibilities that went along with it. A true noble used their power to help people. Lloyd had been raised similarly, but there were far too many nobles who had not. Those were the ones who gave nobility a bad name, and this Anya seemed to be one of them.

Glo gave his friend an understanding nod. "So, what do you propose we do?"

Lloyd was silent for a few moments, chewing on his lower lip as he thought it through. "Well, we can't just leave the monolith un-guarded, but someone needs to go down there and have a heart-to-heart with this so-called 'Princess.'"

The young warrior's hands came to rest on his sword hilts.

"Give me the crown for the Colossus and I'll stay."

All eyes turned to Elistra. The seeress' eyes were ablaze, her tone as hard as steel. "Just let anyone try to sneak in here, and I'll give them a welcome they won't soon forget."

Glo let out a short laugh despite the gravity of the situation. El-istra's determination was heartening to say the least. Aksel had given Glo the crown that controlled the huge golem, just before he left with Ruka. The wizard doffed his pack, pulled out the crown, and proffered it to Elistra with a wry smile. "Woe be to anyone who crosses paths with you, my dear."

Elistra accepted the crown with a gracious curtsey and a wry smile of her own, her response in a mock lofty tone. "Why thank you, my elvish lord."

Glo stood up and dusted his hands off, his mind racing all the while. Even with the Colossus at her command, he was still loath to leave Elistra here alone. "So, who else stays behind?"

Cyclone folded his arms across his chest, and cast a hard stare around the group. "I'm going. If she has dragons, I'm fighting them."

"Me too," Lloyd said before anyone else could speak. "I think Glo should come as well."

Glo mulled it over for a moment, and found he agreed. The three of them were the most likely to be effective against a dragon. Still, he half wished Ruka was here, though if the Princess really could control dragons, then she might be more of a liability than not.

Elistra interrupted his train of thought, an impish smile on her lips. "It's fine with me if the three of you want to go, but good luck telling Alana she has to stay behind."

Donnie had been silently circling around the canopy, searching for the invisible wizard when the Princess cast a spell upon Elladan.

Donnie watched with trepidation as he saw his friend shrink down in size, his fingers growing shorter, his face longer, and his ears extending. When it finally stopped, Elladan had been turned into a little grey bunny!

Donnie nearly choked. *This would be comical in any other situation.* If they got out of this alive, Donnie was not going to let Elladan live this one down.

The scarlet-clad woman scooped Elladan up and handed him over to the Princess. 'Bunny Elladan' tried to bolt, but Anya held him firmly against her bosom, cooing to him and softly stroking his fur. "Now, now, Elladan. Don't be scared. I'm sure your friends will soon be here to rescue you."

The red-haired woman in scarlet scoffed at the Princess' remark. "A lot of good that will do them."

Anya gazed up at her attendant, and softly clucked her tongue at her. "Now, now, Mallona, we shall give them a fighting chance."

The Princess turned her head, and raised her voice. "Sigfus, send for Kalkolith, Dazzle, and Scortch."

At first there was no response. Anya spun her head the other way, her expression growing quickly perturbed. She opened her mouth to speak again, when a disembodied male voice responded to her, in a semi-strangled tone. "Your majesty… are you certain you want them specifically?"

The voice had come from the other side of the table from where Donnie stood, a short distance from where the Princess sat.

Ah ha! Found you! Donnie thought in triumph. The slight elf began to circle around behind Anya, toward his intended target.

Meanwhile, Anya responded to the wizard, her displeasure with him quite apparent in her tone. "Did I ask you for your opinion?"

The chastised wizard remained silent. A smug expression crossed Anya's exquisite features as she spoke once more. "Good then. Summon those three. I want to see what these 'Heroes' can do with them."

Donnie arched an eyebrow as he continued to circle around the Princess' seat. Anya had been toying with them all along. She already knew who they were, and further, what they were doing here. Donnie just hoped that she didn't know the truth about Ruka. If she were to get her hands on the bronze dragon girl…

Donnie suddenly stopped in his tracks as a strange sensation came over him. His surroundings seemed to shimmer and fade, the meadow and everyone in it slowly disappearing, until he was surrounded by nothing but a barren gray landscape. Donnie swiveled his head around, seeing nothing but gray rock and sky in all directions, when he abruptly felt a presence behind him. The slim elf spun on his heel and saw a huge figure towering over him. It was a ghostly, semi-transparent form in the shape of a huge dragon.

Donnie froze, his blood running cold. The thing was impossibly large—it was bigger by far than any dragon he had ever seen. Donnie stood there frozen in place as the huge beast opened its enormous maw and bent down toward him. It drew closer and closer, its great ghostly teeth pointed directly at the hapless elf. Donnie felt absolutely helpless as he saw his certain demise.

Lloyd's jaw was firmly set as he skimmed over the treetops, toward his fateful meeting with the Princess of Lanfor. Glo and Cyclone flanked him on either side, the wizard having cast fly spells on the both of them. They were traveling at a fast pace, Glo finally having mastered the art of flight, and Cyclone, though his first time in the air, taking to it like a fish to water. At this rate, they would reach the meadow in a matter of minutes, hopefully before the wayward Princess could turn any more of their friends into fluffy little bunnies.

The trees began to part ahead, signifying they had nearly reached their goal, when a familiar black form shot across the sky in front of them. It was Raven. Lloyd screeched to a halt in mid-air, signaling for the others to follow suit.

Raven flew up and hovered before them, crying out a warning in elvish. "*Ta naa neuma! Eller ier ramaloke!*"

Glo's eyes went wide, his voice charged with excitement. "*Ramaloke? Sut nir?*"

The small bird squawked a single word answer. "*Nelde.*"

Lloyd shifted his gaze from the black bird to Glo. "What's she saying?"

Glo's face had turned into a stony mask, his lips pressed tightly together. "She says it's a trap. There are dragons ahead. Three of them."

Cyclone hovered in the air nearby, his eyes narrowed. "That doesn't add up. If there were three dragons, they would be hunting us, not waiting in ambush."

He turned his gaze toward Glo. "Ask her how big these dragons are."

Glo turned to his familiar and spoke once again in elvish. "*Sut alta ier ro*n?"

The constant beat of Raven's small wings kept her aloft as she responded to her master's query. "*Il ai. Il ure.*"

Glo arched an eyebrow as he swept his gaze back to Lloyd and Cyclone. "Not small, but not large either."

Lloyd's brow furrowed into deep creases as he tried to make sense of the black bird's vague description. "So, what does that mean? They're medium sized?"

Cyclone's mouth twisted sideways. "Heh. Just as I thought. They're juvenile dragons at best. Probably no bigger than that bronze you hang around with."

"Interesting," Glo drawled, his eyes widening as if he'd just had some sort of revelation.

Lloyd cocked his head to one side. "What are you thinking, Glo?"

Glo glanced from Cyclone to Lloyd, a slim smile on his lips. "Apparently, this Anya can somehow control dragons, but what if her influence only extends to younger ones?"

Lloyd nodded his head in understanding. That would make the Princess far less formidable than he had thought a few moments ago. Still, this was no time to sit here and examine her shortcomings. "That's a good theory, but right now we need to focus on this trap."

A wicked smile stretched across Cyclone's face. "I say we turn their own trap against them."

Lloyd's eyes narrowed as he stared at the dragon hunter. "What do you have in mind?"

Glo's insides were tied in a knot as he crept around the large thicket of brambles at the north end of the meadow. His hands were at his side, cupped around a bright ball of red light—a welcoming gift for the dragons that lay in wait. The thicket suddenly dropped away, and three large forms sprung up before him, all letting out a challenging roar. They were three young dragons, a red, a white, and a blue, all standing easily three heads above him.

It took all the courage Glo could muster not to cut and run right then and there. Yet somehow, he managed to stand his ground. He suddenly remembered the spell that was held in check between his palms. The frightened wizard thrust his hands toward the white dragon in the middle of the three, the vague notion in the back of his mind that it was an ice type.

"*Augue.*"

The single word fell from his lips, a split-second later, the angry red ball shooting from his hands and speeding across the clearing at its intended target. It traveled so fast that none of the dragons had a chance to react. In mere moments, the bright red ball expanded to ten times its size, exploding as it made contact with the ice dragon.

A storm of flame erupted from that point, the white dragon disappearing with an excruciating roar. The fiery hemisphere swiftly expanded outward, catching both the red and blue dragons with its edge. The smaller red dragon hardly flinched, but the blue dragon leapt away, roaring in pain.

A few seconds later, the flames winked out. The ice dragon had fallen to its knees, its white scales smoking and singed from the fiery blast. Three pairs of serpentine eyes then fell upon the elven wizard, all filled with dark malice.

Glo struggled to maintain his composure, his arms moving in practiced arcs as he swiftly readied another spell. Just as the dragons prepared to pounce, two blurs shot from the trees on either side of the clearing, one red, and one blue.

Cyclone landed on the back of the blue dragon, the long, sharp halberd buried deep into the creature's spine. Lloyd had flashed past the red dragon, his black blade leaving a deep gash along its upper torso just below the neck. Thick red blood spurted from the wound as both dragons let out roars of pain.

The blue dragon proceeded to thrash around, trying to buck the dragon hunter off its back, but Cyclone's muscular legs were clamped on tightly, his halberd buried deep. No matter how hard the blue dragon tried, it could not shake the determined hunter.

At the same time, Lloyd spun swiftly around to face the red dragon. The angered creature lunged forward and snapped at him, but Lloyd slashed its snout with his razor-sharp black blade, opening another gash across the dragon's jaw. The dragon flinched, pulling back quickly from the red warrior.

Meanwhile, the white dragon had risen to its feet. It cast a wicked glare at Glo, then swiftly spun about to snap at Lloyd. Glo had to do something fast, but his friends were in too close for another ball of fire. The elven wizard halted his spell and pointed a finger at the ice dragon, two words swiftly passing his lips. *"Radius Ardens."*

A red-hot beam of light leapt from his fingertips and flashed across the clearing, catching the white beast square in the side. The dragon halted in its tracks, roaring in pain as smoke erupted from the point of contact. A scorched circle swiftly fanned out from that spot, the white scales around it turned black and blistering.

The white dragon spun back around, and fixed two malevolent eyes on the elven wizard. Glo took a deep gulp and prepared for the fight of his life.

Donnie remained frozen in place as the huge ghostly dragon bore down upon him. The great jaws drew closer and closer, blotting out everything from his field of view. In moments, his life would end with one giant snap. Yet something nagged at the back of his mind— something wasn't quite right. What was it?

The sandy-haired elf chided himself. *Think, Donnie! Think!*

Where had this huge dragon come from in the first place? There was no way something this big could have hidden in the woods. Yet they weren't in the woods—there was nothing around him but a barren landscape. Had he been teleported somewhere? No, Donnie had experienced teleportation before. There was always a feeling of disorientation after instantaneously traveling a long distance. That meant he was still in the woods, and this was all just… *an illusion!*

The realization struck Donnie just as those impossibly huge jaws closed upon him. Abruptly they faded away, and he was back in the meadow. On the other side of the table, in the direction he had been headed, stood a dark-bearded figure in royal blue robes. The wizard was looking straight at him with an expression of disbelief.

Donnie immediately recognized what had happened. The wizard had been able to see him even though he was invisible. He had observed Donnie sneaking around the Princess, and had cast a spell to kill him.

Donnie was livid. The contemptible wizard had immediately resorted to lethal force. Yet before the elf could move a muscle to react, his attention was drawn across the clearing. Loud roars erupted from that end of the glade, where three young dragons were engaged in battle. Cyclone sat astride the blue dragon, while Lloyd slashed the red one, and Glo fired off a scorching beam at the white. It was a brutal encounter—someone would end up dead if it wasn't stopped soon.

The Princess Anya was not five feet from where Donnie stood, watching the battle with a fierce intensity as she held Elladan, still in rabbit form, tightly against her bosom. Her attendants were also fixed on the battle—no one paying any attention to Donnie except for the loathsome wizard.

Donnie reacted immediately, bolting forward as the wizard let out a strangled cry. "Watch out!"

It was too late. Donnie covered the space between himself and Anya in less than a second. The Ruchan swiftly appeared in his hand as he grabbed the Princess around the waist and brought the dragon-scale dagger up to her throat.

Donnie held the Princess in a tight grasp as he spun his head back and forth and cried out in a loud voice. "This is a lightning dagger! One move and your Princess gets fried!"

Anya's attendants all turned to glare at him, their expressions a mixture of anger and surprise. At the same moment, the Princess dropped Elladan. The little grey bunny fell to the ground and bit the Princess in the leg, then scampered away under the table.

"Ouch!" Anya cried. "That wasn't very nice, Elladan."

Donnie tightened his grasp around Anya's waist and neck. "Don't worry about him, Princess. Call off your dragons now before anyone really gets hurt."

A soft giggle escaped Anya's lips. "Very well done. You 'Heroes' do live up to your reputation."

Donnie arched an eyebrow at her comment, but did not let up. "That's all well and fine, Princess, but first call off your attack, and then we can talk about reputations."

A satisfied smile spread across Anya's lips. "Very well." She raised her voice and shouted across the clearing. "Stop!"

The three dragons froze in place, the white and red slowly backing away from Lloyd and Glo. The blue one sat completely still, even with Cyclone's halberd still stuck in its back.

"But Princess…" the blue-robed wizard cried, his eyes filled with concern.

Anya turned her gaze toward the dark-bearded man, and fixed him with a hard stare, her voice like steel. "I said stand down, Sigfus."

She swiveled her head all around, and added. "That goes for all of you."

The wizard backed away, his expression chagrinned, though his hate-filled eyes were still fixed on Donnie. "As you wish, Princess."

The other attendants backed off as well, though the scarlet-clad redhead remained the closest. Anya then turned her head to the side and spoke to Donnie.

"You can drop the knife now." A mischievous grin crossed her lips. "Of course, you don't have to let go of me, if you don't want to."

As Donnie's knife dropped away, Anya snuggled into his arms. The slight elf began to blush furiously, something no woman had been able to do to him in ages. Donnie enjoyed the warmth of her soft body pressed against his for maybe a moment longer than he should have, then he let his grip on the Princess go, and took a step backward.

Anya spun around and gazed at him, her eyes dancing with amusement. She looked him up and down and said, "My, you are a handsome one as well. I hope you enjoyed our little embrace as much as I did."

Donnie struggled to maintain his composure. This Princess Anya was more than a handful. He covered his discomfort by introducing himself with a deep bow. "Donatello, your majesty, at your service. I meant no disrespect, but my friends' lives were at stake."

Anya continued to appraise him, a slender finger going to her chin. "Oh, you'll do. You'll all do."

She spun around, and with a negligent wave of her hand, yelled across the clearing once more. "You can all go now!"

The red and white dragons turned to look at her, then slowly spread their wings and lifted off the ground. Cyclone carefully removed the long shaft of his halberd from the blue dragon's back and dismounted, his weapon held ready just in case. Yet the blue dragon paid him no heed, instead unfolding its wings and lifting off the ground to join its comrades.

The three young dragons rose into the air, then spun around and shot away in the direction of the airship a few miles south. Anya then spun back to Donnie, stepped forward, and placed a slender hand on his chest.

"Satisified?" she asked him in a playful tone.

Donnie cleared his throat. "Ahem. Well… um… yes, your majesty. So then… do you want to explain what this was all about?"

A small giggle escaped the Princess' slim throat. "Oh. This," she said, spreading her hands out to either side. "This was just a test. As I was telling your friend Elladan earlier, I need you to do something for me."

Donnie's face scrunched up into a skeptical expression. "Really? And what's that?"

A coy smile spread across Anya's face. "I need you to destroy the Colossus."

15

IN THE WRONG HANDS

So, you are still mad about thhe whole rabbit thing

Lloyd Stealle fought for his life against the young red dragon. The creature was fast, Lloyd barely able to deflect its maw with each assault. He had sliced it a few times now, leaving deep bloody cuts across its jaw, but the wounds he had inflicted thus far had only served to further anger the beast. The dragon had not yet tried to breath fire on him, but Lloyd knew it was only a matter of time.

The creature's long neck snapped toward him again with amazing speed, when a voice rang out from across the field. "Stop!"

The dragon's head came to a screeching halt only a couple of feet from the red-clad warrior. The long neck then slowly retracted, the dragon's gaze turning toward the source of the voice. Lloyd chanced a quick glance in that direction, and saw a slender blonde woman, dressed in black, being held from behind by Donatello. The sandy-haired elf had a knife to her throat. A moment later he let her go, the young woman spinning around to face the slight elf.

Lloyd snapped his eyes back to the red dragon, but the creature stood its ground, its gaze firmly fixed on the woman in black. The young warrior swept his eyes across the field. The white dragon had done the same as the red, and the blue dragon now sat docilely with Cyclone still sitting on its back. Lloyd exchanged a glance with the pair, Glo with an eyebrow arched, and Cyclone's expression impassive.

Back across the meadow, Donnie and the young woman were locked in an earnest conversation. A moment later, she spun around and waved her hand at the dragons. "You can all go now!"

The red and white dragons immediately obeyed, unfurling their large, bat-like wings and slowly lifting off the ground. The blue dragon followed suit as soon as Cyclone leapt off its back. The three young dragons then took off toward the airship hovering in the sky south of the meadow.

Lloyd slowly sheathed his swords and strode over to join Glo and Cyclone, both of whom wore wary expressions. Lloyd's brow was furrowed, the young warrior totally perplexed by the sudden withdrawal of the dragons. "Anyone have any idea what just happened?"

Cyclone let out a short snort. "Humph. I think that nut job of a Princess just happened."

Glo gave them a short nod. "I agree. Donnie had her by the throat, but she didn't appear the slightest bit worried. Perhaps Elistra was right."

Lloyd's eyes narrowed. "You mean she was testing us?"

Glo shrugged. "There's only one way to find out."

The trio marched as one across the field toward Donnie and the Princess. Several other folks surrounded the area—her retainers, most likely. Lloyd's gaze swept across them—there was a man in blue robes, a woman in white, another woman dressed in scarlet, a third woman carrying a bow, and one last woman, garbed in black silver-studded leathers.

Lloyd's eyes settled on the woman in black. From her carriage, and the two silver-hilted swords that hung from her belt, she was most definitely a warrior. The black-clad warrior sized him up with a burning intensity in her eyes. Lloyd found himself suddenly itching to test himself against her, but this was neither the time nor the place.

A clapping sound drew his attention away from the female warrior. The Princess Anya of Lanfor applauded as they drew closer, calling out to them in a welcoming voice. "Well done. Very well done."

The trio drew up in front of the monarch, Donnie shuffling around to join them. Lloyd cast a quick glance at the others, then responded to the seemingly irrational Princess. "Thank you, your majesty, but I'm not quite certain what we did."

Anya laughed, the sound like tiny bells ringing in the meadow. "Why, you are just too modest."

She reached up and flipped the end of her long blonde hair over her shoulder as her amber eyes fixed on him, and slowly looked him up and down. "You must be Lloyd—Stealle is it?"

Lloyd suddenly felt very uncomfortable. He shook off the awkward feeling with a low bow, not taking his eyes off the Princess and her attendants. "Yes, your majesty. Lloyd Stealle, of the Penwick House of Stealle."

She continued to eye him with a smoldering stare. "My, my, you are a handsome young lord, aren't you—and it's Anya. You may call me Anya."

Anya's gaze swept across the four of them. "In fact, you all may."

At that moment, the squire, Lamorn, crawled out from under the table, holding a little grey bunny in his arms. He gazed around uncomfortably, edging his way over between Lloyd and Glo.

Glo gave the young squire a reassuring smile, then responded to the Princess with a nod toward the furry little creature. "That's very gracious of you... Anya. Now, would you mind?"

Anya's eyes fell on Glo, lighting up with recognition. "Ah, and you must be the elven wizard... Glolinda, was it?"

Donnie snorted at the mangled way she had mispronounced Glo's name. Glo arched an eyebrow at the slim elf, then turned back to Anya and executed a short bow. "Glolindir Eodin, of the Elven House of Eodin, at your service."

Anya cocked her head to one side, her hands going to her hips as she eyed the elven wizard up and down. "You are a tall one for an elf—and rather blonde."

A strained smile graced Glo's lips as he shifted uncomfortably from one foot to the other. "Um, yes. Well, that is fairly typical for a Galinthral elf."

Anya's brow knitted, her slim nose scrunching up into a serious expression. "A Galinthral elf?" She cast a brief glance at the man wearing the blue robes. "Sigfus, I thought you said they were extinct."

"Evidently not," the sour faced man replied, casting a dark look at the elven wizard.

Lloyd nearly choked at the callousness of the exchange. They were talking about Glo's people as if they were some sort of endangered species. Glo, however, did not seem fazed in the slightest by their insensitive attitude. He met Sigfus' dark stare and responded coolly, "We have merely been secluded away from the world for the last few hundred years or so."

Anya's eyes narrowed. "And yet, here you are—the first Galinthral elf to be seen in ages."

A slender finger went to her pointed chin. "One has to wonder the reason behind this sudden appearance."

Glo's expression remained stoic. The elven wizard glanced once more at the little grey bunny in Lamorn's arms. "That is a discussion for another time, I'm afraid."

Anya followed his gaze, a pert smile gracing her pouty lips. "Yes, of course. I liked him better the other way, anyway."

Lamorn bent down and gently placed the little rabbit on the grass at his feet. The Princess then waved her hands around in a practiced circular motion, a single word falling from her lips. *"Dimissionis."*

The little rabbit abruptly began to grow. The ears shortened, the arms and legs elongated, and the grey fur disappeared. Moments later, Elladan was standing before them again. The elven bard slowly dusted off his white outfit, then turned his gaze on the Princess, flashing her a quasi-smile. "I thought we were friends, Anya. Now what did you have to go and do that for?"

Anya raised a slender hand to her bare upper arm, and rubbed it as she gazed at the handsome bard. "Oh, my dear Elladan. We are friends. As I promised, not a hair on that gorgeous head of yours was harmed."

Lloyd shifted uncomfortably on his heels. He was getting tired of this all this banter back and forth. "But you still haven't explained what this was all about, Anya. Can you please get to the point?"

Anya shifted her gaze back to Lloyd, her eyes gleaming with amusement. "A man of action. I like that."

She waved a hand at the table behind her. "Very well. Please come sit with me and I will explain everything."

The Princess spun around on her heel and waltzed over to the head of the table, gracefully planting herself in an ornate mahogany chair. She looked up at the companions with a sickly sweet smile. Lloyd exchanged a brief glance with the others, then decided to follow suit.

As they all took seats around the table, Anya's eyes swept over them, falling on Cyclone. Her gaze traveled up and down the large halberd now strapped across his back. "My, that's an awfully long spear you have there."

Cyclone stared back at the Princess, his face a stony mask. "It does its job."

A slight smile crossed Anya's lips, her tone suggestive. "And what job is that, mister…"

"Cyclone… and its job is skewering dragons."

Both of Anya's blonde eyebrows raised this time. A soft growl emanated from the woman in scarlet who stood beside her. Anya swiveled her head toward the fiery redhead. "Now, now, Mallona, no need to get testy. These gentlemen are all our guests."

Mallona shifted her gaze to the Princess and gave her the briefest of nods. Her eyes then turned back to Cyclone, and fixed him with a malevolent glare. The dragon hunter seemed completely unfazed.

Lloyd, still impatient with all the side talk, shifted his gaze back to Anya and cleared his throat. "Ahem. Exactly what is it you want?"

Anya's eyes turned toward Lloyd as she reached forward and plucked a grape from a nearby bowl. "It's simple, really."

She paused a moment to pop the grape into her mouth. "As I told Elladan and Donnie here, my advisors have warned me about the Colossus hidden away in the monolith. It is a danger to us all, and must be destroyed."

Lloyd's eyes widened at her declaration. *How in all of Thac did she know about the Colossus? Not even the Serpent Cult seemed to know what was hidden under the monolith.*

Lloyd exchanged a brief glance with Elladan, Donnie, and Glo. The wizard seemed equally surprised. A short silence fell over the table until Glo broke it, addressing the Princess sharply. "How does the Colossus present a danger? It is completely under our control."

Anya turned a cold gaze on the elven wizard, folding her arms across her chest, her tone rather condescending. "My dear Glolin—dir, the Golem Master can supersede any control device you might have found. If he were to come within range of the Colossus, he would regain mastery of it as if you weren't even there."

Anya sat forward in her chair and gave her head a single shake. "I simply cannot allow that to happen, even if it means bringing the entire monolith down upon it."

Lloyd eyed the Princess uncertainly. He knew a bit about ships and the kind of fire power they carried—an airship couldn't be that much different. "And how do you intend to do that? Even with a full complement of cannons, it would take more rounds than you could possibly carry to destroy something as large as the monolith."

Anya spun her gaze toward him, a smug smile spreading across her porcelain features, as she spoke with clear pride. "Ah, but I don't have just any old cannons. The Wind Hammer is outfitted with six mage cannons—easily enough to take down that grandiose monument to Larketh's ego, and bury the Colossus beneath it."

Mage cannons? Lloyd's eyes went wide with astonishment. He had never seen a mage cannon before, but he had heard of them. A regular cannon, or ballista, launched a cast-iron ball via a high-torsion spring mechanism, but a mage cannon was powered by arcane magic. It could fire devastating spells far more powerful than any regular cannon.

Lloyd's father and brother captained two of the most powerful vessels in the Penwick Navy, the *Crusader* and the *Avenger*. Each ship carried a complement of close to thirty ballista cannon, and one large trebuchet that launched magical spheres, called the Hell-shot. Yet Anya's airship had enough raw firepower on board to hold its own against a Penwick ship of the line. Lloyd suddenly had little doubt that the Princess could take down the monolith if she so desired.

The Princess plucked another grape, then sat back and lounged leisurely in her chair. Her golden eyes swept over the table from under her light-blonde locks, carefully gauging their reactions. Glo had steepled his hands in front of his chin, something Lloyd noticed the wizard tended to do when he was deep in thought. After a few moments of silence, the elven wizard responded to her assertions. "You make a compelling argument, Anya."

Glo peered from Elladan, to Donnie, to Cyclone, and finally to Lloyd. "What do you think, gentlemen?"

Surprisingly, the normally silent Cyclone was the first to answer. The dragon hunter gazed around the table, his eyes intense. "If you don't think a seventy-foot golem is dangerous, then you're all stupid."

Lloyd was momentarily taken aback by the hunter's harsh words, but then caught himself. Despite his callous attitude, Cyclone was right. Lloyd cast a quick glance over at the Princess. Anya raised an eyebrow at the mention of the Colossus' actual size, but otherwise remained silent. The young warrior shifted his gaze back to Cyclone, and fixed him with a hard stare. "You're right. I think it could destroy an entire town, or even an army if it came to it."

Donnie, silent for some time now, weighed into the conversation. "I have to agree. If the Colossus ever fell into the wrong hands, it would be very bad for all of Thac."

He nodded at Anya. "Even a flight of dragons, like the Princess here seems to have, wouldn't stand a chance against it."

Anya responded with a curt nod of her own, her slender arms folding across her chest. Cyclone shifted his gaze toward the Princess, his eyes narrowed. "What about all those mage cannons you bragged about earlier?"

Anya opened her mouth to respond, but Glo cut her off. "I'm afraid not. The Colossus generates an antimagic field around it. Mage cannon fire would not even scratch it."

The Princess exchanged a brief glance with Sigfus, both seemingly surprised at that revelation. Lloyd found that interesting. *So, they didn't know everything. There were holes in their information.*

Elladan had listened to the conversation with a skeptical expression. His eyes swept across the gathering as he finally decided to voice his opinion. "Now hold on there. I agree that the Colossus would be deadly in the wrong hands, but we're the ones who currently control it."

Elladan's gaze fell on the Princess. "No offense Anya, but how do we know that your information about the Golem Thrall Master is accurate?"

Anya sat forward, fixing Elladan with a withering stare. Yet before she could say anything, Glo spoke up once more. "We don't, but can we really take that chance?"

Anya turned to the elven wizard and gave him a gracious nod, then sat back in her seat once more. Donnie planted his hands on the table, gazing from Glo to Anya, his eyes coming to rest on Elladan. "Glo is right. If there is even the remotest possibility that Anya is correct, and the Colossus does get loose, then the destruction of Thac would be our fault."

Mixed emotions played across Elladan's face. After a few moments, that familiar semi-smile returned to his lips. He swiveled his head toward the Princess. "Begging your pardon, Anya, but what is the source of your information?"

A slim smile spread across Anya's lips. She waved a nonchalant hand as she answered his question. "Our good friend and advisor, Theramon. He has spent his entire life studying history, including the Thrall Wars. So far, his information has been accurate. After all, he was the one who pinpointed the location of the monolith, and the existence of the Colossus."

Lloyd's brow furrowed at hearing of this Theramon. Based on what Elistra had told them, Lloyd had assumed it was the black knight with the ancient green dragon who had told Anya. They had all suspected he was the Dragon Thrall Master, and that's how he knew where the monolith was. Yet, from the sounds of it, this Theramon was not the black knight, but instead some sort of scholar, or wizard perhaps.

The companions all exchanged glances, each appearing as surprised as Lloyd. Yet Elladan was still not convinced. "It does appear that this Theramon knows a lot, but can you be sure of all his information? After all, the Thrall Wars were over a hundred and fifty years ago."

Anya raised an eyebrow, but Donnie interjected before she could speak. "You're just mad about the whole rabbit thing."

Elladan turned his gaze toward the sandy-haired elf, and fixed him with a strained smile. "How would you like it if she turned you into a little grey bunny?"

A wicked grin spread across Donnie's features. "You didn't seem to mind a few minutes ago."

Anya gazed at the duo with an appreciative smile. "You did seem rather comfortable, Elladan, nestled against my bosom."

Elladan responded with a short laugh. "I won't deny it, but that has nothing to do with this question about the Colossus."

Lloyd let out a deep sigh. This conversation had gone on far too long. He stood up and raised his voice. "This is getting us nowhere."

Lloyd swept his eyes around the table, his gaze settling on Anya. "Princess, can you give us a moment?"

Anya puckered her lips, answering with a slow nod. "Why of course."

"Thank you," Lloyd responded with a short nod of his own. The young man then marched away from the table, motioning for the others to follow. He led the group about a dozen yards across the field, then stopped and spun around.

Glo, Elladan, Donnie, and Lamorn gathered around him. Even Cyclone had joined them, though his arms were crossed and his expression stony.

Lloyd swept his eyes around the group. "Look, we need to face facts. The Princess has enough firepower on that ship of hers to take down the monolith anyway. The real question is, do we lose the Colossus or the entire monolith?"

Elladan cocked his head to one side, eyeing Lloyd intently. "Are you okay? It's not like you to give up without a fight."

"Lloyd's right," Cyclone interjected before the warrior could answer.

All eyes turned to the stoic hunter.

"I got a good look at the deck of that airship on the way over here. I counted at least three more dragons on board."

Lloyd did a double take. That was at least seven dragons at Anya's disposal. He had already counted the three dragons they had faced, as well as her formidable-looking entourage. This made any battle with her almost impossible to win.

Glo steepled his hands in front of his mouth. When he spoke, there was an ironic lilt to his voice. "So, what you're saying is that there's no way we could take over her ship."

"Not likely," Cyclone answered flatly.

Elladan peered around the group, his hands in the air, his expression incredulous. "So, that's it? We just let Anya destroy the Colossus?"

Lloyd let out a deep sigh. It was not in his nature to give up without a fight, but this time was different. Even if they battled the Princess, he wasn't sure they would be on the right side. He gazed at Elladan, his mouth twisting into a wan smile. "I think you're missing the point. Anya could have blown the monolith to smithereens when she first showed up. Flaky as she seems, she is the Princess of Lanfor, an upstanding nation that has always been a force for good."

Donnie's lips twisted into a wry smile. "So, she's not just some despot bent on taking over Thac?"

Elladan cocked an eye at the slight elf. "I think the jury's still out on that one."

"So, you are still mad about the whole rabbit thing," Donnie teased the bard.

Once again, Lloyd grew exasperated with the constant banter. He threw his hands into the air, drawing everyone's attention his way. "Gentlemen… what I think we need to be asking ourselves is, could the Colossus be a threat to Thac?"

Elladan and Donnie both went silent, the bard's eyes filled with doubt.

Lloyd shifted his gaze to Glo. "What do you think?"

The elven wizard stood with his hands still steepled in front of his mouth. After a brief pause, he nodded. "Yes."

Lloyd turned his eyes toward Cyclone. The dragon hunter responded with a flat, "Already said my piece."

Lloyd then peered at Donatello. The slim elf's expression was grim. "Yes, I do."

Lloyd finally shifted his gaze back to the elven bard. "Elladan?"

Elladan was silent for a few moments, then grudgingly responded, "Yes, it could be dangerous… in the wrong hands."

"I agree as well," Lloyd said with a curt nod.

"So…" Donnie's voice hung on the one word.

Lloyd spun his gaze toward the wiry elf, noting the deep concern in his eyes.

"… you said something before about losing the Colossus or the monolith. Does that mean the monolith doesn't need to be destroyed?"

Lloyd peered sympathetically at the slight elf. He assumed Donnie was worried about Alana and Elistra, both their friends waiting for them back inside the monolith. Yet before he could respond, Glo answered Donnie's query.

"Probably not. Remember that room above the Colossus? Well, it's right above a gigantic stalactite that hangs from the ceiling of the cavern, and it's filled with explosives. My guess is if that stalactite falls, it should be enough to split the Colossus in two."

Donnie's eyes narrowed, his lips pursing together in thought. "So, the Golem Master built in a failsafe?"

Glo shrugged. "It would seem so."

Lloyd waited a moment, then swept his eyes around the group once again. "So, are we all in agreement?"

He was met with a round of reluctant nods. A strained smile crossed the warrior's lips as he led the party back to the table. Once there, he told the Princess of their decision and had Glo explain about the failsafe.

When Glo was done, Anya sat forward in her seat, a triumphant smile on her lips. "I'm glad you see it my way."

The Princess placed her hands on the table and stood up, her eyes sweeping around the small gathering. "Well then, let's get this done already."

She raised a hand and motioned to her red-haired attendant. "Mallona, join us."

The scarlet-clad Mallona drew up next to the Princess. Her fiery eyes swept across the group with a dark stare, challenging anyone to cross her benefactor.

Anya gazed at them all with a sickly-sweet smile, then proceeded to saunter away from the table, motioning for the companions to follow. "Shall we?"

16

BEAUTY AND THE BEAST

Do you expect me to just walk through the forest?

Glolindir trotted along the forest path headed north toward the monolith, just behind the Princess Anya and Elladan. The duo was engaged in an animated conversation as if old friends. Glo had to give the bard credit—not many would be so glib after being turned into a rabbit, but Elladan seemed as charming as ever as he rode beside the unpredictable Princess.

The lively pair sat astride strange, semi-transparent mounts, the creatures beneath them in the shape of ghostly horses. In fact, the entire party rode along the path with them, mounted on those weird spectral steeds. Donnie led the way, while Mallona trotted silently next to Glo, her dark gaze fixed firmly on Elladan's back. Cyclone, Lloyd, and Lamorn brought up the rear, the latter two sharing the last ghostly mount.

The spectral creatures were a conjuration of Anya's attendant, Sigfus. The irritant wizard initially protested the Princess' request, but Anya had fixed him with a cold stare and spoke rather pointedly. "Do you expect me to just walk through the forest?"

Sigfus had immediately withdrawn his objections, and produced the ghostly horses for Anya and the others.

Glo was familiar with the spell he had used—it was aptly named Spectral Steed. The basic spell allowed the caster to conjure a ghostly horse-like creature, complete with saddle, bit, and bridle. The spectral horse was very fast, and could travel over rough terrain with no decrease in speed.

A more experienced caster could conjure multiple mounts that might ride over water or traverse obstacles, such as a wide chasm, as if walking on air. The ghost horse carried its rider to its destination, then disappeared once it had been reached.

Glo had arched an eyebrow when Sigfus conjured those mounts. The multiple form of the spell was of the fourth order. Glo himself could currently cast only third-order spells. Thus, Sigfus was more advanced at spellcraft than he. Glo made a mental note to be careful with this irritable wizard if it ever came to a confrontation.

Up ahead, Elladan continued to keep the Princess entertained, launching into a vivid account of the battle at Ravenford Keep. "… and then, seven huge serpents popped right out of the ground, their huge gaping jaws exposing deadly fangs and nasty forked tongues as they hissed their dreadful greetings. Four mages dressed all in black sat astride those serpentine mounts, nothing of their features visible behind their cold, dark hoods."

Anya seemed completely rapt in Elladan's flamboyant description of the encounter. Her amber eyes were wide open, alight with keen interest at his portrayal of the horrific monsters. Yet the red-haired Mallona did not appear impressed in the slightest. Glo heard a low, but distinct, *humph* from under the scarlet-clad attendant's breath.

Glo arched a single eyebrow, silently wondering what power the disdainful redhead possessed. Mallona wore no visible weapons, yet if she was some sort of caster, she had yet to show even a hint of magic. Still, she had to be powerful, as evidenced by the fact that Anya chose her as her single protector, even over the wizard, Sigfus.

In the meantime, Elladan continued with his account. "Seven

pairs of huge yellow glowing eyes turned to fix on the lone forms of Lloyd and Donatello, the only thing standing between the gathered gentry and the evil presence that had interrupted their celebration. It was a bone-chilling sight."

Donnie, ahead of them all, spun his head around, choosing that moment to chime in. "Too bad you didn't have a nice little grey fur coat to keep you warm back then."

The Princess Anya burst out into gay laughter at the sandy-haired elf's jab. Elladan, however, seemed less than amused. He fixed a dark eye on his elven friend. "You sound jealous there, Donnie. I'm sure Anya here would be more than happy to turn you into a rabbit if that's what you really want."

Elladan cast a sidelong glance at the Princess, and gave her a sly wink. A mischievous smile spread across Anya's lips as she shifted her gaze toward Donnie, her tone playful. "Why of course, Elladan. It would be my pleasure."

Donnie swept his gaze from Elladan to the Princess, flashing her a bright grin. "No, no, that's quite alright. The sight of Elladan as a bunny was more than enough to make my day."

The slim elf's response drew a round of laughter from all the riders. Even the brooding Mallona let out a laugh, though it sounded more wicked than cheerful.

Elladan fixed his friend with a dark stare, his voice dripping with sarcasm. "I'm so glad my predicament kept you entertained." Before the sandy-haired elf could respond, the bard turned back to the Princess, his expression immediately lightening. "Anyway, where was I?"

Elladan went on with the story of their battle at Ravenford Keep, without any further interruptions. It served to pass the time along the rest of their short journey.

Glo half-listened to the tale, his mind elsewhere. Elistra and Alana needed to be warned of their impending arrival with the Princess. Despite their current "alliance" with the monarch, Glo did not really trust her.

At first, he thought maybe Martan could advise them. Even after things had calmed down in the meadow, there had been no sign of the tracker, Martan sensibly keeping to the woods. His decision to remain hidden might have worked in their favor, if Anya had not had those steeds conjured for them.

At that point, there was no way for Martan to keep up with the riders. So, instead, Glo sent out Raven ahead of them. Elistra had proved to know a bit of elvish. Glo could only hope that it was enough to prepare the two women for their imminent return.

As the monolith finally drew in sight, Glo let out a soft sigh. *Elistra, I hope you're ready.*

Aksel Alabaster stood silently at the entrance to the Darkwoods monolith, waiting for his friends to return. He had arrived only a short while ago, leaving Ruka, Maya, and Cal hidden a short distance away in the Darkwoods.

Ruka had wanted to accompany him, but Maya insisted on tagging along as well. Yet, after Glo's warning about the Princess of Lanfor, the exasperated teen realized she could not expose her younger sister to the mysterious monarch. Thus, Ruka reluctantly agreed to stay behind.

Upon reaching the monolith, Aksel was greeted by Elistra, Alana, and the squire Syndir. They informed him of Elladan's predicament, and how Lloyd, Glo, and Cyclone had flown off to the bard's rescue.

Moments later, Raven arrived and squawked to them excitedly in elvish. Thankfully, Elistra was able to make sense of the bird's message. It seemed that everyone was on their way back, including the Princess. After a short discussion, they sent Syndir off to find and stay with Ruka, while Elistra and Alana went below to wait in the cavern with the Colossus. In the meantime, Aksel stayed at the entrance to greet their "guests."

Aksel did not have to wait long. Perhaps a quarter of an hour later, a group of riders appeared at the head of the trail at the southern end of the clearing. The travelers sat astride strange, ethereal mounts that appeared to be ghostly horses.

"Ho, Aksel!" came a call from the head rider.

It was Donatello, the sandy-haired elf leading the entourage. He was followed by Elladan, and a pale young human woman, with long blonde hair. The woman wore a regal, if revealing outfit, of black cloth trimmed with gold, and frilly white lace. Aksel immediately surmised that this was the Princess of Lanfor.

The Princess turned her cool gaze on him, her golden eyes looking him slowly up and down. After a moment or two, she gave him a casual nod.

Behind the duo sat Glolindir, the tall elf accompanied by another human woman. This one had fiery red hair, and was covered from head to toe in a scarlet, in sharp contrast to the Princess. The woman turned her intense gaze on Aksel, practically making his skin crawl. He sensed something dark about her, but he could not put his finger on exactly what it was at that moment.

Cyclone, Lloyd, and Lamorn brought up the rear, the tall warrior sharing a ghostly steed with the squire. The group of riders crossed the clearing, halting a short distance from the entrance to the monolith. There, they all dismounted, except for the Princess, the monarch calling over to Elladan.

"Attend me?"

"Of course, Anya." The elven bard strode to her ghostly mount's side, and took the Princess by the hand.

Anya then leapt down off her horse and practically fell into Elladan's arms with a flirtatious giggle. She pressed her body up against his, her hands on the elf's chest as she gazed up at him with a smoldering stare.

"Thank you, Elladan," she said in a breathy voice.

Aksel cocked his head to one side. This Princess was certainly not one for propriety. A moment later, she pushed away from Elladan, fixing him with a lingering smile.

To Elladan's credit, he handled the entire situation without batting an eye. He bowed to the Princess, merely responding, "Anytime, Anya."

Moments later, the ethereal mounts all blinked out of existence. Aksel was still marveling at the sight when Donnie strode up to him.

"Where's Ruka? Is she alright?"

Aksel cast a quick glance at Anya, but the Princess seemed disinterested in their conversation, having been pulled into a private exchange with her scarlet-clad attendant. Nonetheless, he kept his response to Donnie terse. "She's fine. She had personal business to attend to, so she decided to stay behind."

Donnie gazed at Aksel questioningly, but before he could ask anything further, he was interrupted by Elladan. "Gee, Donnie, you must be losing your touch. A couple of days ago, you couldn't pry her away from your side."

Donnie fixed Elladan with a dark stare. Yet before he could retort, he was interrupted by the Princess, who strode up to join them, arm in arm with the scarlet-clad woman. "Who couldn't be pried away from whom?"

Elladan winked at Donnie, then spun toward the Princess. "Donnie's just having girl trouble is all."

The fiery-haired woman hanging off Anya's arm looked over the slight elf with a condescending stare. "Can't say I'm surprised."

Elladan practically snorted out a laugh, while Donnie's mouth fell agape. Yet Aksel was not amused in the slightest—there were serious matters at hand. He shifted his gaze to the Princess and said, "Is anyone going to introduce us?"

Elladan, still trying to suppress a laugh, performed the formal introductions. "Anya, this is Aksel Alabaster, Cleric of the Soldenar. Aksel, this is the Princess Anya of Lanfor…"

Elladan was unceremoniously interrupted as the redheaded woman stepped forward, reached out a single scarlet clad arm, and forcefully pushed him aside. "That's Anyabarithia Ulteshto Farbican, the Lady of the Amber Mount, Mistress of the Crystal Towers, and Princess and sole heir to the Kingdom of Lanfor, you dolt."

Elladan's mouth hung open, but Anya reached forward and placed a slender restraining hand on the scarlet-clad woman's shoulder, gently chiding her. "Now, now, Mallona, that's no way to treat our new friends…"

The Princess turned her gaze toward Aksel, her tone rather lofty. "…and anyway, titles are so boring, don't you think, Cleric Aksel? You may call me Anya."

The rude exchange had caught Aksel by surprise, but he quickly recovered by executing a low bow to the Princess. "Just Aksel then, Anya."

Anya continued to survey him, her eyes dancing with amusement. "I don't think I've ever met a Cleric of the Soldenar before. Tell me, what's she like?"

Aksel spiked an impressed eyebrow. Anya must have been rather well studied in the Ralnain mythos, the pantheon of the material gods and greater powers, to know that the Soldenar was a female deity. Once again, he kept his response short. "She's demanding, yet fair."

Anya's eyes narrowed shrewdly at his simple reply. "Well spoken. I can see you like to get straight to the point. I admire that." The Princess let out a long, dramatic sigh. "It has been a long journey for me, and I'd like to get this over with already."

Aksel scrunched his nose and narrowed an eye, his head cocking to one side. "Get what over with?"

Anya's face took on a bored expression, her tone correspondingly weary. "Why, the destruction of the Colossus, of course."

Aksel felt all the blood drain from his face. *The destruction of the Colossus? Is she crazy? How in the world did she intend to do that? An even better question—why did she want to?*

Anya waved a dismissive hand in the air, signifying that their conversation was over. "I'll let your friends explain things to you." She then turned to Elladan and held out a pale, slender hand. "Attend me?"

Elladan cast a sympathetic glance at Aksel, then took the Princess by the hand. "Of course, Anya. Right this way." The bard then led the Princess past a bewildered Aksel, and through the archway that led into the monolith, Donnie and the scarlet-clad Mallona following closely behind.

Aksel, still flabbergasted, spun to face Glo, the wizard having just strode up with Lloyd, Cyclone, and the young squire, Lamorn. Aksel stared at them incredulously, trying to speak, but instead stumbled over his words. "Des… destroy… the Colossus? Would someone please explain to me what in Thac is going on here?"

Aksel rushed down the stairs from the sub-basement to the cavern that held the Colossus, striving to catch up to the Princess Anya and the others. Glo and Lloyd had explained to him all that had transpired while he was away, including the sighting of the airship, the exchange of messages, their plan to meet with the Princess, Elladan's transformation, Anya's 'testing' of them with her dragons, and the subsequent discussion concerning the destruction of the Colossus.

Aksel had listed carefully to all they had told him, swiftly realizing this Princess Anya was not to be trusted. When the trio was done with their story, Aksel sent Lamorn off to stay with Ruka and Syndir. The little cleric then spun on his heel and hurried into the monolith, waving for the rest of them to follow.

Aksel's mind raced as they dashed up and down the monolith to catch up with the others. He intrinsically understood all that Anya had told them about the dangers of holding onto the Colossus. The huge construct truly was a weapon of mass destruction, and in the wrong hands it could certainly be used to destroy all of Thac—possibly even the entire world of Arinthar.

Still, he had to question Anya's source of information. Even if she was telling the truth, he was not certain of this advisor of hers, Theramon. Perhaps he was the expert Anya claimed him to be, but then again, perhaps not. Aksel had read some of the ancient texts from the time of the Thrall Wars. Having come from many sources, they were filled with contradictory information. Thus, it was hard to tell what was true, and what was a specific author's fanciful creation. Experts on the subject seemed to agree that Dreamweaver's chronicles were the de facto source on the Thrall Wars, but even those texts contained questionable passages.

There was one story in particular that Aksel always found hard to believe. In the last battle of the war, Dreamweaver claimed the prince of all demons appeared on the field, a huge creature nearly twenty feet tall. He then went on to detail how the demon prince was defeated in an epic struggle by a single warrior. Try as he might, Aksel could not imagine a lone warrior triumphing over the mightiest of creatures from the Abyss.

Aksel's musings were cut short as they reached the bottom of the stairs. He came to a sudden halt—Anya, Mallona, and Elladan were all stopped in front of him at the edge of the alcove, the Princess' mouth agape.

"That thing is huge!" Anya managed a strangled cry.

Mallona stood protectively next to the Princess, regarding the Colossus as if it were a direct threat. An almost inhuman growl escaped her throat as she glared up at the huge golem defiantly.

Aksel swiftly gazed around the cavern, his eyes sweeping across the walkway. Alana stood a little more than halfway across the bridge, shield in one hand, her other hand resting on the hilt of her sword. Donnie had crossed over to join her, the slight elf speaking avidly with the lady knight.

The little cleric continued his sweep, searching for Elistra, his eyes widening as they rose to the top of the Colossus. Elistra sat comfortably upon the stone throne—the seeress had removed her black and red cap with the yellow stars, and in its place, wore the golem's crown upon her comely brow. She gazed down upon them as if a goddess from on high, though her expression was hard to read from this distance.

Anya must have noticed the seeress at the same time as Aksel. She lifted a pale slender finger and pointed toward the top of the Colossus, her voice filled with suspicion. "And just who is that?"

Elladan followed her gaze, his face registering his surprise. The bard immediately recovered, responding to the Princess in a reassuring tone. "That? Oh, that is just our friend, Elistra."

Anya was not mollified by his answer, her eyes remaining firmly fixed on the seeress. "And just what is she doing up there?"

Aksel had been wondering the same exact thing. Yet Elladan took her question in stride, responding smoothly with an answer probably not very far from the truth. "Elistra? She is merely protecting the golem's control mechanism."

Anya turned her narrow-eyed gaze upon Elladan, her voice still filled with distrust. "Really? Well, she might want to get down from there, since you are planning on destroying the creature."

Elladan responded by turning up the charm, flashing the Princess his patented half-smile. "I'm sure she will, but first, wouldn't you like a closer look at the Colossus?"

Another growl emanated from Mallona's throat, but Anya held up a slim hand, her face flushing slightly as a sensual smile spread across her lips. "Easy, Mallona. Elladan is quite right. This 'Colossus' intrigues me. I believe I would like a closer look before it is demolished."

Elladan continued to wear that smile as he offered his arm to the Princess. "Well then, shall we?"

Anya took his proffered arm, and then allowed Elladan to lead her across the walkway. Mallona reluctantly followed, her eyes still glued to Elistra on the throne above them.

Aksel glanced over his shoulder before striding after them, and whispered softly to the others. "Stay close."

He was not quite sure what was going to happen, but Aksel trusted neither Anya nor her scarlet-clad servant. If either attempted to wrestle control of the Colossus away from Elistra, he wanted everyone nearby and ready to thwart them.

The Princess, Elladan, and Mallona slowly crossed the walkway, halting to gaze over the side at the body of the Colossus. Anya leaned over the rail, marveling at the seventy-foot-tall creature, her pale features flushing even further. "My, my… that is enormous."

Elladan leaned next to the Princess, still wearing that charming smile as a short laugh escaped his throat. "Heh. I think we said the same thing the first time we saw it."

Anya shifted her gaze to the bard and locked eyes with him. She said nothing further, but it was obvious, even to Aksel, that Anya was quite interested in the handsome young elf. The scarlet-clad Mallona remained close at hand, practically seething at the attention her liege was giving to this newcomer.

About a minute passed before Anya finally stood up, and took Elladan's arm once again. The pair resumed their march across the walkway, with Mallona following close behind. The trio had nearly reached Alana and Donnie when they crossed the halfway point and entered the Colossus' antimagic field.

Elladan and Anya continued on, but Mallona abruptly halted, a low moan escaping her lips. Anya immediately whirled around, thoughtlessly pushing Elladan aside. "Mallona, what's wrong?"

It was the first sign of genuine concern Aksel had heard the Princess utter. Mallona clasped her hands on either side of her head as if she was in agony.

"I… I can't hold it!" she cried, her voice filled with pain and fear.

Abruptly her body began to glow. It grew brighter and brighter, until it was hard to look at with the naked eye. The intense white light began to swell in size, forcing everyone to back away down either side of the walkway.

Aksel shaded his eyes as he retreated, unable to tear his gaze from the alarming transformation. He watched with growing fear as the torso shifted onto all fours, the neck drastically elongated, and a pair of large, bat-like wings sprouting out of the back. The brilliance swiftly faded away, leaving in its wake a rather large red dragon.

17
COLOSSAL DESTRUCTION

You shall not pass, foul beast!

Aksel stared in awe at the fearsome creature that stood before them. Easily thirty feet long, the red dragon was covered from the top of its serpentine neck to the tip of its long, sinuous tail in thick leathery crimson scales, all except for the underside, which was a rich brown. Long, tapered, bat-like wings extended from the creature's back, a deep scarlet color, but with a burnt-blue tint along the bottom edge.

The fierce dragon reared up its neck, lifting its large head well above the walkway. Two massive brown horns swept back atop the skull, flanked by a pair of crimson-fringed ears. The head was capped by a backswept scarlet crest that ran down the neck and along the spine, all the way to the tip of its long, twitching tail.

Small flames came alight across the beast's nostrils and eyes. It opened its beaked snout, a forked tongue flickering in and out between wicked dagger-like teeth, as it let out a terrifying roar. The bone-chilling sound reverberated off the cavern walls, forcing Aksel to cover his ears. As the sound died down, the distinct odor of sulfur and pumice reached the little cleric's nostrils.

"Mallona!" Anya cried, her voice rising nearly an octave. The Princess, looking rather nervous, put her hands out in front of her as she took a step toward the angry red dragon. "It's okay, Mallona. Everything's going to be okay."

The great head swiveled around on its serpentine neck, as the large beast focused its attention on the Princess. Aksel wasn't sure if she was calming the creature down, or irritating it further. Elladan must have thought the same thing.

"What are you, crazy?" the bard cried.

Elladan reached forward and grasped the Princess by the shoulders.

She twisted her upper body from side to side, trying to pull away from him, but the dark-haired elf drew her back nonetheless.

Anya swiveled her head around and yelled at him. "She's my friend—she needs me!"

Their argument seemed to anger the dragon even further. The great head moved in closer, a low growl emanating from its throat as the flames in its nostrils and eyes grew larger.

Abruptly, two forms brushed by Glo and Aksel, one red and one blue. Lloyd and Cyclone swiftly moved in toward the dragon's flank, the former drawing his two long blades, the latter with the tip of his razor-sharp halberd pointed in front of him.

At the same time, Alana and Donnie pushed past Elladan and Anya, placing themselves squarely in the path of the angry red drag-on. The lady knight wore a fierce look of determination, her shield readied and holy sword gleaming as she glared up at the monster. "You shall not pass, foul beast!"

The dragon's terrible gaze fell upon Alana, another growl ema-nating from its throat. Donnie stood beside the lady knight, watching the beast warily, an ironic smile forming on his lips. "If you wanted her attention, I think you've got it."

A large clawed limb suddenly shot toward them with incred-ible speed. Alana barely pulled back in time, the sharp claws raking against her shield as they passed through the spot where she had just been standing. Still, the force of the glancing blow nearly knocked Alana off her feet.

Donnie tumbled out of the way as the clawed limb passed over him, coming up next to Alana. The slight elf let out a deep breath. "Whoa! Now I know what a fly feels like when it's being swatted at."

Alana cast him a sidelong glance, then the duo set themselves for another swipe. At the same moment, the Princess Anya's voice rang out from behind them.

"Mallona, calm down! I did not come here to fight."

Yet it was too late for that. As soon as the dragon swiped at their friends, Lloyd and Cyclone charged into battle. The red warrior dashed forward, dodging around the dragon's tail, while Cyclone vaulted high into the air, landing on the dragon's back.

Mallona spun her head around, her flaming eyes falling on the dragon hunter. The great head shot toward him, snapping at the blue-clad warrior, but Cyclone fended it off with his long, pointy halberd. Meanwhile, Lloyd zeroed in on a hind leg, slashing at it with his black blade. The weapon bit deep into the dragon's leg, red blood spurting from the wound.

Mallona roared in pain, pulling away from the red-clad warrior, her large wings flaring out on either side. The red dragon spun around, trying to both throw Cyclone off and turn to face this new threat who had drawn her blood.

Aksel watched the entire scene unfold as if it were surreal. He could not believe just how quickly things had escalated out of hand. Beside him, Glo had begun to weave a spell when a dark shadow fell over the walkway. Aksel's head snapped up to see a giant hand reaching over the battle, the huge appendage headed straight for the red dragon. Yet Mallona did not seem to notice, her attention focused on Lloyd and Cyclone.

Anya, on the other hand, noticed it immediately. She gazed up at the colossal hand, her eyes wide with terror, her voice sticking in her throat. When she finally found it, the monarch screamed at the top of her lungs. "Mallona, watch out!"

The red dragon froze in its tracks, the large head swiveling upward, but it was too late—the colossal hand was now directly over her. The startled dragon spun around again, the great wings beating wildly as it tried escape from underneath that huge hand.

At the same time, Cyclone launched himself off the dragon's back, deftly landing on the catwalk below. Both he and Lloyd scrambled away as fast as they could from the frightened dragon.

Mallona nearly got away, but the enormous hand was too close. Giant fingers wrapped around the dragon, and inexorably drew it into the Colossus' grasp. Mallona let out a frightened roar as she writhed around in the golem's grip, but to no avail. The huge hand closed tighter around her—the red dragon was caught.

Mallona continued to roar in fear, but Anya's voice wailed above her cries. "Don't hurt her! She was only frightened! She's not even an adult yet!"

Aksel gazed over at the monarch, and noted her face was streaked with tears. Her emotional reaction to Mallona's imprisonment painted the Princess in a whole new light. From everything Aksel had heard, Anya was just another rich, spoiled noble. Yet it appeared that she really cared about her dragons—or Mallona, at the very least.

Glo must have come to the same conclusion. The wizard cupped his hands around his mouth, and called up to Elistra, the seeress still seated atop the Colossus. "Just hold her there for now—don't hurt her!"

Elistra's arm was held out in front of her, her hand in a fist. The seeress turned her gaze upon Glo, paused for a moment, then responded with a grim smile and a nod. Glo smiled back, then glanced back down at the Princess. "See, your friend won't be harmed."

Anya, red in the face, swept her gaze from the red dragon to the seeress, the two women locking eyes for a few moments. The Princess then returned her gaze to Mallona. The red dragon seethed in the Colossus' grasp, but otherwise seemed fine. Anya took a deep breath, her color slowly returning to normal.

Aksel, Glo, Cyclone, and Lloyd all strode over to join the others. The Princess' eyes swept across them all, finally settling on Aksel. "Very well. Now what? Are you going to renege on your deal?"

Before Aksel could respond, Alana spoke up, her eyes hard and her voice vehement. "You all saw what happened. Red dragons are inherently evil. It would be sheer folly to let it go."

Donnie reached over and placed a hand on Alana's armored-plated shoulder. When the slim elf spoke, his voice was subdued. "That may be, but we gave her our word we would destroy the Colossus."

The lady knight turned her head toward Donnie, mixed emotions playing across her comely features. As a Knight of the Rose, Alana was fully aware of what giving one's word entailed. The lady knight hesitated for a moment more, then let out a deep sigh, her gaze shifting to Aksel. "I see. I will not counsel you to go back on your word, but I do advise caution."

Aksel's eyes met hers, his hand gingerly rubbing his chin. Letting the red dragon go might indeed be folly, but backing out on their deal with the princess of a great nation such as Lanfor was equally foolish. It was not a decision to be made lightly. The little cleric peered over at Cyclone.

"You're the expert on dragons. What do you think?"

The dragon hunter casually held his long halberd in one hand, as his gaze shifted to the red dragon. Mallona still seethed in the Colossus' grasp, yet otherwise remained still. Cyclone eyed the dragon, his face a stony mask. "If you're asking me, I agree with the lady knight. Kill it and get it over with."

Anya fixed the hunter with a dark glare. If looks could kill, Cyclone would have been struck dead right then and there.

Aksel responded with a slow nod, then swept his eyes around the group. "Anyone else?"

Elladan, still holding the Princess, spoke in a soft, but steady voice. "I say a deal's a deal."

Lloyd sheathed his blades, his voice strong and certain. "I agree with Elladan and Donnie… a man is only as good as his word."

Glo was the only one who hadn't voiced his opinion yet. Aksel now turned to the elven wizard. "Glo?"

Glo's eyes were fixed on the Princess, staring at her intently as if trying to read her mind. "What do you say, Anya? Can you promise to keep your 'friend' in check?"

Anya eyed him darkly from under her long blonde tresses. When she responded, her voice was as hard as steel. "She will listen to me,"—she cast a scathing stare at the captured dragon—"won't you, Mallona?"

The red dragon stopped seething, its large horned skull slowly bowing down to its mistress. "Of course, my lady," came the deep, rumbling reply.

Anya turned her hard gaze back on Glo, her tone dripping with sarcasm. "There, you see?"

A feeble smile crossed the wizard's lips. He cast a glance at Aksel with a nod. "Then I agree with Donnie, Elladan, and Lloyd. We stand by our word."

Aksel took a deep breath, and turned an eye toward the Princess. "Very well, we will stand by our agreement. However, you will agree to keep your dragon at bay."

Anya stiffened in Elladan's arms, the monarch obviously not used to being told what to do. She regarded Aksel haughtily for a moment, then her shoulders sagged and she gave him a silent nod.

"Thank you," Aksel replied as graciously as possible. "We will place her outside the antimagic field, and she will change back to her human form."

"She can't," Anya responded in a barely audible whisper.

Aksel cocked his head to one side, his face scrunching in confusion. "Can't what?"

Anya let out another deep sigh. "She can't transform herself. She hasn't learned yet."

The admission caught Aksel by surprise. He opened his mouth to respond, then stopped himself. Mallona wasn't the first dragon he'd met that couldn't change its shape. Ruka had confided to him only a short while ago that Calipherous had never learned to do so.

"Then who does it for her? You? Sigfus?" Glo asked the Princess.

"I do," Anya admitted with a wan smile. She cast a swift glance at the red dragon and added, "But only until she can do so for herself— and she is getting better at it, aren't you Mallona?"

Her declaration was met with a hollow grunt, the dragon spinning its head away from its mistress. Aksel had to suppress a laugh. He found himself liking this Anya more and more, despite her unpredictable temperament. Still, he had to ensure the safety of his friends. "Very well, you shall change her into human form and then Cyclone, Lloyd, and Alana will stand with her. If she tries anything threatening, they will stop her once and for all."

Anya cocked her head to one side and eyed him warily. "And you will live up to your bargain—you will destroy the Colossus?"

"Yes," Aksel said simply.

Anya responded with a curt nod. "Agreed."

Aksel silently hoped they were doing the right thing. He turned to Glo and said, "Care to do the honors?"

The wizard eyed him sharply, then took off without a word down the walkway toward the Colossus. Aksel did not envy him the task of trying to explain their decision to Elistra. Meanwhile, the little cleric motioned to the others. "Let's all exit the field."

Aksel led the group back down the walkway and out of the anti-magic field. They all then spun around and saw Glo, already on top of the colossal head, having an animated discussion with Elistra.

"She doesn't look very happy," Donnie noted with a wry expression.

"Why do you think I sent Glo to tell her?" Aksel responded under his breath.

After a short exchange, Elistra barked at Glo, the word *fine* reverberating around the cavern. The elven wizard then stormed off, disappearing from atop the Colossus. A moment later, the giant hand opened, the red dragon unceremoniously dropping through its fingers. The large dragon swiftly beat its wings, slowing its fall and then regaining altitude.

Aksel peered at Anya. "Well?"

Anya cast him a sidelong glance, then called out to the dragon. "Mallona, land and stand down!"

The large red dragon hovered in the air for a few moments, the great head glaring down at its mistress. Finally it moved, gracefully landing on the walkway below.

Anya turned her head to the side and spoke softly to Elladan, her playful side resurfacing once more. "Much as I am enjoying our embrace, I need my arms now."

Elladan let out a short laugh. "Heh. Sorry, Anya."

The bard let go of his grasp on the Princess and stepped back. Anya, finally free, wrapped her hands around her upper arms and rubbed them gently, then turned her attention to the red dragon. The Princess' hands spun in a circular pattern, at the end of which she spoke a single word, "*Mutatio.*"

The red dragon began to glow, brighter and brighter, until the light became blinding. The larger form shrunk down, the long neck shortening, the wings disappearing, as well as the tail. When the spell was done, Mallona stood before them once more, clad in her bright scarlet dress.

Anya called to her attendant in a commanding tone. "Mallona, come here. You are not to move unless I tell you to. Understand?"

Mallona cocked her head and eyed her mistress for a moment, then responded in a tone dripping with acid. "Yes, your majesty."

The dragon woman limped forward favoring her uninjured leg as she past the others, and parked herself in between Lloyd, Cyclone, and Alana. She gazed briefly around at the trio, then tilted her chin upward with a decided *humph.*

A moment later, Glo's voice rang out from down the walkway. "Well, let's get this over with."

Aksel spun about to see the wizard striding toward them at a fast pace. He seemed rather agitated. Glo halted a few feet away and motioned for them to move backward with both hands. "Why don't you all park yourselves in the alcove." The wizard turned his gaze toward Lloyd. "Care to help me set off an explosion?"

Lloyd cast a glance at Aksel. Mallona and Anya seemed to be behaving themselves at the moment, so Aksel did not see a problem with Lloyd accompanying Glo. He nodded to the tall warrior. "Go ahead."

A bright smile crossed Lloyd's lips at the thought of flying. The young man grabbed his cloak and invoked its spell. A moment later, he and Glo took off up toward the top of the cavern. They were soon out of sight, disappeared into the darkness above.

The little company waited in awkward silence for Lloyd and Glo to return. It became that much more uncomfortable when Elistra strode across the cavern to join them. The seeress and the Princess locked eyes, the air between them practically sizzling with tension. Finally, Elistra walked past them all, a soft comment passing her lips. "I think I'll wait farther back. The air in here has a tainted smell."

Anya, not to be outdone, waved a dismissive hand in the air, her tone purposely lofty. "Nice dye job, honey. Too bad you're not a real blonde."

Thankfully, Elladan interrupted them before any more shots could be fired. The bard pointed upward and cried, "Here they come!"

Aksel glanced overhead to see Lloyd and Glo gliding back down toward them. The duo landed on the walkway a short distance from them and hurried over to join the others.

"What happened to the big kaboom?" Donnie asked glibly.

Glo fixed the sandy-haired elf with an acid stare. "We set a fuse…"

"…and it should go off any second now," Lloyd added, motioning for the others to step back even farther.

The companions and their 'guests' all crowded into the alcove just in time. A few moments later, a loud *boom* sounded from somewhere far above them. It was followed by several subsequent *booms*, each causing the cavern around them to shake violently.

Aksel was hard pressed to stay on his feet, till someone lent him a steadying hand. He looked up and saw Lloyd, the tall warrior hanging onto him with one hand and Glo with the other.

Outside in the cavern, the rumbling continued. Dust filtered down from the ceiling above, followed by small chunks of rocks. Abruptly Glo pointed to a spot over the Colossus. "Here it comes!"

A chunk of rock, in the shape of an immense conical dagger, came into view, falling out of the darkness above. Aksel watched in awe as the enormous stalactite rushed downward, seconds later slamming into the Colossus' head with an earth-shattering *boom*.

The entire cavern rocked once more, a huge cloud of dust rushing outward from the point of impact in all directions. Aksel buried his head in his cloak just before the dust storm washed over them. Several seconds passed before the rush of air died around them.

Aksel cautiously stuck his head out and glanced around. The cavern was still filled with a thick cloud of dust, the Colossus nowhere to be seen. The others around him slowly uncovered themselves, Donnie spitting dust out of his mouth. "Well that was fun."

"You have a strange definition of fun, my friend," Elladan responded, brushing a thick layer of dust off his white outfit.

Anya seemed equally put out. She looked over her dust-covered clothes with a critical eye. "This will never do." The Princess waved her hand and spoke a single word, "*Congue.*"

A slight breeze kicked up around them, sweeping all the dust out of the alcove and back into the cavern.

Elladan glanced at the Princess admiringly. "Nice trick there, Anya." He cast a mischievous eye at Glo. "Why can't you be useful like that?"

Glo stared back at the bard with a deadpan expression. "Do I look like your butler?"

Out in the cavern, the dark dust cloud had begun to settle. The catwalk leading out into the cave slowly became visible again. Part of it still stretched across the cavern, but beyond the halfway point, there was nothing more than a jagged edge. Further out into the cave, a large dark shadow appeared in the haze. A few more moments went by until the dust cloud completely parted, revealing the Colossus' head still intact, the only thing missing being the throne from its enormous brow.

Donnie let out a low whistle. "That is one thick-headed golem."

Aksel was stunned that the golem still stood after that devastating blow. Everyone around him appeared equally dumbfounded.

Anya, however, seemed to take it in stride. "Well, at least you tried. Now it's my turn."

Aksel spun toward the Princess, uncertain what she meant by that, but the monarch was already on the move. She grabbed Mallona by the arm and spoke two words, "*Ianuae Magicae.*"

In the blink of an eye, the two women winked out of sight.

Lloyd, Donnie, and Cyclone all nearly crashed into each other in the space where the two women had just been.

"She teleported away," Elistra's voice came from the back of the alcove, her tone thick with sarcasm.

"So now what?" Donnie asked. His eyes swept around the group, filled with foreboding.

As if in answer to his question, a muffled *boom* erupted from the entrance to the stairwell next to them. A moment later, the entire cavern began to shake. Everyone grabbed onto each other once again, tensing their bodies until the shaking subsided.

Elladan fixed Donnie with a piercing stare. "You just had to ask, didn't you?"

A few seconds later, another *boom* reached their ears, the cavern rocking along with it. As they rode out this next quake, Glo called out from the back of the alcove. "I think Anya's making good on her threat—she's bringing down the entire monolith!"

Alana, grasping tightly onto Donnie, cried back to the wizard, "Can she do that?"

"She's got enough mage cannon on her ship to sink a small fleet," Lloyd answered, the young warrior's face lined with apprehension.

Aksel realized they were all in mortal danger. His eyes swept across the group as the latest quake subsided. "I don't think we're safe down here. We need to get out while we still can."

Glo immediately responded to Aksel's suggestion, barking out orders. "Lloyd, take Alana. Cyclone, take Donnie and Elladan…" He spun to face Elistra, his arms still wrapped around the seeress. "My concentration is wavering—not sure how many more spells I can cast. Can you take the rest of us?"

Elistra responded with a grim nod. The duo parted, swiftly casting dual spells as Lloyd invoked his flying cloak. As the next salvo hit, Lloyd disappeared into the stairwell with the steel-clad Alana in his arms. Cyclone was right behind him, with Donnie in one arm and Elladan in the other.

Elistra had conjured a flying mount that looked like a giant hummingbird. She hopped on, Glo right behind her, and Aksel behind them both. They all held on for dear life as the seeress spurred her flying mount forward, through the archway and up the spiral staircase at breakneck speed.

18
A STEALTHING WE SHALL GO

What he saw was not the face of a snake, but rather that of a man

Kalyn took a deep breath, steadying her nerves and keeping her fingers at the ready on her bowstring. She was still trying to wrap her head around the idea that she was on a reconnaissance mission with one of *the* Heroes of Ravenford. If her brothers could only see her now, they'd eat every word they said to her before she left Deepwood Fort. But she couldn't be too pleased with herself yet. The game was still afoot, and she had to tread lightly and make sure she didn't botch it.

Kalyn had the feeling that Seth was on to something big. If she played this right, she'd be able to find all the missing Deepwooders and bring them home. Well, not all them. There was one that she'd never be able to bring back.

Kalyn shook her head, forcing herself to refocus.

"Something wrong?" Seth asked.

Kalyn shook her head again, not looking at him. "Nothing. Just had some hair in my face."

She and Seth had made it to Serpent's Hollow over an hour ago. They left the dragonflies a short way off and walked the rest of the way on foot. They couldn't get into Serpent's Hollow proper, because there was a gate with two ominous looking serpent statues on either side. A fitting, if creepy welcome. Upon seeing them, Seth had said something like he *'didn't need to be a wizard to know they were magical.'* So, they avoided the statues. Kalyn trusted his judgement.

The duo climbed up the mountainside to find a better vantage point. Kalyn thought it would take them longer than it did, but thanks to Seth's nimbleness, they made quick work of the trek up. Now, they could look down at the entire valley sprawling out before them.

It was an enclosed valley, surrounded by craggy cliffs, with the only way in or out being through the creepy gate they'd seen before on the southeastern end of the valley. A sheer wall of high cliffs bordered the western edge of the valley, with a large, glittering waterfall falling over them near the south, not far from the gate.

Kalyn estimated the valley to be three miles long, running north to south. Heavily wooded at the south end, the center of the hollow had been cleared. Several small wooden structures stood there, surrounding four larger structures that, in turn, encircled a fountain at the very heart of the small town. The fountain appeared to have a fallen statue along one side of it, though it was hard to tell from this distance.

Two plowed fields stood on either side of the town. Numerous figures, dressed in white, tended the fields, with a few figures dressed in black interspersed between them, acting as if they were overseers.

Kalyn spotted a road running serpentine from the gate at the southeast end of the valley, through the town and then northwest to what appeared to be the entrance to a large cave at the north end of the hollow.

Kalyn sighed. "I don't see any way to get down, other than the natural way... falling." She glanced around the valley once more, then looked at Seth.

Seth narrowed his eyes. "Uh-huh. I think I'll pass on that. I'm short enough as it is."

A wide grin spread across Kalyn's face. "Well, darn. I had a great plan to launch you off the side of the cliff. I was hoping you'd come up with a witty one-liner as you fell, to make it all the more memorable."

Seth's mouth lifted on one side. "How's this for a one-liner…"

"Aaaahhhhh!" he cried while waving his arms in the air over his head.

Kalyn covered her mouth as she buckled over in laughter. When she was finally able to breathe again, she wiped a tear from her eye and sighed. "Unfortunately, that's not gonna be very stealthy. So, scrap that idea and feed it to a rust monster. Got any other ideas?"

Kalyn watched as Seth scanned the hollow again, his sharp brown eyes going over every visible detail.

"I think we need to fly in."

Kalyn rubbed her hands together, grinning. "Okay, hold on. I'll launch you over the edge and you can start flapping your arms."

Seth rolled his eyes. "I meant on the dragonflies. But if you want to go the other way, ladies first." He ushered over the edge with his hands.

Kalyn giggled, taking a step away from the edge. "Eh, the dragonflies do sound a tad less painful. Let's do that."

Seth glanced over the valley again, then nodded toward the south. "This side of the valley looks like it's got the most cover."

Kalyn nodded in agreement. "Yeah. I think we should shoot for the waterfall over there." She pointed west toward the twinkling ribbon of cascading water. "It would mask the sound of our hummers."

Seth rubbed his hands together. "Sounds like a plan."

Half an hour later, they were in the woods near the roaring waterfall. The first thing that Kalyn noticed about the area was the large number of snakes. They were everywhere. Luckily, the snakes were startled by the dragonflies and slithered away, keeping a safe distance from the giant bugs. Once she and Seth entered the forest, though, no matter where they walked, one of the slithering creatures was in their path.

Kalyn jumped to the side and bumped into Seth as a long, green grass snake hissed at her.

"Snakes! Why did it have to be snakes?" she whined.

Seth moved past her, knelt and, quick as lightning, grabbed the snake by the head and flung it away. "I don't know what the big deal is. Aren't you some sort of animal guru?"

Kalyn rubbed her arms, feeling suddenly cold. "That's Fran, not me! 'Sides, snakes aren't animals. They're… something else… demons. Yeah! Demons."

"Well, I'm not fond of them either, especially after the last couple of weeks." Seth's lips stretched into a wicked smile. "There was this one time where I opened this hatch on a covered wagon, and all I saw was these two, huge, glowing eyes, staring up at me in the dark." Seth's voice took on an eerie tone.

Kalyn gulped, a terrifying picture forming in her mind. "Eyes? What kind of eyes?"

Seth's eyes twinkled with devilish amusement. "They were huge, yellow, with dark, crescent-shaped pupils."

Kalyn shuddered and scratched her fingers across her scalp. "Oh no, no, no, no! How big was that thing?!"

Seth did his best to stifle a laugh. It was clear he was having way too much fun at her expense. "Oh, I don't know for sure, but the biggest one I saw was about ten foot tall reared up, which would make it… what? Thirty feet long?"

Kalyn could feel the blood draining from her head, making it light and fuzzy. "Thir… thir… thirty feet long? *Are you serious*?"

Seth swiped his hands in the air. "Shhhh! Keep it down! Unless of course you want one of those giant things to find us?"

Kalyn shuddered again. "Look, I know I said I'd help you out with this recon thing, but I got to admit—I'm having second thoughts."

Seth folded his arms over his chest and gave her a hard stare. "Oh, come on! I was just teasing."

Kalyn blinked and relaxed just a bit. "Really? You were? You mean, you didn't see a snake that big?"

"No. It was that big, all right. But there was only one, and it's dead now." Seth seemed so casual about it, like it was an everyday occurrence to kill a giant snake. But then, he was one of the Heroes of Ravenford. They did amazing things like that all the time.

"Which one of you killed it? Lloyd? Glolindir? It was Glolindir, wasn't it? A fireball again?"

Seth half-snorted, half-laughed with amusement. "Heh. Unfortunately, not this time. Actually, the Boulder ripped it in half."

"The boulder? You mean that big stone giant I've heard about?"

"Nah, not a giant, just a regular golem. We kind of adopted him." Again, Seth seemed so nonchalant.

Kalyn sighed, pushing down another shiver as it crawled up her spine. "Well, I sure wish we had your giant adopted stone buddy here with us now, because where there is one big snake, there is sure to be more."

"Yeah, well, we'll just have to kill them, too." Seth shrugged.

Kalyn dipped her chin and knit her brows, looking at him as if he were crazy. "I'll leave that to you. For my part, I'll be shaking behind a tree somewhere."

Seth shook his head. "Whatever. Let's go, we don't have all day."

Kalyn nervously skipped over snakes as they walked, trying desperately to ignore them, until they made it to the edge of the tree line, just outside of town. They hid in the shadow of a large fir tree as they scanned the town and the fields. It was clear now that the figures dressed in black were overseers, as they held whips and took turns shouting orders at the white-robed people. Kalyn squinted, trying to see if she recognized anyone in the field, particularly anyone in white robes, but all of them were hunched over their work and moving too much to be able to see their faces clearly.

A light tap on the arm made Kalyn look down at Seth. The halfling motioned for her to follow him back into the trees. She took a last look at the fields, then silently followed Seth until he stopped under a giant pine.

"We need a closer look at what's going on." Seth said.

Kalyn nodded. "I agree. But how?"

"Looks like those guys in the black cloaks are in charge. If we find some black cloaks of our own, then we can be in charge, too."

Kalyn's eyebrows slowly floated to the top of her head. "Oh! Swell idea! Since the gate is the only way in or out of here, we could wait by the road and snatch the first ones we see going by."

Seth nodded. "Exactly what I was thinking."

"Devilish minds think alike!" Kalyn grinned and winked. "Let's go! I want a boss cloak!"

The duo backtracked through the trees for a while until they were about halfway to the creepy gate, stopping when Kalyn spotted an old oak tree with branches that hung out over the road. She climbed the tree and perched herself comfortably on a sturdy branch that was decently concealed. She pulled a couple of arrows, then waited silently. The minutes dragged on until Kalyn almost lost track of time. She dangled her legs over the branch she was perched on and began to kick them in the air.

This is more boring than fishing in the Singing River in the winter.

Abruptly, two hooded figures dressed in black appeared around a bend in the road, coming from the direction of the gate. They walked closely together and seemed deep in conversation.

It's about bloody time! Just what the cleric ordered—two healthy bad guys in black robes.

Kalyn took a moment to adjust the fletching of one of her arrows, then she nocked both onto her bowstring. She pulled the string back, counted to three, then let the string slip from her fingers. With barely a sound, the arrows zipped through the air, the one with the fixed fletching veering off to the left just slightly, until an arrow plunged deep into each figure's chest. One of the figures slumped to the ground instantly. The other faltered, stumbling back a few steps, before slumping to his knees, then falling face first onto the packed dirt of the road.

A sudden cry rang out from down below. "Watch out!"

Kalyn snapped her head in the direction of the gate just in time to see a red ribbon of light flash off the fingertips of another figure in black. Without thinking, she ducked to the side and slipped off the branch, wrapping her hands around a thin limb to break her fall. A split-second later, a scorching hot stream of fire hit where she had been sitting, passing so close that she was sure it singed the hairs off her arms. Kalyn dropped to the ground with a gentle bend of her knees, only to find the corner of her green tunic was ablaze.

"Dragon fire and Dunwynn unda'pants!" she screamed, batting

at the flames. A second later, she dropped to the ground and rolled around in the dirt. As the flames went out, she caught a glimpse of the black figure out of the corner of her eye. Its arm was pointed directly at her.

Kalyn froze, her eyes going wide. She was about to be on the receiving end of another spell, and there was no way for her to avoid it.

Kalyn cringed, waiting for the worst, when suddenly the caster stiffened, a strangled cry escaping his lips. Just as abruptly, he went silent and slumped to the ground. A short, solitary figure appeared behind the caster, a bloody dagger in his hand.

A smug smile crossed the familiar figure's lips. "Fried Kalyn for breakfast, anyone?"

Kalyn glared at Seth as she slowly got to her feet and brushed herself off. "Took ya long enough, pint-size. What's a girl gotta do to get some decent help around here?"

Seth nonchalantly strolled over to the grass and wiped his blade off in it. "Maybe next time, I should let the nice black mage shoot you first."

"Aw, you wouldn't let a nice girl like me get whooped by a mage, now, would ya? Gotta rush in and save the day, right?"

Seth's mouth bent into an ironic smile. "You've got the wrong hero there, lady. You must be thinking of Lloyd, or even Glo. Of course, if that were the case, the entire forest would be in flames by now."

Kalyn grinned despite herself. "Guess I got the short end of the stick, then, huh?" she said with a wink.

Seth shook his head. "Saved your life, and what do I get for it? Short jokes." With that, he went over and looted the mage, stripping off his cloak.

Seth stuck his fingers through the bloodied hole in the back of the cloak. "Well, this one's shot." He folded it up and stuffed it into his pack with a sigh. "Guess I'll hold onto it anyway."

Kalyn turned the other two bodies over. "Well, these robes are in perfect condition! I wonder who we have to thank for that?"

Seth fixed her an acid stare. "If you're done bragging, can you give me a hand dragging them off the road?"

Kalyn slung her bow over her shoulder and helped him pull the mages, one at a time, off the road and a safe distance into the trees, then she ran back to the road and covered their tracks up. When she returned to where they had deposited the bodies, Seth had already stripped them of the other two cloaks and was examining them.

He pressed his lips together and gave her a subtle nod. "Not even a nick on them. I guess they'll do."

Kalyn glanced down at the bodies and froze when she spied a snake tattoo on the right arm of each mage.

"Aw, was that your sister? Would you like to join her?"

Kalyn felt the blood drain from her face as the eerie voice rang through her mind. The vision of an arm with that same tattoo reaching for her flashed before her eyes, sending shivers up her spine.

"Hey!"

Kalyn snapped back to the moment and turned toward Seth as he snapped his fingers.

"You spaced out there. You okay?" he asked, a hint of concern on his face.

Kalyn opened her mouth, but nothing came out. It was the same vision that had haunted her night after night for years now. It was a rare occasion when she didn't wake up in the middle of the night in a cold sweat. The young woman took a deep breath and calmed her nerves. This was no time to be freaking out over the past. In fact, that was the very reason she was here in the first place—to get revenge, and she'd never been so close as she was now.

Kalyn steeled herself and reached for one of the cloaks, looking it over carefully. "Well, you have got a problem shorty—these 'I'm-in-charge' cloaks are longer than you are tall. They might be a bit too big for me, too."

She slipped the cloak on, then held her arms out in front of her, flopping the oversized sleeves around for emphasis. "Help me! My arms have disappeared!"

Seth let out a deep sigh and shook his head. The halfling then spread his cloak out on the ground, pulled out a knife, and cut the hem of his cloak down to his size. Once he was done, he rolled the sleeves up, then picked the cloak up and slipped it on.

He pulled the oversized hood up over his head and let it drop over his face. "How's that?"

Kalyn giggled with glee. "It's the halfling without a face!"

Her expression abruptly turned serious, her hand going to her chin and she appraised his makeshift outfit. "Well, as long as you can see your feet and don't trip, I guess it'll work."

The young woman then pulled her hood up as well, and tucked her hands into her long sleeves. "So, how do I look?"

Seth pushed his hood back a little, watching as she turned a circle. "Looks like you're a Serpent Cult choir member."

Kalyn knit her brows together as she eyed him sharply. "Is that a good thing or a bad thing?"

Seth cocked his head to one side and shrugged. "You look fine. Let's go."

The duo moved out to the road, walking side-by-side as they headed toward the town.

"Remember to act natural, but keep your head down. We don't want any attention." Seth cautioned softly.

"Right." Kalyn nodded. A moment later, a frown crossed her brow. "What does 'natural' look like?"

Seth shook his head slowly and murmured under his breath. "Oh gods, what have I gotten myself into now?"

"Oh boy. I've made one of *the* Heroes of Ravenford resort to prayer." Kalyn held back a nervous giggle.

"Would you just shut up and try to blend in?"

Kalyn was too nervous to argue, so she tucked her quivering hands into her sleeves, crossed her arms, and focused on keeping in step with Seth.

Kalyn's anxiety grew as the town came into sight and steadily drew closer. As they passed by the fields, she couldn't help but turn her head and look once more at the people. Her stomach jumped into her throat when she recognized three men from Deepwood. One of them had only been missing a week or so, and was a soon-to-be first time father.

As Kalyn stared, she noticed that all the people dressed in white robes had blank expressions and vacant eyes.

"What have they done to them?" she whispered in horror.

Seth hissed, reminding her to quit staring and keep her mouth shut, even though her gut rattled around like it was full of snakes.

Kalyn kept close to the halfling and followed his lead into town. She did her best to appear unassuming, especially as they passed by several black-cloaked figures and walked through the center of town. A group of white-robed, blank-eyed slaves were working around the fountain, trying to repair a large fallen statue of a snake.

Kalyn peered at the spectacle with keen curiosity. *I wonder who broke it?*

The young archer risked a quick glance around and noticed several pairs of black-cloaked figures going to and fro from the large stone buildings surrounding the fountain. That was when she noticed how grand the stone buildings appeared. In fact, they were so magnificent that she couldn't help but stare at them. They were some of the largest buildings she'd ever seen, with tall, beautifully carved pillars and wide sweeping steps leading up to their doors.

"Wow. Nice rock houses," she whispered.

"Looks dwarvish to me," Seth remarked softly.

Kalyn glanced at the buildings again.

So, that's what Dwarf houses look like? I want one. Wonder where I could hire a Dwarf to build me one? I'll have to ask Seth later where I can find me a Dwarf. I'll also have to ask him what halfling houses look like. Or do they live in holes?

Seth's voice shook her from her thoughts. "Looks like a temple."

She glanced at him, then peered at one of the larger buildings. It had a domed top, and a giant bronze symbol of a serpent hung in the archway of the oversized door. A slight shiver passed up her spine. Whatever god they worshiped there, she was sure she never wanted to meet it.

Kalyn followed Seth as he crossed over to the northern road and left the town behind. As soon as they passed the last building, she spoke up. "What are we doing?"

"I want to get a better look at that cave."

"Okay… but wouldn't that be considered a risk? Remember, Fran didn't want us to take any risks."

Seth kept his eyes forward, his tone rather sharp as he responded. "Fran ain't here, and I don't take orders from her anyway."

Kalyn raised an eyebrow, but just nodded. "Well, she did say we were to find out what everyone was up against, and we can't find that out unless we see what's going on in the cave, too."

"Not 'we.' Me," Seth responded. "I'm going into the cave to have a look around. You're going to sit outside of the cave, out of sight, and watch my back."

A frown crossed Kalyn's brow. "Now, hold on just a second! I can do that better if…"

"There might be snakes in the cave. Really big ones."

"…and I'm gonna find someplace to hide outside of the cave and watch your back from out there." Kalyn softly cleared her throat. She could practically hear Seth grinning from underneath his over-sized hood.

Silence fell between them as the cave came into view. As they grew closer, she saw that the entrance was guarded by several black-robed figures. People dressed in white slowly filtered out of the cave, carrying baskets full of rocks, which they dumped into a pile alongside of the road before turning and walking dumbly back into the cave.

The guards were mostly interested in watching the slaves work, seeming unconcerned with the few other black-cloaked figures that came and went.

"This might just work," Kalyn whispered as she watched the guards wave several dark cloaked figures back into the cave. She bit her tongue, though, when a guard stopped one of them, checking his face under his hood. "Nope. Never mind. Abort. Abort."

Seth hissed at her again. "Shut up and follow me."

The halfling veered off the road without missing a beat, Kalyn quickly following him. They skirted around several large piles of rock and rubble, then climbed up a small embankment until they reached a small grove of trees. Kalyn finally relaxed as she moved behind one of the trees, concealing herself in its shadow.

"How are you going to get in there?" She looked down at Seth and watched as he shrugged off his black cloak, then straightened another cloak that she recognized from the stories she'd heard about the Heroes. He said a strange word that she didn't recognize, and then vanished from sight.

"Stay here, be quiet, and keep an eye out. I'll be right back," Seth's disembodied voice said.

Kalyn nodded and watched as a few leaves moved just the tiniest bit, the faintest of impressions left behind in the earth by tiny boots. "Yeah, sure thing, but you better be quick, or I'm coming in after you, snakes or no."

She watched with growing anxiety as the faint footprints moved away toward the cave.

Sneaking into the cave was easier than Seth thought. The black-robed guards appeared more concerned with the dopey-eyed slaves than the possibility of an invisible person walking right past them.

The inside the cave was well-lit, with torches placed periodically on the wall. The floor angled slightly downward for about three hundred feet, then leveled off, just before Seth came to a split in the path. Three tunnels branched off the main cavern, one leading right, one turning left, and the last pushing straight forward.

Screams and wails drifted from the left branch, so Seth turned down there first. He didn't have to walk far before coming across a tall portcullis. It stretched across the length of the tunnel, blocking any further progress. Behind the portcullis was a small cavern.

In the middle of the cavern stood a post with someone chained to it. The person screamed and writhed as a figure dressed in a black-hooded robe held large, dark snakes up to him. The creatures wrapped themselves around the victim and squeezed, or sank long double rows of teeth into his flesh. The dark-cloaked figure laughed as the man screamed and pleaded for mercy.

Seth gagged in revulsion. *That's just sick. I'd love to put a dagger to that guy's throat.*

Seth had to look away before he threw up. Peering around the room, he saw there were four cages, two on either side of the cave. Inside one of them was a group of humans, but the other three held strange, grotesque, half-snake beings. Some had human bodies and snake heads, and others had snake bodies and heads with human torsos. They beat against the bars of their cages, their hisses echoing in time with the tortured man's screams of agony.

Seth suppressed a shudder. What they were doing in there was sick and twisted. *If Lloyd was here, he'd have that portcullis open in a second.*

Seth would take great pleasure rushing in and ending the life of that demented tormentor. *Better yet, Glo could just fireball the entire cavern… after we rescue the few humans left,* he quickly amended.

Thoroughly disgusted, Seth made a mental promise to come back here and end this twisted game. The halfling then spun around and made his way back to the main cavern as swiftly as possible. At the tunnel crossroads, he saw a man dressed in a black robe leading two white-robed slaves down the right tunnel. The slaves were carried an ornate chest that appeared quite heavy.

Seth quietly fell in behind the trio, following them from a safe distance. The tunnel ended at a thick iron door. A pair of guards dressed in black leathers stood on either side. The dark-robed figure motioned to them, and one of the guards produced a key, unlocking the door. He pushed it open, allowing the slaves and their overseer to pass through. Seth got just close enough to peer through the doorway. The room was filled with numerous chests and racks of weapons.

Armory. Possibly a treasury. Maybe both.

With that thought, Seth spun around and headed back to the crossroads. Once there, he turned down the center tunnel. Seth followed it for a short way until it suddenly opened into a fair-sized octagonal room.

Unlike the rest of the caves and tunnels he had seen down here, the walls, floor, and ceiling of this room were all made of smooth, carved stone blocks. Those blocks were finely polished, the flickering light of multiple wall torches glimmering off the shiny stone. Directly across from him stood a wide pair of ornate double doors, with the symbols of a serpent carved into the framework. Both doors hung open at the moment, but guarding the entrance on either side were two large, evil-looking snake statues.

The invisible halfling froze in his tracks. *I bet those are magical.*

Seth slowly crept forward across the polished stone, but came to an abrupt halt when the statues' red jeweled eyes began to glow.

Yep. Magic.

Seth took a step back—there was no way he was getting past those statue sentries. He stayed where he was, and peered into the room ahead. From this angle, it appeared to be a similar chamber to the one he was in, but far larger. At the far end of the room stood what appeared to be a huge altar, though it was partially buried under rock and rubble. White-robed slaves scurried around, scooping up chucks of rubble into baskets. A couple of black-garbed overseers stood nearby, whips in hand.

So, that's where they're moving all the rock from. I'll bet this altar was buried during that ancient battle Fran told us about.

Seth moved to the side and pressed himself against the wall as a few of the blank-eyed slaves filed out from the room, carrying baskets full of rocks. As they passed by, Seth peered back into the room, and froze in shock at what he saw.

Just around the corner of those open doors stood a creature that sent chills up his spine. It appeared to be a giant snake, perhaps as large as the one the Boulder killed, but as Seth's eyes scanned up its powerful dark red and blue coils, he got a glimpse past the creature's hooded head. What he saw was not the face of a snake, but rather that of a man, its expression dark and serious. The creature's muscles rippled as it drew in its sinewy coils, leaned back and gazed down at the floor. The end of its great tail twitched gently back and forth, as if it were deep in thought.

Tearing his eyes away from the strange creature, Seth saw a man standing beside it, dwarfed by the huge man-snake's impressive size. The man was dressed in fine black robes, trimmed in red, but what drew Seth's attention was his bald, uncovered head. The entire left side of the man's face was covered by an ominous grinning skull tattoo.

That must be the dark mage Kalyn mentioned. When she said he had an unforgettable face, she wasn't kidding.

Seth mentally snickered to himself. *Though she forgot to mention how ugly he is.*

Seth's attention was then drawn to the air beyond the man and snake creature. There was a purple, glowing hole floating in the air before them. *A portal!*

The pair appeared to be speaking to a dark figure on the other side of the portal. Seth shifted his position to see if he could get a glimpse of who, or what, they were talking to. Abruptly, the figure's face came into view. Perhaps it was a distortion of the portal, but if it wasn't, he was staring at the face of a giant, beautiful woman.

The woman had pale, porcelain skin, framed by long, raven-black hair. Her nose was thin and she had extremely high cheekbones and blood-red lips. Her blackish eyes shifted between the man and the snake creature, and as she spoke, Seth could see two sharp fangs hanging from her top jaw.

Even though Seth couldn't hear what she was saying, he could tell that she had a fierce demeanor, and positively radiated power—a *lot* of power.

Seth suppressed a cold shiver. *That's the woman from the black gem!*

A vision of their battle with the Barghest in the Darkwoods flashed through Seth's mind. Afterwards, he had retrieved a black gem from the creature. Later, when Glo examined the gem, his mind had almost been taken over by a powerful dark sorceress. The face Seth now stared at looked remarkably like the one Glo had described.

I've seen enough.

The halfling spun around, and without a glance backward, quietly hurried back up the tunnel. Seth paused when he came to the mouth of the cave and peered around, making sure his path back to Kalyn was clear. Just as he exited the cave mouth, a flash of movement caught his eye.

Up where he had left Kalyn, a figure wearing an oversized black cloak darted out from behind a pile of rubble. It grabbed a passing female figure dressed in white, wrapped a long sleeve around her mouth, and jerked the girl back behind the rubble without a sound.

Seth halted in his tracks, and firmly set his jaw. *I'm gonna kill her!*

The halfling swiftly glanced around in a circle, making sure that no one else saw what just happened. Thankfully, no one did, apparently all of them too preoccupied with their work.

Seth quickly moved around the mountains of rubble and rocks and climbed up the embankment to the trees. He watched Kalyn drag the thrashing slave into the shadow of a grove and practically disappear, the slave still struggling the entire time.

Seth took after the pair in a hurry. *I am SO going to kill her.*

19
PARTING OF WAYS

*Do we look stupid enough to get on a ship with someone
who just tried to kill us?*

Rukastanna ta Yatharia Greymantle watched in horror as the tall monolith began to crack and crumble, the boom of cannon fire ringing in her ears. Less than an hour had passed since she first observed the large airship slowly floating in from the south. She had continued to study the vessel carefully as it drew up next to the great structure, yet the ship had just hovered there, doing nothing for the last half hour.

Maya had been fascinated by the flying vessel at first. She sat next to her older sister on a high limb of one of the tallest trees in the nearby forest, chatting away as the vessel approached.

"Oh, that's so pretty…"

Ruka had merely nodded her head.

"Look at the big blue ring!"

"Uh huh…" Ruka had responded, not really paying attention, her eyes fixed on the airship.

"I wonder what it's made of…"

Ruka just shrugged, the dragon teen narrowing her eyes for a better look at the deck of the vessel. It was frustrating—in dragon form, her vision would have been ten times sharper, but then she would be far easier to spot.

"…and how does that thing stay in the air without wings?"

"I don't know," Ruka responded tersely. There were things moving around on the deck of that ship—large things of not-so-friendly colors.

"Maybe we should fly over there and see…"

"No!" came the immediate response from both Ruka and Cal on the forest floor below.

Ruka shifted her gaze toward her little sister just in time to see the pout forming on her lips. Maya's face screwed up into a ball as she folded her tiny arms across her chest. "Humph. You two are no fun! Ves would let me go and see it."

Ruka fixed her little sister with a hard stare. "You know very well that Ves would not let you do that. In fact, she probably wouldn't even let you sit up here in this tree."

Maya glared back at her older sister for a few moments, her cherub face still pouty, then turned her head away, and leapt off the tall branch they were sitting on.

"It's no fair!" her voice trailed off as she fell toward the forest floor some hundred feet below.

Ruka watched her fall with little concern, not batting an eye as her youngest sister landed on the ground like a cat. She stood up, dusted off her cute little dress, and stormed off into the dark forest.

"I'll keep an eye on her," Cal called back up, the copper dragon disappearing with surprising grace and speed after his youngest charge. The two young squires, Syndir and Lamorn, sat at the base of a nearby tree, watching the entire exchange wide-eyed.

Ruka called down to them with a short laugh. "Heh. Don't worry—it's just a hissy fit. They'll be back soon."

The two squires peered up at her, both wearing expressions of astonishment. Her attempt to mollify the young humans had obviously not worked at all.

Half an hour had passed since then, during which the flying vessel had done nothing but hover there. So why in the names of all the gods was it suddenly bombarding the monolith? Ruka's heart thumped wildly with each boom of those great cannons. It felt as if her heart was going to jump out of her chest. *He's still in there.*

Her immediate desire was to change into her natural form and charge the ship, blasting it with her powerful lightning breath. She wasn't worried about those stupid cannons. She was far too quick for those balls of energy to hit her. The problem was the other dragons on board that vessel.

She had counted six so far—two blues, two blacks, and two whites. None of them were much larger than she, probably all young adults like herself. Still, one on six was not good odds. Even with Cal at her side they would be woefully outnumbered, and Cal was not a fighter. Even worse, Maya would want to join them, and she could not allow that.

The onslaught of the dark monolith continued, the relentless booms of cannon fire and subsequent explosions not letting up. Large cracks now formed down the sides of the great structure, pieces of dark stone falling to the ground below. The tall spire wouldn't hold up much longer. *Where the heck are they? Donnie, get out of there!*

Ruka felt a stinging sensation on her cheek. She put a hand to her face and pulled it away, a bead of salty moisture sitting on her fingertips. *Tears? What in the world is happening to me?*

I'm a dragon! A Greymantle! Daughter of Yatharia and Rodric, pride of the Glittering Isles. I have long beautiful wings and bright shiny scales. I can soar through the skies with the greatest of ease, higher than the clouds. I can swim the deepest waters faster than any fish. I can call down the storms and breathe lightning as if it were air. So why in all Thac, do I feel so helpless right now?

The young dragon hung her head, no longer able to hold back the tears that streamed down her face. *Why do I feel so empty when he's not around?*

Ruka lifted the pale fleshy stump that served as a hand for these small creatures. She twisted it back and forth in front of her, staring at it with a fierce intensity. *Is it this body? This small weak, fleshy form? Have I been a human too long?*

Ruka struggled to fight back the tears. She wiped her arm across her face, drying her eyes as best she could. Suddenly something caught her eye—something red and silver shot out of the top of the monolith! Ruka sat forward on her branch, all else forgotten.

The dragon teen narrowed her eyes. It was two figures, one carrying the other. *Lloyd and Alana!*

Seconds later, three more forms flew out of the monolith. The blue one in the center carried a white figure and… a brown one! *Donnie…*

That had to be Elladan next to him, and that new guy, Cyclone, carrying them both. Moments later, a large amorphous creature shot out of the top of the spire. On its back sat three figures—one in red and black, a second garbed in purple, and a smaller form all in white. *Elistra, Glo, and Aksel.*

Ruka let out a long, deep sigh. That was all of them. They were safe. The dragon teen launched herself off the branch and fell to the ground below, landing with a soft *thud* on the forest floor. She gazed at the two young squires, still sitting up against the same tree, both staring at her with wild eyes.

Ruka's mouth twisted as she stood up. She motioned to them with a single hand as she strode off into the forest. "Come on. It looks like things are about to get interesting."

Martan watched in disbelief as the monolith began to crumble before him. His mind was numbed from all the crazy things he had seen today—strike that, the last few days. Ever since the company of knights had been massacred by that green dragon, Martan's view on reality had been turned upside down.

It astounded him that the dragon hunter had managed to get them by the great beast. He was further shocked to find out that Ruka was a dragon herself. It seemed almost beyond belief that Donatello was able to sweet-talk the green dragon into such a compromising position. Yet Martan was incredulous that he and his companions had killed the great beast where an entire company of knights had failed.

Martan thought he had seen it all at that point, but was yet again astonished when that floating ship appeared, carrying a princess from some foreign land. In his gut, he knew things would end badly, yet he was still surprised when she turned Elladan into a little grey bunny.

Against his better judgement, Martan almost shot the monarch, but that was when the invisible stalker began to hunt him. Martan never got a glimpse of whoever, or whatever it was, but he felt its presence nonetheless. The occasional sound that didn't fit in the woods, the silence of nearby wildlife, the odd flowery smell—all these things confirmed his suspicions.

The archer began a deadly game of hide and seek with his invisible foe, moving as silently as possible from place to place in the surrounding woods. His opponent was good—whenever Martan found a new place to hide, it would not take his stalker long to close in again.

Their game of hide-and-seek continued until Glolindir, Lloyd, and the dragon hunter showed up. The ensuing battle seemed to draw his stalker's attention away, but it was short-lived. As soon as the fight ended, it began tracking him again.

Martan considered showing himself at that point. The others had appeared to reach an agreement with the princess, but it was against Martan's nature to take risks. So, he continued to hide until the others left on those strange, ghostly horses. Martan followed, leaving the meadow behind, and thankfully his stalker as well.

It took Martan less than an hour to reach the monolith, but when he got there, there was no one in sight—neither the party nor the princess. Yet the airship had followed them as well, now hovering just above the tall black structure. Martan decided to keep to the forest, wondering what would happen next. His question was soon answered in a most chilling way, when the floating vessel opened up with cannon fire upon the monolith.

Martan's body went cold as he watched the tall structure begin to crumble. He could only assume that his companions were inside. The dour archer sat by, watching the wanton destruction helplessly from his hiding place in the trees. With no other recourse, Martan resorted to prayer. It was only the second time he had prayed in years, both in the last few days. Still, his first prayer had been answered in the form of Cyclone. So what could it hurt?

Goddess Synopei, I know I don't pray much, or really at all if I'm being honest, but if you are listening, please help my companions. They are good folk, a little strange at times, but their hearts are in the right place. Don't let them die like this, buried under all that rock.

Martan suddenly felt foolish. Would a goddess like Synopei really care what he thought? The dour archer shook his head, then abruptly went wide-eyed. Something shot out of the top of the monolith! It was red and silver. Martan narrowed his keen eyes. *That's Lloyd, and he's holding Alana!*

Moments later something brown, white, and blue flew out behind them. *That's Cyclone!* The dragon hunter was carrying Donatello and Elladan.

Not a second later, a huge bird-like creature shot out of the top of the spire. On its back sat three figures—one in red and black, a second garbed in purple, and a smaller form all in white. *Elistra, Glo, and Aksel!*

Martan let out a huge sigh. Somehow, by the grace of the gods, his prayers had been answered. An ironic smile crossed Martan's lips. *Perhaps there was something to this prayer stuff after all.*

Ruka and the two squires slipped swiftly through the dark forest, somehow managing to maintain their footing despite the ground shaking beneath them. The sounds of cannon fire and rumbling of stone echoed through the trees as they went. Though the thick foliage blocked her vision, Ruka pictured the rest of the monolith crumbling to the ground in her mind's eye. Even to a dragon, the thought of something that huge being demolished was staggering.

It took just under ten minutes for the trio to pass through the half-mile of woods. A few dozen yards from the clearing, Ruka threw her hand up and signaled for a halt.

The cannon fire had suddenly stopped. The sounds of crashing stone had also died down, replaced by only the occasional rumble. Ruka motioned for the squires to wait there, then slowly moved ahead through the brush.

At the edge of the clearing, the teen caught sight of a lone figure crouched behind a bramble of thickets. It was a dark-haired man garbed in brown and green leathers, a bow and quiver slung across his back.

Martan.

Ruka adjusted her course toward the solitary archer, swiftly drawing up next to him. As she did so, the trees parted, revealing the clearing beyond. The glade had all but disappeared, replaced with a towering cloud of black dust and smoke. The thick veil of dust rose high above the trees, blocking everything else from view. There was no sign of the monolith or her friends.

Ruka felt her throat tighten, and fought hard to choke back a sob. *Donnie…*

Abruptly she felt a light tap on her shoulder. Ruka turned her head toward Martan. The tracker wore a grim smile as he pointed to a spot off to their far left.

Ruka gazed past him, her keen eyes narrowing as they pierced through the thick black dust. About a hundred yards away, near the edge of the forest, a small group of figures huddled close behind the trees. Red, white, brown, purple, and blue, the familiar colors elicited a deep sigh from the young teen. *Thank the gods, they're alright.*

Ruka stood up and slipped past Martan, motioning for the tracker to follow. As the pair skirted around the edge of the clearing, the wind kicked up, swiftly dissipating the thick cloud.

Ruka's eyes went wide. The monolith was completely gone, in its place a high mass of broken black boulders. The immense pile spread out so wide that it nearly filled the once-open area. *That would have crushed anyone, even a dragon.*

Ruka and Martan had nearly closed the gap when the companions finally filtered out of the woods. Ruka's keen ears picked up their words.

"Well that was close," Donnie quipped. There was a slight quiver in the elf's voice that belied his attempt to be nonchalant.

Elladan brushed off a thick layer of black dust from his normally white outfit, his anger thinly veiled. "A little too close if you ask me."

Aksel, as usual, spoke in a calm tone, though he eyed the huge pile of black rubble with obvious trepidation. "Let's count our blessings. We're all alive and in one piece."

"No thanks to the Princess." Alana sounded more agitated than Elladan as she wiped off some black smudges from her silvery armor.

Ruka silently agreed with Aksel. *I'm just thankful you're all alive.*

It was strange how much these small people had come to mean to her in such a short time. They were not even of her species, but they felt more like family than her own in many ways. Maybe it was their bravery, or the way they all cared for each other. Perhaps it was merely their willingness to actually do something.

The dragons she grew up with were boring, stuffy, judgmental creatures, obsessed with protocol and ancient history. They were more likely to talk you to death than do anything to help themselves, let alone anyone else.

Ruka and Martan finally reached the section of forest behind their friends. They were just about to exit the woods when a strange voice made them both halt in their tracks.

"Now that wasn't very nice," a feminine voice said in a mildly accusing tone.

Ruka swept her gaze across the glade, settling on two forms, about twenty feet back in the direction they had just come from. Neither had been there when they had passed that point mere moments ago.

The first figure was a slim, pale-skinned woman with long, flaxen-blonde hair that reached almost down to her waist. She wore a long, tight-fitting black dress trimmed with gold designs and white ruffles. Yet despite its length, her dress managed to reveal great portions of the woman's skin.

Ruka's lips twisted sideways. *Nice outfit, lady. Looking for attention much?*

The woman's slim nose was slightly upturned, displaying both an air of dignity and offense at Alana's words. Ruka could only surmise that this questionably-dressed human female was the Princess Anya of Lanfor she'd been warned about.

Next to the Princess stood another woman with bronzed skin and a wild mane of curly red hair that dangled down to her shoulders. This other woman was garbed completely in scarlet, a tight-laced leather bodice over her long-sleeved dress and full skirt. Though unarmed, she carried herself with an air of supreme confidence.

A growl nearly escaped Ruka's lips. For some reason, she felt an immediate dislike for this woman in red.

Elladan was the first to respond, his head cocked to one side as he glared at the Princess. "Well, leaving us in the basement of the monolith wasn't very nice, either."

Alana drew up next to the bard, fixing the petulant monarch with a hard stare. "Not to mention nearly bringing it down on our heads."

Anya appeared unfazed by the accusations. Her demeanor remained cool as she waved a slim finger at the lady knight. "Nearly is the operative word… plus, I only used the starboard guns. I figured that would easily give folks as resourceful as you enough time."

Alana's eyes went wide as she mouthed the words, *Only the starboard guns…*

The lady knight appeared as if she were going to say something more, but Anya cut her off with a negligent wave of her hand. "Anyway, I did not come here to quibble. I am leaving shortly, and since you are now out in the middle of nowhere, I've decided to offer you a ride."

Ruka's eyebrows shot up in astonishment. *Is she daft?*

The young dragon girl swept her eyes around the group. Everyone appeared as shocked as she by the unexpected offer. Even the stoic Cyclone arched an eyebrow. Alana, however, exploded into a vehement rant.

"A ride? From you? Are you insane? Do we look stupid enough to get on a ship with someone who just tried to kill us?"

Once again, Anya seemed unperturbed by the lady knight's outburst. She gazed calmly around the group, a delicate smile slowly creeping across her dark pink lips. "Don't look now, good Dame, but I do believe your companions may not all agree with you."

Alana eyed the Princess darkly, before sweeping her gaze across the others. Ruka did so as well. Apart from Alana and Cyclone, the rest of the group wore mixed expressions.

Alana placed her hands squarely on her hips and gazed heatedly at her comrades. "You can't be serious. You want to go with her?

After what she did? Not to mention that evil creature she travels with."

The lady knight waved an armored hand at the woman in red next to Anya. Ruka narrowed her eyes as she returned her gaze to the scarlet-clad woman. *Evil creature?*

The truth dawned on her all at once. *Oh… she's a red!*

The sudden revelation explained Ruka's immediate dislike of the woman. Chromatic and metallic dragons had been sworn enemies for ages. It was so ingrained in them, that their scorn for each other had become a subconscious reaction.

No one responded at first.

Elistra, next to Glo, whispered something in the elf's ear. His eyes widened ever so slightly, then a strained smile spread across his lips. "The monolith and all that was in it is gone, but the Cult is still out there."

Lloyd drew up next to the tall elf and crossed his arms, his expression grim. "Glo's right. We can't leave Ravenford unguarded."

Aksel glanced briefly at Glo with a single eyebrow raised. The elf nodded to him almost imperceptibly. Aksel shrugged, then faced the agitated Alana with a wan expression. "I'm afraid I have to agree with Lloyd and Glo. The longer we take to get back, the more time the Cult has to plot its next move. Not to mention that Seth is out there on his own."

Alana eyed the trio sharply, then shifted her gaze toward Elladan. "What about you?"

The bard eyed the Princess dubiously, a single eyebrow raised. "Well, if she promises not to turn anyone into a bunny…"

A girl-like giggle escaped Anya's lips. She responded to the bard in a highly suggestive tone. "Ah, but Elladan, you were just *so* soft and cuddly."

Elladan's eyes softened as he gazed at the flirtatious Princess, his hardened resolve melting away. A familiar semi-smile abruptly spread across his lips.

Alana let out an exasperated huff, and turned her eyes instead toward Elistra. "Surely you don't agree with this lunacy."

Elistra pursed her lips together as she silently regarded the lady knight. When she finally answered, her tone was carefully measured. "While I am not a fan of the Princess, all things considered, the situation does call for expediency."

Alana's mouth dropped open ever so slightly. That was obviously not the reaction she had expected from the seeress. The lady knight swept her eyes around the rest of the group, her expression one of extreme frustration. "Well, you can all do whatever you want. I, for one, want nothing to do with this crazy Princess and her evil entourage!"

With that, the lady knight spun on her heel and stormed off into the woods, walking almost headlong into the hiding Ruka and Martan. The dragon girl swiftly backed further into the trees, holding up a single finger to her mouth. Alana came to a quick halt without saying a word.

Meanwhile, Anya ignored Alana's declaration, amiably addressing those still in the clearing. "Well, my ship leaves in an hour. If you wish to join me, meet me in the meadow south of here."

Ruka stepped silently around Alana, and peered out through the trees. The Princess and her dragon friend had disappeared, leaving the party alone to talk amongst themselves.

Ruka spun back around and motioned for Alana and Martan to follow her. She led the pair further into the woods, back to where she had left the squires. After a quick reunion, she spoke to Alana.

"I couldn't agree with you more. They are fools to go along with the Princess."

Alana's shoulders relaxed, a grim smile spreading across her lips. "Thank you. At least someone besides me sees reason."

Ruka let out a small sigh. She did agree with the lady knight. Traveling on a ship full of chromatic dragons, and someone who could enslave them, was dangerous at best. Yet she also understood the others' concerns.

She, Maya, and Cal could fly out of these woods in less than a day. The others could not soar through the air like she and her people could. They were earth-bound, and thus stuck in these dark woods. Nor did she and Cal have time to ferry them all out of here. They had to start looking for Ves soon or the trail might run cold.

Ruka paused to scan the thick forest around them. There had been no sign of the horses back in the glade, nor out here in the woods. Without them, it might take the others a week just to get back to Vermoorden. She really didn't want them going on that ship. Yet, if they did, she wanted someone with them who would not be easily swayed by the Princess.

Seth was gone, and Elladan seemed just a bit too smitten with Anya. Donnie, Lloyd, Aksel, and Glo were too good-natured, and Elistra had done nothing to dissuade them. As for Cyclone, the dragon hunter was still too much of an unknown to trust.

Ruka took a deep breath, then carefully explained her concerns to both Alana and Martan. She finished with her pitch. "If they are going on that ship, someone with sense needs to keep an eye on them. I would do it, but I would be taking a huge risk, and Maya would want to follow me…"

Alana held up an armored hand, stopping her in mid-sentence. "Say no more. You cannot put your family in such danger, and anyway, you need to find your sister. So, I will go with them… but on one condition."

Ruka cocked her head to one side and eyed the lady knight curiously. "And what's that?"

"I won't have Lamorn or Syndir setting one foot on that evil ship. I was going to take them back to the Wind Tower, the home of our order, but…"

This time Ruka interrupted Alana. "Not a problem. Since it's just the two of them, Cal and I can carry them to Vermoorden. From there they can travel by horse."

A slight smile graced Alana's lips—she was rather pretty when she smiled. "As you say, someone with sense needs to keep an eye on them."

Ruka let out an ironic laugh. It still amazed her, the level of feeling she had for this little group, especially for Donnie. If the dragons back home only knew, they would call her crazy. *Who am I kidding, they already think I'm crazy.*

The dragon girl shifted her eyes to Martan.

The dour archer stood there wearing a gloomy expression. "Not sure how much sense I have, getting involved in all this in the first place… but as you said, someone needs to keep an eye on them."

Alana clasped the humble tracker on the shoulder. "You're a good man, Martan."

Martan turned a skeptical eye toward the lady knight. "Not exactly sure about that, but I'll do what I can."

Ruka's mouth curved into a lopsided smile. "Anyway, let's get back to the others before they decide to leave without us."

When they arrived back at the clearing, the others were still there discussing what to do. As soon as Ruka broached the treeline, Donnie came rushing over to her. "Ruka!"

The thin elf wrapped his arms around her and hugged her tight, slowly rocking her back and forth. Ruka felt a sudden warmth flow up through her body, and into her cheeks. She imagined her face to be as red as that dragon lady's dress.

She nearly lost herself in Donnie's warm embrace, the smell of his body having an almost intoxicating effect on her. Yet, her anxiety pushed back on those feelings, leading the teen to gently extract herself from the object of her desire. "I'm fine, Donnie. Really."

She took a step back from him, hardly able to wipe the stupid smile off her face. *Damn. Why do I have to be so attracted to him?*

Aksel strode up to them as well, sweeping his eyes from Ruka to Alana. "We're glad to see you… all of you."

Ruka glanced around the clearing and attempted to hide her discomfort with sarcasm. It had become a standard defense mechanism for the dragon teen, especially when dealing with her feelings. "What, I'm gone for like a day and you go and blow up the entire monolith?"

Alana, standing next to her, let out a derisive snort.

Elladan gazed at her with a warm smile, half-laughing as he responded. "Now hold on there, little lady. Don't go blaming us for this mess."

Before Ruka could say a word, Alana stepped forward and answered for her. "She knows. I already told her the whole story."

Aksel gave the lady knight a firm nod. "Good, that'll save us time."

Donnie, however, eyed Alana carefully, seeming far less certain than Aksel. "What exactly did you tell her?"

Ruka forced herself to smirk at the handsome elf. *Damn, why do you have to be so darned cute!*

"She told me you idiots were thinking of flying away with the Princess... the same Princess who nearly brought the monolith down on your heads."

"Yup, that about sums it up," a gruff voice agreed with her. Cyclone stood off to one side, his arms folded across his chest.

Donnie peered at Ruka, his lower lip sticking out ever so slightly. "Did she at least tell you why we were thinking of going with the Princess?"

Stop that, Ruka thought to herself. *How am I supposed to maintain my tough demeanor when you do such adorable things?*

"Oh, I told her," Alana answered for Ruka. "She still agrees with me that you are idiots."

Elistra stepped between them all, a strange expression on the seeress' face. "Don't blame them—it's my fault."

Ruka cocked her head to one side and stared at Elistra in disbelief. "You?"

The seeress nodded, her expression turning grave. "I had a dire premonition. I can't explain it, but I know that we must get on that ship."

Alana's mouth dropped open. The lady knight stood there speechless at Elistra's surprising confession.

Ruka narrowed an eye at the seeress, not sure what to make of her pronouncement. Ruka was well aware of the power of prophecy—a particularly dark one hung over her own head. In fact, it was one of the reasons she was shunned by her own people.

Elladan, ever the peacemaker, strolled up next to the seeress and placed an arm around her shoulder. A familiar half- smile graced the handsome bard's face. "Just remember, keep your friends close and your enemies..."

Alana, her expression suddenly bemused, placed an armored hand on the bard's shoulder before he could finish. "It's fine, Elladan. We already decided that Martan and I are going with you all."

"You did?" came the surprised reply from Elladan, Donnie and Aksel in unison.

Alana cast a quick glance at Elistra. "Far be it from me to ignore a premonition from our illustrious seeress."

Elistra tilted her head toward the lady knight, a thin smile on her lips.

Alana then went into a brief explanation of her discussion with Ruka and Martan. She ended with the dragons' need to search for Ves.

Glo turned his gaze to Ruka, his eyes filled with more than a touch of concern. "Why? What happened to your sister?"

Aksel answered him before Ruka had a chance to speak. "With all the commotion, I nearly forgot. Their home was attacked by a flight of chromatic dragons. Ves led them off, but hasn't been heard from since."

"A flight of chromatic…" Glo began, but then stopped and peered up into the sky.

Ruka followed his gaze toward the Princess Anya's airship. The vessel was already over the forest south of them on its short journey to the southern meadow. Ruka had to admit, ever since she heard about the Princess, she wondered whether she was involved in the attack on the Glittering Isles. Still, her home was a long way from here, and there was also that black knight who could control dragons.

Either way, she and Cal had reached an agreement. Their best bet was to retrace Ves' steps, hoping they might find a clue as to her whereabouts.

Ruka abruptly found herself blushing as Donnie closed the gap between them once more. The charming elf grabbed her hand and gazed down at her with those big blue eyes of his. "I promise you, Ruka, if Anya had anything to do with the disappearance of your sister, we will find out."

Ruka looked away from his gaze, and stammered a reply. "Th– thank you, Donnie."

Inwardly she cursed herself. *Get a grip on yourself, dragon. Stop acting like some weak little girl.*

She forced herself to look back up into his eyes, but her knees went weak once more. Thankfully, Cal and Maya chose that moment to reappear.

Her younger sister came traipsing into the clearing, her eyes as wide as saucers as she stared at the huge pile of black rubble.

"Cool…" the single word fell from her lips.

"Trust me, kid. It wasn't so cool on the inside."

Maya spun around and stared up at Cyclone. The normally impassive hunter gazed down at her with what was almost a smile.

Maya looked Cyclone up and down, a wide grin spreading across her lips. "Ohhhh… you must be Donatello."

Her eyes positively glittered as she peered over at Ruka. "No wonder you like him."

Ruka pushed Donnie away from her, her cheeks suddenly feeling as if they were on fire. Elladan, a pearly grin on his face, strolled over and knelt in front of Maya.

"That's not Donnie… that's Donnie." The bard pointed toward the sandy-haired elf.

Maya peered past Elladan, the smile abruptly fading from her cherub features. "Oh. Then I don't get it."

Elladan burst into laughter. He was joined by Glo, Elistra, and Alana. Even Lloyd and Aksel were smiling.

Ruka glared at her younger sister. *I'm going to kill her.*

Thankfully, Cal chose that moment to interject with his deep rumbling voice. "Much as I am a fan of merriment, we really need to be on our way."

Aksel gave the coppery dragon a curt nod. "As do we."

Ruka cast a furtive glance at Donnie, then strode over and grasped Maya firmly by the wrist. "Come on, short stuff—before you give away any more secrets."

Maya squealed in protest as Ruka marched off with her. "What did I say? You do like him, don't you?"

Ruka declined to comment. She led her sister away from the others, and commanded her to change into her natural form. After a brief explanation to Cal about the squires, Ruka followed suit.

Alana led the squires over, Lamorn and Syndir seemingly reluctant at first. At the lady knight's insistence, they each picked a dragon, and scrambled up until they were firmly seated on Cal's and Ruka's backs. Alana strode back a few steps and called up to them, "Godspeed."

The rest of the companions gathered around the lady knight, wishing them luck as well. Donnie in particular waved and smiled that charming smile that made Ruka melt. "Take care of yourself, Ruka! May a star shine in the hour of our next meeting!"

Ruka recognized the formal elven salutation. It was supposed to imply that they would meet again sometime in the near future.

The three dragons slowly lifted off, keeping low to the trees so as not to be spotted. Ruka cast one last look down at the sandy-haired elf, then shot out over the forest with Cal and Maya, silently wondering to herself if she would ever see him again.

20
ABOARD THE WIND HAMMER

Family? Anya is my only family. I need no other

The small company reached the southern meadow just as the airship lifted off. Upon seeing them, the ship halted its departure, settling back to the ground so their party could board. As Glo stepped onto the airship, he carefully swept his eyes around the deck. He had to admit, it was rather impressive. From aft to stern, Glo estimated the vessel to be about two hundred feet in length, and probably about a quarter of that from port to starboard.

Much like a sailing ship, the airship was divided into multiple sections. There was the main deck where they currently stood, the forecastle, and the sterncastle. Yet unlike a seagoing vessel, there were no masts or sails above them. Instead, there were three long fins that jutted out in a triangular shape from the top and sides of the hull. The tips of those fins generated the elemental ring that propelled the ship.

Glo also took note of the large cannons dispersed across the vessel. There were two mounted near the rail not far from them, two across the main deck, and one mounted up at the bow. Anya had said there were six altogether, so Glo assumed the last one was fitted to the stern of the ship.

The party was ushered aboard by three people they had not met before. One was a thin young man in dark leathers, with a hawk nose, dark hair, and dark eyes. The second, a pale youth with white hair and icy blue eyes, wore a puffy white shirt and white leather pants. The last was a pretty young blonde garbed in a brilliant blue dress, with electric blue eyes. None wore weapons of any kind. All three studied the companions with keen intensity as they led them across the deck.

Donnie, walking between Cyclone and Alana, whispered to the stoic hunter. "I suppose those are more dragons?"

"Duh," Cyclone acknowledged with the barest of nods.

As they approached the sterncastle, Anya exited the door from below decks, her entourage from the meadow in tow. The Princess welcomed them with genuine glee. "I wasn't sure you were going to accept my invitation. I'm very glad you did."

The monarch's eyes swept over them all, finally settling on Elladan.

The bard exchanged a brief glance with Aksel, then stepped in front of the rest and executed a lavish bow. "How could we resist such a gracious invitation?"

Though Anya seemed delighted to see them, her entourage was another matter. They fanned out beside her, the blue-robed Sigfus practically hanging over the Princess. The wizard openly scowled at Elladan, brooding at the way Anya eyed the handsome bard.

The scarlet-clad Mallona had positioned herself on the opposite side from Sigfus, her malevolent gaze fixed on Cyclone. The dragon hunter returned her stare unflinchingly, his muscular arms folded across his chest.

Anya's cleric had situated herself next to Sigfus. Still adorned in her formfitting white and gold robes, she eyed Alana curiously, her hand resting on the golden sword hilt that hung at her waist. Next to the cleric stood the slim woman in brown and green leathers, her long bow slung over one shoulder. Her green eyes fixated on Glo, a fact that made the elven mage more than a little nervous.

On the other side of Mallona stood the fit woman dressed in black-studded leather, an ornate sword strapped to each hip. She stared at Lloyd with an almost feral intensity, as if prepared to pounce on him at any moment. The young warrior regarded her with a practiced ease, though his hands never strayed far from his own sword hilts.

Anya finally tore her eyes from Elladan, spreading her arms wide as she addressed her guests. "Welcome aboard the *Wind Hammer*. My apologies, but we are not currently set up for passengers. Normally a vessel this size could hold up to seventy, but the ship has been 'modified' for use by the royal family of Lanfor."

Other than the cannon, Glo had observed no obvious signs of modifications on the upper decks. *What, does she have cages for her dragons down below?*

The elven wizard cast a brief glance at Elistra, but the seeress' paid him no heed, instead gazing with a fierce intensity at the Princess. It appeared almost as if she were trying to read Anya's mind.

"That's alright, your highness," Donnie chimed in glibly. "Some of us have traveled on ships before. A simple hammock would be more than fine."

Anya's amber eyes fell upon the sandy-haired elf, her lips curling into a sickly-sweet smile. "Oh, no, no, no. That will never do."

She barely turned her head toward Sigfus as she issued the mage a command. "Have the area below the quarterdeck cleared for our guests."

Sigfus cast a dark look at the companions, his tone shrill as he responded to the Princess. "But, your majesty… what about the crew?"

Anya responded with a negligent wave. "Move them down to the main cabin on the lower deck."

Sigfus jaw went abruptly slack. "B–but your majesty… that's where I sleep!"

Anya spun around to face the disgruntled wizard, a slim hand going to either hip. "And that's my problem how, exactly?"

Anya's cheeks had turned a slight shade of red. Sigfus took an involuntary step back from the angered monarch, nearly colliding with the cleric behind him. His voice altered to a placating tone in response to her ire. "It–it's not, your majesty. I'll just find somewhere else to bunk for the duration."

Anya glared at him a moment or two longer, then spat out a single word. "Good!"

The irked monarch turned back to her guests, her angry expression transforming into a pleasant facade as if she were changing masks. "Well, now that that's settled, I have important matters to attend to. In my absence, feel free to roam the deck."

Anya gave them all a saccharine smile, then spun on her heel and strode for the door below decks. "Oh, but do avoid the cannon," she called over her shoulder. "I wouldn't want anyone to get… hurt."

Sigfus shot them all one last glare, then took off after the Princess. The rest of her entourage followed suit, each in turn eyeing the companions darkly.

Glo and the others were left on the main deck with the three dragon youths to 'escort' them. The elven wizard decided to pay them little heed. *I still don't trust this Princess of Lanfor, but it's not like we're planning on trashing her vessel in retribution.*

Above and around them, the great blue ring flared to life. A few moments later, the *Wind Hammer* finally lifted off.

With not much else to do, Glo made his way to the nearest railing for a better view. The rest of his comrades followed, Elistra planting herself on his left, and Elladan on his right. Lloyd and Cyclone did so as well, but both propped their backs against the rail, not taking an eye off their silent dragon escorts.

The tall elf leaned heavily over the rail, watching with mixed emotions as the meadow slowly receded away. Ruka was gone now, just like Seth. A deep furrow creased his brow as he thought about their halfling friend. It had been nearly two days since Seth had taken off after that black mage. With all that had transpired, there had been no time to contact him, but Aksel said he would try first thing in the morning.

The airship soon rose above the clouds, leaving the Darkwoods far below. It slowly turned east, the late afternoon sun now behind them. As the airborne vessel effortlessly plowed its way through the sky, Glo silently wondered to himself, *just what in Thac have we gotten ourselves into?*

A short while later, the area below the quarterdeck had been cleared per Anya's orders. It turned out to be one large cabin, the entire length and breadth of the quarterdeck, with separate bunks for each crew member. A long wooden galley table ran down its center, with benches of equal length on either side.

The party stored their gear there, and then took turns roaming the upper deck in groups of two or three. Elistra joined Glo, the couple strolling around arm in arm as if on some pleasure cruise.

As they started out, Glo immediately noted two men standing guard in front of the door below decks. Both wore deep purple naval uniforms laced with golden trim. They were the same color as the Lanfor flag, thus Glo assumed they were crew members, and not dragons.

Each group that roamed the decks was escorted by at least one dragon in human form. The young blonde in blue chose to follow Glo and Elistra. She was rather quiet at first, but after a while the seeress managed to draw her into a conversation. Her full name turned out be nearly unpronounceable, so she shortened it for them.

"It's Ysauraithus, but you can call me Ysa if that's easier for you."

Glo watched with clear admiration as Elistra worked her magic on the dragon girl. Before long they were chatting as if long-lost girlfriends. Elistra had let go of Glo, and now walked arm in arm with Ysa as they continued their stroll toward the front of the ship.

Glo trailed behind the two ladies, listening with one ear as he swept his eyes carefully across the deck. Other than the companions and their escorts, the upper decks were empty. The only additional people in sight were solitary figures watching over the large cannons.

Much like their escorts, these people were garbed in fine clothes of the shades blue, black, and white. Obviously more dragons in human form, they appeared a bit older than their escorts. Where Ysa and her comrades seemed like very young teens, these others appeared somewhere between Ruka and Ves in age.

Again, like their escorts, the cannon guards were comprised of two males and one female. Yet within this group, the white dragon was the female. Her long white hair had an almost silvery sheen to it, perfectly matched by a glittering white dress draped so perfectly over her tall, lithe figure. As the three of them approached, the older dragon teen motioned for them to keep moving along.

Once they were passed, Ysa spoke in a confidential tone to Elistra. "That's Irovnia. Did you see how her dress sparkles? I wish I could get mine to do that."

Ysa's young features turned into a pout. Elistra patted the young dragon girl softly on the hand. "There, there. Shape-shifting is an art, my dear. You're very pretty, you know. Give it time and I'm sure you'll get the hang of the dress as well."

Ysa's cheeks flushed pink. "You really think I'm pretty?"

Elistra shrewdly regarded the young dragon. "Why of course, dear. Doesn't Anya tell you so?"

Ysa fervently shook her head. "Oh no, no, no. No one is as pretty as the Princess. Not even Mallona, and she's her favorite."

Elistra cast a brief glance at Glo, then spoke softly to Ysa. "How long have you known Anya, dear?"

Ysa's brow furrowed slightly at the question. "Why, as far back as I can remember."

Elistra's violet eyes narrowed. "What about your family?"

Ysa's eyes suddenly went blank, her voice becoming hollow. "Family? Anya is my only family. I need no other. Anya loves me. She takes care of all my needs."

Elistra peered sharply at Glo. The elven wizard returned her gaze, as mystified as she. It was almost as if the dragon girl were hypnotized, but that was supposed to be impossible with dragons. *Impossible for anyone but the Dragon Thrall Master.*

Abruptly, they passed Aksel and Lloyd, the pair being followed by the hawk-nosed young dragon escort. The youth in black eyed Ysa and Elistra with clear concern.

Elistra must have seen it as well. Glo heard her whisper to Ysa. "Don't look now, but I think your friend over there disapproves of us."

Ysa suddenly came out of her trance, her electric-blue eyes shifting in the direction of the hawk-nosed man-dragon. A bell-like giggle escaped her lips, all evidence of her former state gone. She leaned close to Elistra and spoke in a hushed voice. "That's Munwithurix. Pay no attention to him. He's a party pooper."

Elistra grinned at her co-conspirator as they continued past the glaring young dragon.

The threesome eventually wound their way past the bow and then toward the aft of the vessel. Up on the quarterdeck, Glo observed the captain at the helm with the pilot and the navigator.

Ysa cautioned them to give the helm a wide birth "for their own safety." When she spoke those words, her voice once again took on a hollow tone.

Glo arched an eyebrow as he exchanged yet another glance with Elistra. It seemed far more than mere hypnosis. *It's almost as if she's been brainwashed.*

Elistra seemed to catch his thought, responding with a barely perceptible nod.

Glo knew that chromatic dragons were supposed to be evil, but Ysa seemed pleasant enough. Perhaps the scholars had it all wrong. Maybe chromes were not inherently evil, but were in fact raised as such. Either way, the apparent brainwashing of the young dragon girl was a definite strike against Anya in his book.

As Glo suspected, the last mage cannon was mounted at the aft of the airship. Yet unlike the others, this one stood unguarded. Ysa stopped them before they could get too close, once again parroting those hollow-sounding words about "their safety."

Elistra expertly steered them away from the cannon, while asking Ysa a pointed question. "Shouldn't someone be guarding that cannon?"

Ysa cocked her head to one side. "That's normally Karnikogth's job, but he's out on an errand for the Princess."

The young dragon girl's brow furrowed. "It is strange though that he hasn't returned yet."

Glo narrowed his eyes as he gazed at Ysa. "Tell me, dear, what color is your friend?"

Ysa responded with a derisive snort. "Friend? Karnikogth is no one's friend. He thinks he's better than everyone else."

The young girl's hand abruptly went to her mouth. "Oh, I'm sorry. I shouldn't talk that way about my fellow dragons. We are all Anya's family, after all."

Glo and Elistra both smiled at the young dragon teen.

"That's okay, dear," Elistra said in a comforting tone. "Even family sometimes has their differences."

Glo gazed at the seeress curiously. Her voice had taken on a clear tone of irony with that last statement. Elistra never talked about her family, but perhaps like him, she had issues with hers.

His thoughts were interrupted by Ysa. "Green."

His mind a million miles away, Glo peered at Ysa uncomprehendingly. "What was that again?"

"You had asked about Karnikogth's color. It's green."

"Ohhhh." The word passed through Glo's lips as his mouth dropped open. *A green dragon that Anya had sent out, but that hasn't returned?*

Glo's eyes suddenly went wide. *The one we killed back at the monolith!*

The elven wizard peered guiltily at Ysa, but thankfully she hadn't noticed his reaction. Elistra had smoothly drawn the young teen's attention away. *So, that was Anya's dragon. She must have sent it ahead of her airship.*

A feeling of dread abruptly came over Glo. Had Anya ordered the dragon to kill whoever it found at the monolith, or had it been acting of its own accord? Anya seemed more reckless than cold-blooded, and, as Lloyd had pointed out, she was the Princess of a well-renown nation.

Perhaps someone else had given the order. Maybe Sigfus? The wizard had tried to kill Donnie with a spell.

Either Anya had less control over her dragons than she thought, or someone in Anya's retinue was a killer—someone who could order her dragons around. Whatever the case might be, Glo and his friends were all in extreme danger.

Later that evening, the companions reconvened in their cabin for dinner. Anya proved once again to be a gracious host, serving them a sumptuous, multi-course meal. Glo's appetite was quite sated when they were finished, yet it had done little to quell his apprehension.

After dinner, Aksel motioned for them all to remain seated. He then asked Elladan to play them some "nice" music.

Elladan responded with a knowing smile. A golden lute suddenly appeared in the bard's hands, his fingertips dancing as they gently strummed the strings. Soothing music spread out across the room, each note laced with bardic magic. Glo could practically feel the web of sound being slowly woven in the air around them.

After a few stanzas, a partial smile graced the bard's lips. "There, that should keep us from being overheard."

Aksel thanked Elladan, then proceeded to share observations with everyone in the group. No one had seen Anya, Sigfus, or the rest of her entourage since the party had first come aboard. For unknown reasons, the Princess and her followers had sequestered themselves to the lower decks.

The discussion then turned to the upper decks. They talked about the guards to the door below decks, the mage cannons, the dragons guarding them, and their dragon escorts.

Glo and Elistra shared with the others what they had found out from Ysa. The pair went into detail about the dragon girl's hypnotic reaction to certain questions.

When they were done, Aksel sat quietly rubbing his chin. "It does appear as if Anya's control over the dragons only exerts itself in certain situations."

The gnome got up and started pacing around. "If that control isn't constant, perhaps some external means was used to condition the dragons."

Aksel shifted his gaze toward Elistra. "You're the expert on this. What do you think?"

Elistra sat back in her seat while placing a slim finger on her chin. "I think... that would explain a lot."

The seeress sat forward again, sweeping her violet eyes around the room. "Ever since we came on board, I've been sensing some very powerful psionic emanations. If what Aksel suggests were to exist, it would have to be very potent indeed. As I've said before, the will of a dragon is a tremendous thing, and it is not easily bent."

Donnie shot up from his seat, and slammed a hand down on the table. "Well that cinches it. Anya is definitely up to something with these brainwashed dragons. I say we should check out the lower decks. Whatever Elistra is sensing has to be down there."

"Does that mean you're volunteering?" A wry smile crossed Elladan's lips as he stared innocently at the slight elf.

Donnie shifted his gaze toward his elven friend, his expression resolute. "As a matter of fact, I am."

Alana, quiet up 'til now, stood up and placed a hand on Donnie's shoulder. Her eyes were filled with extreme concern. "I'm not sure that is such a good idea. Anya and all her cronies are down there. The chances of you being spotted are too great."

Donnie turned to face the lady knight, his expression melting as he took her hand into his own. "I greatly appreciate your concern, my dear, but I am rather good at sneaking around… and anyway, Glo can make me invisible again."

"You still need to watch out for Sigfus. You were invisible last time, but he still managed to spot you," Elladan reminded his friend.

"Duly noted," Donnie replied with a grateful nod to the elven bard.

Aksel softly cleared his throat, drawing everyone's attention back to him. "I have to agree with Donnie—it does appear that Anya is up to something with these chromatic dragons. I also believe it a good idea that we clandestinely search out the lower decks, for any evidence of her plans or the possible mechanism of her control. But perhaps it would be best to wait a while. The later it is, the more likely everyone will be in their cabins."

Donnie responded with a slow nod. "That's probably true. Still, Anya is unpredictable. It would be better if she were distracted…"

The wiry elf wore a sly look as his eyes turned to Elladan. "She seems to like you. Maybe you can keep her entertained?"

Elladan cocked his head to one side, and fixed Donnie with an acerbic stare. "Sure, why not? Maybe she can turn me into a bunny again, and we can play hop scotch."

The conversation broke down after that. Everyone went to their bunks except Lloyd, Cyclone, and Alana. The trio sat quietly at the long table, sharpening their weapons.

Somewhere just before midnight, there was a knock on the cabin door. Everyone gathered around as Lloyd went to open it. A single guard stood there and announced, "the Princess requests Elladan's presence."

Donnie fixed Elladan with a sly grin. "See, I told you."

Elladan cast a prickly smile at his elven friend, then gathered his cloak and headed for the doorway.

"Lead the way," he motioned to the guard as he pulled the door closed behind him.

21
LOVE IS IN THE AIR

She spun on her heel, bent down, and kissed the elf
on his full, luscious lips

Alana watched with a growing sense of dread as the cabin door closed behind Elladan. Sure enough, as soon as he was gone, her worst fears came to fruition.

Donnie turned to Glo and rubbed his hands together. "Shall we get started?"

Alana thought she would have to intervene, but thankfully the sensible Aksel came to the rescue. The little cleric put his hands up in front of him and made a halting motion. "I'm not so sure that's a good idea just yet. Let's give it a bit longer, just to be on the safe side."

Donnie grudgingly gave in, the thin elf slowly trudging over to his cot and throwing himself on it like he had been reprimanded. Alana let out a soft sigh. The crisis had been averted for the moment, but she knew it wouldn't last forever.

Unable to sleep, the lady knight offered to take the first watch.

She sat at the long table, praying to her god, Cormar, for both patience and guidance in this absurd situation. Alana did not trust Anya, or anyone else on board for that matter. Glo and Elistra seemed to think that the young dragon girl, Ysa, was alright, but Alana knew better. She was a chromatic dragon, and all chromes, as Ruka called them, were evil.

The lady knight fervently wished her companions had listened to her and not gotten on board this airship, but that was water under the bridge. They were here now, and Ruka had tasked her with watching out for their friends. Alana swore to herself, come hell or high water, she would do just that.

The lady knight swept her eyes around the cabin. Silence had fallen over the large room, the rest of her comrades now asleep. Even Donnie had finally closed his eyes, though he seemed rather restless, fidgeting in his cot.

Elladan followed the guard down a steep flight of stairs to the lower deck. The stairwell ended on one side of a long corridor that ran the entire length of the ship. The hallway was lined with numerous cabins, culminating on either end in an ironbound wooden door.

The guard strode straight ahead toward the stern of the ship, motioning for Elladan to follow. The elven bard stayed close behind the man, counting the number of cabins as he went. There were six in total on the one side, though on the other he counted only four.

One door stood apart from the others, encompassing the same area as three cabins. Elladan assumed that was the 'main' cabin Anya had referred to earlier—the one from which she had evicted the smug wizard, Sigfus. A slight chuckle passed Elladan's lips as he recalled the wizard's shocked expression.

When they reached the door at the end of the corridor, the guard signaled for a halt. On closer inspection, Elladan observed it was not a plain ironbound door. The iron wrought carvings twisted and curved into flowery, ornate patterns up and down its length.

The guard raised a hand and tentatively knocked on the ornate door. At first there was no answer, then the familiar voice of the Princess sounded from behind it. "Yes?"

The guard nervously cleared his throat. "I have brought the bard Elladan as you commanded, my lady."

"Send him in," came the immediate response.

The guard opened the door and gestured for Elladan to step inside. As Elladan stepped through the threshold, Anya's voice sounded once more. "Oh, and I am not to be disturbed further this night."

Elladan cast a side-long glance at the guard, but the man's expression remained impassive. The bard silently wondered if he were used to the Princess 'entertaining' guests in her private chambers.

As the door closed behind him, Elladan took in his surroundings. He stood in a short, lushly carpeted corridor with two doors on either side, and a wide archway at the other end. The arch opened to a large room with a long table, covered with maps from end to end. A huge window framed the back wall, ornate purple curtains with gold trim drawn across its width.

Anya's voice came from the open door to his right. "Elladan, care to join me?"

The elven bard took a few steps forward and peered through the open doorway. Beyond the door stood a luxurious room, decorated in gold and purple, with a large four-poster bed set against the opposite wall. His eyes swiftly fell on the Princess, his heart nearly skipping a beat.

Anya lay draped across the bed in a silky black crossover nightgown with gold lace edging. The gown had two thin straps that practical fell off the monarch's creamy white shoulders, revealing far more of her bosom than before, if that were possible. As if that weren't enough, the bottom of her gown was spread open wide, displaying Anya's shapely legs well past her upper thighs.

Elladan took a deep breath, forcing himself to retain his composure. "Thank you for the invite, my lady. I thought you might have forgotten about me."

Anya sat up and gave the bard a smoldering stare, her one strap falling dangerously down her arm. "Oh Elladan… how could I possibly forget about someone as handsome as you?"

A tiny laugh escaped her lips as she eyed the bard with blatant desire. Elladan felt his temperature rising, yet continued to meet her eyes, his tone smooth and low. "You are hard to forget as well, my lady."

The flirtatious princess waved an arm at a small table next to her bed, playing further havoc with the straps of her gown. "Would you like something to drink?"

Elladan wasn't quite sure just how much more of this he could take. He didn't really trust Anya. At best, she was crazy. Yet, crazy or not, Anya was a beautiful woman, and his resolve was swiftly fading. The bard tore his eyes away from the exquisite princess, observing what appeared to be a full decanter of red wine on the table. Two empty glasses sat next to it.

Thankful for something else to focus on, the elven bard strode for the little table. "I'll pour us some wine."

"That would be lovely," Anya purred, laying back down upon the bed.

Elladan poured a small sample into his glass and swirled it around, sniffing the wine's bouquet. It had a fruity smell to it. He lifted the glass to his lips and tasted a sip of the red liquid. It was indeed fruity, with a hint of a smoky aftertaste.

"This is quite good," he called over his shoulder.

"I'm glad you like it," Anya responded. "It's from my family's personal vineyards."

Elladan filled both glasses halfway, then steeled himself as he spun around. Anya lay across the bed with even more skin exposed than before. Elladan had thought to take out his lute, and delay things with a tune or two, but now he realized there was no keeping Anya at bay.

Well, Donnie asked me to keep the Princess entertained.

Elladan climbed onto the bed next to Anya and handed her a glass of wine. She sat up partway and took the glass, her entire top finally giving in to gravity. Elladan took a sip from his own glass, then gave her one of his most charming smiles, resigning the rest of the night to fate.

A couple of hours passed when Donnie's eyes snapped open

again. The wiry elf sat up and glanced around, then stole over to where Alana sat. He leaned in close, querying her in a soft voice. "Any sign of Elladan?"

Alana shook her head. "He has not returned."

Donnie gave her a short nod, then quietly went over to wake Aksel. Alana followed close behind. The little cleric woke and sat up, still somewhat bleary-eyed. He gazed up at Alana and stretched, asking with a half-yawn, "What time is it?"

Alana folded her arms across her chest. "About two in the morning."

Aksel, still somewhat fuzzy-headed, half-mumbled, "I guess that's enough time…"

Donnie immediately took that as a 'yes' to go ahead. "Good. I'll get Glo."

The slight elf spun on his heel, but Alana immediately stepped in his way. If Aksel was too tired to think straight, she would have to reign in the impetuous elf herself. "Invisible, or not, how do you intend to get past the guards? The moment you open the door, they'll know something is up."

Donnie halted in his tracks, and gazed up at her questioningly with those light blue eyes. His answer was glib as usual. "I'm sure I'll think of something."

The thin elf went to step around her, when Alana reached out and grabbed him by the arm. She thought he might react this way and had prayed for a solution. Luckily, Cormar was feeling exceptionally generous this night. He had given her an idea that would most definitely work on both Donnie and the two male soldiers guarding the door below decks.

"I've already thought of something," Alana told him, turning toward the doorway and dragging him with her.

"Alana, wait!" Donnie hissed. "Just what do you have—"

He never got to finish his words. She spun on her heel, bent down, and kissed the elf on his full, luscious lips. She had intended to merely shut him up, but nearly lost herself in the moment.

Donnie's mouth was warm to the touch, and his scent was heady at this close proximity. Alana wanted nothing more than to drink him in, but she forced herself to pull away. When she spoke, her tone was far firmer than she felt. "That will be our cover."

Donnie gazed up at her with a boyish grin. "Oh. That will work."

Alana merely nodded, not trusting herself to say more. That short, simple kiss had left butterflies in her stomach. She quietly led Donnie out the door and onto the main deck of the *Wind Hammer*.

It was warm outside, a gentle breeze blowing across the deck on this clear mid-summer night. The inky blackness of the night sky was alight with the stars of numerous constellations. Yet their light was drowned out by the incandescent blue of the elemental ring that spun high above their heads. Its bright glow cast an eerie sheen across the flying vessel.

The main deck was clear at this late hour, except for two figures leaning casually on either side of the door that led below. Both figures snapped to attention as soon as Alana and Donnie stepped out onto the deck.

Not missing a beat, Donnie gave the naval men a smooth nod, then wove his arm through Alana's and led her over to the rail. Once there, Donnie gazed up at her, his expression only partially visible in the dim blue light. When he spoke, his voice was barely above a whisper. "I owe you an apology."

Alana wanted to chastise him for his behavior earlier, but the thin elf suddenly moved in closer, wrapping both arms around her waist. He was surprisingly strong for one of his slight stature.

Alana answered carefully, not trusting her own voice. "Apology... accepted."

The handsome young elf pulled her even closer, then leaned in, his head tilting ever so slightly. Without realized it, Alana responded in kind. Their lips met and the rest of the world faded away.

Elistra Moonglow lay in her bunk, silently watching the cabin around her. She had tried closing her eyes, but sleep somehow managed to evade her this night. The psionic emanations she had felt before only grew stronger as the night progressed, as if someone were slowly turning up a dial.

When the Princess of Lanfor first appeared, Elistra assumed her an apprentice of the Dragon Thrall Master. Yet it was unlike the Thrall Masters to share their secrets. Now that they were aboard Anya's ship, her control over dragons began to make sense.

From what Elistra knew of psionics, the Princess might indeed be able to bend young dragons to her will. It was not impossible, but it would take an immense amount of psychic power—far more than any one individual could produce. So, either an entire group of powerful psionicists were at work here, or there was some sort of artifact involved that could augment psionic energy.

Elistra's money was on the latter. Individuals with that kind of psychic power were few and far between, and most did not get along well with others. Still, Elistra knew of only one person who could obtain such a rare artifact and show someone how to use it. *My brother.*

A chill ran up Elistra's spine at the thought. Her brother was a dangerous man. He was not necessarily evil, but he wasn't good either. He would do whatever it took to achieve his goals, and woe be to anyone who got in his way. *Even his own sister.*

If her brother were indeed involved with the Princess, then they were all in danger—far more danger than from a handful of young dragons and a few mage cannons.

The seeress' shoulders sagged in defeat. It appeared her time here was almost up. It was a shame, really. She liked this persona she had developed—the seeress, Elistra. It had served her well, but she could no longer justify the pretense if it put the Heroes in danger. They were not quite ready to face her brother. *Not yet, anyway.*

Elistra pushed up off her cot, and peered around the wall that separated her from the next bunk. A pair of familiar blue eyes stared back at her.

"I guess you couldn't sleep, either," Glo whispered.

A genuine smile crossed Elistra's face. "Uh-uh."

She slowly sauntered around the wall, then suddenly threw herself onto Glo's bed. She landed with a soft laugh, her head falling into his lap.

The flaxen-haired elf stared down at her, his eyes lit with mirth. A smile graced his usually stoic features. "I don't think I've ever met anyone who made me laugh as much as you."

Elistra grinned up at the young elf, her voice hushed. "I could say the same."

He reached down and stroked her hair, crooning softly as he did so. "Dear lady, I do believe you have stolen my heart."

Tears suddenly welled up in the seeress' eyes. Gods, she would miss him. No one had made her feel this alive in ages. In fact, she had nearly forgotten what it was like to feel at all. A pang of sorrow abruptly ran through her, wrenching her gut. For a brief moment, she sincerely wished she were this Elistra. As a simple seeress, she would most definitely have been happy with Glo.

"What's the matter? Are you crying?" Glo's brow furrowed as he stared down at her.

Elistra blinked, wiping the back of her hand across her face, then slowly shook her head. "No, just got something in my eye."

The forlorn seeress reached out and touched Glo's face, her heart nearly breaking as she did so. Unfortunately, happiness was not in the cards for her—she had other responsibilities. The main one at the moment was curtailing Anya's control of these dragons. If her brother were truly behind this as she suspected, then that would throw a wrench into his plans.

Glo lifted her hand from his cheek and kissed the palm. "You, my dear, are a terrible liar. You know you can tell me anything. If something is wrong, maybe I can help."

A pained expression crossed her face. She really wished she could tell him the truth, but then he would insist on going with her and protecting her. He was a such a giving soul. She absolutely loved that about him.

Love? Did I actually just use that word? You are getting soft. Keep this up, and your brother will catch you for sure.

"It's nothing, really," she lied once more. "I think I'm just tired is all."

"Then rest here with me."

Glo shifted on the bed behind her, pulling her down with him. The look in his eyes practically melted her heart, but the warmth of his body aroused her in other ways.

Elistra lifted her head up to his and tilted it slightly until their lips barely touched. A feeling like electricity coursed through her body, making her tingle all over. She then proceeded to kiss him in earnest, their lips dancing all around each other.

She lost all track of time, not knowing whether a minute or a lifetime had passed when she finally pulled her lips from his. Her breath came in short ragged bursts, the two of them lying there with their foreheads touching. A grin spread across her face that just wouldn't go away.

"Is that any better?" he whispered softly as he grinned back.

"Much," she practically purred in response.

The seeress spun her body around and snuggled into him, allowing the handsome blonde elf to cuddle her from behind. A contented sigh escaped her lips as he wrapped his strong arms around her torso. It was the safest and most loved she had felt in a very, very long time. Yet her inner voice would not let her enjoy it for long.

You're not safe, you know, and neither is he. If you really love him, you need to let him go.

Elistra let out a regretful sigh. There were things far greater at work here than any of them realized. The Thrall Wars had never really ended. At least two of the great Thrall Masters had resurfaced, maybe even three. Add her brother to the mix, and they would snuff out this world and everything in it. It would take a miracle for Arinthar to survive.

It will if I have anything to say about it.

Across the room, Donnie rose and strode over toward Aksel for the second time that night. On his first attempt, he had woken the sleeping cleric, only to be dragged out on deck by Alana. The duo returned a short while later and reported the door to the lower decks was still under guard.

Upon hearing their account, Aksel had decided it best to wait a while longer. Now, it appeared the impatient elf wanted to try again. After a brief discussion, Aksel rose and the duo headed their way, Alana trailing close behind.

Glo and Elistra sat up to greet them, the slight elf the first to respond in a hushed voice. "It's around four in the morning. If we don't do this thing now, we'll lose any chance we have."

"What about the guards?" Alana asked, her voice laced with apprehension.

Elistra noted the protective way Alana stood over Donnie. The lady knight's eyes were filled with far more than mere concern. Elistra's own relationship was doomed, but these two at the very least deserved a chance at love. The seeress pushed herself up off the bed. "I'll take care of them."

Alana's dark eyes turned toward Elistra. "And how are you going to…"

She abruptly stopped her query, her eyes going wide as she watched Elistra. The seeress stripped off all her clothes except for her undergarments.

"What are you doing?" Glo's voice sounded both confused and concerned.

The seeress spun around and put out a hand toward the tall elf. "Can I borrow your robe?"

"Um… sure…" came the mystified reply. Glo grabbed the purple garment strewn at the base of his bunk and proffered it to her.

A wry expression crossed Donnie's face as Elistra wrapped Glo's robe around her torso. "Oh, I see. You're going to be the distraction."

"Exactly," Elistra said with a nod. The tall elf's vestment was large on her, but she compensated by rolling up the sleeves and hiking it up around her waist. When she was done, she swept her eyes between Glo and Donnie, motioning for them to move. "Well, get on with it already. We don't have all day."

Elistra strode past the others, toward the door, calling back over her shoulder. "I'll go on ahead. Hurry up and follow me."

With that, the seeress opened the door and stepped through the threshold. It was still dark at this early hour, but the deck was bathed in the soft blue glow of the elemental ring that propelled the vessel. The door below decks stood not five feet away, next to it a solitary guard. The airman glanced up at her as she exited the door.

A brief vision of Glo's hurt face passed before her eyes, but then the seeress hardened her resolve, pushing it away. She sauntered forward toward the waiting guard, purposely letting the front of her robe fall open.

Fix her? Who is she? How is she broken?

"Stop squirmin'! Don't move!" Kalyn hissed at the struggling slave. Instantly, the girl stopped moving and her hazy eyes stared blankly at Kalyn. Kalyn dropped her hand from the girl's mouth and felt her throat tighten up.

The girl looked to be about sixteen. She was thin and clearly malnourished. She had long, unkempt honey brown hair, and her facial features, especially her button nose, reminded Kalyn of someone.

Kalyn's eyes drifted down to the girl's neck, where a dirty necklace hung. She reached out and gently picked up the pendant, running her thumb over a filthy and cracked stone that had been carved into the likeness of a turtle. She turned it over, and her eyes filled with moisture when she saw the mark of her grandfather on the underbelly of the turtle.

She looked back up and into the girl's eyes, and realized there was no mistaking her. Although she had matured some and was terribly thin, she still looked the same as she had when she was four years old.

"What's your name?" she asked softly.

The girl blinked her blank eyes before whispering in a monotone voice. "Kia."

Kalyn's lip began to tremble. She brushed some of the dirt off the girl's cheek and combed a matted strand of hair back. "Kia, it's me. Don't you recognize me? I'm your sister, Kalyn."

The girl blinked, her blank eyes shifting away and staring into nothing.

Kalyn's heart sank. "What have they done to you?"

"We live to serve." The girl whispered again, her voice taking on an eerie edge to it.

"*What* in the *hell* are you doing?! I told you to stay here, out of sight!"

Kalyn whirled around and found Seth standing next to her, hands on his hips and an expression on his face that could have made an orc bleed to death. She wiped her left eye, clearing away the tears that had collected on her lashes. "Seth, I thought she was dead. Half Skull took her away from me when she was four years old. They've done something to her. She doesn't even know who I am."

Seth tilted his head to one side, and eyed her darkly. "What are you talking about? Who is this?"

Kalyn swallowed the lump in her throat. "This is my baby sister, Kia. I thought I'd lost her forever."

She pulled Kia in close against her chest, her tone bordering on hysterical. "I won't leave her again! Never again! You can't make me!"

"Your sister?" The anger suddenly faded from his face, his mouth hanging agape. The halfling's face screwed up as he swore softly under his breath, "Dragon dung!"

His eyes closed, and his brow furrowed as if deep in thought. "Alright… alright… this is what we're going to do…"

Before he could finish his statement, Kalyn interrupted him. "Wait, don't you have that damaged black cloak in your pack? We can conk her on the head, put that on her, and I can carry her like she's drunk, or something!"

Seth's eyes snapped open, and he glared at her, his arms folding across his chest. "Or *something*? That's the worst idea ever! Nobody's going to buy that."

The halfling paused and took a deep breath. After a moment or two, his dark eyes shifted toward Kia and his expression softened. "We can use the robe, but we aren't going to knock her out and carry her like we've all just spent the weekend on a private island."

He dropped his pack to the ground and pulled out the robe and some rope. "We'll put this on her and tie the rope around her wrist, then hope we can lead her out of here real quiet-like."

With that, he slipped on his robe, then pulled the hood over his head, before looking Kia in the eyes. "You are going to follow us without a sound, no questions, no talking, and no struggling. You will talk to no one else. Do I make myself clear?"

Kia blinked her eyes again. "Yes, Master."

Kalyn helped Seth put the robe on her. Once Kia was dressed, they pulled the hood over her head, then tied a short length of rope around her left wrist.

"If something goes wrong, let go of the rope and run," Seth said as he helped Kalyn conceal the rope with Kia's oversized sleeve. He looked up at Kalyn, his dark eyes softening a bit more. "Got it? Just drop it and run."

Kalyn responded with a short nod, though she had no intention of abandoning her sister ever again.

Seth rolled his eyes. "Yeah. Right. Why do I even bother? This is the stupidest thing *ever.*"

Kalyn put her hands on her hips. "Yeah, you're with a Rhan. We do stupid a lot, and we're good at it."

Seth gave her an acid look. When he spoke again, there was a dangerous edge to his voice. "Well, you better be really, really good at it today. Otherwise, when we get caught, I'll feed you to the big snakes in that cave *myself.* Now, keep your head down."

Seth motioned for them to follow, then crept down the hill toward the road. Kalyn gripped Kia's hand, keeping close behind the halfling.

As they went, Seth continued to mutter under his breath. "This is *so* stupid."

Once on the road, Kalyn let go of Kia, but kept a tight grip on the rope. She then straightened her sister's hood and made sure it properly concealed her face. Dropping her hands to her side, she kept close to Kia so that their sleeves fell over the rope and hid it from view. Kalyn straightened her shoulders and hoped she looked calm and natural, even though her hands were shaking like a leaf and her stomach was churning. An icy chill crawled up her spine as the town came into view.

Seth shot her a warning look just before they reached the first buildings. Kalyn responded with a curt nod, and braced herself, swallowing hard to calm her nerves.

The first thing she noticed was that there were more people wandering around than there had been before. Slaves still worked on the fountain, but the number of overseers had doubled. It appeared as if they were changing shifts, and they had paused to talk to each other. Furthermore, a large group of black hooded figures approached the temple.

Hopefully, with the extra activity around here, we'll just blend in.

As they neared the fountain, Kalyn inadvertently glanced at one of the overseers. Before she knew it, she made eye contact with the man. Her first instinct was to look away, but instead, she forced herself to glare at him. He returned her gaze in kind, then proceeded to stride in their direction.

Kalyn's heart thumped like a crazed rabbit in her chest. She cast a sidelong glance at Seth and saw the halfling square his shoulders.

Thankfully, luck was on their side. Just as the overseer closed in on them, a dark-robed person called out from behind him. "Hassan! I need to speak to you!"

The overseer stopped and spun to face the robed figure.

Seth quickened his pace, Kalyn matching him while pulling Kia along. It felt like an eternity, but they finally reached the other edge of the town. Seth then slowed down, but kept an even pace until the town was out of sight. At that point, they broke from the road and slipped into the forest. There, they paused just long enough for Kalyn to run out to the road and cover their tracks.

When Kalyn returned, Seth gave her a dark look. "That was by far one of the stupidest things I ever let myself get talked into."

"Stupider than burning down the Cape Marlin lighthouse?" Kalyn asked with a half-grin.

A slim smile spread across Seth's lips in spite of himself. "Yeah, well I wasn't there for that, but this definitely ranks up there with it."

Kalyn broke into a full grin as she took Kia's rope back from him. "At least it worked."

Seth cocked his head to one side and eyed her sharply. "I'm not celebrating until we're in Bendenwood."

Kalyn's grin swiftly faded, her mood sobering. "Yeah, that's probably a good idea."

The three of them made their way through the forest as quietly as possible, though Kia's shuffling feet made more branches snap than Kalyn would have liked. As the sound of the waterfall reached their ears, something nagged at the back of Kalyn's mind about the forest around them. She had just helped her sister around a large rock, when it suddenly struck her.

"There aren't any snakes. This place was crawling with them before. And I don't hear any birds, neither. Something's not right here."

"Very perceptive, young lady."

Kalyn swiftly spun around, her hood falling off with the sudden movement. The dragonflies sat a short distance ahead, the waterfall careening loudly down the cliff side behind them. Standing directly between them and their mounts were two women in dark robes.

Kalyn froze in her tracks, her normally chatty tongue suddenly feeling thick in her throat. The first woman barked at her, while the second subtly began to weave her hands in the pattern of a spell. "Who are you? Where do you think you're going?"

"Uh…" Kalyn cast a sidelong glance at Seth, but the halfling had disappeared. Stalling for time, she sputtered out an answer while casually slipping her bow off her shoulder. "I… um, we… were just coming to investigate… a rare species of bug that showed up here this morning. Looks like you already found them. Good job."

"Don't patronize me!" The first woman snarled. "You aren't a part of the cult, are you?"

Kalyn shrugged. "That depends which cult you're talkin' about."

The dark-robed woman narrowed her eyes, her voice taking on a deadly edge. "There is only one cult."

Kalyn let out a loud laugh, infuriating the woman even further. "Boy, you don't get out much, do you? Haven't you ever heard of the Cult of the Twisted Tree?"

The dark-robed woman opened her mouth to reply, but was abruptly cut off. The woman next to her let out a sharp cry, then slumped to the ground, a small, shrouded form crouched behind her.

The first woman spun around, her hands twisting to cast a spell. The shrouded figure swiftly darted for her, but Kalyn was faster. Before either could strike, the young archer doffed her robe, drew an arrow, and sent it sailing across the distance, right between the woman's eyes. The dark-robed figure stood there for a moment, blank faced, then fell straight backwards, landing with a dull *thud*.

Seth halted in mid-leap and flipped his hood off his head with a snort. He spun toward Kalyn, his lips warping sideways. "Heh. Cult of the Twisted Tree?"

Kalyn shouldered her bow, then grabbed Kia and pulled her up to the dragonflies. "Yeah. The Twisted Tree is my ma and pa's tavern. The only tavern in Deepwood Fort, and the first thing that came to mind."

Seth shook his head, then quickly mounted his dragonfly. "I think your sister should ride with me."

Kalyn gave him a questioning stare. "Why?"

"I'm smaller. You're bigger. Our hummers can only take so much weight."

Kalyn tilted her head, then sighed and nodded. "Yeah, good point."

She turned to face Kia, looking her in the eyes. "You will get on behind Seth, you will hold on tight, and you will stay quiet. Do you understand?"

Kia blinked once. "We live to serve."

Kalyn helped to seat her sister behind Seth, then quickly mounted her own dragonfly. They took off without hesitation, quickly leaving Serpent's Hollow behind.

The sun was long gone, and the stars twinkled brightly in the night sky when the massive trees of Bendenwood finally came into view. Glowing lights beneath the tree-line gently illuminated the canopy of the forest. As the dragonflies drew closer, Seth could make out treehouses wrapping themselves around the massive trunks, and wooden bridges weaving through the air to connect the houses to one another.

A shadow entered the corner of Seth's eye. He turned to see a giant eagle draw up beside them, the creature soaring through the night air on unwavering wings. It peered at him and Kia, then shifted its focus to Kalyn a short distance ahead. The eagle gently beat its wings, pulling ahead of Seth and coming even with Kalyn.

Kalyn whipped her head around and started at the sight of the massive eagle, nearly losing her seat. She quickly righted herself, then nonchalantly saluted the eagle, motioning for it to take the lead.

Seth let out a derisive snort. *Yeah. Real smooth, Kalyn.*

The eagle made a piping chirp sound, then took the lead. It gently banked and angled for an open platform on the nearest tree. Interestingly enough, the dragonflies followed it of their own accord.

The eagle landed well before they did. Seth watched curiously as the creature gave a mighty shake of its wings, and with a flurry of feathers, twisted and shrank, transforming into the girl that he recognized as Raina. Raina quickly moved to the side and watched the dragonflies land, tugging at one of her dreadlocks nervously.

As soon as the dragonflies stopped buzzing, Kalyn jumped off hers and ran up to Seth's, ducking under its twitching wings, and grabbed Kia.

Raina suddenly appeared at Kalyn's side, helping her with the small, frail girl. "What's going on? Who is this?"

"We can explain later. Right now, I need to see someone who can fix her," Kalyn said as she pulled the black robe off her sister and straightened the white one that had been underneath.

A puzzled expression crossed Raina's face. "*Fix* her? Who is she? How is she broken?"

Seth jumped off his dragonfly, landing softly on his feet. "Her mind is basically mush. Oh! And, she's Kalyn's sister."

Raina's face snapped toward Seth, her brown eyes nearly bugging out of her head. She immediately shifted her gaze back toward Kalyn. "Your sister?"

Kalyn glared at the halfling while letting out an exasperated huff. "Really, Seth? I said we'd explain later. I don't wanna tell the whole story fifty times."

Seth folded his arms and shrugged, the corner of his mouth lifting slightly. "Eh, that's a you problem."

Raina positioned herself in front of Kia and looked the girl in the eyes. "I think I know what's wrong with her. And, I think I know just the person to fix it."

"The High Druid?" Kalyn asked in a hushed tone.

Raina peered at Kalyn and grinned. "Well, normally, yes, but I know someone better."

Seth cocked an eyebrow at the druid girl. "Better than the High Druid?"

This I gotta see…

Raina turned on her heel and marched toward a nearby rope bridge. "You said it, not me! Just don't tell the High Druid I said that."

"Who in the blazes is better than the High Druid?" Kalyn asked, sounding completely mystified as she pulled Kia along in pursuit of Raina.

As Seth fell into step behind Kalyn and her sister, an interesting thought crossing his mind. It was something he had suspected for a couple of days now. "It wouldn't be *Fran*, would it?"

Raina let out a soft giggle. "Seth, remind me to give you a piece of cake. You earned it."

A wide grin spread across the halfling's lips. "I'll never turn down cake!"

"What?" Kalyn exclaimed, sounding even confused than before. "I know Fran is good at a lot of stuff, 'specially at being strange, but better than the High Druid? Isn't that stretching it?"

"Oh, you'll see." Raina said with a mysterious lilt to her voice. "Besides, Fran isn't busy at the moment. Well… not *real* busy, anyway."

The small party went silent as Raina led them across the bridge to another tree. This second tree was encircled with a walkway that had multiple bridges connected to it.

Seth gazed at the forest floor below as they followed Raina around the wide trunk. The lights from a few dwellings shone up at them, running in a fairly straight line. One of the buildings appeared larger than the rest—an inn, perhaps. Seth imagined it was the one they stayed at the last time they were in Bendenwood.

The halfling let out a short sigh. That seemed like ages ago. It was back when he, Aksel, and Glo had first set out from Tarsmoor on the caravan headed east to Ravenford. The three of them had noted the lights in the trees above them that eve, but were told the upper town was strictly off limits to outsiders.

Kalyn mirrored his thoughts as Raina led them across another bridge. "I ain't never been to the upper town before. How come you've never brought me here?"

Raina continued without turning her head. "That's because you haven't come to Bendenwood in years, Kalyn! I'm the one who's always going to Deepwood to see you. Besides, the Druids live here in the upper city. Very few people are allowed to come here."

Raina glanced back over her shoulder and smiled. "You guys have special permission to be here. Fran said so."

Kalyn seemed taken aback by her statement. She grabbed Raina by the arm and whirled her around, placing her hands on her hips. "Fran said so? Doesn't the High Druid get a say in this?"

Seth snorted, amused by the whole conversation. This only further confirmed what he had thought all along. Still, he wasn't going to miss an opportunity to needle Kalyn. "Well yes, but only after Fran says so, obviously."

Raina let out a high-pitched laugh, then held up two fingers. "Two pieces of cake for Seth!"

"Bonus!" Seth cried, pumping his fist in the air.

Kalyn huffed in exasperation. "What am I missing here? I know Fran is bossy and has a lot of cards up her sleeves, but…"

Seth said nothing, but it was Raina's turn to be exasperated. She placed her hands on her hips and narrowed her eyes at her friend. "Oh, come on, Kalyn! Think about it!"

"I am! I don't get it!" Kalyn said through gritted teeth. "What is she? A druid?"

Seth peered up at Kalyn, his mouth bending into a lopsided smile. "Ya think?"

Raina rolled her eyes at Kalyn. "You probably know her better than anyone else, and you've never guessed?"

Kalyn swept her eyes from Seth to Raina, her face turning a bright shade of red. "Why would I need to guess? She's never said she was a druid, she doesn't live here in druid-ville, she doesn't act like a snooty, goody-two-shoes druid—no offense—and I ain't never seen her do any druidy things, aside from eat mushrooms. Besides that, she's *blind*. Don't magicky people, druids included, need to *see* to cast spells?"

Kalyn's tantrum was interrupted by a familiar voice. "There are more ways a-seein' than with yer eyes, child. Ya knows that."

Everyone looked up as Fran came into view from around the tree, leaning on the arm of a thin old man. The butt of her staff tapped against the wooden catwalk gently as they approached. "There's more ta the world than what we can see. Fer land's sake, the stuff we can't see is what holds this world from fallin' ta pieces and make tha magics work."

The old man raised a hand, waving it around for emphasis. "It surrounds us and binds us! You must feel it around you…"

He groaned and buckled over as Fran jammed her staff into his gut. "Shut up, Qualar. That weren't what I was talkin' about."

The old man frowned. "Now, listen here, ya cantankerous ol' woman! You is always interuptin' my speech 'bout…"

He jumped slightly as Fran cracked the end of her staff on the catwalk beneath them. "Yer jabber about the forces that surround us is as washed-up and old as you is, and nerbody here cares 'bout it. So shut yer pie hole."

As Fran spoke, Qualar held his free hand up in the air and pretended like it was mouthing her words. If Fran had any indication he was doing so, she chose to ignore him, instead addressing the others. "Na-then. Aside from tha idea that I'm a goody-two-shoes druid, what's got my Kalyn's feather's all ruff…"

Fran abruptly halted, her mouth hanging open and her eyes squinting in concentration. "No… is that… yer lil sista?"

Kalyn looked twice at Fran, her mouth falling open. Her eyes shifted toward Raina, then down to Seth.

Seth was not surprised in the least that the old druid sensed the presence of Kalyn's sister. He folded his arms over his chest and stared back up at Kalyn with a slight twist of his lips. "Told ya."

Kalyn appeared as if she were about to reply, but then stopped herself and shook her head. With a roll of her eyes, she grabbed her sister by the shoulders and stepped forward. "Yeah. I found Kia."

Fran's eyes narrowed even more, her brow furrowing. "And something's not right 'bout her, is there?"

Again, Kalyn glanced down at Seth, but the halfling chose to merely smirk back at her this time. Kalyn let out a short sigh, then looked back at Fran. "You're full of surprises today. You know, you could make money at this. Next time the carnival is in town, I'm taking you."

Fran snorted, a smile turning up her lips. "Wouldn't be tha first time I played soothsayer at a carny. 'Cept, that blonde always took the fun out of it. All I got was the girls wonderin' when they's gonna get married, while ol' purple eyes got all the boys."

Seth's eyebrow shot up. He cast a sidelong glance at the old blind druid. *Purple eyes? Now that's interesting. I wonder what the odds are of another blonde soothsayer running around with those color eyes?*

Raina cleared her throat, drawing everyone's attention to her. "Back to the point, I think her mind has been enslaved in some way by magic."

"She was a slave at Serpent's Hollow, which we've got a mess of information on, by the way." Seth swiftly added.

Fran immediately straightened her posture. "I knows what needs ta be done. Foller me. To the High Druid's study!"

23
TWISTED SISTER

*Every month I would cry your name, because it was
the only name I could remember*

Seth peered up at Kalyn from the knife he fiddled with. She squatted beside her sister's seat, staring at her wide-eyed, while Fran worked her magic on the younger girl. She'd been sitting that way for an hour now.

Jeez, Kalyn. Take a breath of air before your eyeballs pop out of your head.

Fran sat directly in front of Kia in an ornate, high-backed wicker chair that she had pulled from behind a large desk made of the same material. The old man, Qualar, stood behind Kia, muttering a chant in time with Fran's, assisting her in the druid magic. Raina stood next to Kalyn, hands folded together, watching every movement the two older druids made.

Seth watched with keen interest as a glowing aura began to shimmer around Kia's form. It appeared for only a moment, then abruptly faded. The young girl closed her eyes and took in a deep breath. Her eyes slowly flickered back open, as if she were waking from a deep sleep. She glanced around, confusion slowly crawling over her features.

Kalyn took her sister's hand. "Kia?"

The girl looked down at Kalyn, her brows knitting together. "Where am I?"

"You're safe. You're in Bendenwood. Seth and I brought you here."

Seth leaned against the doorsill as the girl glanced at him. She gave him a strange look, then turned her gaze back toward Kalyn. Without warning, she pulled her hand away from Kalyn and scooted backwards.

"Who are you?"

Kalyn swallowed hard, her expression turning fearful. "Why, I'm Kalyn. Don't you recognize me?"

Recognition dawned on Kia's face, just before her features turned hard as stone. Her voice was icy as she responded. "No, I don't recognize you, but I remember your name."

Kalyn leaned forward an inch, her eyes widening. "You do?"

Kia scooted back a bit more while nodding her head. "I remember it because I screamed it a lot. You left me alone, and the bad guy got me."

Seth felt a pang of sorrow as Kalyn's face fell and her eyes filled with moisture. He knew the feeling of letting someone down. It was not pleasant, and it never went away.

When Kalyn responded, her voice was so soft they could barely hear it. "Yes. I did. And I am so, so sorry for that. So sorry. Not a day goes by that I don't regret it."

Fran tapped her foot on the floor. "Now then, child'n. Both of ya was tiny lil grapes way back then. Kalyn couldn't 'a done nothin' to stop the bad man, same as you, missy." She reached forward and poked Kia on the knee. "Ain't no reason for holdin' a grudge. In fact, ya should be happy to see your sister! She saved ya!"

Kia scooted back as far as her seat would allow. "She didn't save me. She just fixed her mistake a bit too late." She fixed her eyes on Kalyn, glaring at her darkly. "Every month, I would wake up from the magic they put on me, and every month I would cry your name, because it was the only name I could remember. You never came."

Kalyn's voice cracked with emotion. "I did come! I came today! I didn't even know you were alive until today!"

Kalyn paused a moment, swallowing hard as her eyes brimmed with tears. "I've never forgotten you. When I saw you, I knew who you were right away, even though you'd changed. I risked everything to get you out and save you."

Kia's face softened just for a moment, but then she looked away, setting her teeth together. "Still too late."

Kalyn's eyes darkened, her eyebrows knitting together as her lower lip trembled. She stood to her feet without another word, and bowed her head, turning away, her hands curling into fists.

Raina placed a comforting hand on Kalyn's shoulder, then took a step past her toward Kia. "Hello, Kia. I'm Raina. I know you must be dreadfully tired and hungry, so I will take you to a nice room to eat and rest. Would you like that?"

Kia looked up at Raina and blinked, her eyes widening with anticipation. "Oh, yes! I am so very hungry!"

Raina smiled kindly at the young girl. "Good! Before we go, though, I was wondering if there was anything you can remember about the cult that enslaved you?"

Kia's brow slowly formed a line, her hazel eyes filling with thought. "I… I can remember some things, but… they're fuzzy. I remember lots of snakes, and mean men with whips."

Her face abruptly took on a frightened expression. "…and a big snake with a man's face!"

Just as swiftly, her expression changed to one of confusion. "Wait… that's odd… can a snake have a man's face?"

"They sure can," Seth said with certainty. "Saw it myself."

Kia swiveled around and regarded him for a moment. "How can a snake have a man's face? That's just silly."

Seth responded with a shrug. "Not so silly when they're trying to kill you."

Kia continued to look at him oddly.

Fran let out a long sigh. "Raina, dear, take the poor thing to my room and feed her something that'll put some color into her face again, will ya? I gets the feelin' that Seth may know more 'bout the goings on in that pit than the lil' one."

Raina nodded, then gently took Kia by the arm and helped her up, ushering her to the door. Kia glanced back at Kalyn, mixed emotions clearly reflected in her face. She opened her mouth as if to say something, but was distracted when a thin woman with prominent elven features and an abundance of red curly hair walked into the room.

"What is the meaning of this?" the woman asked, peering at each person in the room with her sharp green eyes.

Kalyn spun around and stood to attention, quickly wiping her sleeve across her eyelashes.

Qualar raised his hand and pointed to Fran. "It was her idea!"

Fran crossed her arms and leaned back in her chair, the corner of her lips turning upward.

Raina gracefully bowed to the red-haired elven woman. "Forgive me, High Druid. I was just leaving with this girl, Kia. She was enslaved, and her mind dominated by a snake cult for the last several years. She has just been freed, and is in need of nourishment and rest."

The High Druid scanned Kia up and down, then dipped her chin in a slow nod, saying something in a language that Seth did not recognize. With another bow, Raina pulled Kia out the door, which the elven woman then promptly closed behind them.

The High Druid spun around and narrowed her eyes at Fran, her tone hissing like acid. "I see my study has once again proven useful to you."

Fran's smirk widened, making Seth appreciate her all the more. "Yep! Good thing ya has it, Lysandra. Don't knows what I would do without it."

The High Druid, Lysandra, closed her eyes and dipped her chin. She raised her hand and rubbed the bridge of her nose, a nearly silent growl escaping the woman's throat. When she finally looked back up, she glanced first at Seth, then at Kalyn. "And who is this tracker and Halfling that you have invited into my office?"

Kalyn executed a deep bow. "I'm Kalyn Rhan of Deepwood Fort, ma'am. And the short feller is my friend, Seth, one of the famous and highly praised Heroes of Ravenford."

The High Druid focused on Seth, her bright eyes narrowing. "I've heard some tell of them."

Seth responded with a barely perceptible nod. He wasn't quite sure what she had heard of him and his friends. If anything, it probably came from that old druid back in Ravenford.

The elven woman raised her eyes and chin, slowly walking toward the large desk. "I am Lysandra Melassul, High Druid of Bendenwood, as I assume you have already guessed."

She stopped beside the high-backed chair and glared down at Fran, "Do you mind if I borrow *your* seat?"

Fran didn't bat an eye. "Don't mind t'all. I needs to stretch my twigs and branches anyhow."

The old druid slowly stood, stretched, then sat down in Kia's vacated seat. Seth found himself liking this old woman more and more. He had yet to form an opinion of this elven woman, Lysandra, but she seemed rather uptight. The corners of his mouth upturned slightly. *Kind of reminds me of Glo.*

The High Druid took her chair and moved it back behind the desk. She slowly sat down and readjusted the seat to her liking, then soundlessly began to reorder the things on her desk. Everyone watched in silence until she was done. Lysandra then leaned back, propped her elbows on the arms of the chair and interlaced her fingers, folding her hands together.

Seth had to repress a snort. *Definitely reminds me of Glo.*

Lysandra took a deep breath. "Now then… I assume Kalyn and Seth are the two *chosen ones* that you sent to investigate Serpent's Hollow?"

Her tone was smooth and quiet, though it dripped with ridicule.

I take it back. She's even more uptight than Glo.

Fran nodded. "Sho is! N' they brought us back 'a mess of information,' as young Seth put it."

Lysandra's emerald green eyes shifted to Seth, her expression rather bored. "Well?"

Seth glanced at Kalyn, to see her rubbing her hands together. She smiled at him, though her eyes were dark and missing that familiar twinkle that normally lit up her entire face. "Another hero story, and this time, I'm in it!"

Seth peered back at the High Druid and narrowed his eyes. There was something about this woman he just didn't trust. "Sorry, but I don't just blurt information out to anyone."

Lysandra sat up taller in her seat. "Oh? Only those you trust, I assume? And I am not one of those."

Seth shrugged. He wasn't about to placate this pompous woman, High Druid, or not. "I don't trust the old guy either. Sorry, but not sorry."

Qualar did not seem to take Seth's slight to heart. "Great! This means I can go do something fun now, like eat cake and drink cider. Raina did mention cake."

Seth amended his initial impression of the old guy. He did seem to have his priorities straight.

Fran grabbed Qualar by the arm as he turned to leave, spinning him back around. "Not so fast, you ol' goat! You is a representative of the fire maniacs, and you is gonna want to knows what the young'ins found in Serpent's Holler."

Qualar raised a finger toward Fran. "First off, it's Circle of the Sun, not the fire maniacs! Next, you're always bossin' me around, you moon lover!"

"That's 'cause you'd be lost if I didn't."

Qualar placed his fists on his hips. "Oh really? And just what do you think I do when you ain't around to boss me around?"

A wide smile split Fran's face. "Get lost and burn stuff down, I'd imagine."

Qualar opened his mouth to protest, but stopped, thinking better of it. He merely shrugged and nodded. "Ya got a point."

The High Druid let out an exasperated sigh. "Are the two of you done yet?"

Fran grinned at the red-headed elven woman. "Fer the moment, we is."

The old blind druid then swiveled in her seat to face Seth. "Now, young feller, let me tell ya somethin.' Qualar might have a few bricks missing in that ol' noggin o' his, and the High Druid 'n I def'nitely butt heads…"

Fran leaned forward in her chair. "…but they is druids, tried n' true. I trust the two of 'em with my life. So, if we is gonna do something about the cult, then you is gonna have to tell 'em all ya knows."

Seth really liked this old druid, Fran. He was warming to Qualar as well, though he still didn't like this snooty elven woman. His mouth twisted to the side. "Maybe. But I don't think they need to know all I knows…"

A smile turned up one corner of Fran's mouth. "We don't car 'bout yer past or yer love life or anything in-between. Just anything that has ta do with snakes."

Seth let out a derisive snort. He could just imagine this feisty old woman in a deep discussion about the order of things with Aksel. She would be sure to drive the little gnome crazy. The thought caused a wicked grin to spread across his face. "Remind me to introduce you to a good friend of mine one of these days. You two would hit it off just perfectly."

Fran snorted back at him. "Sure, why not. Now what's it ta be, young feller?"

Seth took a deep breath, then shrugged. "Fine."

He moved next to Kalyn, then launched into an account of their time in Serpent's Hollow. Kalyn occasionally interrupted him, adding a few short observations of her own. Yet once he recounted what he had seen in the caves, everyone grew silent.

Lysandra leaned forward, propped her elbows on her desk and steepled her fingers, resting them against her lips like Glo did. Seth arched an eyebrow as he spoke. *The resemblance is uncanny.*

In the end, Seth told them most of it, but he left out the part about Glo's previous encounter with the dark woman in the portal. As he said, these folks didn't need to know everything.

When he was finished, the High Druid closed her eyes and sighed. "All that you have just described greatly disturbs me. I feel this is something that must be brought to the council's attention."

Fran slapped her knee. "Now yer talkin'! But there's just one lil hiccup with that."

The High Druid closed her eyes and winced. "Here it comes…"

"The council is too slow!" Fran said, tapping her foot impatiently on the floor. "Sounds to me like this cult is nigh ready to do whate're it is they is wantin' ta do, n' I gets the feelin' we don't has the time to get the counsel stirred up 'bout it."

Lysandra held a hand up to stop her. "There is nothing we can do about it, though. Until the council is informed and understands the threat, the druids will not move."

Kalyn shifted on her feet, "What about Seth's friends?"

Seth cast a side-long glance at her. "'Friends' is a loose term."

Still, she has a good point.

Kalyn waved a hand dismissively at him. "Whatever. The point is, we could call in the Heroes of Ravenford. They're a small enough group. They could sneak in without much trouble, unlike an army of bears, but they're powerful enough that they could really put a hole in the cult's boat, so to speak."

Lysandra shifted her gaze from Kalyn to Seth. "Would they? There is a high probability of failure and death."

Seth let out a short sigh. If he knew his friends, they'd jump at a chance to take down the cult. Especially Lloyd. The young warrior was set on taking down every last cultist to protect the Lady Andrella. "Somehow that never seems to stop them. Trust me, I've tried."

"Would you really want them to?" Kalyn said with mock seriousness.

The side of Seth's mouth curved into a lopsided smile. "Probably not."

Lysandra looked between the two of them, then turned to Fran. "I trust you can handle this, Fran? I have more sane things to do, like calling a council meeting together."

Fran saluted the High Druid. "Leave the insanity ta me."

Lysandra reached into her desk, pulled out a piece of paper, and stood. "Very well, I shall leave you to it. If you can find the kindness in your soul, do keep the ink from splotching my desk."

With that, she strode across the room and left, closing the door behind her. Seth felt the air in the room turn far less stuffy with her departure.

Meanwhile, Fran got to her feet and moved around the desk, sitting down in the chair. She felt for the paper, then for the quill and inkwell.

Seth exchanged a glance with Kalyn. *Can the old woman really write?*

"Uh, Fran?" Kalyn moved around the desk slowly.

"Don't worry! It ain't normal paper. This here is magic paper. It'll get a note to them thar heroes in the blink of an eye!" Fran dipped the quill in the ink and traced her fingers over the top edge of the paper, then set the quill down and began to write.

"Fran!" Kalyn exclaimed, "You can write letters?"

Fran's quill stopped moving. "Jus' what do ya think I'm doin'?"

"Keeping me from eating cake, that's what." Qualar folded his arms and huffed.

Fran glared in the old man's direction. "Oh, go fill yer pie hole with cake, ya ol' screech owl."

Qualar smiled, flashing a mouthful of yellowed teeth around the room, then glanced down at Seth. "I'll bring ya some."

Seth held up two fingers. "Raina said I get two pieces."

Qualar nodded, his expression turning serious. "Alright, then. I'll grab a whole cake. Two pieces for you. Two for me. We'll split what's left after that."

Seth's impression of the old man just went way up. "Now you're talking."

Qualar spun on his heel and hurried outside, slamming the door behind him.

"Fran, how can you write a letter without seeing what you're writing?" Kalyn insisted.

"Like I told ya, child! Ya don't need sight for lots o' things!" Fran paused her scribbling and pushed the letter toward Kalyn. "Would you like to try?"

Kalyn shook her head, a mischievous smile growing on her face. "Not with my eyes closed, but I would like to write something!"

A wicked grin crossed Seth's lips. *This ought to be good.*

Kalyn took the pen from Fran, and with slow, careful strokes, wrote a few lines down on the paper, then pushed the pen back into the old woman's hand, a satisfied smile on her face. "There! Done. What does your part say?"

Fran traced her fingers down the paper, smudging some of the ink across it, then she started to write again. "I said 'Wher'er y'all is, make all yerselves scarce 'n get to where ya can talk to some druids!' What did you put?"

Kalyn looked over Fran's shoulder at the paper, "I put "Oh my gods. I can't believe we're sending a message to the Heroes. I love you guys."

She smiled, then frowned, still staring at the paper. "What are you writing down now?"

"I'm saying "S'cuse my friend. She wrote that. I didn't. Now, get yer tight fannies o'er here, 'n make it snappy!"

Seth thought he would bust a gut. He fell to the floor, laughing uncontrollably.

"What?" Kalyn asked in an accusing tone. "What's wrong with it?"

Seth took a deep breath, holding his sides from laughing so hard. "Nothing! Send it like it is! I can't wait for them to get it."

"Well then, here ya go. Send it off!" Fran rolled the paper up and held it out in Seth's direction. "Just think about who ya wants it to go to, and it'll go. Just picture their face, their name, or whatever works for ya."

Seth picked himself up off the floor and took the rolled paper from Fran. He glanced over it quickly and saw that it had a familiar spell written above Fran and Kalyn's scribbling. He had seen Aksel use it to contact Sir Craven when they were still aboard the *Rusty Nail*. It's how they had set up their rendezvous with the Knights of the Rose back in the Darkwoods.

Seth closed his eyes and pictured Aksel. With a *poof!* the paper disappeared from his hands, the scroll invoking its magic. Seth then opened his eyes and rubbed his hands together, a wicked smile on his face. "I wish I could be a fly on the wall when they get this message."

24

UNDER THE HAMMER

Suspended in mid-air hung a man-sized, translucent, blue crystal

Donnie stared after Elistra with stark disbelief. The lovely seeress was about to use her body to distract the guards, and from what he had just seen of her, he had little doubt she would be successful doing so.

A pair of hands suddenly grasped him from behind and spun him around. Glo stared at him, the tall elf just a bit wild-eyed. "Come on, Donnie. You heard her. Let's get this done with."

"Okay," Donnie said with a nod. He faced Glo and prepared to be turned invisible.

The tall elf took a moment to compose himself, then began to weave his hands in a circular motion. Donnie felt sorry for Glo. What Elistra was doing certainly had the elven wizard rattled. Donnie supposed he would feel the same way if Alana were acting as the distraction. The thought of Alana stripping down to her underwear made the thin elf suddenly blush.

Abruptly, Glo's spell released, and Donnie felt the magic course over him. When it was done, Donnie could still see himself, but knew that the rest of the world could no longer.

"Come on, Donnie. Go already," Glo urged him.

"Okay. Going," Donnie answered as he headed for the door.

Donnie slowly turned the handle and pulled the door inward a crack. He peered outside and saw two figures standing by the entrance to the lower levels. The first one was a single guard, and the second Elistra. The seeress stood there with Glo's robe wide open, casually chatting with the guard. The second guard was nowhere to be seen. Donnie slipped through the doorway, then carefully pulled it closed behind him.

Elistra must have noticed the door's movement. The sexy seeress grabbed the guard by the hands, and pulled him in the opposite direction, away from both entryways. The guard went along rather willingly.

Donnie stole over to the next doorway as the seeress continued to work her magic. He silently turned the handle, then pushed it in just enough to squeeze through. Donnie had just made it inside when he heard a distinct slap from the other side of the door.

"Just what kind of girl do you think I am?" Elistra's voice wafted through the open doorway. It was followed by the sound of footsteps stomping across the upper deck.

A wide grin crossed Donnie's face as he silently pulled the door closed behind him. Elistra was quite the actress.

Still grinning, the thin elf silently climbed down the steep flight of stairs. At the very bottom stood a solitary form slouched against the wall, its head bowed. Donnie approached the figure cautiously. It was another guard, dressed in the purple and gold uniform of Lanfor. From his rhythmic breathing, the guard was either asleep or pretending to be.

What are the odds? Donnie thought wryly.

Donnie held his breath as he soundlessly crept past the man, but the guard gave no indication of waking from his slumber. A thin smile graced the slight elf's lips. *Lucky for me, but not so lucky for him if that wizard catches him. He doesn't quite seem like the forgiving type.*

Once past the guard, Donnie got his bearings. He stood in a long hallway that ran from the bow to the stern of the ship. The corridor was lined with numerous doors, the two largest ones on either end. Donnie paused a few moments, deciding which way to go, when a muffled cry reverberated down the hall. It had come from the large door at the bow.

Donnie cocked his head to one side, a single eyebrow arched. *That sounds like someone in pain. Well, Anya is a strange one. Perhaps Elladan is still entertaining her…*

A second muffled cry interrupted his thoughts. Donnie cast a sidelong glance at the guard, but the man had not moved an inch. The thin elf shook his head. *Either you're the worst guard ever, or this kind of thing happens down here all the time.*

Either way, the thought was disconcerting. Donnie crept down the corridor until he had nearly reached the end of the hall. The large door in front of him was ironbound and looked rather thick. As he examined the doorway, another cry came from behind it, this one weaker than the rest. It was followed by a shout of triumph.

"Yes! Yes! It worked! It finally worked!"

The other cries had been higher pitched, almost definitely female. Yet that last shout had been a much deeper tone, most decidedly male.

Abruptly, the door in front of Donnie flew open. The wiry elf threw himself against the wall just as a familiar blue-robed figure crossed over the threshold. It was the irritant wizard, Sigfus, the dark-bearded man mumbling to himself as he fiddled with a large ring of keys. "I must inform the Princess."

Donnie peered through the slight crack the wizard had left between the door and its frame. His eyes went wide as they fell on the naked form of a woman, her limp body suspended by two chains that held her wrists to the wall.

I was right! They are up to something down here, but I didn't think it was torture. Donnie strained his eyes, but the captive's face was covered by her long blonde locks.

Abruptly, the door closed the rest of the way. Sigfus had finally found his key and pulled it shut, locking the door with a sharp click. The preoccupied wizard pocketed his keys, then hurried down the corridor, muttering to himself as he went. "She is going to love me for this. That pretentious bard will be yesterday's news."

Donnie raised an eyebrow. *It seems this Sigfus has a thing for the Princess.*

In Donnie's estimation, it was a far reach. He couldn't imagine that the Princess would ever be interested in a toadie like Sigfus.

Once the wizard was far enough down the hall, Donnie peeled himself from the wall. The lock was a rather simple pin and tumbler mechanism—he had it unlocked in mere seconds. The agile elf then slipped swiftly inside, closing the door behind him.

Donnie swept his eyes around the room. It appeared to be some sort of laboratory. It was rather large, filled with a couple of long tables covered with piles of books, as well as flasks and vials filled with various colored liquids. Yet his eyes were almost immediately drawn to the very center of the room. Suspended in mid-air hung a man-sized, translucent blue crystal, the large gem radiating a brilliant blue light.

Donnie began to feel woozy as he stared at it, but then swiftly wrenched his eyes away. Suddenly remembering the woman on the wall, Donnie shifted his gaze toward her. She had not moved at all. The wiry elf hurried over to the woman and lifted her chin, his eyes going wide as he stared into a familiar face.

Ves!

Getting over his initial shock, Donnie whispered frantically to her. "Ves, can you hear me?"

There was no response. Donnie gently patted her face.

"Ves!" Donnie whispered urgently.

Just as the young woman began to rouse, Donnie heard a key being thrust into the door lock. The wiry elf quickly dropped Ves' chin and scurried to the wall behind the entryway. A moment later the door flew open.

"I could have sworn I locked it." Sigfus' voice was full of suspicion.

Donnie peered from behind the door just in time to see Anya blithely striding into the room. The monarch's tone was markedly annoyed. "You probably forgot, in your haste to interrupt my pleasant evening."

Sigfus followed closely behind Anya, his beady eyes sweeping around the room. "My apologies for interrupting your fun, Princess, but I tell you, she is broken."

Donnie retreated completely behind the ironbound door. Though he was still invisible, he hadn't forgotten how the wizard had spotted him back in the meadow.

"She better be," Anya retorted, the threat in her voice not so thinly veiled.

The room abruptly went quiet. Donnie peered out from his hiding spot and saw Anya standing before Ves. The petulant monarch held the young woman's chin in her hand, roughly moving her head from side-to-side. Sigfus stood a few paces behind Anya, his foot tapping nervously against the floor.

Anya dropped Ves' chin and took a step back, her hard demeanor softening. "Yes, I believe you're right."

She motioned to Sigfus with her free hand. "Go fetch the collar."

"Yes, your majesty."

Sigfus scurried over to a nearby bench, swiftly returning with a black metallic collar. He handed it to the Princess, who then took the collar and fastened it around Ves' neck. It clicked into place with a loud *snap*.

Anya's finger went to her chin as she eyed Ves curiously. "Wake up."

Ves' eyes abruptly opened.

"Who is your master?" Anya asked in an expectant tone.

"You are, mistress."

Ves' response sounded hollow. It reminded Donnie of the young dragon teen, Ysa. Glo and Elistra described her as sounding the same when they had broached certain subjects.

Anya abruptly clapped her hands together, her voice filled with glee. "Very good. Very, very good."

Donnie didn't get mad often—he had a devil-may-care attitude on life—but now his blood boiled. It was one thing to enslave all those chromatic dragons, but Ves was their friend. He watched Anya darkly from behind the door as she waved her hand at Sigfus.

"Release her."

Sigfus rushed forward to unlock the chains, then swiftly stood back.

"Now sit down," Anya commanded Ves.

The young woman slowly walked over to a nearby bench and seated herself.

A smile of pure delight crossed Anya's face, almost like that of a young child who had been presented with a new toy. "This is excellent news! Well done, Sigfus."

"Thank you, your highness," the dark-bearded wizard responded, his expression so smug, he practically preened like a peacock.

Donnie had the sudden urge to punch the arrogant man in the face. Had it not been the two of them there, he just might have.

Anya spun on her heel and headed for the door, signaling for Sigfus to follow. "Come with me. I want to inform *him* of what we have accomplished. Now he has to take me seriously."

Donnie retreated behind the door, not moving until it had been closed and locked. His anger swiftly faded, replaced by a sense of bewilderment. *I wonder who she is rushing to inform? Perhaps that black knight? Or maybe that advisor she previously mentioned?*

Either way, it seemed rather odd that a Princess of Lanfor was so eager to impress someone else. Still pondering over the strange notion, Donnie hurried across the room toward Ves. The young woman hadn't moved a muscle since Anya and Sigfus left.

Donnie spoke the word Glo had taught him to turn him visible once more. "*Dimissionis.*"

Ves' eyes spun toward him as the invisibility spell faded away, her face lighting up with recognition. "Hello, Donatello."

Donnie eyed the young woman carefully, keeping his tone as nonchalant as possible. "Hi, Ves. How are you feeling?"

"I'm fine, thank you for asking."

She sounded calm—far too calm for someone sitting naked in front of him, wearing that collar, in the lower decks of Anya's ship.

Donnie merely nodded. "I'm glad to hear that. So, what are you doing here?"

"I'm waiting for instructions from my mistress," Ves explained to him as if that should have been obvious.

Donnie arched a single eyebrow. *Yep, she's brainwashed.*

Had there been any doubt at all in his mind, it was gone now. Donnie hadn't really thought it possible, despite all the dragons that appeared to be under Anya's sway. The young elf cast a furtive glance at the large blue crystal suspended in the middle of the room. As soon as he did so, his head began to feel fuzzy again.

Donnie wrenched his eyes away. Whatever that thing was, it appeared to have a mind-numbing effect. *Could this crystal be the mechanism that Anya uses to control her dragons? If so, why did they put that collar on Ves? None of Anya's other dragons have collars.*

Donnie would love to know what Glo or Elistra would make of all this, but there was no time for that now. He had to get Ves out of here. The question was how? She obviously wasn't going to move unless her mistress told her to.

A sudden idea came to him. "Ves, the mistress sent me with instructions for us."

Ves cocked her head sideways and narrowed her eyes at him. "Really? What are they?"

"You're to accompany us. The rest of the companions are here aboard the Princess' vessel. We have formed… an alliance with her."

Ves grasped both his hands, a bright smile crossing her lips. "You mean Glolindir is here? And Martan?"

Donnie flashed one of his pearly white smiles at the young woman. "Yes, they are all here. Aksel and Lloyd, too. The Princess wishes to ally herself with the Baron of Ravenford, as well. Since we know him, she asked if we would speak with him on her behalf."

Ves nodded her head in understanding. "Why, of course. Anything for the mistress."

Donnie cast a quick glance over his shoulder, then leaned in close to Ves, his tone turning conspiratorial. "There's only one problem. There's a Dunwynn dignitary aboard this ship. After what happened with the Duke in Ravenford, she doesn't want him to know what is going on. So, we have to leave in secrecy."

Ves whispered back to him. "I see. All things considered, that makes sense."

The young woman stood and signaled for Donnie to go ahead of her. "Very well then, lead the way."

Donnie got up, his eyes briefly passing over Ves' naked form. The thin elf felt the blood rising to his cheeks. He quickly doffed his cloak and held it out toward her. "I think you might need this."

Ves glanced down at her torso, then blushed profusely, her hands going to her cheeks. "Oh, my!"

The young woman's brow abruptly furrowed and her body began to glow. It turned bright for a few moments, then the brilliance swiftly faded. When it was gone, Ves stood garbed in a form-fitting bronze dress. She ran her hands down her sides while looking herself over, then let out a sigh of relief. "That's better."

Ves lifted her gaze to Donnie, a warm smile gracing her lips. "Thank you for being so chivalrous."

Donnie's eyes met hers, the heat in his cheeks slowly dissipating. "It was nothing, really. Now follow me."

Donnie led Ves to the door, completely uncertain what to do next. His plan had worked thus far, but how would he get Ves past the guards? Further, what if Anya or Sigfus caught him with her in the hall?

As they reached the doorway, Donnie's hand brushed against the dagger at his waist. It was the dagger that belonged to…

Ruka! That's it! That's how they would get out of here.

Donnie spun around to face Ves. "Oh, I almost forgot. The Princess asked if we could rely on your sister for help."

Ves stared at Donnie, her brow creasing and her eyes narrowing. "My sister? You mean Ruka?"

Donnie gave her a curt nod. "Yes. The Princess felt that your sister might help if you asked her to."

Ves folded her arms across her chest and gently rubbed her upper arm. After a moment's pause, she nodded. "I could do that. Anything for the mistress."

Donnie flashed her another pearly-white smile. "Very good. Let's find a quiet place, then I'll use the dagger to summon your sister."

Ves stared at Donnie, her brow still creased. He thought he detected the slightest hint of uncertainty in her eyes. Donnie pursed his lips, but said nothing. Perhaps Sigfus' brainwashing wasn't all that complete after all. If they could just get Ves away from here, perhaps they could break her out of it.

Ves finally broke the silence, though this time her voice wavered slightly. "Very well. Lead on."

Donnie unlocked the door, then cracked it open, peering gingerly down the long hall. There was no one in sight. If the solitary guard were still there, he was hidden behind the stairwell.

The slim elf seized Ves by the hand, and led her out into the corridor. Donnie halted and listened carefully at the first door they passed. He heard chanting as if someone were deep in prayer. The elf moved on to the next door. The sound of snoring came from the other side.

At the third door, there was nothing but silence. Donnie tried the handle, and it was unlocked. He swiftly ushered Ves inside and closed the door behind them. The slim elf swiftly swept his eyes around the room. They were in a decent sized cabin, easily as large as some of the double rooms he had stayed in over his many years of travel. A cushy-looking bed stood against one wall, a dresser against the other, and a wardrobe against the third.

Two portholes were inset into the outside wall. Through them, they could see the sky starting to lighten. It would be dawn soon. Donnie gave Ves a brief smile, then pulled out Ruka's dagger, the Ruchan. He closed his eyes and concentrated all his will, repeating the same set of words over and over in his mind. *Ruka, I need you. Please come at once.*

At first nothing happened, but on the third repetition, he detected something bright through his closed lids. Donnie's eyes snapped open. A pinpoint of light had appeared in the very center of the room. It swelled and grew into a familiar form, and when it finally faded, Ruka stood there gazing at him with mixed emotions.

"Donnie, why did you…"

Her voice suddenly trailed off, her eyes going wide as they gazed past him. "Ves!"

The young teen rushed past him, throwing her arms around her missing sister in a completely uncharacteristic display of affection. Ves appeared startled at first, but then wrapped her arms around her younger sister, hugging her tight.

After a few moments, Ruka pulled back from the embrace. She grabbed Ves by the shoulders and stared at her, her voice taking on an accusatory tone. "We've been looking all over for you. You had us worried sick."

Ves responded with a genuine smile. "I've been fine. The mistress has been taking care of me."

"The mistress…" Ruka's voice took on a strained tone. She shifted her eyes toward Donnie, concern written all over her face. Donnie met her intense gaze with one of his own, his voice carefully measured.

"As you already know, we formed an *alliance* with the Princess Anya. Ves is going to help us petition the Baron of Ravenford to ally with the Princess as well."

Ruka cocked her head to one side and eyed Donnie carefully, but Ves interrupted her before she could question him. "It's true, sis. Anya has been very good to me, and I want to help her."

Ruka shifted her gaze back toward her sister. There was a dangerous edge to her voice. "Oh really? The Princess has treated you well?"

"Why, yes," Ves responded as if the answer to that question were obvious. "She even gave me this fine collar to wear."

Ves' hands went to the metallic black collar around her neck. Ruka eyed it carefully, then spun her gaze toward Donnie, her eyes filled with apprehension. Donnie responded with the barest of nods, having no choice but to continue with his original ruse.

"Indeed, the Princess has turned out to be rather… nice. That is why we agreed to do her this favor. Unfortunately, there is a Dunwynn dignitary on board. Do you remember Sir Fafnar?"

Ruka let out a derisive snort. "Yes, I remember him. The pompous ass from Dunwynn that Lloyd trounced in the tourney."

A slight smile spread across Donnie's lips as he recalled the epic battle between the nobleman and the warrior. "The very same. If

Fafnar were to find out about Anya's plans concerning Ravenford, he would look to block them. Therefore, we need to get off this ship without him, or anyone else, seeing us."

"Ohhhh." Understanding dawned in Ruka's eyes.

"We were hoping you could help us with that," Ves added.

Ruka glanced from Donnie to her sister, the tension in her shoulders finally dissipating. "Sure, Ves. I'd be happy to help you out."

Ves gave her sister an affectionate smile. "I knew you would."

Ruka stared back at Ves for a moment, then shifted her gaze toward Donnie. Her eyes still mirrored his own concern. "Okay, what do you need me to do?"

Donnie swiftly thought things over, a daring plan forming in his mind. He grabbed Ruka by the shoulders and looked her in the eye. "Of all of us, Sir Fafnar is least likely to recognize you. Could you check the hallway and make sure the coast is clear?"

Ruka tilted her head slightly, eyeing him with uncertainty. "Is that all?"

Donnie gave her a meaningful stare. "You might also want to check with the guard at the bottom of the stairs. He might have seen something, if he's not dozing on the job. Still, I wouldn't be *shocked* if he was."

Understanding abruptly dawned in the young teen's eyes. A familiar smirk crossed her face. "I can definitely do that."

"Very good," Donnie said, fighting the urge to wink in front of Ves.

The thin elf went to the door and listened, but it was all quiet out in the hall. He opened the door and stuck his head out, but the corridor appeared empty. Donnie then stood back and motioned Ruka out the door.

The young teen slipped past him and stole down the hall toward the stairs. Donnie watched from the doorway as she disappeared around the stairwell. A moment later, there was bright flash of light, and then Ruka reappeared and waved him on.

Donnie whispered over his shoulder. "Ruka just signaled—the coast is clear."

Donnie felt a slim hand slip into his own, then stole quietly out into the hall and down toward the stairs. When they rounded the corner of the stairwell, the slight elf noted the guard there slumped against the wall. There was the faintest smell of ozone in the air.

Ruka shook her head, the side of her mouth upturned slightly. "Asleep on duty, just like you said."

Donnie cast a sidelong glance at Ves. The young woman regarded the 'sleeping' man with a raised eyebrow.

"Poor Anya. I guess good help is hard to find," Donnie noted glibly.

Ves shifted her eyes toward him, a look of disdain on her face. When she spoke, it was barely above a whisper. "I'll have to report him to the mistress when I have the chance."

Donnie let out the briefest of sighs, relieved that Ves had bought the ruse. "Agreed, but for now our mission is more important."

With that hurdle averted, Donnie peered at Ruka once more. "It might be best if you check the upper deck as well."

Ruka gave him a knowing nod, then silently climbed the stairs ahead of them. A half minute later, she came back down, a wide grin across her face. She glanced at Donnie and whispered, "It appears things on deck are already well in hand."

Donnie eyed her curiously, then climbed past her, to the door at the top of the stairs. He cracked it open, his eyes widening at what he saw.

The second guard sat on the deck, fast asleep, with Elladan standing over him. The bard stared back at Donnie with that all-too-familiar half-smile of his. Behind the bard, the rest of their companions had gathered over by the ship's rail.

Donnie stared at Elladan in amazement, a single word falling from his lips. "How?"

Elladan let out a soft laugh, his voice barely above a whisper. "Sigfus was so pleased with himself that he let a bit too much slip. So, when Anya sent me back to my room, I told the others. We figured you might need a hand."

"And just how did Sigfus slip?"

Donnie spun around as Ves and Ruka came up on the deck behind him. The older Greymantle stood there with her arms folded across her chest, her eyes suddenly filled with suspicion.

"Ah… um…" Donnie stammered, his mind racing for some answer that would allay her suspicions. He had come so close to spiriting Ves away. It would be disastrous if she were to turn on them now. Yet before he could utter another word, fate took over for him.

"Ves!" came a familiar cry from across the deck.

Donnie spun around and saw Martan waving his hands their way, his normally glum features alit.

"Martan!" Ves cried back with delight, all her suspicions forgotten at the sight of the archer.

Martan started forward when all of a sudden, he seemed to lose his balance. The archer teetered there for a moment, his face taking on a panicked expression. Abruptly, he fell backwards over the rail with a loud cry. "Ahhhhhhhhh……"

Ves let out a strangled cry of her own, then sprinted across the deck, her body shimmering as she ran. Ruka immediately took off after her, starting to shift as well. Donnie and Elladan exchanged a brief glance, then plunged after both girls.

At the same moment, a loud shout erupted from the direction of the railing. "Watch out! She pushed Martan!"

Elistra stood beside the others, pointing to the empty space where Martan had just been standing. Donnie squinted his eyes, but couldn't see anything. *Martan's attacker must be invisible!*

As Lloyd, Alana, and Cyclone drew their weapons, Ves finished her transformation. The huge bronze dragon unfolded her wings and soared over the others, diving after the falling archer.

"Go after them, Lloyd! We've got this," Alana shouted.

Lloyd hesitated the briefest of moments, then launched himself over the rail after Martan and Ves. Meanwhile, Ruka had finished transforming. Donnie leapt forward just as she lifted off, grasping tight onto her tail. With a sharp flap, Ruka shot across the remaining deck.

Boom!

A fiery explosion erupted directly in their path, the angry red ball of flame expanding out in front of them. Ruka banked sharply to avoid the conflagration, whipping Donnie around as she did so. Abruptly they were past it, and out over the open air.

Unfortunately, Ruka's sudden maneuver had jarred Donnie rather hard. The slight elf felt his grip on her slip away from between his hands. Donnie abruptly found himself falling unchecked about two miles above the earth.

"I think she forgot us!"

Donnie peered back over his shoulder to see Elladan falling through the air just above him. An ironic smile crossed Donnie's lips. "Guess we both fell for the wrong woman!"

25
WHEN HEROES FALL

A group of dark, winged figures had launched off the airship, and were speeding down in their direction

Glolindir peered from the rail of the Wind Hammer in utter confusion. Donnie had reemerged from below decks, but the sandy-haired elf was no longer alone. Beside him stood both Ruka and Ves. A dozen questions passed through the tall elf's mind, but he never got to voice any of them.

"Ahhhhhhhhh……!"

Glo's thoughts were shattered by the frightened cry. He spun around to see Martan a few yards away, the gaunt archer inexplicably teetering at the rail. The entire scene felt surreal, as Martan lost his balance, then fell backwards, disappearing over the side of the ship.

The archer's fall was immediately followed by a strangled cry. Across the deck, Ves vaulted in their direction, the expression on her face mirroring Glo's own sense of horror. Without warning, his arm was seized by a frantic grip.

"Watch out! She pushed Martan!"

Glo nearly jumped out of his skin. Elistra had grabbed onto him, while pointing at the spot from where Martan had just fallen. Though he could see nothing, Glo's body reacted on its own, his hands instinctively weaving into a familiar pattern.

Lloyd, Alana, and Cyclone responded similarly, the ringing sounds of drawn weapons accompanying the wizard's spell. Yet before any of them could take a step forward, a huge bronze blur whooshed overhead.

Glo involuntarily flinched, nearly losing his grip on the magic coalescing between his hands. Beside him, Alana's voice cried out, "Go after them, Lloyd! We've got this."

Glo did not turn to see his friend launch himself overboard after the others. Instead, the wizard struggled to keep his grasp on the fiery red ball forming between his palms, lest it get away and harm them all. With a herculean effort, Glo wrestled the spell back in line, sending the arcane ball of flame hurtling away.

Boom!

The spell went off with a bang, just a bit closer than Glo had anticipated. The angry red ball swiftly expanded into a hemisphere of brilliant flame, the fire coming so close that they had to turn away and shield their faces.

At the same moment, Glo felt a large presence whoosh over them. Still shielding his face from the flames, the elven wizard cracked his eyes open. He was just in time to see a winged bronze shape dive over the side of the ship, with two smaller forms desperately clinging to its tail. Glo watched in horror as both figures suddenly lost their grip on the dragon, then plummeted out of sight.

"That was Donnie and Elladan!" came Aksel's sharp cry.

A moment later, the flaming ball winked out. Glo started for the rail, but a red and black figure inserted itself in front of him. A pair of violet eyes met his, and he suddenly found himself in the midst of a deep, passionate kiss. The kiss ended almost as abruptly as it started, Elistra swiftly pushing him away.

Glo gazed at her dumbfounded, not quite noticing the mist in her eyes. "What was that for?"

Elistra responded with a forced smile. "For luck…"

The seeress' mouth hung open, her eyes searching his for a brief moment, then she pushed him onward toward the rail. "Quick, after the others!"

Glo hesitated. Something didn't feel right. There was a strange tenor to Elistra's voice. Yet his hesitation only made her push him again. "I said go! The others need you!"

Elistra was right. Aksel, Alana, and Cyclone had jumped after the others, and none of them could fly. Glo gave the blonde seeress one last look, then spun around and vaulted over the railing after his friends.

Martan plummeted backwards through the dawn sky, his arms flailing, his hands grasping at empty air. He was not really sure what had happened. He had been waiting with the others at the ship's railing, when Donnie finally reemerged from below deck.

Martan's eyes went wide when he saw who was with the slim elf. *Ves!*

The archer's heart skipped a beat at the sight of the lovely young woman. Ves had saved Martan's life back on the shores of Cape Marlin. He remembered falling down a cliff face and then everything went black. When he woke up sometime later, the first thing he saw was the face of the beautiful blonde hovering over him. She had saved his life, and he had called her his "angel."

Yet now Martan was falling again, and not even his angel could save him this time. Someone had pushed him over the rail. He had neither seen nor heard his attacker, but in all fairness, he had been focused exclusively on Ves.

The dour archer stopped his flailing, resigning himself to his fate, when his gaze fell on something above him. Whatever it was, it was quite big, and growing larger by the second. The rising sun glinted off the figure, revealing a warm, yellow-brown torso, with a pair of large, bat-like wings protruding from either side.

Martan's eyes went wide as he realized what was chasing him. *A dragon!*

The bronze dragon swiftly closed the gap between them, till it was only a few feet away. Martan's eyes fixed on the large maw as it slowly opened to reveal a vast row of razor sharp teeth. The thing was huge—easily as big as the green dragon back at the monolith.

The gaunt archer gulped. *That thing could swallow me in one bite!*

Panic overtook Martan. He screamed, flailing uselessly at the dragon. "G–get away from me!"

The dragon's mouth open wider, but instead of swallowing him, it spoke. "But Martan… it's me! Ves!"

Martan's eyes practically bulged out of their sockets. "Ves?"

He shook his head with disbelief. Yet, there was something in the voice that sounded familiar. "B–but you're a dragon!"

The creature let out a deep, rumbling sigh. "Yes… I'm a dragon. Now hang on. I'm going to catch you."

Before Martan could utter another word, the dragon shot past and banked so that it would pass directly beneath him.

"Grab on!" the creature roared.

Martan quickly peered beyond the dragon—the treetops were rushing up fast. If he didn't grab onto her now, he would plummet past and be dead within seconds. With no choice, the archer braced himself as he collided with the dragon, immediately wrapping his arms and legs around the scaly neck. It was surprisingly smooth to the touch.

As soon as he had grabbed hold, the dragon gave a huge flap with its great wings, propelling them forward. Martan hung on for dear life as they picked up speed. Chancing a peek below them, he saw the forest canopy passing by only scant yards below. The dragon had saved his life! *Could this creature indeed be Ves?*

Martan let out a huge sigh as the truth struck him. He had observed Ruka change into a bronze dragon. So, it would only make sense that her sister was one, too. The archer gulped and tentatively called out to the dragon. "Ves? Is that really you?"

The dragon turned its head so that one huge emerald eye fell on him. When it spoke, its voice sounded heavy with sadness. "Yes, dear Martan. This is my true form."

Ves paused for a moment, still eyeing him as the green treetops passed close beneath. "I'm so sorry. I never meant to deceive you, but I was honor-bound not to tell anyone."

Martan's stomach churned with mixed emotions. He was still very fond of Ves, and this dragon that saved him sounded just like her. Yet, she was a dragon, after all.

The dour archer lifted his head and peered out in front of them. A short distance ahead, the treeline abruptly ended, giving way to a huge expanse of grass that stretched off far to the eastern horizon. The sun hung low in the distance, just beginning its daily journey across the sky.

"C—can we land please?" Martan asked, his voice cracking just a bit.

The young lady dragon responded in a surprisingly understanding tone, "Of course. Hang on!"

Martan grasped on even tighter as they veered downward to meet the approaching forest edge.

Elladan and Donnie had grasped onto Ruka's tail just as she went airborne, the bard a few feet behind his agile friend. With a flick of her wings, the trio shot across the deck of the Wind Hammer. Yet before they could clear the rail, a ball of flame exploded directly in their path. They were so close when it went off, that Elladan involuntarily flinched. Unfortunately, it had been at the same moment the dragon swerved sideways.

Elladan's eyes snapped open to find them past the fire and out into the open air. Sadly, the sudden movement that had saved them from burning also caused him to lose his grip. Ruka's tail slipped away from the bard, leaving him falling unchecked about two miles above the earth.

Yet, Elladan was not alone. Donnie had lost his grip as well, the wiry elf falling through the air just a few feet below him. Elladan cupped his hands around his mouth and called out, "I think she forgot us!"

Donnie spun his head around, his mouth twisting to one side. "Guess we both fell for the wrong woman!"

Elladan half laughed and half groaned. *Leave it to Donnie to find humor in a situation like this.*

Below them, the bronzed form of Ruka swiftly pulled away, the dragon teen unaware that she had lost her two stowaways. Still, they weren't completely out of luck.

"Don't worry, my friend. I can cast *feather fall* on us!" Elladan cried.

Feather fall was a basic spell that nearly every bard learned. While not as handy as flying, it allowed you to jump from any height and float harmlessly down to the ground like a feather.

Elladan began to weave the spell, but Donnie interrupted him. "No! That's too slow! We need to catch up with Ruka and Ves!"

Elladan knit his brows together. "Are you crazy?"

Donnie shook his head. "Just cast it before we hit the ground!"

Elladan let out a long sigh. "Okay… it's your funeral!"

Donnie cast a grin at Elladan, then pulled his arms into his sides, at the same time angling his body downward to speed his descent. Elladan shrugged and pulled out his lute, a quasi-smile crossing his face as he fell through the air strumming a lively tune.

Lloyd dove through the air as fast as he could, but he was no match for the speed of a dragon. Thankfully, Ves was quick enough to catch up with Martan. The young warrior watched with relief as the archer caught hold of the bronze dragon's neck, and then sped off together toward the edge of the forest.

At that point, Lloyd halted his rapid descent, his thoughts turning to his other companions. As the young warrior spun about, a bronze blur whooshed past him with the cry, "Go back for the others!"

That had been Ruka. Lloyd peered past the dragon teen, and saw two familiar forms careening down toward him. *Donnie and Elladan!*

Lloyd adjusted his ascent toward the pair, while sweeping his gaze across the sky in search of the others. Far above, raging flames crackled and danced along the hull of Anya's airship. Halfway between Lloyd and the vessel, another group of figures hung in the air. From this distance, he could just make out Alana, Glo, and Cyclone. Aksel and Elistra were nowhere to be seen. *Could they still be aboard ship?*

With Donnie and Elladan nearly upon him, Lloyd had no time to dwell on the matter. Shifting his focus back to the pair, he called out, "Don't worry! I've got you!"

"We're fine! Elladan's got feather fall!" Donnie cried in response.

"Worry about the others!" Elladan yelled, pointing upward.

Lloyd followed the bard's arm. A group of dark, winged figures had launched off the airship, and were speeding down in their direction. *Anya's let loose her dragons!*

Glo, Alana, and Cyclone sat directly in the dragons' path. With a quick "Good luck" to Donnie and Elladan, Lloyd shot past the duo toward Glo and the others. The young warrior flew as fast as he could, but the dragons were far faster. He had barely closed half the distance when the creatures reached his friends.

Miraculously, the dragons buzzed right by them, leaving his companions completely untouched. It suddenly dawned on Lloyd what the dragons were after. *Ruka and Ves!*

A deep unabiding anger welled up inside the young warrior. Lloyd drew his black blade, engulfing it with flames as he sped upward to meet the dragons. Abruptly, four of the creatures veered off, leaving a single large black dragon to face him. The creature roared in challenge as it closed with Lloyd, the large maw baring its razor-sharp teeth.

Yet a white-hot anger now burned in Lloyd's belly. He took that rage and used it to fuel his inner spirit. As the black dragon came within striking distance, Lloyd unleashed all that energy at once. It coursed through him like a raging river, rocketing him forward through the sky as fast as any dragon.

The black beast snapped at him with its huge maw, but Lloyd shot past its mouth and spiraled beneath it, driving his dark blade into the creature's neck. Between the sword's keen edge, the dragon's speed, and his own great momentum, the blade sliced straight down the creature's underside and through its chest, all the way to its abdomen.

A trail of dark blood gushed from the enormous wound, the dragon barely coughing once before its body went limp. The large black creature fell from the sky toward the ground still far below.

Wild cheers erupted from above. Lloyd cast a quick glance in that direction and saw Glo, Alana, and Cyclone fast approaching. Yet

Lloyd paid them little heed. Still seething, the young warrior swept his gaze downward. The other four dragons had reached the tree-tops. Lloyd took off after them, but there was no way he could reach them in time.

A few hundred feet above the ground, Donnie's fall came to a sudden halt. The thin elf floated the rest of the way down, taking off at a dead run the moment his feet touched the forest floor. He twisted and dodged his way through the lush green wood, finally bursting out into the open at the end of his mad dash.

A wide expanse of grassland lay before him, stretching all the way to the horizon. The morning sun hung low over the earth, the bright orb burning a brilliant orange at this early hour.

A huge bronze dragon lay unmoving on the grass a short distance away, its deep rumbling voice laced with sorrow. "Martan... please don't be mad at me."

Donnie followed the dragon's gaze to a small figure seated near the edge of the forest. Martan sat on his knees, his chin in his hands, staring wild-eyed at the sulking bronze.

A second large bronze dragon stood nearby, its gaze firmly focused on the first. "Ves, snap out of it!"

Donnie let out a deep sigh. If dragons experienced emotions like humans and elves, he was certain that Ves' heart was broken. There was little he could do for the young dragon lady in that respect, but he did have an idea about how to break her free from Anya's control.

The slight elf stole over to the smaller bronze dragon and spoke in hushed tone. "Hey Ruka, what's going on?"

Ruka swiveled her head around, an emerald eye focusing on Donnie. Her deep voice was soft as she replied, "I can't get her to listen to me."

Donnie pointed toward the huge dragon's neck. The black collar Anya had placed on her still clung snugly to it. The piece of metal had magically resized itself to her change of form. "See how that collar is still on her? I think that's what Anya's using to control her."

Ruka swiveled her head around, and peered at the black collar. She then turned an eye back toward Donnie. "What's the plan?"

Donnie doffed his backpack and rummaged through it while he spoke. "While she's distracted with Martan, we break it off her."

Ruka eyed him skeptically as he continued to search through his pack. "I assume we're not just going to rip it off?"

Donnie let out a short sigh. "If it were only that simple—ah, here they are!"

The wiry elf pulled a pair of red leather gloves laced with black striations out of his pack. Ruka's gaze shifted to the gaudy-looking gloves.

"Where did you get those?"

Donnie pulled a glove on, and spun it in front of his face. "These? We liberated these from one of Larketh's chests."

Ruka let out a derisive snort, a rather impressive sound from a dragon. "So, aside from being a questionable fashion statement, what do they do?"

Donnie grinned as he pulled on the second glove. "According to Glo, these little babies carry the neat ability to disrupt spells. I figure that collar on your sister's neck has to be enchanted. If I can break the spell, then you should be able to get it off her."

Donnie had never seen a dragon smirk before, but this was Ruka, after all. The dragon girl reached out behind him with a clawed arm and pushed the slim elf forward. "Well, don't just stand there. Get going already."

Donnie threw his hands up in front of him as she shoved him forward. "I'm going, I'm going."

Donnie gingerly strode up to Ves. The huge bronze dragon still lay with her head on the ground, brooding over Martan's apparent rejection of her. Martan still sat at the edge of the forest, but Elladan now stood beside him. The bard's hand lay on Martan's shoulder as he spoke softly with the distraught archer.

The slim elf remained silent, hoping Ves would not notice him till it was too late. He stole up to the black collar and placed a gloved hand on it. Nothing happened. Donnie tentatively reached out and put his other hand on the collar as well. A red aura almost immediately appeared around the black metal, then just as swiftly faded.

Donnie carefully backed away from Ves, and called to Ruka in a semi-hushed voice. "Okay, do your thing."

Donnie watched with fascination as Ruka opened her maw wide. A bright spark ignited in the dragon-girl's throat, and a moment later, a fierce bolt of lightning leapt from her mouth. The bolt shot past Donnie across the grassy plain, hitting the collar around Ves' neck dead-on. The black metal sizzled and sparked, then split in half, falling off to the grass below.

Ves suddenly raised her head, spinning her long neck toward Donnie and Ruka. "What do you think you're…"

Ves halted in mid-sentence and shook her large head. "Wait. What am I doing here? Last thing I remember is… being on that woman's ship… and that crystal… that horrible blue crystal."

Ves' deep voice trembled, her entire body visibly shuddering. Ruka ambled over to her sister and nuzzled her head against her neck.

"It's okay now, sis. We removed that nasty collar they were using to control you."

"And the crystal is back on Anya's ship, which is far away by now," Donnie added in a reassuring tone. In truth, he had lost track of Anya's ship. He lifted his head, scanning the sky for the Princess' vessel, his eyes going wide as they swept over the forest.

"Unfortunately, her dragons aren't!" Donnie swiftly added, urgently pointing toward the woods.

All eyes turned to see four large winged figures skimming over the treetops directly for them. The dragons were still some distance away, but closing fast.

Ves lifted herself up off the ground and spread her large wings. "It's me they're after. Go hide in the forest while I lead them off."

Ruka backed away and unfurled her wings as well. "You're not going alone. I'm coming with you!"

Ves swiveled her head toward her sister. She knew better than to argue with Ruka once the teen had made up her mind. She responded with a simple, "Okay."

Ves then shifted her gaze back toward Martan. Donnie could have sworn he saw a hint of moisture in her large green eyes. "Once again, I am sorry, Martan. I never meant to hurt you. I really do like you. Please stay safe."

Her gaze lingered on him a moment longer, then the great bronze dragon rose off the ground with a few fast beats of her huge wings, her sister following suit. Donnie backed away to join Elladan and Martan, the wind buffeting the three of them as the pair of bronze dragons stirred up the air around the area.

"Take care, Donnie!" Ruka cried down at him. "You know how to reach me if you need me!"

Both dragons then spun around and with a great flap shot across the grasslands toward the rising sun, swiftly picking up speed. Elladan, Martan, and Donnie backed into the woods just in time, as four more dragons strafed overhead, right on the heels of the other two.

The trio watched in awe as all six dragons swiftly disappeared into the distance. It was Martan who finally broke the silence, his voice cracking with emotion. "Think… they'll be… alright?"

Elladan clasped the archer on the shoulder and gave him a reassuring smile. "They're bronzes, and they're headed for the sea. Once they get to open water, the others will never catch them."

26
RETURN TO THE BENDENWOODS

Make all yerselves scarce 'n get to where ya can talk to some druids!

Glo, Lloyd, Alana, and Cyclone all touched down at the same time near the forest edge, not far from where Donnie, Elladan and Martan huddled in the woods. The trio slowly came out from between the trees to greet them.

"Is everyone alright?" Lloyd called out to them.

"Yeah, we're fine," Donnie answered with a nonchalant wave of his hand.

"I just hope Ves is okay," Martan added, his expression even more sullen than usual.

Glo peered closely at the archer. He did look a bit pale. Still, that was not his primary concern right now. "Have either of you seen Elistra or Aksel?"

"Up here!" Aksel's voice drifted down from above.

Glo tilted his head back, but saw no sign of the little cleric. "Where?"

"I'm invisible—and I finally found a use for that ring Seth gave me back in the Ruins!"

A faint smile spread across Glo's lips. He remembered that ring. It was a plain silver band with a small blue gemstone.

"What ring is that?" Elladan asked.

Glo shrugged his shoulders as he continued to scan the skies for the missing seeress. "A ring of feather falling."

"And Seth gave that up?" Donnie asked incredulously.

"He didn't know what it was at the time," Glo answered absently.

"He was supposed to be scouting out the Ruins, but came back with a bag full of treasure," Lloyd explained further. "Aksel was kind of annoyed, so Seth gave him the ring as a peace offering. Let's just say, Seth was not happy when he found out what it actually was."

Elladan and Donnie burst into laughter at the thought of the halfling outsmarting himself. Yet, amusing as the tale was, Glo was now far too worried to enjoy it. He called out to Aksel once more.

"Have you seen any sign of Elistra?"

This time, Aksel's voice came from the ground nearby. "Just landed… and no, I haven't since we left the ship… but she did give me a note to hand over to you."

Aksel abruptly reappeared a few yards from where they were standing. Glo rushed over to his gnome friend, anxiously wringing his hands together. "May I see it?"

Aksel reached inside his robe, and pulled out a small piece of folded parchment. Glo gingerly took the paper from him, swiftly unfolding it. There was a short message written on it, in Elistra's handwriting.

My Dearest Glolindir,

I am so sorry that it has come to this, but I must leave you. Please know that this is not my first choice. Were I to stay, I would be placing you all in grave danger. Do not worry. By the time you read this, I will be safely away. Thanks to the distraction I foresee you providing, Anya will never catch me.

I know this is hard, but please do not try to find me. Trust me, it is better this way. Just know that for the first time in a very, very long time, I felt what it was like to be loved.

You will always have a place in my heart,
Elistra

Glo read the letter again and again, his hand shaking as he read it over. Numbness spread through his entire being as he looked up from that letter, his breath coming in short, ragged bursts. It felt as if the whole world had come crashing down around him.

A gentle hand grasped his shoulder. Glo spun around to see Elladan gazing at him, the bard's eyes filled with compassion. Elladan stepped back as the others gathered around, all of them mirroring the bard's expression except for Cyclone—yet even the stoic hunter had gone quiet.

Alana slowly strode up to him and took him by the arm. When she spoke, her voice was very soft. "She's not coming with us, is she?"

Glo gazed at the lady knight for a few moments, then gently shook his head. "No. She isn't."

Aksel peered up at him with a weak smile. "I'm sorry, Glo, but we need to decide what we are going to do. Anya's ship is heading back this way."

The little cleric pointed a finger toward the northeast. The Princess' airship could clearly be seen crossing the sky, as it banked around back in their direction. It was still over a mile away, but once it picked up speed, it would be on them in no time.

Glo forced himself to forget Elistra for the moment. There would be plenty of time to feel sorry for himself later. Right now, his friends were in trouble, and they needed his expertise. His tone was firm as he answered Aksel's original question. "What we're going to do is hide."

Cyclone folded his arms across his chest. "That won't work against dragons. They'll smell you out as good as if they could see you."

The corners of Glo's mouth upturned slightly. "Not if you're on another plane."

The dragon hunter eyed him sharply. "Not even gonna pretend I know what you're talking about."

Glo responded with a closed mouth laugh, then strode off purposely toward the woods. "Follow me and you'll find out."

Glo led them a short way into the forest, finally halting at a small break between the trees. The wizard shifted his gaze to Elladan. "Do you have any rope?"

"Always," Elladan responded with a bent smile. The elven bard unslung his pack and swiftly rummaged through it, producing a hefty length of rope.

Glo nodded toward the ground in front of them. "Lay it there."

Elladan did so and then stepped back. Without a word, Glo spun his arms in a circular pattern, ending the design with the words, "*Funem Dolum.*"

The magic released, coalescing around the length of rope on the ground. A bluish aura surrounded the coils, then the rope snaked straight up as if it were alive. When it was done, the base of the rope hung a few feet off the ground. The rest of its length stretched upward nearly thirty feet above them, the very top disappearing into a fluffy white cloud.

Elladan clasped the elven wizard on the shoulder. "Ah, the old *Rope to Nowhere*! Very clever."

Cyclone eyed the cloud skeptically. "Ain't that thing a little small to hide all of us?"

Glo grimaced at the stony-faced hunter. "It's bigger inside than it looks."

The companions climbed the rope one at a time, Glo leading the way. As he had told Cyclone, the space inside the cloud was larger than it appeared from the outside, easily large enough to fit all eight of them comfortably.

Cyclone was the last one up. He climbed in next to Glo, and looked down at the dangling rope. "Ain't that gonna look kind of conspicuous just hanging there?"

Glo hauled up the rope and layered the coils next to him, then folded his arms and glared at Cyclone. After Elistra's letter, he was not in the best of moods, and the dragon hunter's questioning him was beginning to wear thin. "Any more comments?"

Cyclone stared back at Glo, completely unperturbed by the wizard's ire. After a few moments of silence, he finally responded. "Just one. This fluffy little cloud is cute and all, but ain't it gonna stand out in this forest like a sore thumb?"

Glo narrowed his eyes at the hunter before answering in a monotone voice. "Once the rope's inside, the cloud turns invisible."

Cyclone leaned back against the cloud and interlaced his fingers behind his head. "Well, ain't that handy."

Glo eyed the dragon hunter darkly, but kept his comments to himself.

Aksel was worried. They had found Ves, but in the process, had lost her again, along with both Ruka and Elistra. Further, they had made an enemy of the Princess Anya, a woman with an erratic temperament—and a small army at her disposal.

To make matters worse, both Martan and Glo were sulking. The former had discovered Ves' true nature, and the latter had been unexpectedly 'dumped' by Elistra.

Yet despite their losses, Aksel needed his friends to regroup and focus on their mission. The Serpent Cult was still out there, not to mention that black knight who could control dragons. Both posed a danger to not only Ravenford, but all Thac.

The Princess Anya was another story. Her anger with them aside, Aksel doubted she would intentionally endanger the citizens of Thac. Anya had her standing as a Princess of Lanfor to maintain, and he highly doubted she would do anything to jeopardize that.

No, we definitely need to concentrate on the Serpent Cult.

That reminded Aksel, he had received a *Sending* from Seth. The magically-written parchment had appeared on his bed in the middle of the night with Seth's name scrawled on the outside. With all that had happened, Aksel never had a chance to read it.

The little cleric reached inside his robe and drew out the letter, rereading the name written on the parchment. *Seth Korzair*. Aksel had been worried about his halfling friend ever since he took off after that black mage. That had only been two days ago, but it felt like a lifetime.

Aksel carefully unfolded the letter, but before he could read it, he was interrupted by Glo. The elven wizard had pulled out the bronze amulet that hung around his neck, the one inset with the large 'Pearl of Friendship' that Ves had given him. Glo stared absently at the moon-colored gem while muttering to himself. "I'm worried about Ruka and Ves. Maybe I should contact them."

"I'm not so sure that's a good idea," Aksel told his elven friend.

Glo shifted his eyes toward him, his normally sharp gaze clouded with indecision. "Why's that?"

Aksel felt a pang of sorrow for Glo. Elistra's sudden departure had shattered his self-confidence and fogged his mind. The little cleric took a deep breath and carefully explained what should have been obvious to the wizard.

"Anya captured Ves, right? And what does Ves carry on her? A pearl just like the one you are wearing. A pearl that communicates with yours, Ruka's, and Maya's."

Glo cocked his head to one side, and raised a single eyebrow. "So, you think Anya took Ves' pearl?"

Aksel pressed his lips together and nodded. "I think it's a possibility we have to consider."

Glo closed his eyes and shook his head, a d expression crossing his face. "Why didn't I see that?"

Alana, seated next to Donnie, stood up and strode across the cloud to Glo. She sat down next to the anguished wizard, interlocking her arm with his. Glo shifted his gaze toward her, his eyes filled with mixed emotions.

When Alana spoke, her words were soft. "May I see the letter Elistra wrote you?"

Glo hesitated a moment, then reached into his robe and pulled out the parchment. Alana carefully took the letter from him and read it over in silence. After a minute or so, the lady knight handed the parchment back to him, her eyes brimming with moisture.

Alana wiped the tears from her face, then reached over and grabbed the wizard's arm, her light hazel eyes fixing upon his. When she spoke, her tone was heartfelt. "You need to stop being so hard on yourself. Elistra obviously cares for you deeply. What she did was an ultimate act of sacrifice."

Alana placed her other hand over the wizard's heart. "Carry that here where it belongs. Let it strengthen, rather than diminish you."

The tall elf's eyes now brimmed with tears. He reached down and placed his hand over the lady knight's, his voice thick with emotion. "Dear, sweet, Alana… thank you. You have opened my eyes. I will endeavor to do as you say."

Alana smiled warmly at Glo, then knelt forward and kissed him on the cheek. Glo's face reddened briefly, as the lady knight sat back down and interlocked arms with him.

Elladan, across from the duo, couldn't resist needling Donnie. "Hey Donnie, I think you just lost another girlfriend."

Donnie fixed the bard with a withering stare. "At least mine isn't trying to kill us."

Elladan cocked his head to one side and spiked an eyebrow. "Anya is not my girlfriend. I don't do crazy."

A wry smile graced Donnie's lips. "Then what were you doing in her cabin all night?"

Elladan stared back at Donnie with a semi-smile. "A gentleman never kisses and tells."

Aksel had kept silent this entire time, trusting in the group's desire to help each other. Alana's words and actions had gone a long way toward healing Glo. Elladan and Donnie's banter had also served to lighten the group's mood. But now it was time to get serious.

The little cleric cleared his throat. "Ahem. Anyway, before all hell broke loose, I received a message from Seth."

Aksel held up the parchment in his hand for all to see. Glo, Lloyd, Elladan, Donnie, and Alana all sat upright and stared at the letter.

"So, what does it say?" Glo asked, the wizard's eyes sharp once more.

Aksel slowly shook his head. "I haven't had a chance to read it."

Everyone except Cyclone gathered around as the little gnome read the contents of the message aloud.

Wher'er y'all is, make all yerselves scarce 'n get to where ya can talk to some druids!

Aksel lifted his eyes and swept them across the group. They all wore mixed expressions, ranging from perplexed to downright astonished.

"If that's from Seth, he must be hitting the ale," Donnie quipped.

"Forget the ale," Elladan countered. "If Seth wrote that, he's gotta be drinking rum."

Lloyd's brow was furrowed into deep creases. "Does it say anything else?"

Aksel responded with a curt nod. "There's a bit more."

Oh my gods. I can't believe we're sending a message to the Heroes. I love you guys.

S'cuse my friend. She wrote that. I didn't. Now, get yer tight fannies o'er here, 'n make it snappy!

Aksel put the letter down after reading that last line, and glanced around the cloud once more. Many of the companions looked just as confused as they had moments ago. Donnie, however, was doubled over with laughter.

"I don't know about you guys, but I kind of like this new Seth."

A broad grin stretched across Elladan's face. "I have to admit, he's definitely more colorful."

Unlike his fellow elves, Glo took the message seriously. He sat there cross-legged with his hands steepled together, and his brow knit in concentration. "I imagine Seth had someone else send that message—a druid, by the sound of it."

Aksel exchanged glances with Glo. There was one place they had been in the recent past that was full of druids. "Do you think he's in Bendenwood?"

"If he is, then we're less than a day's ride from him."

All eyes turned toward Martan. It was the first time the archer had spoken since they had climbed up into the cloud. Martan gazed around at all of them and shrugged. "That's where we are—the eastern edge of the Bendenwoods."

Lloyd stared at the archer with his brows knit together. "Are you sure?"

Martan nodded. "Positive. I grew up here. I know these woods like the back of my hand."

Lloyd's eyes suddenly brightened with excitement. "Well if that's the case, then we should be able to meet up with him later today."

"Well then, get a-crackin' write'n up a response," Donnie said, waving his hand and mimicking the tone of Seth's note.

His imitation elicited a round of chuckles from the group.

Eight hours later, the companions climbed down from the fluffy cloud and re-entered the woods. It was now the middle of the day, the warm rays of the sun peeking through the forest canopy here and there. Martan and Donnie scouted the area, but there was no sign of Anya's airship or her dragons.

Martan then set out to find the east-west road that ran through the Bendenwoods. Aksel had worked out a rendezvous with Seth, along the road where it emerged on the eastern edge of the forest. As it turned out, they were only a couple of miles south of the road, and could easily reach it in time to meet up with the halfling.

Seth was going to bring horses, and from there they would set out for the northern branch of the Korlokesels. The halfling had found the cult's lair, Serpent's Hollow, nestled somewhere in those mountains.

Seth also discovered that the cult was planning some ritual that would loose a great evil on Thac. Due to the limitations of the messages they had exchanged, the halfling was sketchy on the details of this latest threat. From what little they could tell, Seth had tried to get help, but it wouldn't reach the hollow in time. Thus, once again, it was up to the companions to hold off the cult from perpetrating its deadly plan.

Personally, Martan was skeptical about the whole thing. The Heroes had been lucky thus far, but as Martan knew only too well, luck eventually ran out.

Thankfully, Alana agreed to go with them. The lady knight had been reluctant to join them aboard Anya's ship—a sensible notion in Martan's mind—but she did need to get back to her fellow knights afterwards.

The news of her impending departure had saddened Donatello. Just before Martan left, the duo went off into the woods together to talk in private. Martan liked both Donnie and Alana, and sincerely hoped they could work things out. *At least someone should be happy.*

The archer's own experience with love was disappointing at best. Ves' being a dragon had caught Martan by surprise. She was the first woman to show interest in him in quite a long time. *So, of course there had to be something wrong with her.*

The only other girl Martan had ever been close with was a young archer back when he still lived in Deepwood. The girl was a fiery one, full of life and fun, though a bit goofy at times. Still, she was one of the few people that had taken an interest in Martan. Unfortunately, life got in the way of that budding romance.

Martan wasn't a native of Deepwood. Old man Coran had begrudgingly taken him in after rescuing the lad from bandits. As it turned out, Coran was not paternal in the least, although he did teach Martan everything he knew about archery and tracking.

Still, Martan was an outsider. No one in Deepwood trusted him except for that girl. Yet, the girl's family did not approve of their friendship, her brothers in particular making Martan's life a living hell.

Thus, when old man Coran was found dead, Martan was immediately blamed. The girl's brothers used the tragedy to drive him out of town once and for all. Martan never even got the chance to say goodbye.

He could still picture her to this day. The long reddish-brown hair always pushed behind one ear, those sharp gray eyes, and that goofy grin that never failed to make him smile.

The dour archer let out a deep sigh as he trekked his way back to fetch the others. *That's water under the bridge.*

Lloyd Stealle waited quietly with his friends on the road at the eastern edge of the Bendenwoods. It was late afternoon, the golden orb of the sun shining brightly in the clear blue sky as it slowly sank toward the western horizon. The companions had arrived here an hour ago, and had maybe another hour to wait before Seth arrived with their mounts.

Lloyd gazed fondly around the familiar woods. This was the very spot he had met Glo, Seth, and Aksel all those weeks ago. The encounter had changed his life in more ways than one.

Never in his wildest dreams could he imagine all the adventures they had been through together. In that short amount of time, Lloyd had grown tremendously in skill with his blades. Yet that was not the only way he had grown. Lloyd had learned much from Aksel and Elladan about tactics. Elistra had helped him to deepen the connection with his inner spirit. And Glo and the others had taught him the true meaning of friendship.

Then of course, there's Andrella. Lloyd's heart skipped a beat at the very thought of the beautiful young lady. He would go to any length to keep her safe.

One day, if I'm lucky, she might even agree to marry me. The thought made Lloyd arch an eyebrow. Marriage had been the farthest thing from his mind before he met Andrella. He had never been good with the ladies, though he did have some lady friends. In truth, they were mostly his sister's friends.

One friend in particular, Alys, had convinced him to set out on this journey in the first place. Lloyd felt extremely thankful that he had listened to the clever young lady. He was certain if she ever met Andrella, the two would hit it off magnificently.

"Dragon!"

The sudden hiss made Lloyd jump to his feet. Martan pointed up to the sky directly above them. Sure enough, a winged red figure buzzed over the tree tops, circling around their current position. Thankfully, it didn't appear to be all that large.

Lloyd had just started to relax when Elladan called out in a semi-hushed tone, "We can't let it report back to Anya."

Elladan was right. Small, or not, the dragon was still a threat.

"I'll handle it," Lloyd declared, grabbing the edge of his cloak.

He invoked its magic with a single word and swiftly rose into the air. Lloyd stuck to the trees as he carefully drew his ebon blade. On the dragon's next pass, he unleashed his spirit energy the same way he had against the black dragon earlier that day.

Lloyd shot up out of the trees, catching the smaller red dragon completely off guard. His black blade bit deep into the creature's underside, gutting it just like he had previously with the black. The small red dragon never knew what hit it. It was dead before it reached the ground.

Lloyd led Martan, Elladan, and Cyclone to retrieve the body. It really was a small dragon, maybe eight feet in length from its head to the tip of its tail. In the end, they put it in Elladan's *Portal Bag*. Just like Glo's cloud spell, the bag opened to another plane. Thus, it was far larger on the inside than it appeared.

On the way back, Cyclone grunted at Lloyd. "Don't let killing a couple of baby dragons go to your head."

Lloyd's face flushed, a hot retort on his lips, but then just shook his head.

They had just rejoined the others when a group of riders appeared on the road off to the west. The lead rider was a familiar figure in black astride a large dog. He was accompanied by nine riders, one another little person straddling a second dog.

The group of riders halted a short distance from the companions, then eight of them dismounted and shifted into wolves. The eight wolves bolted off into the forest, leaving Seth and the one other rider alone to greet the companions.

"Ho, Seth!" Aksel cried, running forward to greet the halfling.

"Ho yourself!" Seth yelled back.

Lloyd grinned. Seth hadn't changed in the slightest.

The second rider turned out to be a young woman, perhaps in her early twenties. She dressed in the green and brown leathers of a tracker, with a long bow slung across her back. The young woman dismounted, pushing a strand of long reddish-brown hair behind one ear, her mouth agape as she swept her sharp gray eyes around the group.

She clasped her hands together and practically squealed, "Oh my gods! You're the Heroes of Ravenford!"

The corner of Seth's mouth upturned slightly. "Who'd you think we were off to meet? The Duke of Dunwynn?"

The exuberant young woman fixed him with a grin, but before she could reply, Martan stepped out from behind the others.

"Kalyn?" the name barely passed Martan's lips. He looked deathly pale, as if he'd seen a ghost.

The young woman shifted her gray eyes toward the archer, her expression immediately growing hard.

"Martan," she responded icily, as if his name were a curse.

Seth swept his eyes between the two, his smirk widening. "You two know each other?"

Kalyn folded her arms across her chest, her voice remaining cold. "You could say that."

Seth peered at Martan and then back at Kalyn. "Oh, this just keeps getting better and better."

Kalyn looked away from the archer and flashed a big smile at the rest of the group, "Hi! I'm Kalyn!"

Lloyd found himself grinning back at the exuberant young woman. "Hi! I'm Lloyd."

Kalyn's mouth fell open. She gawked at him for a moment, before finding her voice again.

"The red warrior…" She spoke the words as if he were some sort of folk hero.

Lloyd's cheeks suddenly turned hot, his hand going to the back of his neck. He fumbled with a response, but was interrupted by a hand on his shoulder.

"He's been called worse—mostly by our enemies."

Lloyd turned to see Elladan standing there with Glo and Donnie next to him. All three appeared quite amused.

Kalyn's eyes went wide as they shifted to the trio. "By the giant faces of Deepwood—the tales are true! You're elves! Real, honest-to-goodness elves!"

"What gave us away?" Donnie said with a sly grin.

Kalyn abruptly covered her mouth, her freckled face turning beet red.

Alana strode up to the young woman and cast a glare at Donnie. "Ignore him. He thinks he's a jester."

The lady knight then extended a gauntleted hand to the lady archer. "Alana Benefilla…"

"…Knight of the Rose," Kalyn interrupted her, gushing once more. "The lady knight from the Battle of Ravenford!"

Lloyd peered at Seth. "The Battle of Ravenford?"

Seth merely shrugged in response. "That's what they're calling it. It appears we're famous."

Kalyn nodded her head vigorously. "Oh, you are. You all are. Tales of your adventures have traveled like wildfire even as far as Deepwood."

Lloyd knit his brow. *We're famous?*

Elladan, however, did not seem surprised. "I've sung about our exploits in a few taverns now. Stories like that tend to get around."

A few murmurs went around the group before Aksel stepped forward and cleared his throat. "Ahem. That's all well and fine, but we still have work to do, people."

The little cleric then introduced himself to Kalyn. Seth explained she was a tracker from Deepwood and had helped him scout out Serpent's Hollow. He had brought her along to lead them all there.

It was at that point that Kalyn noticed Cyclone. The stoic hunter stood to one side, his arms folded across his chest. Kalyn stared at him for a moment, then snapped her fingers. "You must be Donatello."

The hunter's mouth bent sideways. He pointed a thumb toward the wiry elf. "I'm Cyclone. That's Donatello."

Kalyn shifted her gaze toward the sandy-haired elf, her complexion reddening once more. "Oops. Sorry. My mistake. I just thought— you'd be more like him."

Nearly everyone erupted into laughter. Even Cyclone appeared amused.

Donnie cast a dark gaze around the group. "I seem to be getting that a lot lately."

With the introductions done, everyone chose a mount and saddled up. Kalyn took the lead, Martan trotting beside her, as she led them out of the woods and then north along the forest edge.

Lloyd noted with curiosity the strained silence between the two trackers. It seemed a stark contrast to the new girl's bubbly personality. The young warrior spurred his horse up next to Seth, then whispered to the halfling, "Any idea what's up with those two?"

Seth shook his head. "No idea, but whatever it is, I like it. I've been trying to get her to shut up for days now."

Lloyd couldn't help but chuckle. He hadn't realized till that moment just how much he'd missed the halfling.

27
TALL TALES

Your little mishap has become the stuff of legends

The afternoon wore on as the little band skirted the edge of the Bendenwoods. Seth trotted silently next to Aksel, his mind preoccupied by their missing companions.

The halfling had immediately noticed both Ruka and Elistra were gone from their ranks. Yet between Kalyn's "fan-girling" and Aksel's insistence on moving out, he never got the chance to broach the subject.

Seth brought it up to Aksel once they left the woods, but the gnome refused to discuss the topic. He had covertly glanced at Glo and whispered, "Not now."

From Glo's sullen expression, he was obviously pining away over the missing seeress. Seth decided to drop the subject, but continued to wonder at what had happened. The last time he had seen them, Elistra and Glo were practically inseparable.

Further, none of this explained Ruka's disappearance. The dragon teen had been as glued to Donnie's side as Elistra was to Glo's. It would take an act of the gods to pry her from the slight elf.

An ironic smile crossed the halfling's lips. *These elves have no luck with women.*

The riders followed the edge of the Bendenwoods until a chain of rolling hills appeared ahead.

"Those must be the Vogels," Elladan announced from his saddle.

"Yup. Sure are," Kalyn called back from the head of the riders. The young tracker glanced over her shoulder and squinted at the bard. "Y'all been here before?"

Elladan snorted. "Ha! You could say that. Does nearly being buried in a cave-in count?"

The young woman's face lit up at his mention of the incident. "That was here?" Her eyes swept across the landscape ahead of them. "I heard tales of your run-in with orc bandits. Guess I should'a realized their base was in the Vogel foothills."

Elladan chuckled softly. "Yeah, well, you won't find anything left of it. Titan saw to that. Nearly brought the whole thing down on our heads."

"…and saved our lives in the process," Lloyd added, in defense of their erstwhile companion.

Kalyn practically squealed with excitement. "Titan? Isn't that the lady warrior who went up to Stone Hill with you guys?"

Lloyd grinned. "That's her. She's a regular force to be reckoned with."

Kalyn seemed completely enamored with their old comrade. She spent the next hour pumping them for stories about the lady warrior. Elladan obliged with several tales about their adventures with Titan and her companion Brundon back at Stone Hill.

Seth half-listened to the stories, his thoughts straying back to Ruka and Elistra. While the others were preoccupied, Seth took advantage of the situation. He nudged Aksel in the shoulder and whispered, "Follow me."

Seth reigned in his dog and fell back to the end of the line. Aksel followed shortly thereafter. Seth looked the little gnome carefully in the eye. "So, what happened to the others?"

Aksel held up a finger and gazed ahead. The rest of the party seemed so wrapped in Elladan's narrative that they hardly noticed them back here. Aksel took a deep breath and filled Seth in on their run-in with the Princess of Lanfor.

Seth listened closely, barely commenting during Aksel's recount. He found it rather interesting that this Anya could control dragons, and was not surprised in the slightest that she had kidnapped Ves.

Seth just shook his head when he heard they had boarded her airship. It was all he could do to keep from laughing out loud while Aksel described their frantic fall from Anya's vessel. Ruka's ditching of Donnie and Elladan in mid-air especially amused him.

When Aksel was done, Ruka's departure finally made sense. Seth wasn't worried about the dragon girls, though. He was certain they could handle themselves, other dragons or not. The only thing that nagged at him was Elistra's abrupt departure.

Seth had never completely trusted the seeress. She was far too secretive, but he had liked the way she affected Glo. The elf had loosened up tremendously since he had met her. Yet now her questionable exit had left his elven friend shattered. What Seth really wanted was a look at that letter she had left him. There might be some clues in there as to the reason for her sudden disappearance.

In the meantime, Elladan finished his last tale. "…and so, the mighty Titan departed Ravenford with Brundon by her side, to seek out her place as a Knight of the Rose."

Alana had trotted quietly next to Donnie during Elladan's narrative. Yet now at the mention of her order, she finally spoke. "How long ago was this?"

"About two days before the Lady Andrella's party," Elladan responded. "How long is the journey to the Wind Tower from Ravenford?"

"About four days," Alana said. "We were on the road well before they would have arrived." The lady knight paused a moment, her brow furrowing. "Titan is a warrior name, right? What is her given name?"

"Delara. Delara Ranblade," Lloyd answered.

Alana's eyes widened with surprise. "Delara Ranblade? Well,

praise be to Cormar, we did meet her! At the inn in Bendenwood. She came over and introduced herself. In fact, we even had dinner with them!"

Kalyn snorted. "As my friend, Fran, always says, it's a rinky-dink world." The lady tracker cast a side-long glance at Martan. "Maybe a bit too rinky-dink…"

Seth shifted his gaze between the pair. Martan had turned positively gray after Kalyn's cutting remark. Whatever he had done, it wasn't going away anytime soon.

Meanwhile, Alana swept her gaze around the riders, a wan smile on her lips. "The entire time I listened to your story, I thought this Titan sounded familiar. I should have known when you said Brundon."

Lloyd gave the lady knight a sympathetic smile. "That's alright. We knew Titan for quite a while before she told us her real name."

Alana smiled kindly at the young man and nodded. "I will tell you this, though. From what I saw and heard just now, Delara will rise swiftly through the Knights of the Rose."

A warm chuckle passed Elladan's lips. "Trust me, Alana, of that we have little doubt!"

A short while later, the riders reached the Vogels. The grass-covered hills filled the sky to the east, their green and brown slopes dotted with trees. A sparsely-treed strip of grass, maybe a few hundred yards wide, separated the forest from those hills. The riders wound their way along the strip until they came across a spot that appeared quite familiar. There was an indentation in the hillside like the mouth of a cave, except that it was filled with rocks.

Kalyn's keen eyes noticed it immediately. "Is that the remains of the orc cave?"

Elladan peered sharply at the hillside. "I believe it is."

"It definitely is," Lloyd declared. He pointed to a rather large tree not too far from the cave mouth. "That's the place where the troll had Seth treed."

A slight shiver passed up Seth's spine. He remembered that incident far too well. The blood-red eyes of the troll peering up at him would be forever engrained in his brain.

Kalyn abruptly reigned in her horse and spun around in her

saddle. "What? Seth, treed?" She peered back at the halfling with a wide grin on her lips. "Really now? How come I've never heard that story?"

Seth glared at her darkly, refusing to comment.

Elladan responded with a short, closemouthed laugh. "That's because I wasn't around to tell it. Must have been just before I met these guys."

Kalyn shifted her eyes back to Seth, her arms crossed and a smug expression on her face. "Well don't be shy—spit it out, already!"

Seth fixed her with a scathing stare, his mouth remaining firmly shut. Lloyd, on the other hand, seemed more than willing to fulfill her request. The riders continued along the path while the young man relayed the tale. He vividly described Glo's heat ray arcing through the air as it caught the troll in the chest. Lloyd then launched into how he and Titan tag-teamed the creature until it sent him sprawling with its huge club.

Kalyn appeared completely engrossed in the story. "So why ain't you jelly under a troll's heel? Did Titan save you?"

"Actually, it was Seth."

All eyes turned to Glo. It was the first time the elf had spoken since they had set out on this journey. The corners of Glo's mouth upturned slightly as he continued with the story.

"As you may already know, trolls are weak to fire. So, while the others kept the creature busy, Seth decided to light a torch. When Lloyd hit the deck, Seth ran up behind the creature and shoved that torch right up the troll's butt."

The group of riders came to an abrupt halt, most of them roaring with laughter. Kalyn practically snorted through her mouth. "Oh my gods! That's hysterical!"

All eyes turned to Seth. The halfling shrugged, his mouth lifting on one side. "It was one of my finer moments."

Much as Seth disliked rehashing the past, the story had lightened everyone's mood, especially Glo. The elf remained talkative after that. He and Lloyd finished the troll story, and then went on along with Elladan to detail their adventures in the orc caves.

Darkness slowly blanketed the sky, stars twinkling into existence overhead when the riders finally left the Vogels behind. They continued along the edge of the forest for a few more hours until they spotted a break in the tree line. A smooth cobblestone road led out of the woods and headed off toward the northeast.

Donnie and Alana gazed back and forth along the roadway.

The sandy-haired elf wore a puzzled expression. "I wonder where that leads?"

"I'm guessing it comes from Bendenwood," Alana hazarded.

Kalyn nodded. "Yup. Heads from Bendenwood all the way to Dunwynn."

The young woman turned her head and spit on the road after answering. Seth was curious about the strange behavior, but was distracted by Aksel before he had a chance to comment. The gnome trotted his riding dog onto the road, then spun around to face Kalyn.

"It's getting kind of late. How much farther to Serpent's Hollow?"

The young tracker glanced around, her brow knit in concentration. "Hmm, the mountains are just a stone's throw away. We could reach them by midday tomorrow. From there it's a hop, skip, and a jump to the hollow."

Aksel's brow furrowed in puzzlement, but Seth came to his rescue. The halfling held up three fingers and said, "That's this many hours."

Aksel stared at him, dumbfounded. "How do you get that out of what she just said?"

Seth smirked outrageously. "It's Deepwood-ese. You pick it up after a while. A hop, skip and a jump are an hour apiece."

Kalyn put her hands on her hips and stared at him. "Now what did you have to go and do that for? My directions was just fine. He'd a figured it out… eventually."

Aksel shifted his gaze between the pair and just shook his head. "Anyway… I say we should make camp for the night."

Kalyn gave him a sharp nod. "I know just the place."

The young tracker spurred her horse along the road toward the woods, motioning for the others to follow.

Kalyn led them to a secluded clearing, surrounded by thick pine trees a short way off the road. It was the perfect spot for a campfire.

Martan swiftly had one roaring. Elladan then pulled out his pots and prepared the base for a stew while the two trackers went out hunting.

As Seth predicted, the pair went out separately, Kalyn sticking to her icy treatment of Martan. When they returned a short while later, Kalyn practically crowed with triumph that her stag was bigger than the doe Martan had found.

The air around the little camp was soon filled with the delicious aroma of one of Elladan's stews. Seth would never admit it out loud, but he had missed the elven bard's cooking. Kalyn appeared impressed as well. She gingerly took the first bowl Elladan proffered her and after one bite gushed over its contents.

"This is the best stew I've ever tasted! What in the world did you do to this venison?"

Elladan's eyes glinted with mirth. The bard leaned in close and whispered the same phrase Seth had heard him tell Ruka not so long ago. "Secret seasonings known only to elvish lords."

The side of Seth's mouth rose. Corny as the bard was, it felt surprisingly good to be back with this group. It felt like… home.

Kalyn's response was as predictable as Elladan's. Her eyes went wide and a toothy grin spread across her mouth. "Well I'd never been a huge fan o' venison, but this'n here just made me one!"

The young tracker dug heartily into her bowl and even went back for seconds. Mid-way through dinner, a familiar silver lynx plopped down from the nearby trees. The others were startled at first, but Kalyn swiftly explained it was her companion, Elfar.

Elfar padded over to Kalyn and sniffed her stew with keen interest, but the young woman spun her body away and hovered over her bowl protectively. "Mine! Go get yer own!"

Elfar cocked his head to one side and stared at her quizzically, then the strangest thing happened. Martan called out to the large cat. "It's okay, Elfar, you can have some of mine."

The silver lynx swiveled his head around and gazed at Martan. A deep purr abruptly emanated from his throat as if in recognition, then he swiftly padded over and stuck his head in the proffered bowl.

Kalyn watched the whole scene with narrowed eyes, muttering a single word as the lynx scarfed down the contents of Martan's bowl. "Traitor."

Elfar paused his meal and looked up at her with his large amber eyes, then huffed dismissively and stuck its head back in Martan's bowl. Seth chuckled wickedly at the lynx's reaction. It seems that the large cat did not share her dislike of Martan. In fact, much to Kalyn's chagrin, when he was done, he lay by Martan's side meticulously licking his paws.

A slight smile crossed the tracker's face for the first time since Seth rejoined the group. Martan gingerly stroked the large cat's fur while cooing to him, "Good to see you too, buddy."

Kalyn glared darkly at the pair. Seth could practically see the steam rising from her ears. The halfling lips twisted as he muttered, "Martan one, Kalyn zero."

Kalyn's head spun toward him, her eyes narrowing, but she refused to comment any further on the topic.

Once everyone was done with dinner, the conversation inevitably turned to their destination. Seth sat back comfortably against some rocks and sipped his ale while letting Kalyn explain the layout of Serpent's Hollow. The young tracker painted a vivid description of the tall mountains surrounding the enclosed valley, the forest within, the fields, the village, and the large cave at the other end. She finished her account with the single entrance in and out of the hollow, and the stone serpents that guarded it.

Glo listened silently to the young woman, his brow knit and his fingers steepled in front of him. Now that she was done, he turned to Aksel. "I supposed we'll need to find a way past those guardians."

Kalyn's hands went to her hips, a puzzled expression on her face. "Now hold on there. You're a powerful sorcerer, ain't ya? Can't you just magic us up and over them mountains?"

Glo shifted his gaze back toward Kalyn, a single eyebrow raised, yet Kalyn apparently wasn't finished. She pointed her hands in front of her as if shooting a crossbow. "Or how about just blowing yer way through, like ya did with that lighthouse?"

Seth practically spit out his last sip of ale. Glo's mouth hung open, the elf's cheeks turning bright red in the firelight. A moment later, a round of snorts and giggles erupted from around the campfire.

Glo cast a dark look at his companions, then peered sharply at

Kalyn. "First of all, young lady, I am a wizard, not some hack sorcerer. And secondly, exactly what has Seth been telling you?"

Seth broke out into a wicked grin. He threw up his hands in front of him, unable to wipe the smile from his lips. "Oh, no. Don't blame me. I never even mentioned the lighthouse. Face it, Glo, your little mishap has become the stuff of legends."

Glo cast an acid glare at the halfling. The tall elf sputtered with anger, but Kalyn interrupted him before he could fire off a retort.

The young woman's face had gone pale. She appeared mortified at having offended the tall elf. "I'm truly sorry. I didn't mean to cause you any grief. What Seth told you is true. He ne'er said a word. The story of the lighthouse has been all up and down Deepwood these last couple of weeks."

Glo shifted his eyes back to the young woman, his expression softening just a bit.

Kalyn had trouble meeting his gaze. She glanced down at the ground, shyly digging into it with her toe.

Seth, on the other hand, found the whole situation hilarious. It was all he could do to stop from falling off his boulder and roll on the ground in laughter.

Kalyn found her voice once more. When she spoke it was in a semi-whisper. "Honestly… no one ever said exactly how the lighthouse blew'ed up. Fran and me just kinda guessed it was you…"

That last statement pushed Seth over the edge. The halfling rolled off his seat and fell to the ground in a fit of hysterics.

He went on like that for a few moments before Aksel's voice cut into his revelry. "Alright, Seth, that's enough."

Seth slowly sat up, his sides still hurting from laughter. He peered over at Glo. The wizard had sat down, his head buried in his hands. Seth felt a touch of remorse, but the whole thing was just too easy to poke fun at.

Aksel cleared his throat. "Ahem. Back to the matter at hand. Seth, what is your assessment of the hollow?"

Seth slowly pulled himself together, then launched into his own evaluation of the hollow. Kalyn had effectively covered the layout, so Seth concentrated on the occupants of the enclosed valley. He gave a detailed account of the guards, the slaves, and the robed figures in black. He ended with his encounter of the man-snake, the bald black mage, and the dark, raven-haired woman in the portal.

Glo visibly shuddered as Seth described the sorceress. There could be little doubt—it was the same visage Glo had seen in the black gem.

Aksel gingerly stroked his chin. "So, it appears that we have found the serpent's head, so to speak."

Seth nodded slowly. "Those slaves were busy unearthing that altar. If I had to guess, I'd say they'll be done in the next day or so."

"And you think the altar is a way for this sorceress to cross over from wherever she is into our world?" Glo's brow was furrowed with concern.

Seth nodded once more. "It would make the most sense."

Lloyd jumped up from his seat. "Then we have to stop them! If this sorceress, or whatever she is, gets loose in our world, there's no telling the damage she'll do."

Seth saw the look of fear in Lloyd's eyes. He knew the young man was thinking of the Lady Andrella. The cult had already gone after her once. With their leader in our world, they might try it again. Or they might try something worse.

Alana stood up and placed a hand on Lloyd's shoulder. "I agree. We need to strike as swiftly as possible, before this foul creature enters our world."

"That's all well and fine, but we can't just fly over the mountains, or blow a hole in them," Elladan chimed in.

All eyes turned to the bard.

Elladan swept his gaze around the group. "Listen, it sounds like there are tons of cultists in there, some probably as high-powered as that Voltark character we faced back in Ravenford. So we can't go wasting magic before we even get in there. We need to conserve our resources until we really need them."

"I agree with Elladan." Aksel nodded to the bard. "So, what do you propose?"

The new guy, Cyclone, had sat quietly off to the side listening up till now. Seth didn't know what to make of him yet. Apparently, he was some sort of dragon hunter, and had been a big help back at the monolith and with the Princess. Seth had to admit, he liked the fact that this Cyclone kept his mouth shut. It was a sign of intelligence.

"I normally don't hunt anything but dragons, but it seems to me what you want is to take this 'cult' out at the head. Anything else is just a waste of time."

Glo gave the hunter a curt nod. "I tend to agree. The question is how?"

"I think I might have an idea," Donnie interjected. "Seth and Kalyn were able to move around rather freely in their disguises. What if the rest of us get some as well?"

Seth had to admit, it wasn't the worst idea. Aksel didn't appear to think so either. "What do you have in mind?"

Donnie motioned everyone in closer as he laid out his plan.

28
AMBUSH

Help me, my lady! This tree fell on me, and I can't get up

There was an old folk song in Deepwood about a girl who fell madly in love with an elf and ran away with him. Kalyn never understood what the girl's deal was until now. Now that she'd met not just one elf, but three, she understood how those stinking elves could make a girl's head swim. Elladan could sing a pack of wolves into submission with that pretty voice of his, Glo was about the smartest feller she'd ever met, and Donnie… well… dang… all he had to do was just smile.

Kalyn huffed and rolled her eyes toward Martan, who sat on a branch directly across from her. That stupid elf's smile was the reason she was stuck in this tree, alone, with the last person she wanted to be alone with. She glanced down at his side and glared at Elfar, who lounged comfortably next to the man, his big feet dangling on either side of the branch and his furry lips turned up in a sort of smile.

"That makes two stupid, smiling imps…" she murmured under her breath.

Martan glanced at her, raising an eyebrow just the slightest.

Kalyn quickly looked away and crossed her arms.

They had reached the roots of the Korlokesel mountains about midday. It didn't take long after that to find a worn path that broke from the road and wound its way in the direction of the hollow. Aksel suggested that those who could move around quietly in the wild go and scout out ahead. Naturally, that meant Kalyn and Seth.

Kalyn was thrilled when Donnie offered to go along too. She had been dying to see some of the other heroes in action, but why did Martan have to go? Sure, he was sneaky—too sneaky for her taste. Still, between two heroes and a tracker, they had it covered. So why did they need Martan?

Kalyn held her tongue, though. She merely made it clear to Martan that he stay out of her way, which had worked well. Martan stayed out of sight and out of mind until they reached a sheltered pass surrounded by tall trees on either side.

Seth and Donnie agreed that it was a perfect place for an ambush. Seth decided he would go ahead and scout the rest of the road, while Donnie made his way back to the others and told them.

Kalyn liked the idea, until they both told her and Martan to stay and wait for everyone to meet back here. That was when she put up a fuss, but Donnie just smiled at her. He said something that made sense at the time, keeping that smile on his pouty lips, and next thing she knew, she was sitting in this stupid tree with Martan.

Kalyn whipped her head to the side when a hand gently touched her shoulder. She glared at Martan until he withdrew his hand. Kalyn gingerly rubbed her shoulder, trying to make the warm, tingling feeling go away.

Martan's eyebrows drooped over his sad brown eyes. He swallowed, then pointed to one side. Kalyn's eyes drifted in the direction he indicated until they came to rest on a black bird perched on a branch just above them. The creature cocked its head to one side and gazed at Kalyn curiously. It then swiveled its tiny head toward Martan, twitching its wings with almost an inquiring gesture.

Martan responded with a thumbs-up sign. The glossy black bird cocked its head once more, then with a shake of its wings, flew away and in the direction where the others were waiting.

"That was Glolindir's bird, Raven," Martan whispered.

Kalyn blinked. *He named his raven, Raven? Oh, that is clever! Next lynx I get, I'm naming it Lynx. That will be so much easier for people to remember.*

Kalyn abruptly realized Martan was still watching her. She shrugged and looked away, gazing back up the road in the direction Seth had gone.

"Kalyn?" Martan said softly. His voice made her tense and prickle. "I, uh… how are your brothers?"

"Same as you, irritating as an owl bear with no feathers and not really on good speaking terms with me. Why do you ask?" She swiveled around and locked a stern gaze on him, keeping her arms crossed. "Wanna strike up a conversation now, after five years?"

Martan swallowed again, looking down at his hands.

Kalyn narrowed her eyes. *Yeah. That's what I thought. Coward.*

At one time, Martan had been her best friend. They grew up together and were inseparable as children. At one time, she had thought they were more than friends.

Five years ago, he was accused of murdering old man Coran, the man who had raised him. Kalyn hid him from the angry townspeople and worked for days to prove his innocence. When she succeeded, and even captured the real murderer, she hurried back to where she hid Martan, only to find that he had left. It took her days to accept the fact that he'd run away, like a coward. It had shattered her heart into a thousand pieces.

Martan looked back up at her, a determined look behind his eyes. "Not long after you left, your brothers came and told me to leave. They said everyone knew I was guilty but you, and that a lynch mob was on its way. They said because I was your friend, they'd give me a running start."

Kalyn's eyebrows flew to the top of her head. "That's a load of troll snot!"

A look of genuine confusion fell over Martan's features.

Kalyn unfolded her arms and curled her fists. "I proved that you didn't murder old man Coran! The whole town dropped the charges against you! When I went to the treehouse to give you the good news, you were long gone. And, mind you, that was *our* treehouse. Nobody knew it was there. Not even my brothers."

Martan's confused expression deepened. "Uh, yes they did. They always knew. They used it for a hunting stand more than a few times."

An angry fire rushed through Kalyn's body, mingling with her own confusion and a dozen questions. She was certain her brothers never knew about that old treehouse and why would they lie and tell Martan to run? He had been her only friend. She had loved him. Why would they do that to…

Kalyn's insides suddenly turned to ice. *No. They didn't. They wouldn't.*

Kalyn tried to deny it, but Martan's story rang true. She'd recently caught her *darling* brothers doing almost the exact same thing to another man she had come to like. Now he was long gone, too, but unlike Martan, he had the decency and guts to come tell her to her face that he was leaving.

Kalyn crossed her arms, and glared at Martan. "Face it, you didn't trust me to save you. You didn't even leave me a note with a simple goodbye on it! I don't care what my rotten brothers did or said, you don't just leave a girl hanging like a trout on a string!"

Martan hung his head low, his voice no more than a faint whisper. "They said they'd tell you goodbye for me, since I couldn't read or write."

Kalyn felt her insides melt. She believed he was telling the truth. Kalyn uncrossed her arms and nearly reached out a hand to him, but stopped herself, firmly setting her teeth together.

I want to believe him. If what he's saying is true, my brothers have yet to learn the meaning of pain and suffering. But until I know for sure, I can't give him an inch. No backing down.

"Well, good thing they didn't tell me, because if they had, I would've tracked you down and dragged your sorry rear end back to Deepwood, and… and… done something terrible to you for not trustin' me to do what I promised I'd do."

"I hear tar and feathering is fun."

Kalyn leaned over and looked down at the ground below to find

Seth propped against the trunk of the tree, fiddling with one of his many knives. The young archer shook her head. "Too messy. And do you know how many chickens you have to pluck to get enough feathers?"

Seth tilted his head back and cocked an eye at her. "Sounds like you've given this a lot of thought."

"Maybe…" Kalyn responded with a side-long glance at Martan. The blood drained from the disheveled man's face.

Seth snorted, and with a flick of his wrist, made his knife disappear. He then pushed off the tree and jerked his thumb behind him. "There's a caravan of cultists coming down the road."

Kalyn shifted her gaze in the direction he pointed and frowned. "A caravan? How far back?"

Seth shrugged. "Saw them leaving the hollow. They'll be here in about half an hour or so."

Kalyn nodded, then flipped over backwards and grabbed a branch beneath her, kicking her legs up and swinging down, hooking them around another branch and letting her hands slip off the one above her. She repeated this until she dropped to her feet with a graceful bend of her knees, then winked at Seth. "Child's play."

Seth tilted his head and eyed her disdainfully. "Amateur."

Kalyn ignored him. She puffed up, sniffed, and thumbed her nose. "As for them cultists, no problem! You just step aside, sonny, and let ol' Kalyn handle this. I'll have them outta sight and outta mind in no time t'all."

Seth buried his face in his hands and shook his head.

Martan dropped from the tree behind Kalyn. "Maybe we should wait for the others?"

Kalyn sighed and turned to face him. "I was joking. Seriously, what am I going to do to a caravan full of cultists by myself?"

Seth let out a derisive snort. "Too bad you can't turn into a dragon. Then you could just eat them all."

At the mention of the word dragon, Martan started to cough violently. Kalyn shifted her gaze toward him and saw he was red in the face. Martan put up a hand and sputtered, "I'm… fine… really…"

Kalyn raised an eyebrow, then shrugged and turned back to Seth.

She steepled her fingers in front of her face, doing her best to mimic Glolindir's voice. "Turning into a dragon is a cheap trick for hack sorcerers. I would much rather use a proper wizard's spell, like a fireball."

Seth cocked an eye at her and let out a short closemouthed laugh. Meanwhile, Martan had nearly gotten his coughing fit under control. "In a… forest? Sounds like a… bad idea… to me."

A twisted grin crossed Seth's face. "Yeah, Glo-linda. Burning a forest down just to get some cultists sounds a bit over the top."

Kalyn threw her hands in the air. "Well, how else am I going to top blowing a lighthouse up?"

Seth raised an eyebrow, then burst into laughter. He leaned back against the tree trunk and continued to giggle hysterically.

"What's so funny?"

Kalyn looked up to see Donnie riding toward them, the others right behind him. Everyone was grinning or smiling, just for seeing Seth in hysterics, but Glo's sharp eyes were locked onto the halfling, a little color rising in his cheeks.

"Nothing!" Kalyn and Martan both declared at the same time. Kalyn exchanged glances with him, then awkwardly looked away.

Kalyn covered her discomfort with a smile at Donnie. "Ya know, it's just Seth having a Seth-spazz. Oh! And he said he saw a mess o' cultists coming from the holler toward us, 'bout half an hour out."

Donnie nodded, still grinning. "Seth-spazz, huh? I'll have to remember that."

Aksel moved to the front as the others came to halt. "Well Seth, when you're done laughing at 'nothing,' would you mind filling us in?"

Seth pulled himself together and described seeing three covered wagons. There was an armed driver and a figure in black robes sitting in the lead wagon, two armed men in the second wagon, and a robed figure and armed driver in the third.

Aksel absently rubbed his chin. "I think it would be safe to assume that there are probably a few more in the back of the wagons."

"Not so many that we can't handle," Lloyd said, glancing around the sheltered pass that surrounded them. "After all, the idea was to set up an ambush."

"And this is the perfect spot," Kalyn agreed with the tall, handsome warrior.

Donnie dismounted from his horse. "That was the general idea, although now that I see this place, I think I can add to it."

"Oh, this ought to be good," Elladan said, dismounting his own horse and rubbing his hands together.

Alana walked up from behind Elladan and placed a hand on the bard's shoulder. "Give him a chance to speak."

"Gotta admit, I'm curious what he's gonna come up with this time," Cyclone added gruffly.

Kalyn narrowed her eyes at the slight elf and jerked a thumb back at Martan. "As long as it don't include leaving me to babysit him again."

"You were babysitting him? I thought it was the other way around."

Kalyn turned to glare at Seth. "Yeah, keep talking, short stack."

Aksel cleared his throat. "If everyone is done, let's give Donnie a chance to speak."

Donnie gave Aksel a grateful nod. "Now then, here's what I was thinking…"

Kalyn took a deep breath as she watched the covered wagons come into view. She tensed her arm, testing her bowstring, while keeping the notched arrow held firmly between her fingers. She glanced at Martan, sitting to her right. He sat still, his face a mask of concentration as he surveyed the approaching wagons, already marking possible targets.

Kalyn shifted her eyes from Martan to the road below. A large tree now lay across it, felled rather quickly by some fancy bing-bang-boom stuff that Glolindir had conjured up. Donnie lay 'trapped' under that tree, patiently awaiting the arrival of the small caravan. Elfar hid under there as well, his plush coat providing the perfect camouflage to blend in with the shadows and leaves, making the lynx all but invisible. When the wagons finally drew into view, the sandy-haired elf made a show of struggling against the branches that had him 'pinned.'

The caravan drew to a halt about a dozen yards away from the tree, the lead driver reining in his horses and resting his hand on the crossbow next to his seat. The black-robed figure next to him stood, gnarled wooden staff in hand, and pulled back its hood, revealing itself to be a woman with short black hair and a pale complexion.

Donnie didn't miss a beat. He called out to her, "Help me, my lady! This tree fell on me, and I can't get up."

The words he chose, and the tone of his voice, tickled Kalyn's funny bone. She slapped a hand over her mouth, desperately stifling a giggle. Martan gave her a sidelong glance, but she ignored it, keeping her eyes on Donnie and swiftly moving her hand back to her bow.

By this time, several men had filed out of the backs of the wagons—two out of the lead, two out of the second, and two out of the last. Three more men joined them from the fronts of the other wagons, all stopping at the lead wagon and glancing at the woman. She lifted her head, her eyes narrowing as she swept her gaze around the sheltered pass.

Kalyn froze as the woman squinted at the tree where she and Martan sat, but her dark eyes passed over their hiding place without halting. The dark woman's brow furrowed as she completed her sweep of the area. After a momentary pause, she peered back at Donnie, then snapped her fingers. Two men immediately broke from the group and cautiously approached Donnie with their weapons raised.

Kalyn slowly drew back her bowstring, her fingers touching her cheek as her eyes locked onto one of the ruffians. Then she remembered the lead driver had a crossbow. She cast a quick glance at the man and noticed the position he was in gave him a clear shot at Donnie. Kalyn readjusted her aim, bringing her weapon to bear on the driver instead.

Donnie's a hero, she reasoned. *He can handle himself against the two ruffians… plus, he's got Elfar with him anyway.*

The two men were nearly on top of Donnie when the rest of the heroes revealed themselves. Lloyd, Aksel, and Glolindir stepped out from behind the trees on one side of the road, while Elladan, Alana, and Cyclone stepped out on the other.

"Drop your weapons!" Lloyd's voice boomed around the sheltered pass.

"We have you surrounded!" Alana added.

A grim smile spread across Kalyn's lips. *Meh. You're all gonna die.*

The dark-robed woman whipped her head around in Lloyd's direction. "It's a trap! Get them!"

Her men immediately responded, drawing their weapons and charging the ambushers on either side of the road. At the same moment, the dark woman raised her staff, and with a flick of her empty hand, sent a spell careening in Lloyd's, Glolindir's, and Aksel's directions. Almost simultaneously, another caster stood in the third wagon and jerked his arms up in the air, pointing them at Alana, Cyclone, and Elladan.

After that, everything happened all at once. There was so much movement and confrontation that Kalyn had a hard time taking it all in. The young archer began to hyperventilate when she heard Fran's voice in her mind. *Don't panic now, girl. Them heroes is countin' on ya!*

Real or not, the voice forced Kalyn to catch herself. She took a deep breath and swept the battlefield for marks like she had been taught.

From the corner of her eye, she saw Elfar pounce on one of the men next to Donnie, taking him to the ground where the slight elf knocked him out. On one side of the caravan, black roots shot up from the earth and tangled around Cyclone, Alana, and Elladan's, lifting them up into the air. On the bright side, it forced the guards charging them to halt in their tracks.

On the other side of the wagons, Lloyd suddenly dropped his weapons. She focused on him and watched in horror as a blank look filled his eyes, his shoulders slumping forward. Three guards rushed at him, weapons raised, but still he did nothing. Kalyn drew her arrow back, targeting one of the guards, but before she released it, Glo swept his hand through the air dramatically. Out of nowhere, a wall of flames sprang up between Lloyd and the rushing guards. The three men slid to a halt before the flickering flames.

Kalyn stared at the burning wall in awe. "Ooh! Glolindir sure is a fire lovin' feller, ain't he?"

"Male caster."

Martan's voice shook Kalyn from her fire trance just in time for her to see the caster in the third wagon fall to the ground, an arrow piercing his heart, dead center.

Nice shot.

A moment later, the black roots tangling Cyclone, Alana, and Elladan disappeared, freeing them to fight the four men in front of them. The bard immediately produced his lute and a bracing tune flowed from it, making Kalyn feel as if her limbs were on fire.

Kalyn swept the battlefield with renewed energy, a sudden movement catching her eye. The driver of the first wagon had stood and lifted his crossbow, pointing it in Glo's direction.

"Lead driver." Kalyn called the shot as she let her arrow loose. A moment later the man tumbled, head first, out of the wagon and onto the ground with her arrow protruding from his temple. "Didn't know what hit him."

She smiled smugly, and glanced at Martan while she drew another arrow and nocked it. Back on the battlefield, the dark woman weaved her hands in preparation for another spell.

"Boss lady caster," Kalyn called, planning to wing her.

"Wait! Don't!"

Martan's plea made her hesitate just in time to see a small, dark figure appear behind the lady and wrap a short arm around her neck, putting a knife up to her skin. The lady froze as Seth whispered into her ear, then slowly lowered herself back into her seat. Elfar jumped up into the seat next to her and sat down, glaring at the woman.

Kalyn let out a brief sigh. *That was close. I could've hurt Seth!*

She glanced at Martan, a bit of guilt washing over her that she hadn't predicted Seth doing that, like he had.

"I've got Lloyd." Martan pulled his string tight, taking aim at one of the guards staggering away from the firewall.

"I've got the other side." Kalyn acknowledged.

She began to turn away when a circle of white light suddenly appeared around Lloyd. The red-clad warrior shook himself like he'd just waken from a dream, then stooped down and picked up his swords. "I'm okay! Drop the firewall!"

The fire abruptly disappeared, and the three guards charged Lloyd. The middle one barely made it three steps before Martan's arrow planted itself square into the middle of his back and he went face first into the dirt.

Kalyn frowned. "Only one, Martan? Seriously? Pay attention and watch how a girl gets it done!"

Kalyn drew her bow and turned her attention to the guards fighting Alana and Cyclone. She unleashed her arrow, instantly reaching back and drawing another one, nocking and firing it just before the first arrow made its home in the leg of the man fighting Alana. The shot threw him off balance and allowed the lady knight to finish him off with ease. Kalyn's second arrow plunged into the skull of one of the guards fighting Cyclone, dropping him like a sack of potatoes.

Kalyn cocked her head in Martan's direction and sniffed smugly. "Gotta be quick about this stuff, ya know."

To her utter surprise, Martan grinned at her and laid his bow across his lap. "Just like the good old days."

Kalyn half-smiled at her one-time friend, then quickly returned her gaze to the battlefield. Almost directly below them, Donnie danced around his opponent, taunting him and smiling as if he were having the time of his life. Across the road, both Cyclone and Alana were engaged in close-quarters combat with a guard, while Lloyd was left to fend off two.

Kalyn considered trying to even out the field for Lloyd, until his swords burst into flame. The tall warrior easily gained ground on both guards, beating against their blades mercilessly.

"Wow! Wish I could set my bow on fire like that." Kalyn said to herself.

Martan shifted in his seat, "Your bow? On fire? Uh…"

"Oh, shut up you." Kalyn waved her hand dismissively at him, continuing to watch Lloyd. With a fearsome swipe of his black blade, one of the guards slumped to the ground in a bloodied heap. Kalyn laid her bow across her lap and clapped, then stretched her legs and crossed her arms. "This is more entertaining than lighting a warg's tail on fire!"

"Gods, I've missed your colorful phrasing." Martan leaned back with a smile on his lips.

A fire rose to Kalyn's cheeks. She swiftly turned away so Martan wouldn't see her blushing.

She was just in time to see Alana deal the final blow to her opponent, sweeping her shining blade through the air with an ease and grace that Kalyn found beautiful. "That lady knight could make an orc swoon with how prettily she kills things."

A second later, Cyclone's opponent fell. "Finally! Took him long enough."

"I said… drop… your… sword!" With that declaration, Donnie cleanly severed the hand of his opponent, then ran him through with his pointy little sword. At the same time, Lloyd finished the last guard. The area fell abruptly silent as everyone took a moment to catch their breath.

Kalyn started clapping loudly. "Whoo! Do it again!"

Donnie looked up at their tree with a wide grin before saluting her with his sword and bowing. "Anything for you, m'lady! Your wish is our command! But first, a short reprieve for your humble entertainers?"

Kalyn giggled, then nodded to him, waving her hand in what she thought was a regal gesture. Then she turned to Martan. "He called me "m'lady" like I was a regular princess or something."

She giggled again, then she flipped off her branch and made her quick decent to the ground below where she paused and watched everyone move in closer to the wagon where Seth held the female caster captive. "I got to watch the Heroes of Ravenford win a *real battle*!"

She shrieked and danced around in a violent circle, then ran up to the first wagon, grabbing the horses by their bridles. She looked up at the black-robed woman, who was already neatly bound and gagged. Kalyn smiled wryly at the dark woman. *Seth sure doesn't waste any time.*

Elfar looked at Kalyn expectantly, then huffed and made a throaty growl, laying his ears back in an annoyed fashion.

Kalyn smiled at him. "Good boy, Elfar. You totally put that wicked woman in her place."

The woman shot her a wicked glare, but Kalyn ignored it, instead shaking a finger at her. "They told ya to surrender! But did you listen? Nope! Ya should've known better than to tangle with the Heroes. Serves you right. Now I get to watch them interrogate ya!"

She smiled gleefully at the woman, until Seth groaned. Kalyn turned to him, her hands on her hips. "What? It's exciting!"

Before Seth could retort, they were interrupted by Glo. "Nice going with those arrows. You saved us a lot of trouble."

Kalyn looked at the wizard, then peered at the ground, twisting her boot in the dirt sheepishly. "Shucks, it was nothin. Martan took down a few of 'em too."

"Not as many as you!" Martan called down, still sitting in the branches above.

Kalyn glanced up at him, then swiftly turned away as her cheeks flushed yet again. *That sneaky goblin licker! He's making it hard for a girl to hate him.*

29
PAWNS OF FATE

Take your last breaths while you can. For tonight you will fulfill your destiny

Aksel let out a deep expulsion of air as the last of the caravan guards fell. He hadn't realized he'd been holding his breath, but it didn't surprise him, either. The fighting had been quite intense. The little cleric swiftly swept his eyes around the sheltered pass. Thankfully all his friends were still standing.

The same couldn't be said for the guards. They were all down, except for the dark-robed woman in the lead caravan, but she wasn't going to be a problem. True to form, Seth already had her bound and gagged. The new archer, Kalyn, had dropped down and was harassing her.

It was actually rather amusing, but Aksel only allowed himself a brief smile. They needed to get off the road soon. There was no telling how long it would be before someone else might come along.

Aksel lifted his head up toward the tree where Martan was still perched. "Any signs of movement on the road?"

A moment or two went by before the dour archer answered. "Nope. All clear in both directions."

Aksel gave a curt nod. "Very good. Keep an eye out, just in case."

"Will do," Martan acknowledged.

Assured that the road was clear, Aksel turned his attention to the wagons. Seth had already disappeared into the lead one. Lloyd, Cyclone, Alana, and Kalyn were busy relieving bodies of their black-clad outfits and loading them into the other two wagons.

"A little help here?" Donnie called from behind him.

Aksel spun around and saw the slim elf attempting to drag the bodies of one of the two guards he felled toward the wagons.

"I've got it," Elladan said as he brushed by the little gnome.

"Well that was interesting." Glo said from beside him.

Aksel pursed his lips and nodded. "Quick thinking there. If you hadn't put up that wall of fire when you did, we'd have been in serious trouble."

The corners of Glo's mouth lifted slightly. "I could say the same to you. You freed Lloyd fairly quickly."

Aksel shrugged. "It wasn't too hard to figure out what had been cast on him."

A moment later, Seth popped his head out of the lead wagon. The halfling held his nose with one hand and waved his other in front of his face. "It reeks in there." He turned his gaze toward their bound captive. "Don't you folks believe in cleaning up the blood when you're done torturing your victims?"

The bound woman mumbled something unintelligible through her gag, but grew silent when Kalyn's lynx growled at her. Still, there was a dark look in her eyes that made Aksel shiver. Seth, however, seemed unaffected by it. He leaped down off the wagon. "Nothing we can use in that wagon, but at least we've got what we came for."

He strode off to help the others with the downed guards.

"I should probably help, too," Glo noted dryly.

"You go ahead," Aksel told him. "I want to make sure everyone is all right."

They spent the next twenty minutes or so finishing with the bodies while Aksel healed some minor wounds that Lloyd, Donnie, and

Cyclone had incurred. When they were done, the others took turns donning their new attire.

Seth, already in a black robe, handed one to Aksel. The little cleric swiftly donned it and then went to interrogate the prisoner. With her hood drawn back, he could clearly see her features. She had raven-colored hair, cropped short at the neck, deep brown eyes, a thin nose, and extremely pale skin. Her lips were the shade of blood.

Seth handed Aksel the staff the woman carried. It was a rather plain, gnarled length of wood, except for its head, which was carved in the shape of a serpent.

Aksel turned the staff over in his hands, looking it up and down. When he reached the head, the eyes of the serpent suddenly lit up. The world around Aksel abruptly started to spin. He felt himself falling when a steadying hand caught him by the arm. He looked up and saw Seth standing there, one hand holding him the other firmly clasped over the staff's eyes.

The corner of Seth's mouth was slightly raised. "Thought you of all people would know better than that."

Aksel grimaced as he righted himself. "Yeah, well that's what I have you around for."

The little cleric reached into his robe and pulled out a cloth, which he swiftly tied around the serpent's head. "That takes care of that." He then turned his attention to the owner of the staff. "Let's see what she has to say for herself."

Seth strode over to the dark-robed woman and produced a sharp knife, seemingly from thin air. He cut the gag from her mouth and then stepped back while continuing to toy with the blade. Yet the woman didn't seem scared in the slightest, instead eyeing him with disdain.

"Oh, please," she said, her voice dripping with contempt. "If you were going to kill me, you would have already. You can put your toy away."

Seth glanced at Aksel with a raised eyebrow, then abruptly made the blade disappear from his hand. The woman gave him a smug smile. "Now, isn't that better?"

Aksel cleared his throat. "Ahem. So then, my good woman, what is your name?"

The woman fixed her dark eyes on Aksel and let out a wicked laugh. "My name is Skuld, and I can assure you there is nothing good about me."

Kalyn let out a short chuckle in the background. "Was just gonna say that."

Aksel cast a quick glance at the young archer. Seth snorted and rolled his eyes. Aksel shook his head and returned his attention to the prisoner. "Okay then, Skuld, since you seem so sure of yourself, I'm sure you wouldn't mind telling us exactly who you are."

A faint smile spread across Skuld's blood-red lips. "Oh, I don't mind at all. I am a high-ranking sorceress of the Serpent Cult in service of the goddess, Salisma."

"The goddess Salisma? I don't remember seeing that name in the Ralnain pantheon."

Aksel peered over his shoulder to see Glo had rejoined them. The tall elf looked rather strange garbed in black robes.

"Bah, the Ralnain," Skuld practically spat. "Mere mortals playing at being gods. My mistress has been around since the beginning, and will be here still when the Ralnain are nothing but ash."

Glo spiked an eyebrow at her blasphemous statement. "Okay then, if your mistress is everlasting, where has she been these last few hundred years? Why the sudden resurgence of her cult?"

Skuld fixed Glo with an acid glare, but then her lips spread into a malicious smile. "The answer is quite simple, really. It's because of you."

Glo raised both eyebrows this time. He placed a hand on his chest. "Me?"

Skuld laughed again, an altogether evil sound. "No, not just you, you imbecile. All of you." She swept her eyes around the group as the others rejoined them, her face contorting into a sneer. "Your coming was foretold long ago." She paused a moment, as if relishing the attention. "Now the long wait is finally over. It all ends tonight. Tonight is the night of blood and fire." Her eyes narrowed, her gaze intensifying as she glared around at everyone present. "Your blood. It will be spilled on the altar and it will open the gate, bringing the goddess forth and into this world at last."

As those last words left her lips, the world around them seemed to suddenly darken. Aksel felt a chill run up his spine. *Was there any truth to what Skuld was saying? By pursuing the cult to their lair, had they played right into their hands?*

Seth, however, wasn't buying any of it. He eyed Skuld with clear skepticism. "So glad we could help you with your little plan. I'm assuming you mean the altar in the caves, and by 'gate' you are referring to a portal?"

Skuld shifted her gaze to the halfling and scrutinized him for a moment or two. "You're not as stupid as you look, little man." She peered around the group once more. "Take your last breaths while you can. For tonight you will fulfill your destiny. Your lives will be forfeit in the service of our goddess!"

Skuld let out another shrieking laugh, but it was abruptly cut short when the hilt of Seth's knife connected with the back of her head. The black-robed Serpent cultist slumped down in her seat. The halfling looked up at the others and shook his head in disgust. "I hate fanatics."

"More irritatin' than a rooster at the crack of dawn," Kalyn commented, pretending to clean out her ears.

"At least roosters are good for something," Donnie noted with a lilt in his voice.

Elladan snorted. "Never thought I'd hear you choose a rooster over a woman."

Donnie eyed the archer with a mischievous grin. "Even I have my standards."

Seth gagged Skuld and motioned for Kalyn to come up and give him a hand. He grabbed her by the arms while Kalyn grasped her ankles. The two of them then unceremoniously flipped her into the back of the wagon like a sack of potatoes.

A solid-sounding thump followed from inside the wagon.

"Ouch," Donnie cried with a grin, rubbing the back of his head. "That's gonna leave a mark."

Elfar jumped into the back of the wagon as well, eliciting a giggle from Kalyn. "Ha! He's sitting on her head!"

The corner of Seth's mouth twisted upward. "That oversized cat of yours is starting to grow on me."

Kalyn, Martan, and Donnie then drove the wagons out of the pass and off the road, where they'd be hidden from sight.

While they waited for them to return, the rest of the companions discussed what Skuld had told them. Yet no matter how they looked at it, they really had no choice. They had to get into Serpent's Hollow. Still, Aksel couldn't get Skuld's words out of his head.

Your coming was foretold long ago.

Is the rest of the cult expecting us? If so, are we walking straight into a trap?

If anyone had been standing at the entrance to the hollow, it would have appeared that just another group of worshippers approached the valley. The party consisted of three dark-robed casters and six black-clad guards. Some appeared quite short, others rather tall, and two were most definitely women. A few carried swords and some wore bows, while one guard in particular held a wicked-looking pike. Still, the group did not look out of place, for the cult recruited its members from all races and genders.

The party stopped just short of the tunnel that was the only path to the hollow beyond. They stood before the wrought-iron gate that stretched across the entrance, flanked on either side by the two watchers.

The watchers were a pair of huge serpent statues that guarded the gate from intruders. Two large amber gems were affixed as eyes in either statue, their gaze intersecting a short distance ahead of the gate. If the watchers detected trespassers, an alarm would sound all through the hollow.

Glo had sensed the magic from the twin serpents and warned Aksel from under his dark hood. Aksel had called the companions to a halt and covertly cast a spell of his own. Whatever force resided in those statues was most definitely evil.

"So, what do we do now?" Lloyd whispered impatiently.

Kalyn sighed. "Wish I hadn't left Elfar behind with Skuld. He could've tested it for us."

There was a moment of silence, then Aksel spoke in a hushed voice. "Everyone wait here. I'm going to try something."

The little cleric cast a second spell on himself, one that would protect him from evil, then slowly strode forward. When he reached the point where the serpents' eyes intersected, the amber gems began to glow.

Aksel froze in his tracks.

"You might want to slowly back away," Seth said from over his shoulder.

Without turning, the little gnome slowly retraced his steps. As he did so, the light in the statues' eyes faded. Aksel wiped the back of his hand across his forehead. "Phew, that was close."

Everyone seemed relieved, except for Cyclone. The dragon hunter fixed the others with a scornful stare. "So, now what, geniuses? Are we just going to stand here all day?"

Glo, his emotions still raw, reacted poorly to the hunter's derogatory tone. "And I suppose you have a better idea?"

The duo momentarily locked eyes, but Elladan stepped forward before any further words were traded. "I think I might. What about using this thing?"

The bard produced his portal bag and reached an arm inside, all the way down to his shoulder. When he pulled it back out, Elladan held in his hand Skuld's staff. Aksel had given the rod to the bard to hold onto just before they set out for the hollow.

"There has to be a way for those cultists to get past the watchers," Elladan reasoned.

Kalyn strode up next to the bard and bent over for a closer look at the staff. "Come ta think of it, a few of them robed folks was carryin' these things inside the holler."

Aksel peered at Seth. The halfling nodded. "She's right. I remember seeing them as well."

Aksel pondered it for a moment, then shrugged. "I guess it's worth a try."

"Just one thing. You might want to point that thing away from you this time," Seth noted, one edge of his mouth upturned slightly.

Aksel cast a withering glance at the halfling. "Duly noted."

"Um, maybe if you and Alana tried it together?" Donnie held his arms out toward the black-clad lady knight.

Aksel grasped his chin and peered at Alana speculatively. She was a member of a holy order just like himself. Perhaps Donnie was on to something. Between the two of them, they might indeed be able to control the staff.

Alana stared back at him, her eyes unwavering. "I'm willing to try if you are."

"Yes, that might just work," Aksel agreed.

The lady knight and the little cleric each grasped the staff with one hand and strode forward together toward the watchers. When they reached the point where the eyes intersected, the amber gems came alight once more.

Aksel grasped the head of the staff, and making sure it was pointing away from them, ripped away the cloth he had wrapped around it. Nothing happened at first, but then a dull red glow began to emanate from the staff's head. The light grew increasingly brighter until it was as intense as the glow from the statues' eyes. Still, nothing happened.

"Perhaps if we step closer?" Alana suggested.

"Slowly," Aksel agreed.

The duo carefully took a few more steps. As they drew closer to the gate, the statues' eyes began to flicker.

"I believe it's working," Alana noted with veiled enthusiasm.

The pair took a few more steps toward the gate until the serpents' eyes finally winked out. The moment they did, there was a loud clang and the large iron gate slowly swung inward.

The others rushed up and clasped the pair on the shoulders.

"That was it!"

"You did it!"

"Nicely done!"

"Slicker n' snot!"

Cyclone was the last to join them. He stood there with his lips pressed together and gave them a curt nod. "Not bad. Now can we get a move on before the day is over?"

Aksel glanced at the sky to the east. It was starting to darken, faint twinkles of light appearing here and there on the horizon. Night would be falling soon. A shiver crawled up Aksel's spine as Skuld's words reverberated through his mind.

The night of blood and fire.

By the time they reached the inside of the hollow, night would have already fallen. Still, it couldn't be helped. The companions lined up in pairs and entered the tunnel, toward whatever fate had in store for them.

30
NIGHT OF BLOOD AND FIRE

The Council of the Six are the right hand of the goddess

When the companions reached the other end of the tunnel, night had indeed blanketed the earth. The moon was not quite up just yet, but the evening sky was already filled from end to end with twinkling stars. The light from that breathtaking visage dimly illuminated the world below.

Serpent's Hollow lay stretched out before them, the black silhouettes of the surrounding mountains cradling the hidden valley between them. Their peaks reached up toward the star-studded sky like the fingers of some impossibly immense hand. The hollow itself was dark, except for a gathering of lights in its very center and a dim glow at the northern end of the valley.

The companions swiftly filed down from the cave entrance to the woods that covered the southern part of the hollow. Kalyn and Martan took the lead, fanning out ahead of the others. The small company traversed the woods without incident, quickly reaching the edge of the forest. The fields on either side of the town lay empty, but the town continued to bustle with activity.

Seth and Kalyn took the lead as the group fell into a double-file formation. They followed the pair along the winding road that led through the fields and to the edge of town. They passed through an outer ring of small huts and cabins until they came to a circle of large stone buildings. The small group passed between two of the structures and entered the center of the village.

Glo swept his eyes around the village square. It was exactly as Seth and Kalyn had described it. Four great stone buildings surrounded the square, each with tall, beautifully-carved pillars and wide sweeping steps that led up to a pair of ornate doors. The craftsmanship was so well refined that there was no mistaking their dwarven origins. The structure directly across from them stood out among the rest. It had a domed top, with a giant bronze symbol of a serpent hanging in its archway. It was obviously a temple of the cult's serpent goddess.

Dozens of torches were set around the village square, lighting the area and the buildings surrounding it. In the very center stood a white circular stone fountain, probably ten yards in diameter. It was straddled by a tall wooden scaffolding, with a number of thick ropes draped over it. A few dozen white-robed figures stood with their backs to them, straining against one end of the lines. The other ends were wrapped around an impossibly huge statue of a serpent. The stone serpent teetered precariously over the other side of the fountain.

The air was filled with the grunts and groans of the white-robed slaves as they strained against the ropes. A few black-clad guards were interspersed amongst the crowd, barking orders.

"Pull harder!"

"Put your backs into it!"

"If it breaks, you die!"

Most of the guards had whips, which they cracked in the air to emphasize their point. Unfortunately, the nearest guard decided to aim for a lower target. He caught two of the slaves in their backs, causing them to cry out and shudder in pain.

He pulled back his arm to strike a third target, but never got the chance. Instead, a hulking black form loomed over the guard and caught his arm in a vice-like grip.

Glo thought he recognized that figure. The tall elf cast a swift glance around. Sure enough, Lloyd was no longer with them.

The guard spun around and cried in outrage, "Hey! What do you think you're doing?"

They were the last words he managed to utter. A moment later, a huge fist connected with his jaw.

Crack.

The guard's body lifted into the air, landing in a heap about five feet away. The sound of that crack was so loud that it caused everyone nearby to stop and turn in their direction.

A hush fell over the crowd as they saw the guard lying flat on the ground, out cold. Lloyd stared angrily down at the abusive man, casting aside the whip he had ripped from him.

"Your days of torturing people are over!" the young man declared vehemently. His statement was punctuated by the sound of ringing steel as he drew his twin blades from their scabbards.

"So much for a quiet entrance," Seth murmured wryly.

Glo silently shrugged. Seth was right, their cover had been blown. Still, he could not fault Lloyd for stepping in when he did. Slavery was just plain wrong, but beating slaves on top of that? *That guard was lucky to still be alive.*

The white-robed throng continued to stare blankly at the tall warrior, but several guards separated themselves from the pack, shouting as they stalked the lone figure.

"Who do you think you are?"

"No one messes with the Serpent Cult!"

"Kill the infidel!"

Yet Lloyd didn't stand alone for long. Cyclone, Alana, and Donnie swept past Glo and the others, weapons also ringing as they took up positions at Lloyd's side.

Martan and Kalyn were also on the move. The twin archers spread out wide to either side, bows already drawn and arrows nocked. Eight black figures had lined up against the companions, one of them easily as large as Lloyd.

"Get them!" the big guard cried.

As one, the guards launched themselves forward. Three dropped almost immediately, with arrows protruding from vital spots. The rest continued their angry dash forward, the sound of steel on steel ringing throughout the square as the battle was joined in earnest.

Any trepidation Glo had felt suddenly melted away as the sound of peaceful music pervaded the battlefield. Elladan's fingers glided gracefully across the neck of his lute, the music taking the form of a lullaby.

Almost as one, the cultist guards disengaged from the fight, with drooping eyes and wide yawns. In mere moments, all had succumbed to the bard's charms, slumping to the ground fast asleep.

Glo glanced at Elladan, the bard responding with a nod and a grin.

The sound of clapping abruptly echoed across the square, a strange voice accompanying it. "Nicely done."

A black-robed figure pushed its way through the unusually quiet throng. It was followed by another group of guards. Glo counted twelve altogether.

The robed figure threw back its hood, revealing a dark-bearded man with weathered features. When he spoke, his tone was rather lofty. "We were wondering when you were going to show up. Let me introduce myself. My name is *Paine*."

Elladan cast a quick glance at Aksel, then spoke for the group. "Pleasure to make your acquaintance, Paine."

Paine turned his gaze upon Elladan. "Hmm. You must be the elven bard. That was a nice little lullaby you played my men. You needn't bother trying that on us, though. We are immune to such enchantments."

Elladan pursed his lips and gave the mage a slight nod. "Duly noted—and you should know that we knew you were expecting us. We ran into your 'friend,' Skuld, along the way. She made it quite clear we were tonight's 'guests of honor.'"

"Yeah, and then we sent her packing," Donnie added glibly.

A smug smile spread across Paine's face. His gaze swept between Elladan and Donnie. "Ah yes, dear Skuld. She was the weakest link of the Council of Six. Getting rid of her is no great loss."

Glo exchanged glances with Aksel. *Council of Six?*

Aksel responded with a slight shake of his head. Glo peered back at Paine with a perplexed expression. "What is this Council of Six?"

Paine shifted his eyes to Glo, recognition dawning on his face. "Ah, the elven wizard—the one who likes to light things on fire."

Seth, a few feet from Glo, snorted. "Told you, you have a reputation."

"Not now, Seth," Aksel whispered through gritted teeth.

Meanwhile, Paine went on with his explanation. "The Council of Six are the right hand of the goddess, Salisma, and I have the privilege of being one of them."

"Wouldn't that make him a finger?" Donnie quipped in a soft voice.

"Bet I know which finger he is," Elladan murmured under his breath.

The side of Seth's mouth twisted upward. "What kind of freak has six fingers?"

Glo coughed violently into his fist, all the while trying to keep a straight face. "Wasn't... Voltark... one of your number?"

Paine's eyes narrowed, his expression hardening. "Ah, yes. I am quite aware that you did away with him."

He held his stare for a few moments, then waved his hand dismissively. "It's just as well. Voltark was always too full of himself, vying with the rest of us for Salisma's favor. It appears his ego finally caught up with him."

"That and Lloyd's sword," Donnie quipped under his breath.

"Well at least they're back down to five fingers now," Seth added softly.

Poor Kalyn turned red in the face, trying hard not to react to the comments. If Paine heard them at all, he chose to ignore them.

This time Elladan queried the mage. "If you don't mind me asking, who are the other three?"

Paine nonchalantly shifted his gaze to the elven bard. "The other three wait at the old temple just north of here, but you will meet them soon enough."

With that, Paine motioned his men forward. "Anyway, that's enough talk. Take them."

This new batch of guards launched themselves across the intervening space between them and the companions. Paine faded behind his men, cutting off any clear shot at the mage.

Once again, Kalyn and Martan immediately took out two of their opponents, but these men were more seasoned than the rest. The rest of them dodged the archers' arrows and rushed into close combat.

The sound of steel on steel rang throughout the square once more. Lively music struck up to accompany it. Elladan played with keen dexterity, his fingers flying over the strings of his lute almost faster than the eye could follow.

Lloyd and the others pushed back on their opponents with renewed vigor, but they were greatly outnumbered. Kalyn and Martan spread out to either side, the dour archer searching for an opportunity to take down any opponent.

Kalyn, on the other hand, seemed bent on getting a shot at Paine. She wound her way around the expanding fray until she found an opening. The young archer then let loose one, two, three arrows in rapid succession at the dark mage. Yet all three just bounced off an invisible barrier about a foot away from the mage's head.

Paine let out a wicked laugh. "Ha, ha, ha. You'll have to do better than that, little sniper."

Kalyn snarled at the mage. "Casters. I hate casters!" She glanced over her shoulder at the elven wizard. "No offense, Glo."

"None taken!" Glo yelled back, yet her attack had given him an idea. The elven wizard called out to both archers as he lifted a hand and pointed at the mage. "Kalyn! Martan! Keep shooting at him!"

Kalyn knit her brow and narrowed her eyes, but she didn't argue the point. Martan, on the other hand, questioned his proposal. "You sure?"

"Just do it! Don't let up!" Glo cried. With that, he let loose a most basic spell. *"Nullam Telum."*

Four projectiles of arcane energy immediately leapt from his fingertips, spiraling out across the distance. The purple missiles unerringly wove their way through the ongoing battle and struck their target square in the chest.

A moment later, Paine was pelted with arrows from both sides.

Yet the mage remained completely untouched. Paine laughed again, shouting at Glo over the battlefield. "Ha-ha-ha. Did you really think that was going to work?"

"Not really," Glo murmured under his breath.

"Once more!" he shouted to the two archers.

The three of them hit Paine with another salvo, leaving the mage once again unscratched. This time, Paine's brow creased. "You know, this is getting quite tedious…"

"And again!" Glo cried, releasing a third salvo.

The mage was pelted once more with missiles and arrows. Again he was left without a mark, but his expression had grown angry.

"I said enough!" he cried over the sounds of battle. "Perhaps you'd like a taste of your own medicine!"

Paine lifted a finger and swept it across the square, finally coming to rest on Kalyn. "Sorry sweetie, but you lose!"

The dark mage chanted a spell, a red-hot ray springing from his fingertips.

"Kalyn!" Martan screamed.

"Duck!" Glo cried at the same moment.

The beam arced across the square with the speed of lightning, yet something had gone wrong with the mage's aim. As the ray left Paine's hand, his mouth suddenly dropped open and his eyes went glassy.

The red-hot beam went awry, glancing across Kalyn's arm as she flung herself out of the way. The young archer hit the dirt, rolling in it to put out the flames that had sprung up on her tunic.

Meanwhile, Paine was in trouble. His head tilted back, a strangled cry leaving his lips. A moment later, his knees gave out, his entire body collapsing to the dirt below.

Behind the fallen mage stood a small black-robed figure, a gleaming dagger in its hand.

Glo let out a deep breath, the corners of his mouth upturning slightly. He had noticed Seth disappear a while ago. Knowing the halfling as well as he did, he was sure Seth had set his sights on Paine.

Mage killer. His halfling friend had certainly earned that title today, yet Glo would have to tease him about it later.

Kalyn had put out the fire on her arm, but she held the limb limply by her side. Meanwhile, Lloyd and the others were still engaged in battle. The tall warrior had a few gashes in his armor. Cyclone and Donnie sported visible wounds as well. Only Alana appeared unscratched. *Guess it pays to carry a shield and wear full armor.*

Still, it appeared they were gaining the upper hand. They had felled most of their opponents, each combatant now facing a single remaining guard.

Martan had rushed to Kalyn's side and tried to help her as Aksel tended to her wound. The young woman seemed grateful at first, but then pushed the grim young man away. "Quit your fussin'. I ain't no damsel in distress. Go find someone else to paw."

Martan sighed and slowly turned away from the young woman. A moment later he cried out, his voice filled with clear panic. "Um, guys, I don't think we're out the woods just yet!"

The archer pointed across the square.

Glo followed his gaze and saw more black figures pouring out of the temple. There were dozens of them this time, more than they could handle. Glo's heart leapt into his throat. *There's no way we can stop that many… unless…*

An idea suddenly dawned on him. Glo quickly pulled out a pinch of glowing dust from his belt and weaved his arms in a well-practiced pattern. "Oh well, if they wanted a night of blood and fire, they've got it."

A moment later, he finished his incantation. *"Murum Ignis."*

Glo lifted his arms, palms out, in the direction of the temple. At the base of the steps, a curtain of shimmering scarlet fire suddenly sprang into existence. It swiftly rose up into the air, reaching nearly twenty feet in height. The mass of black-clad figures came to an abrupt halt, the lot of them backing away from the flames.

Yet Glo didn't stop there. The young wizard knit his brow, beads of sweat forming on it as he concentrated. Over by the temple steps, the wall of fire began to move. It climbed the stairs one by one, driving the black-clad figures back inside the stone structure. The flaming curtain finally stopped moving, trapping the cultists inside the temple.

Meanwhile, the battle had ended, the last of the guards fallen at their feet. Everyone now stared at the spectacle at the entrance to the temple.

"Well that's some fancy fire work there!" Kalyn grinned.

"I'm suddenly glad you like playing with fire," Donnie joked.

"They don't call him 'Glo' for nothing," Elladan chortled.

The young wizard grimaced, a short laugh escaping his lips despite himself. He shook his head. "Laugh it up all you want, but I can't keep this up forever."

Aksel, finished with Kalyn, narrowed a single eye at him. "How long do we have?"

Glo pursed his lips together as he thought it over. "Ten minutes, give or take, provided I don't get any further interruptions."

There was a momentary pause as the gravity of their situation sunk in. Glo had bought them a little time, but not much. In less than ten minutes, that curtain of flame would come down, and a host of black guards and mages would come swarming out of the serpent temple.

It was Lloyd in the end who saved the day. He had been staring at the temple intently, then suddenly spun around with his mouth and eyes open wide. "What if we take out those pillars?"

Aksel and Glo exchanged a glance. There were two thick pillars holding up the entrance to the temple. If they were brought down, the entire front of the building would collapse.

Glo shrugged. *It just might work.*

Aksel didn't seem convinced. He squinted at Lloyd, his expression skeptical. "And just how do you plan on knocking down those pillars?"

The tall warrior sheathed his swords and strode over to Elladan. "Can I see your bag?"

Elladan put his lute away and produced his portal bag.

Lloyd reached his arm inside, down to the armpit, and rummaged around for a moment or two. Shortly thereafter, he withdrew his hand—it was wrapped around a long metal handle. The tall man continued to withdraw the handle until a large metal head appeared at the other end.

Glo immediately recognized the weapon. It was one of the war-hammers Lloyd had used back at Stone Hill. The young warrior had dashed a few skeletons to pieces with the sturdy weapon, but could it be used to break down stone pillars?

Lloyd reached into the bag once more and pulled out a second hammer. He hefted the heavy weapons in his hands, spinning the heads over to reveal familiar-looking runes carved into the edges.

"These hammers were a gift from my father," Lloyd said as he admired the weapons. "They are dwarven-made. I'd imagine they're up to the task."

The young man lifted one hammer up and held it out toward Alana and Cyclone. "Either of you care to do the honors?"

The dragon hunter held up a hand. "I don't do hammers." He cast a glance at Alana. "Be my guest."

Alana arched an eyebrow at the hunter, then sheathed her sword and took the hammer from Lloyd. A gasp escaped her lips as she hefted the metal weapon in both hands. "Whoa. That's heavier than I thought."

She widened her stance to compensate, then took a couple of practice swings. A wide grin spread across her face. "Oh, I like this!"

Elladan wore a wicked grin. "Hey Donnie, you might not want to do anything to piss her off just right now."

Donnie tilted his head down and glared at the bard with one eye. "I never do anything to piss her off."

Alana stopped swinging her weapon and stared at the slight elf with a raised eyebrow. "Come again?"

Donnie gave her one of his most charming smiles. "Well… not intentionally anyway."

Glo had been listening to the banter quietly, but his patience was wearing thin. "Can you guys get to it already? We don't have all day, you know."

All eyes turned toward the elven wizard. There were still a few grins among the group, but they swiftly faded as Aksel spoke.

"Glo's right. We should hurry."

The little cleric strode off purposely in the direction of the temple, dispersing the slaves around him as he went. Glo took off immediately after him, the others following as well.

When they reached the base of the stairs, Lloyd and Alana split up, each taking a separate pillar. Aksel had the others shoo away any remaining slaves, while the two warriors began to bang away on their targets. After a few swings, cracks started to form in the thick columns.

Glo breathed a sigh of relief. *It's actually working.*

The curtain of fire was still going strong, keeping the cultists trapped in the temple. Yet dark faces could be seen glaring at them through those flames. The cultists jeered.

"Kill the infidels!"

"Drain their blood!"

"Feed them to the goddess!"

Glo tried to ignore the curses, but Kalyn didn't seem quite inclined to. The young archer grabbed Martan by the arm and dragged him to the base of the steps.

"What are you doing?" Martan cried in alarm. "Don't you know this whole thing is likely to come down on us?"

"Oh, quit your whining," Kalyn admonished him. "They wanna play, so let's play."

The lady archer nocked an arrow and drew it back, taking aim at the temple entrance. Martan raised an eyebrow, but then followed suit. "Just as long as we back away when this thing starts coming down."

Kalyn's mouth twisted sideways. "Quit your worryin'. Live a little."

She let her arrow fly with the words, "And may the best girl win!"

Martan's shot went completely awry, nearly catching Lloyd in the shoulder. The tall man cast a glance back at the dour archer, but refrained from commenting, being so intent on taking down his pillar.

Kalyn, on the other hand, chewed him out. "Shoot the cultists, not the heroes!"

A few cries echoed from inside the building as the two archers continued to send arrows through the flaming curtain. Kalyn kept count as they went.

"One for me, one for you."

"Three for me, two for you…"

Glo was hard-pressed to maintain his concentration during the amusing onslaught. However, things were progressing. A few more swings, and both Lloyd and Alana had cracked chunks off each pillar. Large crevices began to appear in the stone canopy above them.

Unfortunately, their time was nearly up. The curtain of fire Glo had erected slowly began to diminish in size. Sections of the wall began to flicker and fade. He started to squint from the pain, his head feeling as if it were going to explode.

Just when he thought he couldn't take it anymore, Lloyd broke through his pillar. A few moments later, Alana broke through hers. A loud rumbling sound reverberated across the square as the stone canopy above them sagged and began to crack in places.

"Get back!" Aksel shouted in warning.

Lloyd and Alana swiftly backpedaled away from the crumbling structure. Yet Kalyn seemed intent on hitting another target.

"Just one last shot!" the lady archer cried.

Martan threw his arms around her waist and lifted her off the ground as he ran away from the building. Kalyn let one last arrow fly over his shoulder as he carried her away from the collapsing structure.

Glo lost it at that point, his curtain of fire completely failing. With it gone, a multitude of black clad figures poured from the temple entrance. They rushed down the steps just as the entire front of the building collapsed.

Huge boulders crashed to the ground, the earth shaking from the impact. A cloud of dust rushed outward from the site, sweeping over the companions like a wave.

Glo and the others covered their heads and waited for the wave to pass. The rumbling finally subsided. Glo peeked out from beneath his robes. Dust still filled the air, but it was slowly settling back to the ground.

When the dust finally dissipated, they saw that their plan had worked. The temple entrance was completely gone, hidden behind an avalanche of stone. Not a single cultist had made it out of the temple in time. The few who had tried now lay buried beneath a rocky tomb.

Kalyn whistled in amazement at the sight of the devastation. "I think somehow Glo won that last contest."

"Definitely beat his record at the lighthouse," Seth commented wryly.

Glo cast a scathing stare at the halfling, but Seth was grinning. "Not that I'm complaining or anything."

Glo just shook his head. "I'm never going to live this down, am I?"

"Nope," Seth answered with a lopsided grin.

31

SLAVES OF THE SERPENT

*Another figure was chained to the post in the
middle of the small cavern*

Seth was amazed their plan had worked. He thought for certain they were goners after Lloyd cold-cocked that guard. He had hoped they could slip through town and make it to the north end of the hollow unnoticed. However, Lloyd's keen sense of righteousness had dashed any chance of that.

Still, he supposed he couldn't completely blame the tall warrior. The abusive guard did have it coming—and beyond all hope, they had somehow managed to seal most of the cultists in their own temple. With any luck, they would reach the caves before any of them managed to extricate themselves.

Aksel seemed to be thinking along the same lines. He motioned for everyone to gather around. "We need to move quickly. Seth, you keep an eye out for any rogue cultists. Kalyn, Martan, you two go and scout the road ahead. The rest of you stay put so I can heal your wounds. As soon as I'm done, we'll move out."

Kalyn and Martan took off, while Aksel tended to Lloyd, Donnie, and Cyclone. Once they were all healed, the group headed north out of the small village. Seth led the way until they met up with Kalyn and Martan.

"We've got good news and bad news," Kalyn drawled in that thick Deepwood accent of hers.

Seth just couldn't resist asking the obvious question. "So what's the good news?"

"There's nothing between here and the cave except for a few snakes," Kalyn answered almost too nonchalantly, though he detected a slight tremor in her voice. The young woman still hadn't gotten over her aversion to the slippery creatures. He wondered just how she'd react when they came face to face with that snake-man in the cave.

"So what's the bad news?" Donnie just had to ask.

"There are a lot of folks guarding the front entrance," Martan answered this time.

Elladan pursed his lips together. "Just how many is a lot?"

Kalyn and Martan exchanged a brief glance before she replied. "We counted about twenty."

"Almost sounds like they were expecting us," Donnie wisecracked.

Seth fixed the slight elf with an acid stare. "Ya think?"

Aksel stepped back, his face scrunching up with concern. "This is not good. That's far too many for us to handle at once."

Glo steepled his hands together in front of his chin. "What we could really use is some sort of distraction."

Elladan snapped his fingers together and wagged one in the air. "I think I have just the thing."

All eyes turned to the bard as he reached into his pouch. The dark-haired elf pulled out what looked like a small piece of wool, then weaved his hands in an intricate pattern. He ended the incantation with the words, *"Perfecta Deceptionem."*

Seth watched with fascination as Elladan's face began to bubble. It popped and twisted in a few different directions until its entire shape changed. The bard's body followed suit. In mere moments, he transformed into the spitting image of the dark mage, Paine. When

Elladan spoke, his voice even sounded like the smug man. "Ah, you must be the Heroes of Ravenford. So good of you to offer up your lives to our goddess."

Kalyn giggled at the bard's imitation. "Dang, that's really good." The young woman sniffed the air. "You even smell like him."

Seth squinted an eye at the lady archer. "And just when were you smelling Paine?"

Kalyn fixed him with a wicked stare. "It's not like it was on purpose or nuthin'. I just needed to get all them arrows back that I shot at the creep."

Seth let out a short, closemouthed laugh. "Humph. Sure, ya did."

"Anyway,"—Aksel interjected shifting their attention back to Elladan—"what exactly did you have in mind?"

"How about this?" Elladan cleared his throat and waved his hand in the air, pretending to shout in a soft voice. "You! Guards! The sacrifices are getting away! Quick, follow me!"

Soft chuckles sprung up around the gathered group. The corner of Seth's mouth twitched with appreciation. "Not bad. That just might work."

The companions put their heads together and swiftly laid out a strategy centered around Elladan's disguise. In the end it worked like a charm. Elladan drew most of the guards away from the cave entrance into the trees. There, they were able to pick them off in small groups. When they were done, only a small contingent remained in front of the caves.

Donnie, Cyclone, and Lloyd doffed their disguises and pretended to be captives. The others walked them up to the entrance. Once within striking distance, the companions made short work of the remaining guards. Aksel healed some minor wounds they had incurred, then Seth led the way into the cave.

The inside was exactly as Seth remembered it. Torches lined the rough-hewn walls at periodic distances, nicely illuminating their way. The tunnel angled downward for around three hundred feet, then opened into a small cavern. The chamber was empty except for a few torches spaced evenly along the walls. Three more tunnels branched off from there, one directly in front of them and one to either side.

Low moans drifted up from the tunnel on the left, reminding Seth of the last time he was here. Seth felt the blood drain from his face at the memory of what he had seen down that tunnel.

"What's all that racket?" Kalyn whispered softly.

Seth cast a glance at the lady archer. "I'm not sure you want to know."

"So which way do we go from here?" Aksel prompted him.

Seth peered at his cleric friend, torn as to what they should do. Common sense dictated that they continue along the main path, but somehow Seth couldn't bring himself to ignore all those tortured souls he had seen.

The halfling closed his eyes and shook his head. *Damn it. All these goody-two-shoes must be rubbing off on me.*

His mind made up, Seth turned down the path to the left, motioning for the others to follow. He put a single finger to his lips as he went and whispered, "Quietly."

Seth led his companions down the short tunnel until they reached the tall portcullis that blocked the passageway. A few gasps escaped his friends when they saw what lay beyond.

Seth's own stomach turned once again at the sight. Another figure was chained to the post in the middle of the small cavern—a woman this time. A few snakes were already wrapped around her and Seth could see the bite marks on her body.

She moaned and writhed in pain as the black-hooded figure stood before her, chuckling with obvious delight. Someone gagged behind Seth. He cast a glance over his shoulder and saw Kalyn blanch, her face turning deathly pale.

Seth held a finger to his lips and shook his head. The halfling returned his gaze to the small cavern beyond the gate. Three of the cages were filled with humans; Seth counted a few dozen of them. The last cage held about ten of those weird-looking half-snake beings. The creatures hissed and slithered, but they seemed far more docile than the last time he had been there.

Seth backed away from the gate, motioning for the others to follow. They retreated a short distance down the tunnel until they were out of earshot of the dark torturer.

Once they stopped, Lloyd whispered in outrage. "We can't just leave those folks there."

For once, Seth agreed with the tall warrior. "We're not going to… but we can't just rush in, either. If he releases those half-snake creatures, we'll have a heck of a fight on our hands."

Aksel's expression was dreadfully somber. "What do you propose?"

Seth eyed Lloyd speculatively. "How fast do you think you can lift that portcullis?"

Lloyd's expression was positively grim. "Lift it? Heck, I'll smash through it if I have to."

The young warrior set his jaw as he retrieved his warhammers from Elladan once again.

"Be faster if we both do it."

Everyone turned to gaze at Cyclone. Seth found it surprising the dragon hunter suddenly wanted to help. Lloyd did as well.

"I thought you 'didn't do hammers'?'"

The dragon hunter roughly grabbed one of the hammers from Lloyd's hand and brushed by him. "Humph. Let's just get this over with already."

Seth exchanged a brief glance with Aksel. The little cleric just shook his head, his expression mystified.

The party followed Cyclone down the tunnel, and on Aksel's signal, warrior and dragon hunter each swung a large hammer at the gate.

The twin strikes hit the portcullis so hard that it sounded like a gong had gone off. The rock holding the gate in place split in half and the metal structure fell into the cavern beyond with a loud *thud*.

The black-hooded torturer was taken by surprise. It whipped around, the hood falling from its head as Alana and Donnie charged into the room.

Seth momentarily froze as the torturer's identity was revealed. It was a bald-headed woman, her skull and face covered with snake tattoos. She immediately grabbed the snakes off her victim and threw them to the ground between her and her would-be attackers.

"Get them, my petsssss," she hissed in a weird, snake-like voice.

Four large cobra-like snakes sat on the ground between the companions and their target. Alana and Donnie stopped to deal with them. Lloyd and Cyclone swiftly joined them.

While they were preoccupied, Seth stole around the inside wall of the cavern. He was not sure the tunnel was not the only way out of this cave, and he would be damned if he let the torturer get away.

Yet the black-robed woman seemed to have other ideas. While the fighting went on, she slowly inched her way toward the cage with the half-snake, half-human creatures.

Kalyn must have seen it the same time as Seth. Her warning reverberated across the cavern.

"Watch out! She's gonna set them critters loose!"

The lady archer might not have a clear shot, but Seth had worked his way far enough around the cavern wall. He drew a thin black blade from his belt and flung it with deadly accuracy. The sharp blade flipped end over end as it sailed across the small cave, striking its target square in the chest.

The black-robed woman halted in her tracks, her hands going to the knife suddenly protruding from her torso. Her knees buckled and she fell to the ground, landing on her side, all the while still grasping the hilt of the knife. A moment later, she went completely still.

"Nice one, short stack!" Kalyn called from the cavern entrance.

Yet Seth paid her little heed. The others had finished off the deadly cobras. Miraculously, no one had been bitten. Seth led the others over to the cages with the human prisoners. The halfling swiftly unlocked all three and let the captives out. The prisoners turned out to be from all over the surrounding area, including Deepwood.

A couple of them seemed to recognize Kalyn. They exchanged greetings with the lady archer, Kalyn even hugging one or two of them.

"I never gave up on ya! I told the others you guys hadn't up and ran off, but they wouldn't listen to me," Kalyn exclaimed. "I knew I wasn't crazy!"

"Debatable," Seth noted, the corner of his mouth twisting upward.

Kalyn squinted at him darkly, but then returned her attention to the captives. "When you all get back to Deepwood, you tell 'em I was right and set their butts on fire!"

Elladan tapped Kalyn on the shoulder. "Sorry to interrupt this touching reunion, but we should get them out of here as soon as possible. No telling what will happen to these caves when we confront the cult leaders."

Aksel nodded in agreement. "Go ahead and escort them out of here. I want to see if there is anything I can do for these human-snake creatures."

"Good luck with that," Elladan said, his expression clearly skeptical. He then motioned to the freed captives. "This way, folks."

Elladan, Kalyn, Martan, Alana, and Donnie escorted the people out of the caves. Meanwhile, the others turned their attention to the cage with the half-human half-snakes.

Abruptly Seth noticed something was missing. The torturer's body was gone. The halfling practically kicked himself. He usually checked his victims to make sure they were indeed dead. *I must be slipping.*

"Watch it. That torturer's still alive," he warned the others.

Everyone froze in place. A moment later, Lloyd dropped his swords, his hands going to his head as he cried out in pain. Aksel and Glo both reacted to the young man's sudden outburst.

"Lloyd, what is it?"

"What's the matter?"

Yet Seth had a sneaking suspicion. The halfling swept his eyes across the cavern. *There. Behind that cage.*

Seth spotted the torturer. She was lying on the ground behind one of the empty cages. In her hand she held a wand. It was pointed directly at Lloyd.

The halfling immediately drew another knife and launched it at the woman's arm. It struck her just above the elbow, forcing her to drop the wand. He immediately followed it with another knife. This one caught her right between the eyes. The woman sagged to the ground, dead.

Seth spun around to face the others. "Phew, that was clo…"

He halted in mid-sentence, his jaw dropping at the sight in

front of him. Where Lloyd had stood moments ago, there was now something else. The top half still looked like the young man, but the bottom half was all large yellow-green coils, folded in and over themselves.

Andrella's gonna hate this…

The half-man half-snake creature shifted its gaze toward Seth. The eyes were no longer Lloyd's. There were black slits just like a serpent. The creature picked up the warrior's swords and lifted them as it advanced on Seth.

"Seth, quick—turn invisible!" Aksel yelled.

Seth immediately grabbed his cloak and invoked its magic, disappearing from sight.

Having lost its current target, the creature halted. It spun on its large coils and then started slithering across the cavern toward Aksel and the others.

Cyclone pushed the others back and planted himself firmly between them and serpent-Lloyd. "I've been looking for an excuse for this. Don't worry, I won't hurt him too much."

A moment later, Lloyd was on him, and sword met halberd in a heated exchange.

32
LLOYD VS. CYCLONE

*Lloyd's black blade came around again, this time
aimed directly at Cyclone's head*

Glolindir watched in horror as Lloyd transformed into a half-serpent. The upper half of the creature still looked like their friend, but the lower half was all reptilian—large, scaly yellow-green coils that ended in a curved tail. At first, Glo had thought Lloyd might have retained his senses, but then the half-serpent creature advanced menacingly on Seth.

"Seth, quick—turn invisible!" Aksel had warned him.

Seth almost immediately disappeared, confounding the creature, but then it set its sights on them. That was when Cyclone interposed himself between them and what had been Lloyd.

"I've been looking for an excuse for this. Don't worry, I won't hurt him too much."

Now the pair were locked in combat. Lloyd slithered up to the dragon hunter, swinging his twin blades with frightening speed. Still, his fighting style was not quite the same—the creature could not spin its body around the way the warrior normally could.

Cyclone held his halberd in both hands, expertly blocking all Lloyd's attacks.

Meanwhile, Aksel had begun an incantation to change Lloyd back. The little cleric's brow was knit with concentration, his hands weaving an intricate pattern in the air in front of him.

Glo could feel the magic building. It rose in power just before the spell was released.

"Nullam Depelle," Aksel cried as his hands came together and the spell was cast.

A flood of mana filled the air, settling in a circle around Lloyd. The half-man, half-serpent halted in its tracks, its large tail twitching as the magic enveloped it. For a brief instance, the creature's eyes changed back to their normal blue.

Lloyd looked from Glo to Aksel, his expression filled with re-morse. "I'm sorry…"

The magic around him suddenly dispersed, and Lloyd's eyes changed back to those of a serpent. The creature launched itself at Cyclone again with renewed vigor.

All of a sudden, the dragon hunter launched himself into the air, bringing his deadly halberd down in a wide-sweeping arc on serpent-Lloyd. At the very last moment, Lloyd brought his swords together and blocked the attack. Cyclone used the momentum to flip over the snake-creature, landing deftly behind him. The dragon hunter then immediately spun around and caught Lloyd in the tail with his sharp weapon.

Serpent-Lloyd let out a loud cry, spinning around as fast as it could move its large, bulky form.

"You better hurry up, or the next time it's coming clean off!" Cyclone called out to the others.

Glo exchanged a worried glance with Aksel, but the little cleric just shook his head. "I tried dispelling whatever was cast on him. I'm just not sure what else to do."

"Maybe this will help!"

They both turned to see Seth running across the cavern toward them. The halfling held a wand in his hand. "This is what that cult mage used on Lloyd."

Seth stopped in front of Glo and handed him a gnarled wooden stick. Glo reached in his pouch and pulled out the potion that enhanced his senses. He gulped it down, then closed his eyes while holding the wand in both hands.

A vision immediately formed in his mind. He saw a black cloud circle around Lloyd and envelop him. Lloyd's body then began to glow black, shifting and growing until he had transformed completely into a serpent. The entire scene reminded Glo of when Ruka shifted into her dragon form. The only difference was that when Ruka changed, she was surrounded by a brilliant white light.

That's it!

Glo's eyes snapped open. He peered at Aksel and Seth with renewed hope. "It's a spell of *malefic transformation*. A simple dispel won't work. You would need a spell of a higher order."

Aksel's expression was grim. "I can't cast anything higher."

Seth snapped his fingers. "Elladan might."

Glo's eyes went wide. Seth was right. Bards were intuitive casters. They didn't study like wizards or pray like clerics. That limited what they could cast, but enabled them to learn complex spells more easily.

Aksel barked at Seth. "Well don't just stand there. Go get him!"

Seth fixed Aksel with a scathing stare as his hands weaved a short incantation. "Yes, your majesty… *Tempore Duplo*."

Seth released his spell, then shot off down the tunnel faster than a jackrabbit.

Meanwhile, serpent-Lloyd had grown angry. The creature crossed its blades in front of its torso and closed its eyes.

Cyclone did not seem impressed. He glared at the half-serpent creature. "That the best you've got?"

As if to answer his question, serpent-Lloyd's blades suddenly lit up in flames.

Cyclone let a closemouthed laugh. "Humph. That's not gonna do you much good if you can't hit me."

Lloyd launched himself at the dragon hunter once again. He seemed a bit faster this time. Cyclone did his best to compensate, but Lloyd finally broke through his guard. His black blade sliced across the hunter's hand, causing Cyclone to lose his grip on his weapon.

The snake-warrior's second blade immediately followed, flashing across the hunter's torso and leaving a wide gash in its wake.

Lloyd's black blade came around again, this time aimed directly at Cyclone's head. It appeared that the hunter was finished, but at the very last moment, Cyclone managed to deflect the blade with his bracer and in the same motion grab Lloyd's arm.

Serpent-Lloyd struggled to pull away, but somehow Cyclone managed to hold on. In desperation, the half-serpent creature stabbed at the hunter with its other blade. Cyclone somehow deflected that blade as well, and caught hold of Lloyd's other arm.

Serpent-Lloyd cried in out in rage, trying to pull away from the dragon hunter, but Cyclone held him fast. The hunter said nothing, but Glo felt a strange energy emanating from him. The pair stayed locked in that position for a few more moments, when abruptly the dragon hunter struck.

In a lightning-fast motion, Cyclone jumped up and lashed out with both legs at the half-serpent creature. He struck with so much force that Lloyd was sent flying across the cavern. The half-serpent slammed into the wall on the other side of the cave and slumped to the ground in a heap.

Cyclone scooped up his halberd and sped after him, stopping just before the fallen creature. Serpent-Lloyd appeared to be stunned by the impact. He tried to lift himself, but immediately fell back to the ground. Cyclone stood over him, his shoulders tense, then slowly lifted the razor-sharp spear above his head, poised to deliver the killing blow.

"Cyclone!" Glo and Aksel cried the hunter's name simultaneously.

"Stop!" Two more cries were added to theirs as Seth and Elladan appeared from down the tunnel.

Cyclone still held his weapon aloft, but turned his face toward the others. Glo felt a sudden chill go up his spine. Cyclone's eyes had changed. They were no longer human. They looked like black slits—nearly the same as Lloyd's, but even scarier, the whites of his eyes had turned red.

As Glo watched in terror, Cyclone turned his gaze back to Lloyd, then lowered his weapon. The hunter then lashed out with his fist, catching the half-serpent creature across the jaw.

Crack.

The sound of the punch reverberated through the cavern as Lloyd slumped to the floor, out cold. Cyclone then strode away from the downed warrior. He glared at Glo with those eerie red eyes as he brushed by the others. "You better hurry up and fix him, or I'll do it for you."

The dragon hunter then stormed down the tunnel and out of sight.

"What the heck was all that?" Elladan asked his eyes wide. "He didn't get turned, too?"

Glo slowly shook his head. "I don't think so. That was something else entirely…"

"Elladan, can you help Lloyd?" Aksel brought them back on track.

"Um… I think so," the bard nodded.

The four of them hurried over to the downed warrior. Lloyd was out for the count.

Elladan began to weave his incantation. Glo was amazed by the complexity of the spell. He could feel the magic as it rose to a powerful crescendo. Still, it took time to weave, and Lloyd started to show signs of waking before it was finished.

"Hurry," Aksel urged Elladan.

The bard ignored the cleric and finished his last few motions with the words, *"Conteram Augurium."*

A torrent of power flowed from the bard and wove itself around Lloyd, pinning him in place. The half-serpent tried to fight it at first, but the magic held him fast while enveloping his entire body.

Lloyd transformed before their eyes, the serpent half of him shrinking down and turning back into human legs. His eyes were the last to change, fading back to their normal blue. When the magic finally released him, Lloyd fell to the ground in a heap.

Glo and the others rushed to his side. "Lloyd! Are you alright?"

The young warrior's eyes slowly opened and focused on Glo. "I… think so. Is there… anything to eat? I'm starving."

"Heh. He's fine," Seth declared with a snort.

Glo and Elladan lifted the tall warrior from the ground. Glo held onto him while Elladan changed the half-snake creatures in the cage back to their natural form. They turned out to be more men and women from nearby towns.

The companions escorted them out of the caves so they could hide in the trees until the final battle with the cult was over. The entire time, Glo kept seeing the image of Cyclone's red serpent-eyes in his mind.

What exactly is up with the dragon hunter? Where did that sudden amazing strength come from, and what changed him back? Whatever it was, Glo silently hoped the fierce hunter remained on their side.

33

THE SERPENT QUEEN

*The two titans clashed, blades and tail whipping around
almost faster than the eye could see*

Kalyn shuddered as they cautiously stole down the main tunnel that crawled deeper into the mountainside. The torches spaced evenly along the dark walls lent an eerie feeling to the already creepy tunnel, their dancing flames casting odd shadows everywhere.

A short distance ahead, Kalyn could see that the tunnel gave way to a larger room. As they drew closer, she observed two giant serpent statues against the back wall, situated on either side of a pair of closed doors.

Snakes. Why did it have to be snakes? Why couldn't it be an owlbear cult, or a wolf cult, or even a kitty cult? Elfar could have his own cult! Wouldn't that be cute?

Kalyn suppressed another shudder. *Sure wish I hadn't left him back with the wagons…*

The lady archer frowned when she felt a pair of eyes boring into her. A glance to her side proved it to be Martan. The disheveled archer raised an eyebrow in question, but Kalyn merely rolled her eyes and looked away.

Everyone filed out of the tunnel into the large, octagonal room. The two snake statues on the opposite wall appeared to glare at them ominously. It was quiet here. There were no people and no sounds. Just silence.

Kalyn stooped and leaned in toward Seth. "Sure is creepy in here. I thought you said there was a bunch of slaves roamin' around?"

Seth peered sidelong at her. "They must be done with their excavation—and trust me, it was creepier with the slaves."

Kalyn shrugged, "Well, like they say—beauty is in the eye of the beholder."

"Beholder? Where?" Elladan piped up, his eyes peering cautiously around the eerie tunnel.

Kalyn slapped a hand over her mouth. She had inadvertently invoked the name of a terrifying bodiless monster. Given the current situation, it was too easy to imagine such creatures lurking around every corner. Kalyn stood ramrod straight and tried to cover her verbal misstep. "Beholder? Did I say beholder? What I meant to say was 'beholden.' As in I am beholden to y'all for lettin' me come along on this 'venture.'"

The tension left Elladan's shoulders, a partial smile curving his lips. "Oh. Good. I don't ever want to run into a beholder—and you're welcome."

Donnie chuckled, "You just want the beauty and not the beholder, eh, Elladan?"

"I leave that part for you," Elladan retorted.

"No thanks. I have enough trouble keeping my own head straight," Donnie whispered over his shoulder as he crept across the room toward the double doors. The thin elf carefully inspected the floor and the walls, giving the statues a moment of consideration before moving back to the group.

"I don't see any traps," he reported.

Seth snorted derisively. "Really? Maybe you should get your eyes checked."

Donnie shrugged, then ushered Seth forward. "You're more than welcome to prove me wrong."

Seth crept forward, his gaze riveted on the twin serpent statues. Kalyn noticed a dull glow in their eyes as the halfling stole closer. She was about to say something when Seth halted and spun around. The halfling moved back to join them and folded his arms across his chest, a smug smile on his face. "Definitely trapped."

"What kind of trap and how do we disarm it?" Aksel asked.

"The same nasty one that was on the statues at the gate, and I imagine that staff will work on them."

"You could tell all of that just by looking at it?" Donnie asked with disbelief.

"Shhh! Don't question the master!" Kalyn said, half-jokingly.

Donnie held his hands in the air. "Hey, I'm just trying to make sure our lives aren't at risk here."

"Too late for that," Seth said, the corner of his mouth twisting upward.

Aksel cleared his throat. "Ahem! If we could focus on disarming those traps, please?"

Elladan reached into his bag and pulled out the covered snake staff, passing it to Aksel. The little cleric uncovered it, and then he and Alana both grabbed onto it and approached the statues with the staff raised.

While Aksel and Alana worked on disarming the trap, Glolindir started doing some snazzy work of his own. Kalyn watched with appreciation as he wove his hands expertly in the air. Suddenly, Donnie turned invisible.

"Oh, now that is slicker 'n blowing up a lighthouse." Kalyn giggled.

Glolindir dropped his head and shook it with a heavy sigh. "Never living that down."

"Bah! Don't be embarrassed! Own it!" Kalyn gave him a friendly punch in the arm. "I mean, if it ain't you, it's gonna be someone else doin' it and getting' put in the story books, right? So, might as well be you."

Glolindir eyed her skeptically, a single eyebrow arched.

"That did the trick." Aksel said, drawing Kalyn's attention back to their original task.

She glanced at the snake statues. The dull glow in their eyes was gone.

"I'll sneak up to the door and take a peek inside," Donnie whispered, his disembodied voice unnerving Kalyn.

"Be careful," Alana told him, her voice betraying a hint of concern.

"Always," Donnie's voice whispered from a little way ahead.

"That's what I'm afraid of," Alana murmured to herself.

Kalyn held her breath as one of the double doors opened just a crack. It seemed like an eternity before they heard Donnie again. Kalyn nearly jumped out of her skin when Donnie's voice came from just in front of her.

"There's a lot of chanting going on in there."

"Sheesh, elf! You're gonna give me a heart attack."

"Sorry." Kalyn could practically hear Donnie shrug with that stupid grin on his face.

"Did you see anything?" Aksel asked.

"Yep, and you're not going to like it." Donnie's voice sounded grim. "The good news is it's a big room filled with benches and lots of columns running its length, all of which will make good cover."

"And the bad news?" Elladan said with just a hint of trepidation.

"There's a big altar at the back of the room like Seth told us. There are a group of folks chanting around it—four black-robed figures and one tall bald guy with a skull tattoo on his noggin. He seems to be their leader."

"Probably another member of the Council of Six," Elladan remarked.

Kalyn felt a cold chill run up her spine. She put a hand over her heart as her mind started to boil with old, unwelcomed memories—memories of a tall, bald mage with a grinning skull tattoo on the left side of his face.

A vision abruptly passed before her eyes. The dark mage chuckled sinisterly as he cast a spell that sucked her sister Kia, only four years old at the time, into the glowing stone in his hand. Her sister's terrified, pain-filled screams had haunted Kalyn's dreams ever afterward. Skull Head tried to use the same spell on Kalyn next, but the magic mysteriously failed. It was not till much later that she learned she had been protected by the old family heirloom that hung around her neck. To this day, Kalyn wished her sister had been wearing it instead.

A firm, warm hand set itself on Kalyn's shoulder. She looked to the side to see Martan giving her a reassuring nod. The archer then peered in the direction of Donnie's voice. "A skull tattoo? You're sure?"

"Yeah. I'm positive." Donnie paused briefly, "Why?"

Martan removed his hand from Kalyn's shoulder. "He tried to kill Kalyn when she was real little. He took her sister, too. If you ask me, she has the right to try and kill him back."

Kalyn's mouth fell open, surprised that Martan would speak up for her like that.

Donnie seemed okay with the idea as well. "That's fine by me, but we have bigger problems. He and his cronies are not the only nasties in there."

"Spit it out already, Donnie. We don't have all day," Elladan urged the slight elf.

Donnie sounded hurt. "I'm getting to it. Aside from those, there are eight of those big serpents like we fought back in Ravenford. There's also a small two-headed dragon, a half-woman, half-serpent with snake hair, and a large half-man, half-serpent creature. The last one's chanting next to the altar with Skull Head."

Donnie paused a moment. "Oh, and if I forgot to mention it before, there's a bluish-purple portal beginning to form over the altar."

"Nice thing to forget," Elladan chided the invisible elf.

Kalyn had started to shudder at the description of the monsters. She'd never heard of such hideous things, except maybe in childhood stories. She looked at Glolindir and found the elven wizard's face furrowed with concern.

"What are those things?" She looked between him and Elladan and Aksel.

Elladan peered at her sympathetically. "Sounds like a hydra, a medusa, and a naga."

Glolindir nodded in agreement. "And, if I were to hazard a guess, I'd say they are beginning to summon their 'goddess,' or whatever she is, into this world."

"We're sorely outnumbered," Aksel's voice was low and grim.

"That doesn't matter. We've got to stop them," Lloyd declared. The young man swept his eyes around the group, his pupils burning with passion. "We have to do it now. We are the first line of defense. If they summon an evil goddess into this world, there is no telling what will happen or how many lives could be lost."

Kalyn felt inspired by Lloyd's ardent speech. "In Deepwood, we say that if you don't want your scalp on a shaman's pole, you scalp the shaman first."

Cyclone snorted, either in amusement or annoyance. He stood nearby with his arms folded across his chest, but otherwise refused to comment.

"I think the short version of that saying is 'prevention is the best medicine,'" Elladan noted.

Aksel nodded in agreement. "Lloyd is right. I never meant to say we should back away from this. What I meant to say is that we need a plan."

Kalyn smiled wanly at the gnome. "Yeah. Ain't no Dunwynn tea party we're going to tromp on."

Elladan waved everyone in closer. "Gather 'round folks. I think I might just have an idea or two."

Kalyn counted to ten, then slipped through the double doors into the chamber beyond. Seth, Donnie, and Aksel were all now invisible and had gone ahead of her.

The room around her was as Donnie described—rather large, with numerous columns disappearing into the dark ceiling above, and rows of benches spanning the chamber, leading to the altar on the opposite side.

Keeping her footsteps in time with the chanting, Kalyn stole behind a nearby pillar. She noticed two sets of tracks in the dusty floor, leading straight toward the altar.

Kalyn peered around the pillar and locked her eyes onto a tall, bald man in black, with the prominent skull tattoo on the left side of his face. She instantly recognized that grinning tattoo. He was the one who took Kia away from her and turned her into a slave. She glared at the man's back and mentally marked him for death.

Kalyn swept her eyes across the room. Martan stole behind the pillar next to her, the archer's bow drawn and nocked. Across the aisle, Glolindir stood plastered against the pillar directly opposite of them, the tall elf's shoulders tensed with anticipation.

Abruptly, the double doors slammed open, and a blur of red flashed across the room, right up to one of the giant snakes.

Quick as lightning, Kalyn drew an arrow back and shot the snake square in the eye, causing it to reel. Before the creature knew what had happened, Lloyd chopped its head clean off with that razor-sharp black blade he wielded.

A figure in blue charged in right behind Lloyd, and with a massive leap, landed in front of a second serpent. Cyclone thrust his halberd all the way through the unprepared snake, then yanked it out and gutted the giant creature, leaving it to slowly die.

Over at the demolished doorway, two more figures stepped into the room. Alana stood there prepared for battle, holy sword gleaming in her one hand, rose-adorned shield in the other. Elladan entered next to her, the bard's fingers flying over his lute almost faster than the eye could follow. Lively music flowed across the room, in direct contention with the chanting from the altar.

The two-headed dragon creature stomped into view from around a pillar, and with a thunderous roar, charged Cyclone. The tall serpent woman with snake hair slithered around, and upon seeing two of her servants lifeless on the floor, released a shrieking wail.

Alana, shield held in front of her, dashed from the doorway toward the medusa with the cry, "For Cormar!"

A giant snake rushed ahead of the medusa and met Alana, striking at her, but before Kalyn could react, an arrow flashed by her and caught the serpent directly in the eye, causing it to flinch in its tracks. A quick glance over her shoulder showed Martan standing next to his pillar, another arrow already nocked to his bowstring.

Nice shot!

Alana took advantage of the serpent's pause. She rammed her sword through the roof of the snake's mouth, the tip of her blade jutting out the back of its head.

I thought they said these snakes were tough? Ha! Not tough enough to withstand real heroes.

There was a strange sizzling sound followed by a bright flash. Across the aisle, a bolt of lightning burst from Glolindir's hands. The brilliant bolt lanced across the chamber, catching the two snakes next to the hydra, and also striking a caster standing at the altar, blowing the man back several feet.

The stench of burnt flesh filled the air.

"Hot warg, that was slick!" Kalyn stepped out from behind the pillar. She fired two arrows in succession, catching the singed snakes in the eye, dropping both before they could get any closer to Cyclone and Lloyd.

"Wa-hoo! Those lil guys are a piece of cake!" Kalyn shouted excitedly.

Martan stepped out behind Kalyn once more and shot twice in rapid succession at another approaching snake, hitting it squarely in both eyes. The creature let out a loud hiss and dropped to the ground writhing in pain. "Lil guys? You realize these snakes are over eight feet tall, right?"

Kalyn grit her teeth together as she felt the blood drain from her face. "Don't remind me. They're big targets. That's all that matters!"

Why couldn't it have been a bunny cult? Or a squirrel cult? Squirrels can be mean too! Just try stealing one of their nuts.

Martan drew his arrow back and fired at the caster Glo had blasted. Yet before the arrow had sailed half the distance, the caster waved his hands in a swirling circle and disappeared from sight. The arrow Martan had fired passed through the air where the mage had just been, continuing on as if there were nothing there.

Kalyn and Martan both ducked back behind the same pillar.

"I told you before not to miss!" Kalyn shoved him in the shoulder.

"Sorry. I tried my best," Martan said apologetically as he drew another arrow.

"Well… can't hit something you can't see, I guess. Still, you're out of practice."

Any retort that Martan may have made was interrupted by a loud cry. "Help! I can't see!"

A chill went up Kalyn's spine. *That sounds like Glolindir!*

Kalyn dashed out from behind the pillar, her bow raised. Glo stood in the same spot directly across the aisle from her, but he was stumbling around and flailing his hands helplessly.

Before Kalyn could move a muscle, Elladan rushed from the doorway and grabbed the flailing wizard, pulling him back just as another giant snake charged them.

"Get back, or I'll turn you into a bunny!" Elladan yelled, waving his free arm at the giant snake.

The creature slowed its approach, hesitating as if uncertain. The momentary pause gave Kalyn the perfect shot. The snake dropped into a writhing heap on the floor in front of the two elves, an arrow protruding from each of its eyes.

She was about to gloat aloud when a sudden cry made her freeze. "Kalyn, look out!"

Strong arms wrapped themselves around her torso and jerked her backwards a moment before a giant wall of stone shot up from the floor.

"Are you alright?" Martan asked breathlessly, still holding her in his arms.

The warmth of his body pressed against hers made Kalyn feel tingly all over. She abruptly unraveled his arms from around her, her cheeks burning with embarrassment. "Quit your worryin' and get back in the fight before they kill everything on us!"

Kalyn grabbed Martan by the arm and practically dragged him around to the other side of the stone wall. They made it back around just in time to see Aksel appear out of thin air. The little cleric cast a spell in the direction of the naga, causing a shimmering aura of radiant light to surround the large creature. At the same time, Lloyd carved a deep gash across the back of the large snake-man's hooded head.

The naga stopped its chanting and threw back its head, a tortured scream escaping its lips as the aura of light burned the wound across its back. The creature whirled around, nearly tripping Lloyd with its muscular coils, then pushed him away from the altar. A wicked-looking curved sword magically appeared in its hand as the tall warrior recovered his balance.

The two titans clashed, blades and tail whipping around almost faster than the eye could see. Kalyn didn't dare try a shot. They were too close and moving too fast to take the chance.

A shimmering in the air behind the duo caught Kalyn's eye. Donnie suddenly appeared at the altar, standing behind one of the dark-robed men. He stabbed with his pointed sword, right through the mage, killing him instantly.

Another chanting caster suddenly screamed and slumped to the floor as well, Seth appearing directly behind him. Without pausing, the halfling flung a knife through the air, catching another mage right between the eyes.

They seemed to have things well in hand, and Lloyd was still locked in close combat, so Kalyn swept her gaze around the chamber.

Across the room, Alana squared off with the medusa. According to Glo, the creature's gaze could turn its adversaries to stone. Thus, the lady knight skillfully used her shield to hide her face while parrying the tall creature's double swords. Yet with that handicap, she didn't appear to be making any headway against the snake-woman.

Kalyn decided to lend her a hand. She drew back an arrow and let it fly for the medusa's head, but at the last moment the monster raised its weapon and ruined the shot. The arrow penetrated completely through its arm and speared a few small snakes in its hair, but missed its head completely.

The medusa screamed and reached up, gingerly touching the dead little snakes in her hair. Luckily, the distraction was enough for Alana to carve a deep gash into the medusa's hide.

On the other side of the chamber, Cyclone battled the hydra. The plan had been for the hunter to handle the dragon-like creature, but somehow he had managed to climb onto the creature's back. The hydra snapped at him with both sets of wicked-looking teeth. Cyclone slammed the heads with either end of his spear, momentarily stunning the creature.

A sudden movement caught Kalyn's eye. Another serpent was

closing in on Seth and Donnie, but the duo appeared to have their hands full with the last caster and Skull Head. Kalyn rapid fired two arrows at the giant snake, each landing firmly in an eye, killing the creature instantly. Three more arrows whizzed past Kalyn, embedding themselves into the last snake in the room, dropping it before it could reach Aksel.

The lady archer let out a brief sigh. *That's a relief.*

Yet the battle was far from over. Kalyn focused back on Cyclone just in time to see the hunter sweep his wicked-looking blade down and lop off one of the hydra's heads clear off its neck.

Kalyn's jaw dropped. It was the one thing Glo had warned them against. "Dragon dung! Now he's gone and done it."

Martan's jaw dropped open. "Oh no."

"What are you doing?" Elladan and Aksel both yelled at the hunter.

"What is who doing?" Glo cried with frustration.

Elladan grabbed Glo's arms and started shaking them. "Prepare a fire spell. Prepare one now!"

"But I can't see!" Glo screamed.

"Just do it!" Elladan urged him. "I'll be your eyes!"

Cyclone raised his halberd again, aiming the blade for the second head.

"Stop!" they all screamed at once.

Just then, the stump that Cyclone had cut split into two pieces. A pair of buds bloomed from them and swiftly burst into two new heads. Both heads swiveled around and glared at Cyclone with angry hisses.

Cyclone smirked and readied his halberd for another swing.

Kalyn's head nearly exploded. "He's gonna keep doing that until it has more heads than the Duke of Dunwynn has issues!"

She watched in horror as the hunter swept his blade down lopping off yet another one of the heads. "Somebody do something quick!"

"Working on it!" Elladan yelled back.

Suddenly, there was a bright flash and a burst of heat filled the room. Kalyn whirled around just in time to see a beam of fire leave

Glolindir's hand and scorch the newly-severed hydra head, stopping it from splitting into new ones.

Elladan stood behind Glo, holding the wizard's arms and aiming them. "Get ready."

The hydra roared as Cyclone lopped yet another head from its body.

"Fire!" Elladan cried as he swiveled Glo toward the fresh stump.

Glo said the magic words and a beam of fire burst from his fingers, searing the bloody wound on the monster.

Kalyn started to cheer with glee when a loud shout interrupted her.

"Kalyn!"

She spun around, but something rammed into her, sending her sprawling on the floor. Kalyn looked up to find Martan standing over her, his hand clamped around a raised arm and his eyes looking directly into the face of the medusa. The monster screamed and dropped her sword, but her arm was firmly caught in Martan's grasp. It desperately tugged against the archer, but Martan had become unmovable, stiff, and completely gray. He had been turned to stone.

"Martan!" Kalyn screamed, even as she realized her cry was falling on deaf ears. She jumped to her feet with an angry scream, tears brimming over her eyes.

The medusa raised its other sword to break Martan's stony grip on it, but Kalyn lifted her bow and fired an arrow into the monster's raised arm. The medusa screamed, its sword dropping from its hand. The creature glared in Kalyn's direction, but Kalyn avoided her gaze by ducking behind Martan.

The lady archer nocked another arrow and rolled out from behind Martan. Yet before she could fire, a gleaming blade sailed through the air with a whoosh, slicing clean through the medusa's neck. The snake-haired head went tumbling off the tall creature's body as the rest of it slumped to the floor.

Alana stood behind the fallen creature, heaving heavily. She glanced at Kalyn, a grim smile on her face, her eyes filled with sorrow. Suddenly, her eyes flicked up and looked past Kalyn, growing wide with fear.

"Donnie!" Alana screamed.

Kalyn whirled around, her breath catching in her tight throat as she watched Donnie sail through the air and collide with a pillar, falling to the floor with a loud *crunch* before finally going still.

"Ahhh!"

The loud cry drew Kalyn's attention toward the altar. Lloyd was still locked in combat with the naga. The creature had broken through the warrior's defenses, its wicked curved blade embedded deep in the young man's left arm. Lloyd dropped his sword, swiftly beating back the naga's weapon with his black blade, then staggering backward.

Kalyn drew an arrow back and let it fly into the monster's coils, but the creature just shrugged it off. Yet instead of pursuing Lloyd, the naga turned away, knocking the young man down with its tail.

"This blood will suffice for my mistress," the monster hissed as it slithered up to the altar with its red-stained sword.

Skull Head spun to watch, the battle around him all but forgotten. His face took on an exultant expression as he cried out with glee, "Yes! Yes! The goddess can now come forth!"

Yet he had dropped his guard. A moment later, Seth appeared behind the bald man and sliced two knives across the backs of his knees. The cultist screamed and dropped to the floor, groping at his legs.

The naga glanced down at the man and halfling for a brief moment, then chose to ignore them. It slithered closer to the altar and hissed, "Come, my mistress, and feed on their…"

Out of thin air, Lloyd appeared between the naga and the altar. His black blade burst into flames as the tall warrior jammed it into the monster's torso.

The large snake-man visibly shuddered, then gasped, the blood-ied sword falling from its hand just short of the altar. Lloyd yanked out his black blade as the naga crumpled to the floor in a coiled heap.

"Mistress… I have… failed… you…" It gasped, and then all went silent.

Kalyn glanced around the chamber. The hydra was now a smoldering corpse. Cyclone sat on the ground a short distance away, badly burned. The cultists were now only corpses, scattered all around the altar. Giant snake bodies littered the room. Alana knelt next to Donnie, who lay still unmoving. The medusa was dead, and Martan…

Kalyn turned around and peered at the gray statue of Martan. His posture was a protective one, his feet set wide apart, his bow hand behind him to protect her and his posture leaning back to provide a shield. His stony hand was still wrapped around the medusa's limp arm, and his face was permanently frozen with a strange look of terrified determination. He had been scared to death, but he still stepped between Kalyn and that monster.

Kalyn tried to choke back a sob, but was unsuccessful. "Martan. Oh, Martan, why?" She stumbled up to the statue and wrapped her arms around him, her inner armor slowly crumbling away until a torrent of sobs and tears finally escaped her and trickled down the stony edges of Martan's clothes, dripping off and mingling with the medusa's blood beneath him.

"What have you done, you fools?" a man's voice echoed around the cavern, raking against Kalyn's nerves like nails on slate. "You've ruined everything!"

Kalyn let Martan go and turned around, focusing on the bald cultist with the skull tattoo.

"Hey, you're the ones who invited us. It's your funeral," Seth smirked at the skull-headed cultist.

Skull Head leaned back against the altar and glared at the halfling. "You think you've won? Well, think again. You can't stop it from happening. One way or another, my mistress will rise again."

Kalyn took a step forward, then stopped as her boot brushed against something. She glanced down to find the medusa's head lying face down on the floor. Without really thinking it through, she stooped and grasped it by the snake hair, lifting the oversized head. Kalyn then strode purposefully up to the cultist, stopping just in front of him.

She looked down her nose at the kneeling cultist, her tone deathly quiet. "What is your name?"

He looked up at her, his eyes drooping just slightly, "What's it matter to you?" Slowly, his brows knit together. "Oh. I see! You're that little brat that I tried to take from Deepwood all those years ago. Tell me, do you still wear that cursed elf stone around your neck?"

Kalyn gripped the hair of the medusa's head a little tighter and knelt to look him in the eyes. Her voice was as hard as granite. "Name."

Skull Head smiled, his tattoo smiling at her as well. "How's your little sister, eh? Did she thank you for saving her? Did she wrap you into a loving hug and plant a tender kiss on your brow?"

Kalyn's eyes squinted, her hate for this man growing even deeper if that were possible. "Name."

"She was my favorite slave. I only gave her the best treatment, I'll have you know."

"Name!" Kalyn shouted nearly at the top of her lungs.

He glared at her in return, then finally spoke. "I am Ruine."

Kalyn took in a slow, deep breath, before speaking, not trusting her own voice. "Hello, Ruine. My name is Kalyn Rhan. You took my sister from me. Now, you're going to die."

He laughed. It was a hollow, wicked sound. "I know who you are, Kalyn. You have always been the prize that got away from me. How long did it take you to think up that pathetic line?"

"Longer than it will take for me to do this." With that, she jerked the medusa's head up and held it directly in front of Ruine's face.

His eyes widened as he gazed into the medusa's. Ruine grunted as his body slowly started to turn to stone, but then, to Kalyn's surprise, he smiled. "Clever girl. I always knew… you were a prize."

With those final words, and the cracking of stone, he grew still and silent, that crazed smile forever engraved on his gray face.

Kalyn stood to her feet, dropping the medusa's head. "Elladan, can you do me a favor?" She asked, not taking her eyes off the grinning statue.

Elladan stepped up to her side. "Anything."

"Could I borrow one of Lloyd's hammers?"

Elladan hesitated, then he opened his portal bag and reached in, and grunting, drew one of the hammers out.

Kalyn took it, hanging onto it as the heavy head swung down to the floor. She lined her shoulders up with Ruine's head, then, using all her strength, hauled the hammer back and swung it, slamming it into the middle of the grinning statue's face, shattering it into a thousand pieces.

34
STONE COLD TRUTH

I'm sorry, my dear, but I'm not sure we can do anything for him now

An eerie silence fell over the altar room. All sounds of battle had stopped after the naga's declaration of failure to his mistress. Glolindir strained his ears, but could detect no further signs of fighting anywhere around them. What he did hear instead was a faint sniveling sound somewhere off to his right, accompanied by soft murmuring.

"Martan. Oh, Martan, why?"

A little farther off, he could hear Alana's voice. "Donnie… Donnie? Wake up… wake up."

A mixture of fear and frustration washed over Glo as he wondered what had happened to the duo. With his eyes blinded, he couldn't be certain of much.

"What have you done, you fools?" a strange voice echoed around the cavern. "You've ruined everything!"

Glo then heard Seth. "Hey, you're the ones who invited us. It's your funeral."

Glo laughed silently. *Leave it to Seth.*

The strange voice spoke again. "You think you've won? Well, think again. You can't stop it from happening. One way or another, my mistress will rise again."

The words sent a chill up Glo's spine. That was no idle threat. Glo had previous experience with the cult's mistress, and she was quite powerful indeed.

He then heard someone walk across the chamber and soft voices speaking. One was the strange man and the other was Kalyn, yet he couldn't hear exactly what they were saying until Kalyn shouted, "Name!"

The voices went soft again after that, and Glo didn't hear anything else until a loud *crack* echoed across the chamber. It sounded like metal meeting stone. The room went silent again for a few moments until another noise reverberated around the altar room.

Clap. Clap. Clap.

It sounded as if two giant hands were applauding in a slow rhythm. The noise was followed by a chilling voice.

"Well done, *Heroes*. Very well done."

Glo involuntarily flinched at the sound. He had heard that malevolent voice before, albeit only in his mind till now. It belonged to Salisma, the demon 'goddess' of the Serpent Cult.

"Pathetic as he was, my servant was right. You may have won for now, but this is not the only way into your world. So, enjoy your victory while you can. It will be short-lived…"

A whooshing sound filled the chamber, signifying the closure of the portal to the abyss. Yet the demon's last words still hung in the air, sending a chill up Glolindir's spine yet again.

The altar room went silent after that, only to be broken a few moments later by a weak, but familiar glib voice. "Well, she's certainly pleasant."

Glo shook his head, a closemouthed laugh emanating from his throat despite himself. Donnie was alright after all, and apparently hadn't lost his droll sense of humor.

Elladan snickered. "Heh. What's the matter, Donnie? Not your type?"

"I don't think she's anyone's type," Donnie shot back. The slight elf started to laugh, but it swiftly degenerated into a coughing fit.

Alana chided the slim elf. "Easy there, tiger. That was a nasty shot you took. You're lucky you didn't bash your skull in."

Donnie's response was a sarcastic laugh. "Wouldn't be the first time I banged my head against the wall. Luckily I have a thick skull."

The duo's light banter brought the beginnings of a smile to Glo's lips. The tension had just begun to drain from his shoulders when Kalyn's voice blared across the room.

"How can you troll-brained morons joke at a time like this? A man's been turned to stone, and y'all are waggin' your tongues about some demoness? Don't ya have any sense of respect?"

Glo felt his gut wrench into a knot. *Martan? Turned to stone?*

Seth, on the other hand, positively snorted with glee at the duo's berating. "Yeah, you troll-brained morons. Show some respect for the man. After all, he threw himself in front of the medusa to save Kalyn."

Seth's double-edged remark subdued Kalyn's sudden outburst. The young woman's voice was filled with guilt as she mumbled a reply. "Well he didn't have to. I would've been fine."

"Sure, you would," Seth humored her, though his tone was positively scathing.

Kalyn went silent at that point, but Glo could just imagine the dark look she was giving the halfling. Meanwhile, both Elladan and Donnie must have been chagrinned by the young lady's scolding.

Elladan uttered a brief, but sincere apology. "Sorry, Kalyn."

"Yes, sorry we got carried away," Donnie added dolefully.

Kalyn remained silent, but Alana spoke in her stead. "You would think that hitting the wall would have knocked some sense into him."

"Not likely," Seth chimed in.

Alana barely choked back a laugh as she tried to tend to Donnie. "Now hold still while I heal that thick skull of yours."

At the same time, Glo heard purposeful footsteps stride across the cavern in his direction. A moment later, a gentle hand touched his arm and Kalyn's voice whispered to him, "Is there anything you can do for Martan? Some sorta magic stuff to change him back to the way he was?"

That's a good question. Glo didn't answer immediately. Instead he closed his sightless eyes, his brow furrowing as he racked his brain. There was a high-order spell that could turn rock to skin and another one that could do the exact opposite. Yet the medusa's magic was a powerful innate ability, one that far surpassed either of those spells.

Glo finally shook his head and grimaced, his unseeing eyes misting over as he spoke. "I'm sorry, Kalyn, but I'm not sure we can do anything for him now. He may be gone for good."

Glo felt the hand on his arm fall away. Kalyn's voice sounded hollow as she implored the others. "Ain't there anything… anyone can do?"

Aksel answered her plea this time, the little cleric's voice filled with sympathy. "I promise you we will do everything we can for him, but right now we must focus on healing what we can."

Glo heard a short sigh, then Kalyn uttered a glum, "Okay."

Aksel went silent for a moment, then turned his attention to the others. "Cyclone, let me see those burns."

Glo felt a slight twinge of guilt at hearing of the hunter's burns. His fireball had most likely been the cause. Yet Cyclone didn't seem to care. The hunter responded in his typical gruff fashion.

"Nah, I'll be fine. Maybe you should fix Lloyd's arm before it falls off."

Glo's eyes went wide. *What happened to Lloyd?*

Aksel sounded as surprised as Glo. He heard quick footsteps shuffling across the cavern floor, followed by the gnome chiding Lloyd, "Your arm's almost completely severed! When were you planning on telling me?"

Lloyd's reply was rather sheepish. "I didn't think it was that bad, and anyway, Martan's problem seemed a bit more pressing…"

For the first time since Glo had known him, Aksel swore under his breath. In fact, he swore multiple times before getting a hold of himself.

Seth snickered off to one side. "I guess we're rubbing off on him."

The little cleric ignored the side-comments, his focus completely on their severely injured companion. "Now sit down, and hold still! This is going to take a while."

Glo felt the rush of nearby magic as the little cleric invoked his healing power. At nearly the same moment, a strange female voice filtered across the chamber. The accent sounded similar to Kalyn's, but was just a bit thicker. "Well at least y'all are in one piece, more n' less."

"Fran! Raina!" Kalyn shrieked with excitement. Her tone abruptly turned confused. "Elfar? What are y'all doin' here? Where'd you find him?"

Glo heard the sound of multiple feet shuffling across the cavern.

"Thought we'd have to come n' save you, sis," a male voice answered in that same thick dialect. "As for your cat, found 'im with that nice lil gift-wrapped present ya left in them wagons."

There was a slight pause, then Kalyn spoke again in a withering tone. "Decon... Daer... what in the abyss are you two orc-lovers doing here?"

"Now is that any way to talk to your lovin' brothers?" the one who had spoken before replied.

Glo heard a loud *pop*, followed by a cry of, "Ouch! What was that for?"

"For bein' an idiot n' a jerk... n' that goes for the both of you," Kalyn shot back.

"Now, seeing as you is related to us, what does that make you?"

Pop!

"Ouch!"

"N' that's for what you did to Martan," Kalyn added, her tone as sharp as an icy blade.

"Oh..." her brother faltered, "You found out about that too, eh?"

"I don't hear you denying it."

"Nah, nah, chil'ns. This ain't tha time ner tha place," the female voice admonished them.

"Well she started it," Kalyn's brother complained.

Pop!

"Ouch!"

"Enough already!" the female voice roared.

Glo didn't know whether to laugh or be concerned. He assumed the voice he had heard was Fran, the same druid who had sent them the message from Seth. His assumption was confirmed a moment later.

"Lookin' like ya got things t'well in hand though," she continued.

"We do our best, *Mistress* Fran," Seth interjected with just a trace of sarcasm.

"Nice ta see ya too, *Masta* Seth," Fran retorted with a slight lilt to her voice.

The corner of Glo's mouth upturned slightly. It appeared the lady druid was quite familiar with Seth's acerbic sense of humor.

Kalyn spoke next, though the young woman's tone had turned glum once again. "We held our own… mostly. Though Martan didn't fare so well."

"Martan? Martan Folke? What's that low-life doin' here?" Kalyn's brother asked.

"Nothing much. Just saving your sister's life is all," Seth retorted in Martan's defense.

Elfar's low growl echoed around the room.

There was a momentary pause before Kalyn's brother spoke again. "You don't say, short stack. So Martan actually grew a spine?"

Pop!

"Would you stop doing that!" Kalyn's brother snarled.

This time, Elladan interrupted the siblings. "Listen, friend. Martan's been with us for a while now, and he's faced more danger than you'll probably see in a lifetime—everything from wolves to dragons. So, you might want to think twice about what you say about him."

Kalyn's brother, however, did not seem convinced. "Is this true, sis? Did he save your life?"

Kalyn reluctantly answered her brother's question. "Well, yeah, Decon… he sorta jumped between me n' a medusa. Not that I needed the help, mind you, but he did go n' get himself turned to stone trying to keep me safe."

Decon finally seemed impressed. "Well, I'll be…"

"Glo here said there ain't no way to change him back…" Kalyn's voice trailed off.

"That tall elf over there yonder, this Glo?" Fran asked.

"Yes, ma'am," Kalyn answered the lady druid.

A moment later, Glo felt a tingling sensation cross his body. It was very delicate and rather brief, but he immediately recognized it as a magical scan. Whoever the practitioner was, they were very skilled.

When it finished, Fran addressed him again. "You been blinded there, son, and it ain't natural, is it?"

Glo shook his head. "No, ma'am."

"Raina, werk ya magic on tha poor lad. Kalyn shows me this medusa that went n' stoned Martan. Decon, Daer, keep an eye on that cave entrance. There may'n be some cult-cysts still lurkin' 'round."

"Eh, not likely. Ya druids probably et 'em all." Decon sighed.

The noise of scuffling feet filled the chamber once more, when Elladan's voice rang out next to Glo. "I think I'll join you two. I'd love to hear about Martan's days in Deepwood, and I can tell you more about his adventures with us."

"Whatever floats your boat," Decon answered, though the Deepwooder didn't exactly sound thrilled.

The sounds of retreating footsteps died away when Glo felt a small pair of hands on his shoulders. The owner of those hands then spoke to him in a tiny, but firm voice. "Hello, Glolindir. There's a bench right behind you. Please sit down."

Glo felt behind him and found the bench, sitting carefully down on it. A moment later, a light pair of fingers touch his temples. There was a brief surge of magic, then the blackness in front of him suddenly brightened into a world of colors and motion.

The tall elf blinked, his eyes focusing on the unfamiliar freckled face of a small but cheerful young woman with colorful red dreadlocks. Her green eyes danced with amusement, her lips curling into a cute smile. "Now that's better, isn't it?"

Glo beamed at the young lady while taking in her interesting attire. She wore a strange combination of fibers and colors, woven to appear like bark and leaves. Her outfit was further adorned with feathers here and there, but her tiny feet were bare. "Most definitely better. Thank you… Raina, is it?"

"That's me!" Raina's smile widened into a grin. "And you're the infamous fire mage, Glolindir."

Glo felt the blood rise to his cheeks. He felt like denying it for a moment, then hung his head and smiled wanly. "Guilty as charged."

Seth, lounging on another bench across the aisle from them, snorted with obvious glee. "Told you, you had a reputation."

The elven wizard cast a dark look at the halfling, then swept his eyes around the rest of the chamber. Aksel and Lloyd sat over by the altar. The little cleric knelt next to the warrior, brilliant white light emanating from his hands and completely enveloping Lloyd's left arm.

Across the room by a tall pillar, Alana stood over Donnie. A bright light similar to Aksel's flowed from her hands and covered the back of the slim elf's skull.

Cyclone sat alone at the far end of the pews, his skin still covered in burned welts. Yet as Glo watched, those welts slowly began to shrink.

Glo arched an eyebrow at the sight. He had no idea how the young man was healing himself. Whatever was going on with the hunter most definitely warranted further investigation, yet this was neither the time nor the place.

Back behind Glo, Kalyn and a middle-aged woman he presumed to be Fran hovered over the dead body of the medusa. The druid was dressed as he expected, in a patchwork robe of greens, browns, and grays. Yet upon her head sat a straw hat covered with decorative flowers.

Glo mentally adjusted his initial assessment of the woman. She was certainly not your typical druid.

A stone figure stood not far away from the pair. Glo's face fell as he recognized what had once been Martan. From the archer's pose, he must have been terrified when he threw himself in front of the medusa—yet he had done so to save Kalyn.

Glo could only imagine what it would take to make that kind of sacrifice. The young elf had only felt that deeply about a very few people in his life. A vision of bright violet eyes and honey-colored hair briefly flashed through Glo's mind. He quickly pushed it out of his head. That part of his life was over.

Kalyn's sudden screech broke him out of his deep thoughts. "Fran, put that down! You want to turn to stone, too?"

The middle-aged druid cackled with laughter as she juggled the medusa's head in her hands. "This old thing can't hurt me none… or didja furget I was blind."

Though the lady archer shielded her face, Glo could still see the sheepish look on it. "Yeah, guess I did forget for a moment, but that thing ain't 'xactly safe either."

Fran cackled once more. "Well, safe or not, it may jus' be the key ta savin' young Martan here. Bes' we be puttin' this 'way for nah, though, wheres it won't be causin' no more trouble."

The blind druid pulled out a familiar-looking bag from her belt and stuffed the medusa head into it. Though the bag was far smaller than the head, it easily disappeared inside.

Ah, Fran has a portal bag just like Elladan's.

With that squared away, Glo returned his attention to Raina. "So then, when did you folks get here?"

Raina had seated herself on the bench next to Seth, Kalyn's lynx sitting between the two of them. The young druid's hand drifted over and stroked his plush fur as she proceeded to tell them about their arrival in Serpent's Hollow.

In a record vote, the Druid Council had unanimously chosen to marshal their forces and move on the Serpent Cult. The decision had happened so fast, in fact, that the druids were already on the move by the time Seth and Kalyn met up with Glo and the others. The High Druid sent word ahead to Deepwood, and the town snipers also gathered their forces. As soon as the druids reached Deepwood, they joined them on their rushed march north.

The entire company arrived at Serpent's Hollow maybe an hour after sunset. When they reached the village, it was probably about the same time the companions entered the caves. Their timing couldn't have been better. The cultists who had been trapped in the temple had just found their way out.

What ensued was a huge battle between the bulk of the Serpent Cult and the combined forces of the druids and the Deepwooders. Magic, knives, and arrows flew everywhere. Shape-shifting serpents, bears, and wolves clashed in the center of the little village.

The druids and snipers appeared to be gaining the upper hand when the High Druid sent Fran and Raina ahead to lend a hand to the Heroes. Kalyn's brothers, Decon and Daer, insisted on coming along as well.

All the others had gathered around by the time Raina finished her tale. Glo swept his eyes carefully over his companions.

Lloyd's arm appeared completely healed, though Aksel had cautioned the warrior to avoid wielding a blade with it for a while. Donnie's cracked skull was fixed, and Cyclone's welts were miraculously gone.

"Kalyn tol' me most o' what happened here," Fran explained to the small gathering. "'Less you got somethin' else that needs doin' probably bes' we be headin' back to tha village."

"I think we've done all we can here," Aksel agreed with the blind druid.

Fran cast a quick spell to make Martan lighter, then Decon and Daer carried him back along with the others. It turns out the brothers had a change of heart about the vagrant archer after hearing Elladan's stories about his brave exploits. It also didn't hurt that he'd sacrificed himself for their little sister.

Seth and Kalyn led the way back to the village. When they arrived there, most of the fighting had died down. The group was met by a tall, thin elven woman with a thick mane of coppery-red curly hair, garbed in a pale green robe. She was closely surrounded by at least ten druids, who stood protectively around her.

The woman regarded them carefully as they entered the north end of the village. Her deep green eyes scanned the little group, pausing for a moment as they fell on Glolindir.

There was something strikingly familiar about this woman. The regal way in which she carried herself reminded Glo of his mother, Aerandir, or perhaps even the Lady Gracelynn of Ravenford.

Fran called out as they drew up to the druids. "Howdy, Lysandra. How goes the 'party?'"

Lysandra eyed Fran for a few moments. Glo could almost feel the tension passing between the two. It appeared there was no love lost between this pair. Finally, Lysandra exhaled an exasperated sigh. "This is a bloody mess. Good thing we stopped these fiends when we did."

Fran's mouth twisted into a sarcastic smile. "We? If it twarn't for these folks here, we'd be fightin' a hydra, a medusa, a naga, and tha cult's dark goddess."

Lysandra spiked an eyebrow, a puzzled expression on her face. "And what goddess would that be?"

"They call her Salisma," Glo answered in a flat tone.

Lysandra already pale face turned positively white, her body visibly shuddering at the mention of that name. The elven woman wrapped her arms around herself to stop her body from shaking. "No… it couldn't be…"

"What is it?" Raina asked, the young druid's voice betraying her fear at seeing her leader so rattled.

Lysandra dropped her arms and squared her shoulders, forcing herself to stand up tall. Still, Glo could see a tiny bit of fear in her green eyes. "Salisma Tanj is a maralith, a lieutenant of the Lord of All Demons, whose name I dare not utter in such a place as this."

Glo arched an eyebrow at her declaration. He exchanged a brief glance with Aksel, then returned his attention to Lysandra. "I thought that name sounded familiar. The Thrall Lord was a master of demons. According to the tales, in the final battle he even summoned the Demon Lord to fight for him. Yet he also had a number of demon lieutenants at his command."

Lysandra turned her gaze back on Glo and stared at him sharply as if assessing him anew. "You are quite astute. Salisma Tanj was indeed one of those lieutenants who served the Thrall Lord."

Aksel rubbed his chin slowly as he mused aloud. "Then Elistra was right. The Serpent Cult was being driven by more than just the Thrall Master's legacy…"

"Did you say Elistra?" Fran interrupted him.

Aksel nodded to the blind druid, his demeanor remaining serious. "She was a companion of ours until a brief while ago."

"Well I'll be," Fran drawled, her face lit with surprise. "Eh, t'aint no surprise, though. She's always where the fun is."

Glo had momentarily started at the mention of the seeress' name, but his curiosity got the better of him. "Do you know her?"

An enigmatic smile crossed the blind druid's face as she nodded back at him. "Prob'ly as well as anyone knows 'er. She keeps 'er cards close to tha vest, that one."

"That's for sure," Glo agreed wholeheartedly. Still, he couldn't stop himself from feeling excited. If Fran did indeed know Elistra, perhaps she could shed some light as to why the seeress had left him.

Fran interrupted his musings by bringing up Martan. She swiftly explained the circumstances surrounding the hapless archer to Lysandra.

The High Druid listened carefully, then slowly nodded when Fran was done. "There may indeed be something we can do for him, but not here. It will have to wait till we return to Bendenwood."

Kalyn, uncharacteristically silent up till now, expelled a deep sigh. "Thank you, your High Druidiness. Anything you can do for him would be greatly 'ppreciated."

Lysandra arched an eyebrow at the lady archer. She studied her for a brief moment, then a thin smile crossed her lips. "We shall see what we can do, but for now we must finish cleaning up this mess."

With that, the High Druid Lysandra spun on her heel. She strode away while waving the others to follow her back into the heart of the village.

35
BAD NEWS TRAVELS FAST

Something dreadful has happened to the Baron

Glolindir looked up from the thick book in front of him and rubbed his hands across his tired, bleary eyes. The tall elf leaned back in his chair and stretched while sweeping his gaze across the large chamber around him. The room was oval in shape with two levels, the entire walls of each covered with tall shelves. Every shelf in turn was filled with nothing but rows and rows of books.

Elladan, Lysandra, and Fran sat not far away, the table they all shared strewn with open books and piles of texts that they had already read through. The four of them had been at this now for nearly eighteen hours, ever since they had arrived in Bendenwood.

It suddenly dawned on Glo that he hadn't rested in over forty-eight hours. After their initial meeting with Lysandra, the companions had joined in with the druid forces, and by sunrise, the hollow had been completely cleared of cultists. With the battle won, Lysandra tasked her forces with returning the slaves to their homes. She then set out for Bendenwood with the companions, Fran, Raina, the Rhans, and her personal guard.

The small company had ridden hard through the day, finally reaching their destination late that evening. Thoroughly exhausted, most of the companions went straight to bed. Yet Fran and Lysandra had forgone sleep, focusing instead on a cure for Martan. Glo and Elladan offered to assist the pair since neither elf required sleep.

The foursome had spent all night and most of this next day holed up in the Bendenwood library. It contained an impressive collection of texts, though not as big as the libraries in Cairthrellon or Kai Arborous. Still, there were many books here that neither Glo or Elladan had seen before.

Yet now Glo had begun to feel discouraged. It was late in the afternoon and they were still no closer to finding a cure for their stoned friend.

The tall elf sighed, then forced himself to bend back down over the book he was reading. He had only gone through a few more pages when Elladan abruptly called out, "Looks like Fran was right!"

The blind druid glanced up from a text she was somehow scanning with her hand. "O' course I was right. Bout what in partic'lar though?"

Glo got up and gathered around Elladan with the others. The bard pointed to a passage he had discovered. "This section was written by the great hero Valgar, a high priest of Phobas some thousand years ago during the last demon war. In it, he states, *short of a wizard's wish, the only way ever found to dispel the medusa's curse is through the creature's tears.*"

"Well ain't that a kick in the head," Fran drawled, glancing around with a toothy grin.

Glo leaned in close over Elladan's shoulder. "Does it say anything more?"

The bard leafed through the next couple of pages then shook his head. "Nope. That was the only reference to a medusa in this section."

Glo straightened back up and steepled his hands in front of his mouth. This was their first solid find, but something about it bothered him. "So, let's say we drain the medusa's tear ducts and distill the contents into a potion. How do we get that potion into Martan? He can't exactly swallow it."

Silence pervaded the library as the others mulled over Glo's words. Lysandra finally broke the silence. "What if we were to spray the potion over him? Stone is porous after all, and it should absorb most of the liquid."

A line appeared between Elladan's brows. "That might work, but what if it doesn't absorb enough of the potion?"

Glo pursed his lips together. "Elladan's right. A spray may not be effective enough."

The tall elf paced around the room while drumming his fingers on his chin. "If only there was a way to augment the potion's magic, it wouldn't matter how much of it was absorbed."

"I knows a place where tha magicks is thick as molasses," Fran stated with a smile, fixing her unseeing eyes on Lysandra.

The High Druid stared back at the older woman, her eyes going round with disbelief. "No. You can't be serious. We can't bring them there. That site is reserved for druids only."

Fran's smile widened into a toothy grin. "But you're the High Druid, so ain't yas able to make n' 'ception? After all, these folks did jus stop a powerful demon from enterin' tha world."

Lysandra went silent, her eyes growing thoughtful as they swept from Fran to Elladan and finally settled on Glo. Mixed emotions played across her face as she stared at him.

Glo intrinsically understood her dilemma. As the High Druid, she was bound by her peoples' laws and customs. Still, their friend's life was at stake.

"Please, Lysandra," Glo implored her. "Martan is a good man. He proved that by sacrificing himself for another. If there is a way to ensure his recovery, then I believe we owe it to him."

Lysandra appeared to think over his plea, then her eyes softened and a warm smile spread across her lips. "Very well. I will sanction the use of the druid meeting place this one time."

The High Druid's voice turned hard as she shifted her gaze toward Fran. "But this stays between us. I don't need the council getting wind of this. They are hard enough to control as it is."

Fran grinned, then pressed her lips together and drew her hand across her mouth. "My lips is sealed, your High Druidiness!"

Lysandra held her gaze for a moment, then let out an exasperated sigh. "I'm going to need a long drink after this is over."

The moon waxed a shade from full in the inky black sky above. Its silvery light softly bathed everything in sight, casting long shadows around the gathered group.

Glo and the others stood amidst a tall circle of monolithic stones set in a clearing a short distance northeast of the town of Bendenwood. The henge was the meeting place of the Druidic Council, where the head druids of the many circles gathered during the full moon.

Martan's stone form stood in the very center of that circle, placed upon a wide dais normally reserved for the High Druid. Lysandra and Fran stood nearby, carefully loading the potion made from the medusa's tears into a sprayer.

Glo subconsciously rubbed his arms as he waited in silence. He could feel the mana flowing in the air around him and in the ground beneath his feet. It was so strong it practically made his skin crawl.

Aksel and Elladan appeared to be having the same reaction. Glo leaned in close and whispered to the duo. "Lysandra told me this place is built on a point where two ley lines intersect."

Ley lines were lines of mystical force that encircled the earth at regular intervals, both east to west and north to south. While the lines themselves emanated power, the mana levels where two lines intersected was particularly high.

Aksel gazed back at Glo, a look of understanding dawning on the gnome's face. "Ah, that explains a lot."

"You mean that itchy feeling like a thousand fireflies crawling under your skin?" Elladan drawled, the bard rubbing his arms like Glo had moments ago.

Aksel grimaced at Elladan. "Yes… that, and why we were dragged all the way out here to administer this cure."

Earlier that evening, Lysandra and Fran had drained the medusa's tear ducts and distilled the potion they would need. They had then waited until moonrise to journey to the henge, when the magic that ran through the ley lines would be at its peak.

The two druids, Raina, Kalyn and her brothers all now stood in the stone circle. Nearly all the companions had gathered there as well, all except for Cyclone. According to Raina, the dragon hunter had departed town just before noon. He left without leaving any message, or even a word of goodbye.

While it seemed rather gruff, even for Cyclone, Glo believed the hunter's curt behavior had to do with the strange transformation he experienced back in the caves. Perhaps Cyclone had gone off to find out more about what had happened to him.

Glo's musings were interrupted as Lysandra and Fran finished preparing the sprayer. The High Druid then stepped back and bade Fran to proceed.

Raina stepped up to Fran's side, taking her gently by the arm and guiding her forward toward the center of the stone circle. The blind druid pointed the sprayer at the rocky figure of Martan and shrugged. "Well, here goes nothin'."

Fran pumped the handle and a cloud of gas erupted from the tip. The moonlight reflected in a silvery sheen off the mist as it fanned out over Martan's still form. The blind druid circled around the stone figure with Raina's help, spraying it a few more times. She then stepped back with the pronouncement, "That's all of it."

Glo' eyes narrowed as the mists converged on the stone form. They settled onto the porous rock, making it appear wet in sections. Nothing appeared to happen at first, but Glo could feel a surge in the flow of mana around the henge. It felt as if the already-potent magical forces were being focused toward the center of the stone circle.

Abruptly, the layer of 'dew' on Martan disappeared. It was as if it had all been sucked into the rock. An amber aura briefly appeared around the statue, then the entire figure began to glow. The light grew steadily brighter and brighter until it became so intense that Glo had to shield his eyes. The light abruptly faded, and in its place stood Martan, the dour archer miraculously returned to flesh and blood.

Glo felt a sense of awe. It was one thing to theorize about a potential cure, but another thing entirely to see it work.

The silence that had fallen over the circle was abruptly broken by a loud squeal. "Martan!"

Kalyn rushed forward and flung her arms around the archer, pulling him into a tight embrace. Martan appeared taken aback, the disheveled young man still half dazed from his recent transformation.

"Well, this is awkward," Seth commented, his mouth twisted sideways in the bright moonlight.

Kalyn fixed the halfling with a dark stare, then swiftly shifted her grip on Martan, pulling the young man into a head lock. "That was so stupid! Promise me you'll never do something that stupid again!"

"I… promise…" Martan managed to sputter despite the tight grip around his neck.

"Good!" Kalyn let go of him, hauled off, and punched him hard in the shoulder.

"Ouch!" Martan rubbed his arm.

"That's so you don't forget your promise," Kalyn declared, her face flushed. The young lady then stormed off past her brothers.

"Not a word, you two," she cautioned in a hard tone as she stomped past them and out of the stone circle.

"Our lips is sealed. But that don't stop us from thinking." Decon nudged Daer in the arm, winking.

Meanwhile, Elladan strode up to Martan and grasped his hand. "Welcome back to the land of the living!"

Martan, still rubbing his shoulder, glanced around the stone circle with obvious confusion. "What happened? Where are we? Last thing I remember is that snake woman was after Kalyn… and those eyes…"

The young man visibly shuddered.

"Ya turned into stone is'n what happened," Fran responded with a loud cackle.

Martan glanced at the blind druid. "And who are you?"

Elladan clasped Martan on the shoulder. "It's a long story, maybe one best told over a keg of ale."

Martan's hand went to the back of his neck. "That does sound good. For some reason, I am incredibly dry."

"Count us in!" Decon and Daer both chimed in.

Martan gazed at the two brothers with obvious disbelief. "Seriously?"

Decon gave his fellow archer a wry smile. "Let's just say you're not the goblin licker we originally thought ya were."

"Gee, thanks," Martan responded with more than a touch of irony in his tone.

The foursome strolled off together out of the stone circle, toward the path that led back to Bendenwood. Meanwhile, Alana addressed the remaining company. "Now that things are set right, I must head back to the Wind Tower."

Donnie's face fell at her announcement. "Really? Now?"

Mixed emotions played across Alana's face in the silvery moonlight. "Well, probably not until first light."

"Then we still have tonight!" Donnie declared, flashing the lady knight a bright smile.

"Yes, we do," Alana agreed, her mouth curving into a smile.

Donnie wove his arm through Alana's and the duo strode off together out of the circle. As the pair disappeared, Kalyn sheepishly strode past them back into the henge. The lady archer approached the remaining company and said, "So what are you guys going to do now?"

It was a good question. Glo hadn't really thought that far ahead.

Lloyd obviously had, though. "We need to return to Ravenford, of course—to report to the Baron."

Seth snickered. "Sure, the Baron. What you really mean is to see Andrella."

"Maybe," Lloyd responded, his face obviously flushed even in the pale light of the moon.

Lysandra suddenly spoke up. "Did you say Ravenford?"

The High Druid reached into a pocket in her robes and pulled out a parchment. "I found this letter on my desk when I returned to my office this afternoon. It's addressed to the Heroes of Ravenford."

Lysandra held it out to Aksel. The little cleric took the parchment and gingerly opened it as the others gathered around.

"What does it say?" Lloyd asked eagerly, hanging over the gnome's shoulder.

Aksel's eyes drifted over the parchment as he read through its contents. "It's from the Lady Gracelynn. She says that something dreadful has happened to the Baron. She requests that we return to Ravenford at once."

Lloyd grabbed the letter from Aksel's hands, his tone frantic. "Does it say anything about Andrella?"

Aksel gazed up at the young man with sympathy. "That's all it says. There's nothing about Andrella."

Lloyd briefly looked over the parchment himself, then swept his eyes around the group. "We have to go at once!"

Lysandra placed a restraining hand on the young man's arm. "You've all been though a lot. Rest here in Bendenwood this night. We will provide you with all you need to set out first thing in the morning."

Before Lloyd could respond, the High Druid peered at Raina. "Gather whatever they will need—horses, supplies, et cetera. Have them ready at first light."

Raina responded with a swift bow. "At once, your eminence."

The spritely druid spun on her bare heels, and hustled off from the stone circle at a fast pace.

"Thank you, Lady Lysandra. That's more than kind of you," Aksel responded for the companions.

Lysandra gave the little cleric a brief smile. "It's the least we can do."

"Yes, thank you," Lloyd added sheepishly, obviously embarrassed by his sudden outburst.

"Don't worry, Lloyd. I'm sure she's alright," Kalyn said reassuringly. The young woman then glanced down and dug her toe into the dirt. "If you want, I could go with you guys and lend a hand."

Glo exchanged glances with Aksel, Lloyd, and Seth. The little cleric peered at each of them in turn. "Lloyd?"

The young man nodded. "She's been mighty handy to have around in battle."

"Seth?"

The halfling's lips bent sideways. "Eh, she's alright. Annoying, but alright."

Kalyn cast a dark glare at Seth, then abruptly winked at him, the hint of a twisted smile on her lips.

"Glo?"

The elven wizard nodded as well. "She's proven herself these last few days. I think she'd be a fine ally."

Aksel turned back to Kalyn. "Then it's settled. Welcome to the crew."

Kalyn's reaction was delayed as Aksel's words sank in. "Wait, really? You really mean it?"

She jumped in the air and practically did a jig in the center of the stone circle. "Wa-hoo! I get to hang with the Heroes of Ravenford! I can barely stand how excited I am!"

Seth snorted. "That makes two of us."

Kalyn ignored the halfling and danced around for a few moments more until Lloyd finally put a damper on her enthusiasm. "Alright, people. We still have packing to do. Let's get a move on."

The young warrior headed off toward the path that led back to Bendenwood, Kalyn dancing off after him and the others close behind.

Glo started to follow as well, but he felt a soft hand on his arm. He turned to see Lysandra staring at him, a strange look in the druid's eyes. "How about a drink before you go?"

Glo arched an eyebrow at the elven woman. She continued to stare at him, a slight smile gracing her lips.

"It's been a long time since I've seen or spoken with a Galinthral elf."

Glo let out a short, closemouthed laugh. For a moment there, he had totally misread her intent. "Sure, why not?"

Lysandra held out her arm and Glo took it, leading the lady druid down the forest trail back toward town. They talked of many things as they went, but Glo's mind kept drifting back to Ravenford.

It had been barely more than a week since they'd been there, but it felt like a lifetime, between their search for the monolith, the discovery of the Colossus, the battle with the green dragon, their encounter with the Princess, rescuing Ves, and then finally dismantling the Serpent Cult. What could possibly have happened to the Baron in that short time? Glo silently prayed that the little town they had come to call home, and everyone in it, was alright.

Here ends Book Four of
the Heroes of Ravenford
the story continues in Book Five
The Baron's Heart

ABOUT THE AUTHOR

F.P. Spirit writes high fantasy fiction inspired by the likes of Tolkien, Eddings, Brooks, and Piers Anthony. An avid science fiction fan, he became hooked on fantasy the moment he cracked open the Lord of the Rings in high school. When he is not writing, F.P. is either spending time with his wife and sons, gaming, doing yoga, Tai Chi, or walking their dog.

A long-time lover of fantasy and the surreal, he hopes you enjoy his fun contributions to the world of fantasy and magic.

You can learn more about F.P. Spirit by visiting his website at:
Fpspirit.com

www.ingramcontent.com/pod-product-compliance
Lightning Source LLC
Chambersburg PA
CBHW020909110726
47900CB00001B/77